BLACK LEVIATHAN

The First Journey into the Cloudmere

BERND PERPLIES

Translated from German by Lucy Van Cleef

TOR

A TOM DOHERTY ASSOCIATES BOOK

NEW YORK

BLACK LEVIATHAN

Copyright © 2017 by Bernd Perplies

English translation copyright © 2020 by Lucy Van Cleef

Originally published as *Der Drachenjäger: Die erste Reise ins Wolkenmeer* by Fischer Tor Verlag in Frankfurt, Germany

All rights reserved.

A Tor Book
Published by Tom Doherty Associates
120 Broadway
New York, NY 10271

www.tor-forge.com

Tor® is a registered trademark of Macmillan Publishing Group, LLC.

Library of Congress Cataloging-in-Publication Data

Names: Perplies, Bernd, author. | Cleef, Lucy Van, translator.
Title: Black Leviathan : the first journey into the Cloudmere / Bernd Perplies ; translated from German by Lucy Van Cleef.
Other titles: Drachenjäger. English
Description: First U.S. edition. | New York : Tor, a Tom Doherty Associates Book, 2020. | Originally published as Der Drachenjäger: Die erste Reise ins Wolkenmeer by Fischer Tor Verlag in Frankfurt, Germany.
Identifiers: LCCN 2019041689 (print) | LCCN 2019041690 (ebook) | ISBN 9780765398307 (trade paperback) | ISBN 9780765398314 (hardback) | ISBN 9780765398321 (ebook)
Subjects: GSAFD: Fantasy fiction.
Classification: LCC PT2716.E4726 D7313 2020 (print) | LCC PT2716.E4726 (ebook) | DDC 833/.92—dc23
LC record available at https://lccn.loc.gov/2019041689
LC ebook record available at https://lccn.loc.gov/2019041690

Our books may be purchased in bulk for promotional, educational, or business use. Please contact your local bookseller or the Macmillan Corporate and Premium Sales Department at 1-800-221-7945, extension 5442, or by email at MacmillanSpecialMarkets@macmillan.com.

First U.S. Edition: February 2020

Printed in the United States of America

0 9 8 7 6 5 4 3 2 1

FOR EVA,

who reads all my books
even though she can't stand fantasy.
That's what I call sisterly love.

But beware! A shadow will cover you, larger than that cast by any other dragon of this world. Its body is violent, and as black as the night through which it flies. Black as the fog, from which it strikes. Black as the lightless chasm, from whence it was born at the beginning of time. Flee if you encounter this shadow. For nothing can save you otherwise. He is the father of all great dragons, and his name is Gargantuan.

—THIRD BOOK OF THE CRYSTAL DRACHEN ORDINANCE

BLACK
LEVIATHAN

1

Jägers in the Cloudmere

Seventh Day of the Fourth Moon, Year 822

The schooner glided through the air as its wooden hull pierced thick clouds of fog. Delicate wisps of mist crept silently upward, dissolved by the brightly shining sun as they rose. Thicker blankets of fog sank back into the endless whiteness that completely enveloped the small vessel.

At the ship's bow, Adaron set both hands onto the swaying railing, gazing pensively into the unending and all-consuming Cloudmere. The fleece of the blanketing clouds spanned beneath him like freshly fallen snow on a hilly landscape, though the impression was misleading. The ground lay more than a thousand paces below, and perhaps more importantly, no water filled the space in between to buoy a person who fell. Only endless, weightless mist gathering into a thick gray fog as the vessel rose in the sky, until even the biggest creatures below were concealed from view.

These creatures—formidable dragons—were the reason the *Queen of Fog* had been aloft the island-studded Cloudmere for the past two weeks. Before their departure from the port city of Skargakar, Adaron and four of his crewmates—Enora, Ialrist, Jonn, and Finnar—had pawned all unnecessary possessions, many acquired from previous adventures, to purchase the skyship they now called home.

The name was more impressive than the actual vessel, which was relatively small and had barely any room below deck. However, the steering mechanics were in good condition and the kyrillian crystals, which gave the flying ship its buoyancy, were enclosed safely in their metal casings. In fact, the ancient Nondurier ship merchant had even boasted that Adaron wouldn't find a more agile ship anywhere between Skargakar and Luvhartis afloat the Cloudmere's waters.

They were still waiting to test this claim.

With their final few coins, Adaron and his crew recruited three young Nondurier to join their mission. Like so many others these days, the houndlings had been searching for work, but it had been prospect of great fortune from a dragon catch, Adaron reckoned, and not the mere handful of gems that Jonn had pushed into their hands that convinced the Nondurier to board the vessel.

"Lost in thought again, are you?" A woman spoke from behind him.

As Adaron turned to discover Enora standing there, a smile curled his lips. The woman leaned against the railing, her long red hair billowing behind her. She was dressed in weatherworn leather trousers, a lightweight linen shirt, leather boots, and a dark green doublet to shield her from the cool morning breeze. Two Sidhari swords, her favorite weapons, short curved blades that had been gifted to her from a desert elf prince, hung from ornamented sheaths at her hips.

"Well?" she coaxed. "What is going on in there?"

"I'm thinking that at this very moment, my life could hardly be any better," he confessed. "The Three Gods must truly love me to bestow such great fortune."

"Embarking on a journey without a single coin in your purse, on the hunt for the most vicious creatures in this realm . . . you consider *that* to be the greatest fortune?" Enora looked shocked, but the sparkle in her blue eyes proved she was teasing.

Adaron chuckled. "It's all a question of perspective. I think of it this way: aboard one's own ship, in the company of the most loyal crew that I could wish for, we are approaching the most promising realm of Cloudmere. Great adventures, not to mention treasures, await us. And to top it all off, the sun shining from the blue heavens pales in comparison to the smile of the woman standing before me, who has my heart."

"You've got such a flair for the poetic." Enora smiled. "Any bard would turn green from jealousy. Or white with nausea."

Adaron set his hands on his hips. "Well, this much is sure. I won't waste any verses on you in my next epic."

Now Enora laughed. "Settle down. I love you most because of your courage and your good heart. The beautiful words you whisper in my ear only increase that love beyond any shadow of doubt." Her right hand wandered toward the medallion that she wore on a chain around her left wrist, a gift that Adaron had given her last moon cycle. Taijirin had crafted the token, promising protection to the wearer.

"A love that I return," Adaron said, approaching Enora. He wrapped his arms around her, gazing into her eyes. "Now we're just missing one thing to make this moment perfect."

"If you say 'an heir to the family line,' I'll cast myself overboard," Enora warned.

Adaron grinned. "A dragon," he continued, his gaze wandering across the endless white of the Cloudmere that spanned before them. "A dragon to pursue and conquer, and to return home to the greatest laud and honor." With that, the lovers parted and took their places at the railing.

"Well, we haven't had much success on our hunt so far," Enora admitted. "Except for the one bronzeneck that we caught last week, but he was just a buck, and not especially big. If we don't find a full-grown bull soon, we'll return to Skargakar just as poor as when we left."

"Our stores aren't used up yet," Adaron said soothingly. "And anyway, we're approaching the zone where most other jäger ships will surely turn back. Just wait. Soon we'll be alone on the Cloudmere—free to make the catch of our lives."

"What makes you so sure about that?"

"I just know it."

"Comrades!" called Jonn from high atop the crow's nest at mainmast. "Ialrist is on his way back!"

Adaron looked up as Jonn pointed portside. The small, wiry man with wild black hair and the keen vision of a lynx had the withered skin of someone who had spent most of his days under the hot sun and whipping wind atop the crow's nest as he kept a sharp lookout for dragons or other flying vessels.

The flying ships were an awe-inspiring combination of expert crafts-manship and magic. Two half-circle enclosures around the bow and the stern formed a frame, which held six metal cases against the wooden hull. On the underside of these cases, small, gill-like slats opened and closed by way of a rope-and-pulley system from a control stand above deck. These cases contained amethyst-like kyrillian crystals, which held powerful magical properties that propelled them upward when not en-closed by heavy metal. A sufficient number of these crystals could not only lift a ship's hull into the air but could also raise entire rock masses, or lithos, from whose undersides kyrillian was mined. Fanlike sails along their sides enhanced most skyships, while trapeze-shaped ones hung on the masts above deck, to control the vessels' propulsion and steering ac-curacy.

The ability to fly ships was first introduced to the foggy coast near Skargakar nearly a century earlier. On a cool autumn day, a fleet of flying ships first appeared through the fog. Both the humans and lizard-like Drak residing there were stunned. Those ships had been steered by the folk with small frames, red complexions, and heads like hounds. Non-durier were refugees from a distant land where an unknown evil had driven them south. During the first few weeks, the locals feared con-quest and were wary of the outsiders. However, it soon became apparent that Nondurier were not hostile and that both their expertise and their ships could be precious commodities for the entire coastal region. For the first time, the prospect of free flight through the Cloudmere, just as the vogelfolk had always enjoyed, would now be possible for any man or woman without a set of wings.

Thanks to their ships and nautical abilities, the Nondurier quickly de-veloped into highly sought-after employees. The abundance of dragons within the Cloudmere became apparent, and as the many possible uses for those great reptiles were revealed, the coastal folk relinquished the last of their reservations. They built more and more flying ships, supported through an extensive discovery of kyrillian crystals. The coastal region, previously a collection of small, scattered settlements amid the lush wil-derness, practically blossomed overnight. Especially Skargakar, which prospered from its new reputation as a hub for the most formidable jägers and their flying ships. Anyone on the hunt for Great Drachen wound up in Skargakar eventually—just as Adaron and his crew had done.

With a last beat of the great wings growing from his back, Ialrist landed on the deck beside Adaron and Enora. The Taijirin, as the vogelfolk called themselves, did not seem quite as foreign as the Nondurier on board, but no one could have mistaken Ialrist for a human. A fine tan-and-white speckled down covered the man's skin. His large, dark eyes peered out from a gaunt face. Feathers grew from his head in a crest that nearly reached the floor, and powerful wings sprouted from his back that, when extended, spanned nearly four paces. As with most members of his kind, Ialrist had the lean and sinewy build that allowed him to lift into the air by strength alone.

The vogelfolk turned toward the group and called over the wind. "I come bearing good news. I've spotted a silverwing circling a flock of cliff birds not far from here."

"A silverwing?" repeated Adaron. "Now that's a beast worth hunting."

Known for their shimmering scales and glimmering silvery wings—which were fashioned into expensive robes back in Skargakar—silverwings, depending on age could span from ten to twenty paces.

"Where is the beast now?" asked Belhac, the Nondurier who manned the helm.

"Over there," Ialrist said, pointing starboard. The crew could decipher nothing beyond the endless clouds that streamed past.

"That would lead us dangerously close to Death's Bleak," the houndling warned.

"Death's Bleak?" Adaron looked bemused. "That sounds remarkably dramatic to my ears. Who thought of that name?"

"I don't know," answered Belhac. "But I will say this much: any experienced jäger you'd meet in the taverns of Skargakar would avoid that area at all costs. Rumor has it that the mountain peaks hidden beneath the fleece are so treacherous that one wrong encounter could be a ship's undoing. They also tell of firebloods lurking in the fog there, awaiting unsuspecting prey."

"A red dragon." Enora's eyes glimmered with anticipation. "That would be the catch of our lives!"

"You can forget about that," said Belhac, shaking his head. "We aren't prepared for a battle against a fire-breather, and neither is our ship."

"That may be," Adaron cut in gruffly, "but we're the ones who pay your wages. So we'll decide the course of action. I will happily remove anyone who doesn't like it from the deck."

"Who is steering this ship, then?" the Nondurier challenged, eyeing Adaron. "You?"

"Belhac is right," Finnar said—being without a doubt the most sensible person on board. The massive bearded man, who had previously earned a living as a weaponsmith before being dealt a bad hand, crossed his arms in front of his huge chest. "This is our first voyage into the Cloudmere. Let's not go immediately for the most dangerous dragon of all. That can only end badly, and I for one would like to return home in one piece to sell our wares and buy endless barrels of mead with all of the money we earn."

"Wisely said," said Belhac. "My brothers and I share your opinion."

"Fine, then we'll keep a distance from red dragons for now," Adaron announced. "But we shouldn't let any silverwings escape us. You know how rare they are; their scales alone are worth a pretty pile of crystals."

"Maybe we'll even be lucky enough to find a drachen pearl inside its heart," added Enora, wistfully.

"Why not? The chances are certainly higher than with bronzenecks." Adaron's gaze passed over Ialrist, Jonn, and finally Finnar. "I say we follow Ialrist's lead. On the edge of this so-called Death's Bleak, there's only a slight threat of hitting any cliffs. I trust that the Three Gods will know how to keep us from encountering any firebloods on our way."

"I agree with Adaron," said Ialrist, now growing restless. "Let us hunt the silverwing."

"I'm with you," called Jonn from the crow's nest, and Enora nodded.

"Good, then," agreed Finnar. "Let's look upon our riches."

At the order, Belhac steered the *Queen of Fog* into a wide curve, clearly unhappy with the decision. His younger brother, Wuffzan, also looked grumpy and resigned. Only the youngest of the three brothers, Felhim, seemed to have caught the hunting fever. He had already positioned the crystal rudders and now set to work hoisting the extra sail from beneath the bowsprit. Veils of fog rippled around the ship as it picked up speed, gliding toward the unknown.

The sun had passed its zenith, well hidden behind a cluster of clouds, when the crew first discovered the silverwing. The dragon circled elegantly over a stone reef, whose peak stuck out through the mist in two sharp crags, each looming forty paces high and pointing up like an admonishing claw.

At the start of their journey, Adaron had not yet learned to discern whether a piece of land protruding from Cloudmere was the summit of a mountain rooted deep within the earth or a lithos floating in the air from an abundance of kyrillian ore on its underside. Time aloft had, thankfully, sharpened his eye to decipher the subtle movements that set free-floating masses apart from unmoving ones.

The reef, which before the dragon's arrival had been a flock of birds' undisturbed breeding colony, rose and fell gently as if it drifted over the gentle waves of a quiet, ordinary ocean of water. Even today, Adaron could barely believe that hard, heavy stone, often as large as a dwelling and occasionally as massive as an entire village, could hang in the fog, suspended as though weightless. He pushed back his astonishment; they were not there to marvel at the magic of kyrillian crystals.

"Look at him!" called Enora, her eyes wide and sparkling as she gazed at the silverwing. The dragon measured about fifteen paces from its head to the tip of its tail—it must have been a young animal. Its body was a light gray, and the scale sheath, running from its tail, past its back and flank, and all the way up to its neck, glittered in a matte silver. Black scales lined its four legs, indicating the beast was male. Certainly, the creature's wings did its name justice; silverwing—the leathery skin growing between the bony spokes sprouting from its back shimmered, reflecting rays of sunshine into brilliant sheets of silver.

"He's beautiful," said Adaron, awestruck, before turning to the others. "We all know what needs to be done, mates. I'll man the harpoon ballista. Finnar, Enora, you stand ready by the kyrillian buoys. Ialrist, fetch your reaver. And Belhac . . . ," Adaron paused, his eyes aflame. "don't let him out of your sight."

"Don't worry, Captain. We know what to do. The dragon won't get away from us," Belhac answered solemnly.

The *Queen of Fog* picked up speed and leaned into a wide curve to circumvent a mound of cloud and sneak up on the dragon from the side. Adaron stepped up to the harpoon ballista. Attached securely to the ship's bow, the contraption resembled an oversized crossbow on a swiveling gun carriage. He laid the harpoon into the crossbow's shelf and threaded fine, unbreakable Sidhari hemp through the eye at the rod's base. Four rolls of rope lay ready next to him, which would gradually bind the prey, sure and steadfast, to the ship's side. Using a winch, Adaron began to pull back the bowstring, made of tightly wound dragon skin. He raised his head occasionally to gauge when their target would come within shooting range.

Ialrist appeared at Adaron's side. The spear in his hands was nearly three paces long, ending in a flat, sharp, scythe-like blade. On the opposite end, an iron ball topped with a spike, served as a counterweight. Aside from the short bow, used in long-distance battle, a reaver was the most common weapon used by Taijirin in sky battle. In a fight in the winding alleys of Skargakar, Ialrist would surely lose; he needed room for both the reaver's swing and his own wingspan to make the most of weapon. When he had sufficient room, he was a dangerous opponent.

Even a dragon would be wise to be wary; a Taijirin warrior could descend on its prey as quick and sure as a raptor. If everything went according to plan, Ialrist would swoop in, slicing through the muscle fibers at the base of the beast's wings. A dragon that could no longer fly was a far easier target.

One thing was sure: a giant beast in full possession of its strength shouldn't be underestimated. Even if they didn't possess any particular natural weapons, such as spitting fire or deadly acid, they were still immensely powerful. One blow could break bones, and one bite would cut straight through an unarmored opponent without second thought. In addition, dragons were clever and cunning creatures—as this one proved once the wavering mountain reappeared in the *Queen of Fog*'s view.

"Where did he go?" Adaron said, looking around in confusion. The silverwing, which had eaten its fill of the bird colony, had disappeared. Whether the beast was simply full or sensed approaching danger, it was impossible to say.

Jonn's sharp vision spotted the dragon first. "There, he's flying ahead!" called the wiry man pointing starboard, past the cliff's sharp crags.

Adaron squinted. Between clouds far in the distance, he could make out the beast's body glinting in the afternoon sun. "Belhac, take pursuit!" he roared.

"On it, Captain," the gruff Nondurier called from the helm.

"He's not diving," Enora remarked. "He doesn't seem to be leaving because of us." She stood next to the kyrillian buoys, metal cases with gilled undersides similar to those at the hull, which could unleash the crystal's hidden powers in large amounts when opened. These buoys would be employed to give a fishing boat extra lift should a dragon, once shot by a harpoon and successfully bound, threaten to pull the vessel into the depths of Cloudmere, taking its men along with it into the foggy abyss.

"We can't overtake a silverwing with this skyship," called Belhac. "We'll have to follow him until he stops to rest or feed again." He stopped short.

"Why are you hesitating?" Adaron asked.

The hound-headed man curled his lips into a snarl. "He's flying straight for the—" he growled.

"Spit it out, man!"

Belhac bowed forward. A chilling expression loomed on his face. "If the silver doesn't turn around soon, he'll lead us straight into Death's Bleak."

2

Encountering the Beast

Seventh Day of the Fourth Moon, Year 822

The Cloudmere remained unchanged as the crew passed the invisible border into Death's Bleak. The only existing map from this part of the world, an imprecise and tattered account at that, placed them somewhere south of a group of mountain peaks known as the West Bird Islands. As the legends went, one of the Taijirin's largest tribes had founded the island kingdom Aiostra when they settled there centuries earlier. Aiostra Taijirin were known for treating foreigners with hostility, but thus far, none of their soldiers had appeared before the small company on board the *Queen of Fog*.

The silverwing glided lazily past mounds of cloud, not seeming to mind its pursuers—that is, if the dragon even noticed the boat's approach at all. Belhac kept enough distance so that the dragon likely couldn't make out the ship behind its own horn-plated spine and massive wings. Not to mention, the ship's white-and-gray hull was barely discernable from the haze through which it silently plowed.

"When will this creature finally tire out?" Finnar asked impatiently, stroking his beard.

"It seems like he's slowing down," Enora answered from beside him at the bow.

Ialrist shook his head. "You're just imagining that," he said, leaning against the long handle of his reaver.

Adaron shaded a hand over his eyes. "I think he'll rest at that cluster of rocks," he said, pointing toward a structure drawing near.

The *Queen of Fog* began to slow and veered into a turn. Surprised, Adaron turned toward the Nondurier manning the helm. "Belhac, why are you taking us off course?"

"We're flying too close to Death's Bleak, Captain," explained the houndling. "We have to retreat."

Adaron looked at him sharply. "The silverwing has nearly reached his target, and thus so have we. I won't let us quit now!"

"There will be plenty of other dragons," the Nondurier insisted. "Cloudmere is vast, and toying with our lives for a single prize isn't worth the risk."

In a few quick strides, Adaron stood directly before Belhac. "You can't be serious," the captain hissed through closed teeth. "We toy with our lives every day that we continue this mission. That is the price every jäger pays to capture drachen. Our journey has only been quiet thus far because no dragons have crossed our path, other than the measly bronzeneck in the hold. Now we've finally encountered a magnificent silverwing, and you don't have the balls to see the hunt through? If I'd known you were such a coward, I never would have allowed you and your brothers on board my ship."

Belhac muffled a growl, his ears flattening against his head.

"Hey, Adaron, take it easy," Finnar said, setting a hand on the captain's shoulder.

"How can I take it easy when he's letting our prey escape?" Adaron insisted.

"The dragon is flying directly into Death's Bleak," the Nondurier retorted. "It's a very bad place. There are—"

"I know the risks already—treacherous cliffs and red dragons. You've already warned me. But look around." Adaron made a sweeping gesture that cut through the thick fog surrounding them. "Have you seen a single fireblood in all the distance we've covered? Do you really think a silverwing would take shelter here if there were firebloods nearby?"

"But what about lithos?"

"Fly the ship above the clouds," Adaron instructed. "Then nothing will happen to us." Adaron bowed forward. "Trust me. My crew and I have conquered a great many other dangers already. There's no obstacle here that could surprise us."

"Friends!" called Jonn as he nimbly descended the mainmast. "Something strange has happened. Look at the dragon." He pointed ahead toward their prey.

Adaron focused his gaze on the silverwing. Jonn was right. The beast shot hectically from one direction to another. On the end of its long neck, the dragon's slender head darted back and forth, frantically searching for something, while its wings flapped furiously, swirling the white mist around itself.

Belhac recognized the signs. "He seems agitated."

"What does that mean?" Enora asked, joining the group at the helm.

"Surely nothing good," growled Finnar ominously.

Adaron noticed Ialrist still standing at the bow, searching the sky. "Friend, do you see something?" he called.

The vogelfolk shook his head slowly. "Not any immediate danger, no, but the cloud blanket is thickening with too much speed for my liking. And our view of the horizon is weakening, which means that the fog is ascending." He turned toward Adaron and the others. "I may not have been raised on the islands of the Cloudmere, but I know an awful lot about wind and weather. And I've never seen anything like this before."

"There!" called Jonn excitedly. "He's descending!"

With a great beat of its shimmering wings, the dragon tilted sideways and disappeared into the white nothingness.

"Is he trying to flee from us?" Enora asked.

"I don't think so," Adaron answered. "I don't think he even noticed us. It seems like he is escaping something else, a danger much more menacing than our ship."

An ear-piercing scream—half howl, half roar—surged from below. The sound grew shriller, a cry of horrible pain and fear. Then, from one heartbeat to the next, silence surrounded them once again. An air of finality lingered in its place, wafting from below and chilling Adaron to the bone.

"By the Three Gods," murmured Finnar, "what was that? The silver-wing? It sounded like a living body being ripped apart."

"Maybe another dragon," whispered Enora. "Could even be a red."

"That's impossible," argued Adaron. "Firebloods sear their victims with fire. There were no flames in sight."

"Hush," Jonn cut in. He leaned over the railing, listening carefully. "Do you hear that?"

Adaron fell silent and listened into the stillness. He heard the rush of blood in his ears, but, after a while, became aware that the rushing didn't match the beat of his heart. Instead of coming from inside himself, the sound penetrated through the clouds.

"Look there. Something is flying underneath us," murmured Jonn. "Something big."

"I don't like this." Belhac's ears twitched nervously. "We have to go."

"Yes, maybe you're right." Adaron turned toward his crew. "Steer the *Queen of Fog* away from here. The silverwing is lost, anyway. Let's not risk losing anything else."

"You've finally seen reason," answered Belhac. Relieved, he began to pass orders to his brothers. The ship creaked as it leaned into a wide curve, but when the bow veered onto their new course, they met a white wall that completely blocked their path.

"The fog!" cried Enora. "Look how thick it is."

"This cannot be!" cried Jonn in horror. "It goes against nature!"

"Is it possible that the shadow looming in our depths could be to blame?" Finnar asked.

"No dragon that I've ever encountered could influence the weather," growled Belhac.

"But, brother," put in Wuffzan, "what about the old jäger who told us the legend of the great Firstborn, Gargantuan the Horn-Crowned, descended from the Starborn, Ariocrestis the Wise? Gargantuan is known for his powerful strength. They say he is more violent than any fire-breather. For all we know, he could have ordered the skies to turn."

Belhac nodded. "I remember. But Illuminated Wings and Black Leviathans are only legends. Those beasts faded into eternal fog on the edges of our world ages ago."

"That may be true, but couldn't one of them have returned to Endar?"

"Brother, you're speaking of creatures that only live in stories. Who knows if they ever even really existed at all?"

The Nondurier's words reminded Adaron all too closely of his conversation with Belhac over Death's Bleak earlier that day. Then Belhac had been the superstitious one and Adaron the one who had answered in mockery and disbelief.

Ialrist peered into the murkiness that grew thicker around them at the bow. Then he let out a shriek and cried, "Look underneath us!"

Adaron and the others peered over the railing, and their eyes widened. All they could do was clutch the wooden beams for dear life and let fate decide the rest. Without warning, an enormous dark shadow rammed into the hull from below.

The *Queen of Fog* was thrown upward in a whirlwind of shouts and cries. Adaron felt the deck fall from underneath his feet. It took all his strength to cling to the railing. Finnar flew backward and crashed into middle mast, where Ialrist spread his wings to break his fall. A small figure shot over their heads and howled as it disappeared into the clouds.

"Jonn!" cried Adaron.

"No, I'm here!" answered his friend. "It was Felhim."

"Brother!" shrieked Belhac. "Felhim!"

A dark and powerful growl resounded, as if conjured from the heart of the earth itself. A hot stream of air blew against their faces as the monster drew closer, its form still invisible behind the clouds.

"What in the name of Indra, Jerup, and Vazar is that?" asked Enora.

"A Black Leviathan!" Wuffzan answered agitatedly, too excited to be frightened. "I can't believe it. They really do exist. They really do!"

Adaron glanced toward Belhac, who still searched wildly for his brother. "We have to gain some height, man! I think we should break through the fleece. Then at least we can see to face this devil head-on."

"Head-on?" The houndling gasped. "Are you crazy? If he really is a Black Leviathan, then we're as good as dead. Our only option is to accept our end and leave the rest to the gods."

"Would you kindly shut up and open the kyrillian cases?" Adaron snapped. "I don't want to hear about death unless the words are uttered from Vazar's lips alone. Finnar, Jonn, start the kyrillian buoys. We'll need all the boost we can get. Ialrist, tell us when—"

Enora's shrill cry broke his words as the dragon struck the ship a second time. The greater impact ripped the side sails from portside and threw Adaron off his feet as easily as a leaf in a strong wind. He landed on the deck with a crash. The force knocked the breath out of his chest and an ache seared through his left leg.

He pulled himself up and whipped around. Finnar and Jonn, both stone white and smeared with blood, climbed on deck alongside Belhac and Wuffzan. Ialrist hovered atop the bow, his wings flapping.

Enora was nowhere in sight.

The realization struck Adaron like a bolt of lightning. The woman he loved more than his own life was—gone.

"Enora!" he cried and raced starboard toward the ship's ledge. He looked out into the fog, feverishly searching for any sign of life, but he already knew that no one ever found shipwrecks amid the Cloudmere. If anyone went overboard, death was the certain outcome. "Enora!" he called again into the mist.

"Adaron!" a voice called from the stern. "Help!"

He raced to the other side of the *Queen of Fog*. "Enora!"

As soon as he leaned over the railing, Adaron spotted her. His most precious crewmate hung by her side from underneath the hull. The impact from their second encounter with the shadowy monster must have thrown her overboard, but her clothing had caught on the half-broken frame of a crumpled side sail. Her feet dangled into nothingness as she clung to the thin wooden strut with both hands.

"Hold on!" Adaron called out. He reached out his hand but didn't even come close. "Finnar," he called over his shoulder. "Hold on to my legs! Ialrist, help us!" In a feverish rush, Adaron threw his armor and weapons to the deck and swung himself over the wooden railing. When he felt Finnar grasp his feet and legs tightly, he pushed himself over the edge until he dangled headfirst along the hull.

Adaron gave no thought to the fear that Finnar might lose his grip and send him to his death. After surviving so many dangers together already, he trusted his men with his life. From the corner of his eye, he saw Ialrist swoop from below in order to approach Enora from her feet.

Adaron reached again toward Enora, and though he could barely see her through the fog, he clasped a hand around her wrist. "Now let go of the strut and hold on to me tightly," he said.

She hesitated and looked down to the mist below her feet. The fog was so thick that it could be easy to mistake the ground for only a few strides away. Such a mistake would be treacherous, and they both knew it. At the moment, they hovered at least a thousand paces away from solid ground, and somewhere, amid the impenetrable whiteness between them and that ground, the monster—the Black Leviathan—lurked in wait.

"Don't look down," Adaron said, trying to remain calm. "Just focus on me. Trust me. We will make it, I promise." He tried to calm himself, too, as he continued. "We'll survive this just as we've survived all our trials. You know how much the Three Gods favor us, don't you, my love? We can't die. You'll see! And now, come! Give me your hand!"

He watched as new determination filled Enora. She loosened her fingers from the strut and grabbed hold of Adaron's wrist. He pulled her a bit upward until he could reach her remaining hand. As she removed her last grip, a brief moment of uncertainty struck them both—until Adaron's hand closed confidently around hers.

"Very good," he coaxed. "Now listen. Ialrist will come and carry you back on board. When he has you, you have to let go of me. Got it?"

"Yes, all right." Enora looked up at him. Terror flickered in her blue eyes, but amid that terror, trust burned brightly—trust in the capabilities of her crewmates and in her beloved Adaron—that everything would be right in the end.

Ialrist drew nearer from below. The Taijirin wasn't able to hover for long, but he could swoop by, grab hold of Enora, and carry her upward. Earlier adventures had already proven that he could still fly while carrying the weight of one person.

The vogelfolk neared and reached out toward the red-haired woman.

Just then, the Black Leviathan emerged from below.

The fog at their feet darkened to pitch-black as the enormous monster surged upward. Leathery wings, larger than the sails of any ship, beat the wind below them into a furious storm. The beast's body, covered in an armor resembling a stone wall, slammed into Ialrist's side, casting the Taijirin aside. The massive beast, covered in horn-plated armor, opened its jaws wide, brandishing teeth as large as a grown man's forearm.

Time stood still for Adaron. With a clarity that seared every detail into his memory forever, he watched disaster draw near. The beast's hot, foul breath alone nearly knocked him unconscious. A meaty purple tongue slithered in its mouth, and in the depths of its throat, a red ember glowed powerfully—the only sign of the unholy fire blazing inside the monster's belly. However, it was the sharp-horned headdress covering the monster's head that made Adaron certain that bitter death was their only end.

Gargantuan.

As Adaron tried to heave himself and Enora away from the monster's eager gullet, his face contorted with strain, but his effort was useless, and they dangled helplessly.

The Leviathan raised itself up so that Adaron could have stretched a hand out to touch its scaly snout. A cry came from somewhere, but whether from Enora or his own lips, Adaron couldn't say. Catching her eye briefly, he saw only bitter doubt as endless as the fog on the far side of Endar. After all they had shared and everything that they hoped to experience together, the evilest of all creatures would now rip that future to shreds. Neither of them could do anything about it, and they both knew it.

The beast clamped its mouth shut to the squelch of flesh and the crunch of bone, and surged sideways, away from the ship. Adaron watched the colossal body pass by in an unending stream of scales until it finally ended in the flat leaf-shaped blade of its tail. That tail whipped into the air, and its blade shattered the entire stern of the *Queen of Fog* with a casual blow.

The force threw Adaron into the air and over the railing's edge. Finnar groaned from the strain but continued to grip Adaron's legs tightly, gradually pulling him backward onto the fog-damp wooden deck.

In the next moment, the ship tipped sideways, and both men slid downward. Adaron saw shining crystals hit the deck, roll past him, and continue over the side of the ship. The dragon's attack must have ripped some of the kyrillian cases from the hull.

Adaron crashed into the mast and was caught by its flapping sail. Finnar, however, continued sliding.

"Adaron!" he shrieked and reached out. Adaron was too stunned to be of much help, and, he realized, one of his hands was already occupied with the small hand in his grasp. He surveyed the hand matter-of-factly. A chain with a Taijirin medallion of protection dangled on its wrist, the charm's glimmer its own cruel form of ridicule. The body belonging to that hand was nowhere in sight. Enora, his beloved Enora, was gone—swallowed by the Firstborn himself.

No! he screamed wordlessly, staring at the hand's smooth back, delicate wrist, and pale forearm. Just before the elbow, shreds of a linen shirt now shone red as they clung to the wet, bloody stump at the arm's end. *This can't be true! Enora!*

A strange rapture overtook him, which barely allowed him to notice the beast's elusive form still circling the ship. When the dragon struck the ship again, Adaron flew into the air and landed once again on the hard deck. Masts and their rigging, barrels, and a red-haired houndling with his muzzle frozen in a silent cry fell past Adaron and disappeared into the fog. Wind whipped against Adaron's hair and clothes as the *Queen of Fog* plunged into a rapid descent.

Adaron did nothing to break their fall. Any remaining ounce of his awareness recognized that nothing could save them. An adventurer's usual last resort to cling to a kyrillian buoy and rise from danger wasn't worth the effort. Where would he go? And why should he bother? His most loyal crewmates—Ialrist, and Finnar, and his love, Enora—had all lost their lives under his watch. The black beast had robbed Adaron of everyone who had meant anything to him. Death seemed his only mercy. Only then would he be rid of the searing pain of loss.

It took a moment before he noticed the figure standing next to him and the hand shaking his shoulder. "Adaron!" a distant voice called into to his ear. "Adaron, come back! You and I . . . we can still make it!"

Adaron jolted his eyes open. *Ialrist!*

Like a winged messenger of the gods, the Taijirin rose before him. The wings on his back were ruffled and torn, and blood drenched the left side of his face. Miraculously, Ialrist had survived the encounter with the Black Leviathan.

He reached a hand toward the stunned captain. "Come with me. We're the last ones remaining, but by the Illuminated Wings, I won't lose you as well!" He leaned forward and pulled Adaron into the air, holding him firmly against his waistcoat.

The ship's hull creaked and groaned as the *Queen of Fog* fell below them. A torn white sail fluttered like a flag of surrender atop the mainmast. The deck was empty, with no signs of Jonn, Belhac, or Wuffzan anywhere in sight. *By the gods, we really are the last living souls on board,* Adaron thought. *My recklessness has killed every one of them. Belhac, if only I'd listened to you. Then we never would have entered this cursed Death's Bleak.* He had paid the ultimate price.

"Hold on to my harness!" Ialrist called, pulling Adaron back to reality. "I'll get us out of here."

Adaron stared at Enora's hand still clasped in his own—the only part of his beloved that he had salvaged. Her fingers had gone cold, and the skin unnaturally white. Blood ran from the stump and dripped onto the wooden planks below. He stroked the vogelfolk amulet with a finger absently. *She was so young and so beautiful. Gods, why have you taken her?*

But it wasn't the gods that had taken her. Indra, Jerup, and Vazar couldn't be blamed for Enora's death. None but the Black Leviathan bore that deed on his conscience. The dragon's unquenchable hunger and primordial evil had robbed Adaron of the one person more precious to him than all the world's riches.

A spark kindled within his breast that transformed the horror that took hold of him into something new. With every heartbeat, the flame grew into a roaring inferno. As if drawn from a magical amulet, hatred, all consuming and powerful, gave Adaron the strength of ancient forces.

Vengeance! A vow surged through him. *You, Gargantuan, shall meet my wrath for what you have done. I will hunt you, you beast, to the gateway of the dark realm at the end of the world. Even if it is my very last act, I will find you. Upon my life, I will rip your heart out of your body, just as you have severed mine.*

"Do you hear that, Gargantuan?" he cried into the white nothingness. "I, Adaron, will be your downfall!"

Ialrist shook him. "By the Illuminated Wings, be quiet, or you'll attract the monster again."

"I dare him to come," Adaron growled.

"But not today," Ialrist insisted. "We'll get our revenge. I promise you that. But not yet."

The two locked eyes briefly. Then, unflinching, Adaron shoved Enora's arm underneath his waistcoat. With his newly free hand, he grabbed hold of Ialrist's bronze-studded leather armor. "Take us away from here, my friend."

Without another word, Ialrist spread his wings. A gust of wind stirred his feathers and pulled them upward. When Adaron blinked twice and looked down, the destroyed *Queen of Fog* had disappeared from view.

The vogelfolk beat his wings powerfully and stretched his neck upward like a drowning man struggling to reach the water's surface. As they gained height, the persistent howling grew fainter among the clouds beneath them. The Black Leviathan was nowhere in sight. The monster had retreated into the dismal abyss that had spat it out.

Adaron couldn't tell how long they'd been flying when he realized it, but the white fog surrounding them had lessened. Finally, they entered clear sky. A low-hanging evening sun glowed in the east, pouring red light over the cloud peaks as though drenching them in blood. Ice-cold wind whipped against their faces and tore at hair and feathers as it crept underneath their clothing.

"Hold on tightly," the Taijirin repeated, breathing heavily.

Adaron nodded. The pair had flown like this before, even if never under such awful circumstances. He loosened a hold on Ialrist's harness, unbuckled his belt, and threaded it through the leather of his friend's belt. Once bound securely, Adaron no longer ran the risk of slipping away during their flight.

Adaron let his gaze wander. The prospect wasn't very encouraging. Sure, Ialrist had saved him, and the two had survived the Black Leviathan's attack, but now the only sight in every direction, all the way to the horizon, was the lonely, empty Cloudmere. Not a single lithos or mountain peak could be seen through the endless white. Adaron, too, couldn't ignore that Ialrist's strength was beginning to falter.

No, he thought with renewed determination, *I won't die today. Nothing will conquer me until the day we face each other again, Gargantuan.* He raised his gaze toward the blood-tinged fog and sent his pure hatred silently to the black demon. *I'll come for you. You shall pay for the lives of my friends and my precious beloved that you have taken from me!*

3

The Streets of Skargakar

Twelfth Day of the Fifth Moon, Year 841

Under the blanket of night, fog hung heavy in the streets of Skargakar. In the coming early moments of new day, wisps of cloud would disappear in the sun's rays. Until then, however, the city lay shrouded in damp whiteness and shadowed with dark silhouettes. Night in Skargakar was a cold, nightmarish world, where walking a few hundred paces in the wrong direction could lead to being swallowed into endless nothingness.

Lian shivered and pulled his dragon leather cape tighter around his shoulders as he hurried along the narrow alleys of Hafen, the harbor quarter. He walked lightly on the cliff stone paving so that the echo of his clicking footsteps would not wake those lucky souls still asleep in their beds.

He hated having to wake before the night had even lightened to dawn, but as the season for dragon breeding came to an end, more ships set sail every day. It wasn't just the busiest time of the year for jägers, where success depended mostly on courage, but also meant extra work for all at port, especially for a kyrillian carver. Ever since Lian had begun as an apprentice to such a carver nearly twelve moons ago, his walk to work began so early that he passed drunkards staggering to their beds.

Lian turned a corner at a weatherworn house and stooped to pass through a narrow alleyway. Hafen was a maze of winding passages that ran between shingle-covered shacks and low buildings made of cliff stone, with exteriors completely covered in moss from perpetual dampness.

This constant damp, which made summer nights sticky and humid and winters clammy and gray, was the Cloudmere's doing. A newcomer in Skargakar might complain about how the damp crept into clothing, caused armor to rust, turned scrolls to sludge, and made walls cave in. If this gloomy ocean didn't shroud the life in this city, Skargakar might have looked entirely different.

Despite the damp, residents of Skargakar gave thanks to the Cloudmere for their prosperity. No other place offered such a wealth of dragons. Their skin, meat, bones, scales, teeth, and even innards made them high commodities in every land beyond Skargakar. There were even buyers for the most unappetizing parts of a dragon. Sly salesmen had a way of concocting their words to turn superstition and skepticism into coins.

Lian wasn't bothered by any of this. Just like everyone else in Skargakar, he made a living from dragons, even if only as a lowly apprentice.

He turned another corner, then another, and entered a somewhat wider street that opened directly onto the harbor's promenade. From the shadows, he made out the mast of a large ship moored in the harbor. Somewhere to his left, he heard shouts and the groan of a winch. The foul stink of festering dragon flesh hung wet and heavy in Lian's nostrils. The hunting ship had probably docked last night, and its crew was unloading their cargo.

They must have been novices, thought Lian. Experienced jägers would have prepared their catch while still on the hunt. That way, they could salvage more than just the solid parts, like scales and bones and skin. A dragon produced barrels full of meat, but no trader would touch it after it festered on deck for a week.

Maybe they'll be lucky and a merchant will take the whole carcass, he considered. Drak, the lizard-like folk who lived in tribes in the wilderness, had strong stomachs to deal with rotten meat, or so they said.

A few paces in front of him, a wooden sign hung from a short chain that kept it from swinging. The sign read *Waunar's Crystal Carvers* along a row of crystals embedded underneath, which shimmered with kyrillian's unmistakable pale violet. These crystals explained how the sign floated at eye level, rather than falling to the ground whenever passersby ran into it.

Most people took heed not to bump into Waunar's sign when passing by. All the jägers who relied on his skills protected the ancient Nondurier. After all, his carved crystals and sturdy storage cases kept their ships aloft in the clouds. There were other crystal carvers living in Skargakar, of course. The city was large, with plenty of work for everyone, but nobody carved as well as Waunar, whose capable red hands had cut and polished stones in the days before Lian had even entered the world on a chilly winter morning nearly eighteen years ago.

Lian ducked to pass under the low entranceway. Waunar was already busily working at his desk, which didn't surprise Lian in the least. The old master practically lived in his workshop. Only here, where he could devote all his care and patience to a mass of crystal, did he seem himself and at peace with the world. These moments didn't make Waunar agreeable by any means, though. Lian knew that Waunar had a good heart, but he also knew how well the Nondurier could conceal it.

"You're late," the Nondurier grumbled in greeting. His attention remained glued to the crystal in front of him, clamped into a metal brace atop his worktable. He chiseled at it with a thin wand.

Lian scanned the room, bathed in a whitish-blue light from the elven fire burning brightly in the furnace. Two other apprentices—the hunchbacked Jorun and Klaefften, a Nondurier—were missing from their places. "Forgive me, Master. My father wasn't well last night."

Waunar looked up then, his clever eyes studying Lian over the delicate spectacles, crafted by his own hand, balanced upon his wide hound's snout.

"Not well, eh?" he growled. "Did Lonjar look too far down a bloodwater bottle again?"

Lian pursed his lips and remained silent. It wasn't a secret that his father was a drunkard, but he didn't like to talk about it.

Lonjar Draksmasher had spent the first half of his life bounding from one ship to the next atop the Cloudmere. The story of his final hunt was still told in the harbor's taverns to this day. On that fateful night seven summers ago, a fireblood destroyed Lonjar's leg below the knee. The medic on board had insisted that amputation was Lonjar's only option, and Lonjar's days atop the clouds were over. Since then, he hobbled on a wooden leg, and he drank. Strong rum, with its familiar burn, was his drink of choice, especially when spiked with a dangerously high dose of dragon's blood. The concoction was known as bloodwater, because the burn consumed body and soul as it eased unthinkable pain.

"Anyway," Waunar mumbled. "Get to work now, Lian. These crystals have to be ready by this afternoon."

"Yes, Master," Lian answered. He hung his cape on a hook by the door and tied a brown leather apron around his waist. Then, he took his place at the heavy wood bench bolted into the stone ground.

One couldn't be too careful when working with kyrillian. Waunar had once told of an inexperienced carver whose worktable had crashed through the rear wall of his workshop when he had carelessly set aside a box of crystals to inspect his wand.

With a practiced hand, Lian laid his tools out on the table, lit a bowl of dragon oil, and set another bowl holding a clump of sealing wax on top of it to melt. He pulled a casing of carved crystals out from a wooden drawer beside the table and removed the linen towel from the burnished metal rack atop his work space. Then he began setting the stones that he'd worked on for the last two days.

Even in their natural forms, unworked and half-covered in cliff stone from the lithos they grew beneath, the crystals defied gravity. Cleaning, shaping, and polishing the stones improved their potency, thus saving ships from needing to install whole fields of gravel along their hulls. Four to six cases of polished stones were enough to suspend an average-sized ship in the clouds, even if the cases weren't fully opened.

Lian couldn't explain how kyrillian floated. He'd asked Master Waunar once but hadn't been given a straight answer. "It's magic," the old Nondurier had said, "and there's no reason for magic. Well, at least I can't explain it. But I wouldn't want to, either. I'll leave that to the scholars in their academy. The only thing that counts to me is how to coax the stones to do as I want them to."

Lian had struggled to accept this. Contrary to Waunar, Lian's calling wasn't to be a crystal carver. He returned to the workshop day after day because kyrillian fascinated him. For Lian, every crystal had its own meaning. Each glowing stone represented the mystery and promise that stretched across the entire expanse of the Cloudmere.

He carefully slid the lowest slat of the case open, and the familiar soft violet shimmer met his eyes. The crystal glowed, even through the metal lining that stifled its power—yet another mystery that bothered Lian and busied the scholars. Still, he took advantage of the fact that base metals robbed kyrillian of its power so that he could do his work.

The case holding the kyrillian had no lid but instead slid open. Since the drawer narrowed toward the back, Lian could grasp one crystal at a time, but he had to be careful that the gem didn't shoot up toward the ceiling beams. The trick was to rotate the crystal so that the polished side pointed upward, and its power would radiate toward the earth. Only then could the stones be handled at all.

Anyone holding kyrillian for the first time would be astonished by its weight. A typical precious stone of similar dimensions weighed practically nothing in comparison. A tiny fragment of kyrillian, though, had as much weight as a large hen's egg and could raise as much into the air when fastened to it.

He could hold a single crystal in his hand, but it was harder to hold more than one. The stones' weight increased exponentially. A handful of crystals was difficult for a man of Lian's size to carry.

This was how six metal cases containing forty to eighty kyrillian crystals each, depending on the size of the ship, could lift a ship into the sky. It took many men to carry such cases but they were necessary to lift a ship formidable enough to face beasts like firebloods.

Lian had his work cut out for him if he hoped to work through nearly two dozen stones by midday. It would be a stretch, even without a break.

One after the other, he was to fill each setting with sealing wax and lay each stone into place. The wax only served to set the alignment. Metal clamps tightly secured the crystal itself.

While he worked to place the second crystal, Jorun entered the workshop. Jorun was a crooked and haggard little man, about the same age as Lian's father. He was almost always good-natured, even when Skargakar's streets filled with blinding fog for five days straight.

By Lian's fourth crystal, Klaefften finally appeared. His ears hung heavily as though he'd gone yet another mealtime with no bread. "Forgive me, Master," he growled in a hoarse voice. "My brother and his comrades returned from the hunt last night. We celebrated their conquest over a goldscale, and I was stupid enough to stay out too late."

"A goldscale, hm?" Waunar said without looking up. He'd lived on the edge of Hafen so long that he'd heard all the stories a thousand times before. "And how big was the pearl they found?" he added, his eyes twinkling.

"As big as a man's fist," Klaefften answered proudly, balling his furry hand into a fist. "A marvelous find, fit for a king. That's what they said."

Waunar nodded. "Then my congratulations to your brother and his comrades." His pointed ears flattened against his red head. "And tonight you can clean up once the rest of us have set down our tools and gone home."

Klaefften sank his head and ears in remorse. "As you wish, Master," he said sulkily.

He lowered himself onto his workbench behind Lian. With a clatter and a whir, the great polishing stone begin to swing across a leather strap as Klaefften stepped on a wooden pedal to begin his work cleaning raw kyrillian.

Some time later, Lian set his crystal into its frame. He jostled the contraption to make sure all the stones were fastened securely. "Master, the frame is set," he said with satisfaction.

The Nondurier stood from his work space and approached Lian. Straightening his spectacles over his snout, he leaned forward to inspect Lian's progress. With a practiced hand and critical eye, he assessed the work, pausing between each row to mumble softly.

"Very good," he said, standing up. "Run a rag across the frame, and then you can take a break."

Lian nodded. "Yes, Master."

He was still busy polishing the frame when the door jingled open. At the sound of heavy footsteps, he turned. An enormous man, with stringy shoulder-length hair and a bushy beard, towered before him. The jäger wore soldier's armor made from gray dragon scales and a coarse leather cape across his left shoulder. A chain of fangs as sharp as daggers lined his chest, and the crown of a dragon's skull formed his helmet. A long-handled ax hung from a strap across his back and throwing axes dangled from his belt. To the right of his knee-high, cuffed boots, a blade resembling a short sword glinted in the firelight.

"Master Waunar," boomed the newcomer. "I've come to retrieve the new frame for the helm of *Draconia*. Have you finished it?"

"But of course, Captain Koos," the Nondurier answered, pointing in Lian's direction. "There it is."

The hulk of a man approached Lian's workstation, shooting him a critical glance. Then he turned to assess the crystals glittering in their frame. Lian stepped aside, still clutching the polishing rag.

The jäger pulled his hand from underneath his cape. Setting it onto the table, Lian saw that it wasn't a hand at all. Attached to Koos's remaining arm was a cuff ending in a black metal hook, blacker than night from its matte finish. Using his actual hand, the man opened each slat one after the other, carefully inspecting Lian's work.

"Never seen a man with a hook for a hand before?" the jäger growled and continued to examine the fourth row of crystals, not glancing at Lian.

Shaken from his daze, Lian forced himself to speak. "No, uh, I mean yes. Forgive me," he stammered bashfully. "I've just never seen one as black as yours before."

Koos observed Lian and raised his hook. "I buffed it to get rid of the shine. All the metal on board my ship is buffed. Dragons have damned sharp eyes, you know. One ray of sunshine against a naked blade at the wrong time could mean life or death."

Lian noticed that the ax at the captain's back also had a blackened blade.

"Did a dragon do that?" he dared to ask, pointing toward Koos's hook.

Koos grunted. "A gray lizardscale, to be exact. Not very big and still relatively young. But a bloody quick bastard, he was. I was lucky he only cost me a hand."

"Did you catch him?"

A self-satisfied grin curled across Koos's bearded face. "I carry his head as a helmet decoration," he said proudly and pointed toward the skull. Then he slid the final slat closed and turned to Waunar. "The case is in order."

"I'm glad to hear it," the Nondurier answered. "Shall we install it onto the hull for you?"

"No need. My men can manage on their own. I'll take it with me now."

Waunar nodded. "As you wish. I presume you have brought the amount we agreed upon?"

"So I have," answered Koos, reaching into his harness with his good hand to pull out a leather pouch. He tossed it toward the Nondurier, who aptly caught it.

A soft clicking could be heard, not of metal but of stone. Hardly anyone paid with coins in Skargakar. Most business was transacted using precious stones collected from the coast and the floating isles of the Cloudmere. Each one was assigned worth based on purity and rarity.

"Would you like to count them?" the jäger asked.

Waunar tightened his fist around the pouch. "Please don't think that I doubt your word, Captain, but I would prefer that. It's so easy to mistake Amorite with Wavequartz if one isn't used to telling the difference."

Koos laughed. "If you knew how many dragon skulls and barrels of blood that Amorite cost me, you'd trust that I know the exact worth of every stone inside that sack."

"A worth I reciprocate by providing you with a storage case holding the finest carved kyrillian that one can buy in Skargakar," answered Waunar, unimpressed. "Now if you'll excuse me."

Koos waved him on. "Go, then, and count your loot." He chuckled.

The Nondurier disappeared through a small door at the far wall. As the door closed, Lian realized he'd forgotten to ask to take his lunch break. Even though he'd already been told to take a break, he still needed Waunar's permission to leave the workshop unattended. He grimaced as his stomach rumbled. Now he'd have to wait until Waunar returned to go to the tavern.

Unsure what to do, Lian wound the polishing cloth in his hands until he realized that Koos was studying him thoughtfully. Then the jäger pointed his hook toward Lian's chest. "I recognize your face from somewhere. Have we met before?"

"I don't believe so, sir. I'm pretty sure I'd remember you." It wasn't a lie. Sure, there were many drachenjägers in Skargakar, and hardly any were shy and reserved, but a man of Koos's size, who wore a dragon's skull on his head, was a sight that would have remained in Lian's memory.

"Then why is your face so familiar?" Koos asked again pensively.

"Maybe you know my father. He used to sail on jäger ships. They call him Lonjar Draksmasher."

"Draksmasher?" Koos looked surprised. "You are the son of Draksmasher? That name is certainly known to me. More dragons were pierced by that man's spear than by any other weapon. Come to mention it, I see the resemblance. Your face is similar, and you stand the same way. Say, can you throw a spear as surely as your father could?"

"He showed me what he knew," Lian answered elusively. "But I'll never be as good." He hadn't missed the change in Koos's tone. The jäger had begun to address him noticeably less dismissively. Nonetheless, Lian longed to change the subject.

The captain pressed on. "If you're only half as bold as your father, you belong on the hunt. By the Winds, why are you wasting your talents cooped up in this workshop when you could be on the greatest adventure of your life? Any captain would welcome Draksmasher's son aboard his ship."

Lian shook his head and stared at the ground. "I can't, sir. My father needs me here."

"Why?" Koos wanted to know. "What's wrong with him? I thought he'd be sitting on top of his treasure, growing fat and surrounded by admirers."

"You must have been away for a long time, if you don't know," Lian said, smiling sadly. "Lonjar Draksmasher isn't the man he once was."

Koos raised his bushy eyebrows. "What happened? Is he ill?"

"Yes, sir. 'Ill' is one way to put it."

4

Sweet and Destroyed Dreams

Twelfth Day of the Fifth Moon, Year 841

The sun nodded above the western horizon as Lian made his way homeward. His right fingers throbbed from an afternoon spent carving kyrillian. Usually, he was accustomed to the effort required to shape a stone, the unrelenting force of sanding back and forth, and his body adapted over time, but a few days' rest from the sander to prepare storage cases had made his fingers lazy. Now they swelled purple—not so different from the glowing crystal they had carved.

Instead of heading directly to the small and run-down house where he lived with his father, he took a detour. Captain Koos had revived a longing inside him that normally lay dormant, and the harbor beckoned to him. A cool breeze and the call of swallows pulled him forward as he strolled along the way leading toward the steep precipice that signaled the end of solid land and beginning of the Cloudmere.

Lian loved the harbor, and not just because his friend Canzo worked in the slaughter yard at the western end of the market. Cliff House, the tavern where the two friends met at least once a week, wasn't the reason, either.

It was the ships that lured him there.

All along the harbor, whether along the cliff edge supported by bricks, or along the wooden docks that stretched out over the abyss like the winding branches of a tree, ships bobbed in the lapping mist. Some were only skiffs, with one triangular sail and two benches, where men known as Cliff Clippers prowled the treacherous coasts along forbidding rock faces to rob nests, poach moss, and break away any crystals they found. Merchant ships also docked there, whose captains either conducted business among vogelfolk colonies in the isles or set out north, their holds full of dragon scales and precious stones to trade for fabric and spices in Nemred or Maduria.

Jäger ships made the greatest impact at harbor by far. Hunting ships were easily discernible, not only by their white-and-gray-painted hulls but also by the row of shields that lined their railings, the harpoon ballistae at their bows, and the large nets and rolls of rope lining their decks to secure their catches to their hulls.

Lian had spent more than one fresh spring morning or melancholy summer evening wondering what it would be like to set forth across the Cloudmere's white expanse. He dreamed of having no plans except for the task at hand—to catch the greatest prize imaginable. A drachen pearl, that elusive treasure, gave wings to the fantasies of every jäger.

That wish alone lured Lian toward cloudy unknown, to venture where no ship had sailed before, where tales were told of terrible dragons that no person had ever set eyes on.

For Lian, however, the hunt was not the goal. It was the journey itself, sailing through the clouds to discover faraway shores, that was far more alluring to him. Over his entire life, he had never left Skargakar, not counting the occasional ride on a Cliff Clipper's rowboat or a childhood fantasy adventure into untrodden jungles of afar. As he grew older, his longing to flee the cramped city, if only for a few moon cycles, grew within him.

But it isn't possible, thought Lian as he wandered the pier and watched crews busy at work aboard on the decks of their ships. If he were to go, he knew his father was as good as dead. Lonjar Draksmasher wasn't capable of taking care of himself anymore. Sure, some days Lian found it difficult to care whether his thankless father, whose body and spirit deteriorated by the day, lived or died. Then the memory would return of how Lonjar used to be before he'd lost both his legs and his bride. Lian knew he could never abandon his father. There were even a few good days—almost—where Lonjar would push through his drunken haze and become the person Lian remembered.

"Lian! Hey, Lian!"

The call startled Lian from his daze. He turned away from the ships and spotted Canzo waving as he neared. The young man stood nearly a head taller than Lian, and though his upper arms showed the signs of hard physical labor, his belly was proof of his love for food. He wore a sleeveless wool tunic, gray dragon leather pants, and heavy black boots. Brown flecks of splattered blood stained his pant legs and shoes.

"Canzo." Lian smiled. "It's nice to see you."

"Yes, it's always a pleasure," said Canzo formally. "And convenient, too, as I'm on the way to Cliff House. Want to join me?"

For a moment, Lian hesitated as he remembered his father waiting in the dark corner of their main room, his armchair creaking as he grumbled sullenly, a jug of spiked ale sloshing in his hand. He pushed the thought out of his mind and smiled at his friend. "Gladly! It's been far too long since the last time."

"Indeed, three whole nights," Canzo joked.

They turned away from the ships and headed east toward a small hill on the edge of the docks—the best view for seeing what went on at harbor.

"How's the slaughter yard these days?" Lian asked.

Canzo worked as a slaughterman, one of the poor souls who waded knee-deep through blood and innards to collect a dragon's precious scales and skin, as well as horns, teeth, claws, and even their organs and fluids (useful in alchemy). It was a filthy and thankless job, but slaughtermen were very important in Skargakar. Without them, jägers with smaller ships couldn't reap the full benefits of their harvest. Almost all tools, clothing, shields, weapons, jewelry, talismans, and drugs they used in the city were made from dragon parts—not counting the dragon meat that tavern owners kept on the menu.

"Oh, the same as ever," Canzo answered. "Why do you ask?"

"Klaefften told us that his brother arrived with a goldscale last night," Lian explained. "The pearl was supposedly as big as a man's fist. I wondered if you encountered the carcass on your table?"

His friend shook his head. "No, no goldscales under my knife. Our last delivery was two bronzenecks and an old bluetail. Had the most beautiful wings I've ever seen. A ship with sails made from those wings would fly so quickly, it would practically be alive itself."

"You're a true poet," Lian said with a smirk.

"You should hear me after five mugs of ale!"

"I *have* heard you after five mugs. And believe me, it wasn't pleasant," Lian said, and Canzo laughed.

When they reached the end of the docks, they began their way up toward the only dwelling atop the hill. The building's black shingled roof was askew, and moss grew like a rash over the entire surface. The tavern was built so dizzyingly close to the cliff's edge that peering out from windows facing south meant staring directly into the Cloudmere's depths.

As they pushed open the heavy door, they were met by the raw laughter of drunken men. "More beer," bellowed one, and other voices echoed the call. Canzo pushed his way along the bustling counter, and Lian followed.

Even so early in the evening, the tavern was full with customers. Locals and ship workers sat at the many tables drinking, eating, and talking loudly among themselves. They were mostly men, the youngest showing only a shadow of a beard on his chin and the oldest with white beards with wrinkled faces. In the far corner, a bard plucked a lute. The stink of unwashed bodies and scorched dragon meat hung heavily in the air.

To the left of the entrance, Lian and Canzo found places at the counter. Canzo banged a fist overconfidently against the polished countertop. "Anija!" he called to the black-haired barmaid standing at the far end of the counter, who filled stone mugs full with ale from a flowing tap. "Two herb brews over here!"

The young woman glanced toward them and waved to signal that she'd heard their order. After serving other waiting guests, she carried the drinks over to them. "Lian and Canzo. You visit more often lately. So thirsty, or what?"

"We can manage the thirst, but not our longing to see you," Lian crooned. "You know how much Canzo admires you."

Anija laughed lightly and smiled as she glanced at Lian for a moment before locking eyes with Canzo. "Yes, that I know. He's let on more than once. And I hope he'll keep letting on." Her dark eyes glimmered mischievously.

Canzo's cheeks flushed bright red. "Whenever you call on me, I'll be there, my lovely one," he said in barely more than a whisper, grinning awkwardly.

"Then don't stray too far tonight. I might call during the wee hours of the night." She ran a finger across his chin, her eyes still sparkling. Then a customer's call drew her away. "I have to get back to work," she stammered. "Too many parched throats need relief."

Lian raised his mug and, nodding to Anija, took a long gulp. From the corner of his eye, he spotted a familiar figure standing at the kitchen door. Emman, Anija's father and Cliff House's owner, shot an accusing look toward the two boys. Then he reeled around and disappeared through the door into the cloud of cooking smoke that filled his small kingdom.

"He seems in an especially foul mood today," said Canzo.

"Seems about the same to me," added Lian.

Canzo sipped his ale nervously, set his mug on the counter, and wiped a hand across his mouth. "Sometimes I wonder if he knows something about Anija and me."

"Maybe he doesn't want to know," Lian answered. "But it sure seems like he has some grudge against us. He's skeptical of any man who shows interest in his daughter." This observation wasn't quite accurate, actually. Emman's flirtatious daughter offered her warm breast as readily as she gave a cold shoulder to just about any young man, but Lian kept the sentiment to himself. He didn't want to hurt Canzo's feelings. He could see that his friend was still reeling from the thought of having Anija all to himself and didn't notice all the competition that sat around him.

"She is such a beauty. And I am such a lucky man!" Canzo sighed. "I don't have the slightest idea why she gave me her heart. I don't have any treasures to show for myself or a jäger's courage to impress her with. I'm just a lowly slaughterman."

"Maybe it's your strong hands," taunted Lian. "Or the musky scent of hot dragon flesh makes her blood rush."

Canzo looked at Lian, wounded. "You can joke if you want, but I promise you this: you'll be sitting jealously in front of your mug while I'm bouncing a son on my knee. Just you wait."

"I wish you all the luck in the world," Lian said, raising his mug. "Honestly. Just don't get too lost in your fantasies. It might end very differently."

"I doubt that," Canzo said, gazing longingly across the tavern to the young woman who now served a table of Nondurier. "And I don't care how threatening her father is, either. One of these days, I'll take the next step and ask her to marry me. I'll wear my best shirt and give her a bracelet I made using carved Amorite that I collected myself from the islands. That will show her how great my love is. She'll weep with happiness when she accepts me, and we'll be happy for the rest of our days. You'll see."

Lian listened with pursed lips and cupped his mug. He didn't believe in the sort of simple happiness that Canzo described. Not since spotted fever took his mother and his father sank from his heroic jäger's past into the embittered cripple that he was now.

"I hear the winds of your words and am at your service, friend," Lian murmured. He raised his mug and drank the rest.

It was already dark and far too late when Lian finally reached the small house cramped between the others, where he and his father lived. In the reddish shine of a nearby street lantern lit with dragon oil, he pushed the knob of the worm-eaten wooden door and was met with surprise. The door was bolted shut. His father had locked him out.

"Miserable bastard," Lian muttered. He wondered whether Lonjar did it out of anger for returning home so late or whether he'd simply gotten so drunk that he couldn't remember he even had a son at all.

He bashed a fist against the door but refrained from calling out at so late at night. Inside, nothing stirred.

Lian cursed under his breath, then tested the window next to the front door, but that, too, was locked tightly. If his father had gone to such lengths, he must have been at least halfway conscious. Luckily, this wasn't the first time Lian had been forced to break into his own house. At least he was prepared.

He walked to the side of the house until he reached the small gap between his and the neighboring building. It couldn't exactly be called an alleyway; at best, the gap was large enough for a person to shimmy through. Lian groaned as he waded past the trash and muck that filled the space.

His goal wasn't to reach the back of the house but to retrieve a dull and broken sword shard that he had hidden underneath a pile of garbage. Clutching the blade, he shimmied back through the opening and returned to the window. He glanced toward the houses along the street to make sure that nobody ran toward him holding a crossbow, mistaking him for a criminal. In a city like Skargakar, where there were practically more jägers than ordinary villagers, the houses contained enough weapons to lead a small army, but the windows of the nearby buildings remained dark and still. Either their inhabitants were fast asleep or still busy at one of the city's many taverns.

Carefully, Lian wedged the blade between the wooden shutters and pulled upward. With a quiet click and rattle, the latch released. After testing to make sure he could slide the window open, he stowed his blade back in its place.

The window leading into the kitchen had no drapes. Lian and his father weren't nearly well-off enough for that. Instead, a simple curtain made of brown wool hung from the inside to protect from cold gusts of wind and the overly curious eyes of passersby whenever the shutters were open. Lian pushed the material aside and swung a leg over the windowsill. After sliding quietly inside, the curtain fell back into place behind him. For a moment, Lian couldn't see a thing. The oil lamp on the dining table had been put out, and not even a glow from the remaining embers in the stove led his way.

At least Lian was home and knew where to find the box of matches. After lighting the lamp, he turned the wick down to dim the flame as much as possible. Then he headed toward the door to begin the long journey across groaning floorboards to his bedchamber. He had to be up before sunrise again the next morning.

He had reached the sitting room adjoining the kitchen when he heard a menacing growl. When a blade glinted in the lamplight, Lian jumped back. "Father!" he cried. "It's your son, Lian!"

The hand holding the knife neared, but his father's grip was unsteady, and his attack was delayed enough for Lian to move aside. He set the oil lamp onto a nearby trunk. With the next charge, he felt the familiar grasp on his upper arm and the firm blow that knocked air from his chest as his father threw him against the kitchen doorframe.

"Father!" Lian gasped, coughing. "I'm not a thief. It's Lian."

Lonjar squinted through bloodshot eyes in the shine of the oil lamp. His breath and the hairs on his beard stank of herb ale and potato schnapps. He groaned and let the knife fall clattering to the ground. "Lian," he gasped in his dark and raw tone, "I thought you were never coming back."

"I was with Canzo at Cliff House," Lian explained. "We got stuck talking and forgot what time it was."

Lonjar moaned softly and swayed sideways.

"Wouldn't you like to sit?" Lian led his father to the armchair in the corner of the main room, where he always sat with a woolen blanket across his lap. His father fell onto the cushion with a thud. He moaned again and leaned forward, hiding his face in his hands.

Lian glanced around, found the dagger that Lonjar had used to attack him with, and shoved it into the back of his belt. Scanning the room, he saw that his attempt to keep deadly weapons out of his father's reach was hopeless. His father's spear hung over the fireplace, and an ax leaned against the back door. Next to an opened trunk that contained handheld weapons, a sword and scale shield lay strewn across the floor, and Lonjar's scale armor peeked out of another trunk at the far wall.

Lian frowned. His father was certainly never one to keep his home tidy, but he never left weapons lying around carelessly. Actually, Lian hadn't seen any of his father's mementos from his jäger past for years.

"Father, what's going on?" Lian asked suspiciously. He knelt at the chest and picked up the sword and shield.

Lonjar raised his head. "I'm done for," he slurred and buried his head in his hands again.

His father admitting weakness was almost as disturbing to Lian as what he'd been doing with the weapons. Lonjar was almost always in trouble. Either he was in a tiff with a barkeeper or was spewing insults at the city guard, but he never wanted to discuss it. If he did, he only ever blamed the other person.

Lian returned the sword and shield to the trunk and followed with the armor. Then he closed the lid and sat down on top of it. He was afraid to ask—afraid to hear the answer. He would much prefer to go to bed and leave this man, who only had himself to thank for his downfall, alone in his chair. On the other hand, though, Lonjar was his father and the only remaining person that Lian called family. So he asked, "What have you done, Father?"

"I was in Green Dragon," Lonjar murmured. Lian wasn't surprised. His father went to the tavern near the harbor whenever he couldn't find anything more to drink at home. "Everything was s-s-swell. Jeren and Konn kept me company. There wasn' mush g-going on, but that didn' bother ush. We wanted p-p-peace and quiet." He covered his face with his hands again, moaning. "Then C-Casran came in."

Lian sat upright when he heard the name. "Casran Klingenhand?"

Lonjar nodded weakly.

"Oh no. You didn't cross him, did you?" Casran was the son of Odan Klingenhand, a man feared by all in Skargakar. As the story went, he had only hunted dragons for a few moons, when an obsidianscale took his right hand. Afterward, he was bound to the land and took over a harbor slaughter yard at first. He made it his mission, through a mixture of violence, skill, and bribery, to gain influence over the other businesses in town. Today, he owned most of the docks and surrounding workshops, taverns, and whorehouses. The only person who crossed Odan was someone who didn't value his life. His son Casran was an intolerable loudmouth, but to his doting father, he could do no wrong.

"What do you want me to say?" cried Lonjar Draksmasher. "He and his men were at least as drunk as we were. He hadda girl wi' him, against her will it seemed to me. Prob'ly the daughter of some poor s-s-swine who had already met the wrong end of Odan's club. Anyway, Casran tried to have his way with the girl, right there in the middle of the tavern. So I let him have it—but it gets uglier."

Lian felt a hard lump grow in his gut. "You didn't kill him, did you?"

"No, no, no, no, not that. But I don't think he had any pants on when I drove him out of the tavern." His father chuckled.

At that moment, the front door blew off its hinges.

5

Kraghma's Jaws

Twelfth Day of the Fifth Moon, Year 841

Lian cried out in shock as a colossal giant blasted through the wreckage of the front door. The creature's skin was jet-black, as if boiling lava had dried and hardened on his body. With the sound of stones scraping, he turned his distorted skull toward Lian and glared with eyes like embers.

He had heard of Odan's new henchmen through rumors whispered in the streets over the past moons, but he'd hoped that these horrors—monsters black as the night, hard as a mountain, and as violent as an avalanche—were merely stories that Odan had spread to instill fear in his victims and enemies. Now, with the power of a stone fist, that hope was smashed to bits.

Behind the giant, three men streamed into the main room. Their dirty, torn clothing and their grimaces revealed that they'd just come from another fight. The leader, who held a lantern, had an eye swollen shut and crusted blood dried on his chin. His comrades, both carrying clubs, didn't appear much better off.

Lonjar let out an inarticulate cry, jumped off his chair, hobbled toward the fireplace, and grabbed his spear.

But the men were faster. While the first lit his lantern, the other two threw themselves on Lian's father.

"You're done for, miserable drunkard!" one bellowed as his club connected with a dull thud on Lonjar's back.

Lonjar smashed into the stone mantelpiece, gasping for breath.

"You caught us off guard at Green Dragon, but now you'll pay."

"No!" Lian cried. "Leave him alone!" Without thinking, he ripped the dagger from his belt and ran forward, prepared to bury his blade between the man's ribs.

With superhuman strength, a stone hand crashed onto Lian's shoulder. "Not you," the monster growled in a deep rumble.

Lian turned toward his opponent, stabbing with the dagger, but when blade met the monster's black chest, it bounced off with a clang and left no mark.

Another stone hand met Lian's ear. Though probably meant as a light reprimand, the impact felt like running into a castle wall. Stunned, Lian lurched toward the kitchen entryway and grasped for anything to keep him upright.

Behind him, his father cried out in agony while Odan's men laughed and jeered. Out of nowhere, Lonjar let out a menacing growl, a sound Lian had never heard from him before. The watchman called out a warning, then another cried out in pain.

Lian turned at the sound of a crash. His father had brought his chair down onto one of his attackers, who now lay groaning on the tiled floor while blood flowed from a fresh wound on his temple.

In the meantime, Lonjar had busied himself with his second opponent. Heaving the heavy chair back into the air, he attempted to keep the man who charged toward him at a distance. His wrinkled face pinched with pain and effort, and blood trickled from his head and seeped into his beard. It didn't seem like his father could hold out much longer, thought Lian, no matter which battles he'd won in the past.

"Câchurt, finish him," boomed the watchman.

The stone man plowed toward Lonjar.

For a heartbeat, Lian considered throwing himself onto the monster's back and wrapping his arms around his throat in a chokehold, but he immediately scrapped the idea. This monster would swat him off as easily as he might a troublesome insect.

Instead, Lian leaped over the man on the floor and raced to the trunk containing Lonjar's weapons. He ripped open the lid and grabbed the sword. The blade wasn't perfectly sharpened, but the steel was heavy and high quality, fit for a jäger. If his father could slay dragons with this blade, thought Lian, then he could also do some damage to this stone demon's knees.

The monster menacing his father let out a screeching roar like two colliding stone slabs and tore the chair out of Lonjar's hands. Lonjar cried out in surprise and rolled sideways, grappling for his spear. Just as his fingers clasped around the wooden shaft, the monster ripped it from his hands and punched him square in the face.

Lonjar tumbled backward and crashed against the wall.

Lian cried out and attacked, lunging with his sword at the monster's back. With a clash of metal and flash of sparks, pieces of stone flew in every direction, but no flesh appeared below the stony surface, only more stone.

What kind of unholy creature is this? Lian wondered. If the beast was made entirely of living stone, normal weapons wouldn't accomplish anything.

Maybe I can at least hold him off or slow him down, he considered. While the monster grabbed Lonjar's shoulder and head-butted him with a resounding crack, Lian readied himself for the fight and aimed his blade at the back of the monster's knee.

He never had the chance to meet his mark. A blow smashed against the back of his head, and pain spread across his skull as he stumbled sideways. Another blow met his legs and threw him from his feet. Lian fell ribs-first into an overturned table and landed with an agonizing crash on the stone-tiled floor. A foot kicked his hand and sent his sword out of his reach. Lian cried out, pulled his hand toward his chest, and squinted as he looked up.

The watchman stood over Lian, holding his comrade's club over his head. His face shone red in the lantern's flickering light. "Just stay there," he warned. "This has nothing to do with you, but I won't sleep any worse if I have to break all your bones."

Gasping, Lian struggled to stand, but when he felt another kick to his side, he crumpled into himself, panting. "You bastards!" he hissed through clamped teeth. "You'll pay for this!" Tears of fury blurred his vision. His skull throbbed, and his side seared with pain.

"Just shut your trap," spat the watchman. "Unless you want to end up like your wasted father." Kicking Lian again, he brought his club down on Lian's chest.

Through his daze, Lian watched as the stone giant heaved his barely conscious father over his shoulder like a sack of wet laundry.

"We're done here," the watchman growled. "Now let's get out before some overeager vigilante shows up." He laughed mockingly at his own joke and turned to follow the giant out the door. The other two fighters followed suit, one leaning against the other, as they staggered through the door and disappeared from Lian's view.

They'll kill him. Casran will kill him. Who besides Odan's spawn, a crook with wounded pride, would be insane enough to send these fighters?

With crushed body and spirit, Lian would have preferred to lie motionless and hopeless until dawn, but if Lonjar Draksmasher passed one thing on to his son, it was a fearlessness—a fearlessness before colossal enemies that neared the point of self-destruction. Anger for his father's endless foolishness, combined with loathing for the brutality shown by Casran's men, allowed Lian to summon the strength to pull himself to his feet, though he groaned with every motion.

He hobbled toward the mantel, clutching his ribs, to retrieve the weapon that his father had attempted to grasp. Wincing as he reached, he closed his fingers around the wooden shaft that had been bathed in dragon's blood and scalded in dragon fire all those years ago. The runes chiseled into the long, jagged spear blade glinted in the shine of the oil lamp that still flickered on the trunk. Lian ran a finger over the edge, still as sharp as the day it had been forged. Lonjar's sword, shield, armor, and even his own life may have fallen into disrepair, but he had preserved his spear like a holy relic.

Clutching the weapon, Lian passed through the demolished doorway and set out into the night. The sky was pitch-black and thick with fog, penetrated only by tiny islands of red light from the street lanterns to give any indication of the way.

Though they had a slight lead, Lian lost all hope of making out his father's captors in the darkness. Their footsteps were a dull vibration between the houses—if the thumping he heard was even their footsteps at all. Skargakar didn't only stir by day. Even so late at night, there were plenty of people on the street.

What choice remained but to hope that he followed the right men?

Lian raced down the street. His ribs and skull ached, and soon he was panting from fatigue as his heart beat furiously. The dragon spear, though an ideal weapon in battle against winged monstrosities, was heavy and awkward to carry. While its length was ideal for hunting dragons from speeding ships, it certainly wasn't made for chases through narrow city streets.

At an intersection, Lian stopped short. Noise traveling from a corner tavern overpowered every other sound. *Where are they?* He couldn't lose them. He squinted into the blackness, but could see nothing beyond fifty paces. The kidnappers could have taken his father anywhere. Odan had hideouts all over town. If Lian lost track of his father, he would never find him again.

With increasing panic, he approached a small group of men loitering in front of the tavern, too drunk to begin their staggering journeys home. "Have you seen three men and a stone giant carrying an unconscious man across his shoulder?" he asked.

The men looked back at him completely dumbfounded.

"Three men and a stone giant carrying a fourth man?" Lian repeated impatiently.

"S-s-stone giant?" the single Nondurier in the group slurred as though he would likely have trouble recognizing his own name.

"Yes. Enormous. Black with glowing eyes."

At the description, one man's bleary eyes widened. "Yes, a black monster. I saw it break through the fog, just like a demon in a nightmare. But then the fog swallowed it right back up again."

"Which direction did they go?"

"That way." The man's unsteady finger pointed left toward the city limits. "I think . . ."

"Thank you," Lian managed as he started to run again.

From behind, another voice called, "They were heading for Kraghma's Jaws."

Lian's feet froze on the spot as though rooted to the ground. Turning in surprise, he looked at the stocky gray-haired man in leather clothing. A chain of fangs—from small lizardwings, by the looks of it—clacked together as he crossed his strong arms across his chest.

"What did you say?" asked Lian.

"The one with the lantern said they'd meet Casran at Kraghma's Jaws. So you'd better get cracking if you want to save whoever they had with them," he said gravely.

Lian struggled to swallow, his throat keenly bone dry. "Thanks," he managed rawly. Then he whipped back and rushed down the street. Concern that he would arrive too late overpowered his own pain.

Kraghma's Jaws was a remote, sickle-shaped cliff just outside of the city that leaned toward the chasm at the far end of the landfall. Just as along the rest of the Cloudmere's coastline, fog lapped just below the cliff's cracked edge. Pointed rock spires jutted from the depths at the cliff's base, like fangs inside a dragon's jaws—the reason for its name. They said that Kraghma was an infamous fireblood that had roamed the land before the founding of Skargakar.

Supposedly, the only poor souls thrown into Kraghma's Jaws were criminals who committed the most heinous crimes—a fate decided by the city council. Lian doubted, however, that Casran would receive much trouble over the murder of an old drunkard. Half the council answered to Casran's father—either through debts or through bribes. For the other half, Lonjar Draksmasher was merely a figure from stories that jägers bragged about.

Nobody would fight for Lian's father—except Lian.

But why should I? Lian wondered as he rushed down Skargakar's dark passageways. His father was an embittered, wasted, and nasty old man. Lian would probably be better off without him, anyway.

Still, his father was the only remaining family that he had. His mother had been gone for so long that Lian struggled to remember what she looked like. There were no uncles or aunts to speak of, and the only sister that Lian had known had died just after birth in the summer of his father's longest dragon hunt.

Everyone else is gone, Lian thought as the painful memory surged through him. He clenched his teeth, gripped his spear tighter, and quickened his pace. He refused to lose his father, too.

Houses became sparse until eventually the cobblestone street under Lian's feet ended entirely. Earth and gravel crunched under his feet as he left the city limits and began the ascent toward Kraghma's Jaws. The way was steep, and Lian wondered if his urgent worry would be enough to maintain his strength. His steps were already labored, and red spots danced before his eyes.

I can't give up. I can't!

A sudden gust of wind from the Cloudmere swept away the fog, unveiling the cliff's jagged edge. Though he couldn't see the rock shard fangs below, Lian made out seven figures gathered on the cliff side—six human men and a powerful obsidian giant.

The giant held Lonjar Draksmasher's beaten body firmly in its stone grip. Lian recognized the watchman and the two henchmen who had attacked his house. One held his hand against an enormous lump on his forehead, but apparently wouldn't miss the execution for anything. The other figures were Casran himself, with black hair and hardened shadowy features on a wiry frame, and his bodyguard, a powerful bald-headed man.

As he approached, Lian tried to assess the situation. The bodyguard stood absently by, a lantern in one hand and heavy mace in the other, while Lian's father appeared to be reasoning with Casran, but their words disappeared into the fog, and Lian could only guess what they said.

A wild urge to storm the group overcame him. His hands cramped around the spear's shaft. *I have to save him, I have to save him!*—the words hammered in his mind.

His reason quietly reminded him that he was no match for so many enemies—one of whom was an invincible monster of living stone. Even if he were to catch them by surprise, he would only be able to take down two men at best before the others overpowered him.

Lian faltered. Whichever gruesome god deigned to glance on him—the Northern Wind, he feared—must have taken his hesitation for a sign.

Casran raised his hand and gave the signal. The stony giant grasped

Lian's father around the waist, hauled him toward the cliff's edge, and lifted him into the air. Lonjar Draksmasher groaned in distress.

"No!" cried Lian. With all his remaining might, he charged toward the group.

6

The Sidhari

Twelfth Day of the Fifth Moon, Year 841

At the sound of his cry, the men turned toward Lian in astonishment. With the spear before him, he reached the group in just a few paces. The stone monster grumbled in confusion and dropped Lonjar's body to the ground. Casran raised a hand to hold him back.

"Wait," he instructed.

The man's nose was swollen, which made his face appear comical—although Lian didn't think to laugh. Instead, he stared furiously at the man, unsure what he should do now that he stood before him.

Casran observed him briefly, and his lips curled into a sneer. "Well, who do we have here?" he asked.

"That's Lonjar's son," explained the watchman hastily.

"Lonjar's son?" repeated Casran in mock surprise. "Didn't you tell me that he was lying on the floor of his father's house with broken ribs?"

"He's obviously just as pigheaded as his father," the watchman answered, looking at Lian reproachfully. "I told you to stay out of this. Now you'll pay the ultimate price for your foolishness."

"Shut your trap, Sorre!" hissed Casran. "We'll deal with your faults in a moment. You promised that you knew how to properly teach someone a lesson."

The watchman hung his head like a beaten dog, but Odan's son had already turned his attention back to Lian.

"Well, what do you want? Have you come to witness your father pay the penalty for challenging me? Or . . ." He looked shocked. "Did you really think you could stop us? A lad holding an old skewer?"

He laughed sardonically, and his followers joined in. Lian felt the terrifying growl from the throat of the stone giant rumble underneath his feet like an approaching avalanche.

Lian's face twisted with scorn. "I won't let you kill my father, Casran," he insisted, trying to suppress his trembling voice. "I'll stop you, if it's the last thing I do!"

"Oh, really?" Casran stepped closer, until the point of Lian's spear grazed his gray leather shield. "You want to kill me? What? Are you a soldier? Or, no, a jäger even?" He squinted at Lian and shook his head. "I don't see it. I only see a pipsqueak about to mess his trousers."

Lian glanced toward his father. Though barely still conscious, Lonjar Draksmasher seemed to follow what happened through a veil of pain. With clouded eyes, one nearly swollen shut, he looked desperately at Lian. His cracked and bloody lips opened and closed without a sound, but Lian registered the faint motion as his father shook his head. *Don't do it*, the gesture seemed to insist. *Run away. It's too late for me. Save your own life, at least.*

It was possible that Lian had just imagined the motion. It could have been a play of light and shadow from the lantern against his father's bearded face.

I can't just watch, Lian thought helplessly. *I just can't.* His hands shook as he squeezed the spear handle. "Let my father go," he insisted hoarsely.

Casran nodded. "Oh, I will, believe me. He'll go over the cliff as fast as you can say 'please.' You're the last person who will hold me back." He spun around. "Câchurt, let Kraghma's Jaws feast on the drunkard. And, Kort, grab his son and throw him over, too."

"No!" Lian cried in panic. A surge ran through his body like a bolt of lightning. Time seemed to slow. With gruesome clarity, he watched the stone giant lift his father lazily into the air while the bodyguard set into motion. Lonjar Draksmasher let out a drawn-out shriek, a noise that Lian heard coming from his own mouth as well. Then the monster released his load, hurling the man that Lian loved, despite everything that came between them, into the air. Lonjar Draksmasher flew, his mouth and eyes wide open, limbs flailing. Momentum carried him over the cliff's edge, and wisps of fog reached out their arms to welcome him.

Lian reached out, too. Before he could process his actions, the glinting razor-sharp point of his spear met its mark. With nearly hysteric fearlessness, he bore the spear deeper and deeper, until it nearly reached the cross guard at the end of the blade.

Horrified and gasping, he let go of the weapon and fell backward. Casran gurgled and stumbled forward. As he turned, the long wooden end of the spear handle swung behind him. The wounded henchman standing next to him cried out in horror as the handle just missed his face.

Overcome with disbelief, Casran stared at Lian. The spearhead peeked out from his chest, and a dark patch blossomed across his white shirt. His hands grappled at the foreign object that stuck straight through his heart. His head fell forward, and his mouth dropped open as though he wanted to speak. His breath was shallow and rattling. "Are you . . . crazy?" he whispered. A stream of blood trickled from his mouth and down his chin.

Stunned and unable to answer the absurd question, Lian watched the man approach death.

Casran's legs gave out, and he fell to his knees. Falling farther, he crashed sideways into the dust, his face frozen in an expression of sheer disbelief.

The dull impact woke Lian from his stupor. For the first time, he registered what he had done. He had murdered the son of Odan Klingenhand! Casran was much too arrogant to have ever imagined that it could be possible. Surely, the crook had never assumed that Lian could be capable of such an act. To be fair, Lian hadn't exactly thrust his spear with clear wits. It had been an act of frenzied uncertainty and an act that he would surely bitterly regret.

Get out of here! The words flashed through his head, and he spun around and began to run.

The other men rose from their stupors. "Grab him!" cried one, probably Sorre. "But keep him alive. Odan will want to torture him to death himself."

Lian heard the quick crunch of boots on the stony ground as the pursuers followed him. When he realized that he had left his spear behind, his stomach lurched, but it would be no use to him if he were dead, anyway.

Fear clawed at his gut. He raced along the unpaved way, tripped, caught himself, and ran on. It was clear to him that his only chance of escape would be in the maze of Hafen's alleyways, if he could just reach them in time. There, where the houses pressed together and the fog was thick enough to swallow up his view, he might be able to disappear.

By now, Lian's ribs ached worse than ever. His skull throbbed, and his already heavy legs could barely carry him a step farther. Before him, at the foot of the hill, the first building within the city limits glimmered through the shadowy mist.

But he didn't reach the city limits.

A heavy body rammed Lian from behind, and he fell gasping to the ground. As he tried to turn around, the bodyguard Kort pressed him to the ground and held his head in the dust. A few heartbeats later, his second attacker descended.

Together, the two men yanked Lian to his feet. "You won't evade your fate so easily," spat the muscular bodyguard with foul breath. Lian tried to fight back, but caught in the two men's iron hold, he was no longer in control of his strength.

The men dragged Lian back to the precipice where the watchman Sorre, injured henchman, and stone giant stood beside Casran's body. "Should we take him to Odan or lead Odan here?" asked Kort.

"We'll go to him. We can make it to the slaughter yard," Sorre decided. "Câchurt, you carry Casran. The rest of you take the killer." He glared at Lian, full of loathing. "You'll pay for this with flesh and blood. I promise you that. Odan will cut you into tiny pieces and feed you to the dragons.

And he'll decide when you take your last breath so that you can witness every last moment of it."

Lian felt a creeping dread. He had heard of Odan's cruelty before. It would be better to die here and now than end up in that man's hands.

With a strained cry, he reared and kicked, attempting with all his remaining strength to free himself from the men's hold. Finally, he managed to shake free from their grip, but before he could make use of his newfound freedom, Kort loomed over him.

"He still has some fight in him," the bodyguard growled. "But not for long." An enormous fist slammed against Lian's left cheek, and another cracked against his head. The impact threw him into the men behind him, and they all fell to the ground.

Another blow met the pit of his gut, then another to his temple. Lian moaned and tasted bile. Dizziness overcame him, and a black curtain pushed at his line of vision. As bright as the fire of resistance had burned inside him, it already threatened to be completely extinguished. Every body broke eventually.

More blows crashed down on him as he lay crumpled on the ground. He tried to turn his head away, but escape wasn't possible. The men might have wanted to keep him alive, but it didn't seem to matter in the slightest if they beat him unconscious.

Through a curtain of pain and fog, and the blurred figures of his tormentors, Lian made out another form standing in his unsteady vision. The man watched with intent curiosity from his spot a few steps away. His eyes appeared to glow an emerald green, but maybe that was only Lian's imagination. *No, they really are glowing,* Lian realized—glowing and looking directly at him.

Amid the sea of his impending unconsciousness, desperate words formed on Lian's bloodied lips. "Please . . . help me . . ."

The green glowing points vanished. Just as abruptly as he had appeared, the figure vanished. Had he been a fog hallucination?

"Good evening," a voice said then, its sharp tone apparently accustomed to giving orders. Though not particularly loud, the voice caused Odan's men to stop what they were doing.

"Get out of here, sharp ear," growled Sorre. "There's nothing for you to see here."

"I can see plenty," the man answered. When he stepped into the lantern light, Lian's eyes widened.

The newcomer was a Sidhari, a folk not often encountered in Skargakar. Sidhari came from the far eastern deserts north of the forests, where they wandered as nomads across distant sands. Others admired them for their mystery and traditions. The few Sidhari who happened to end up in Skargakar kept to themselves. Nobody could explain which wind had blown them there or what they wanted. Sidhari also served on hunting ships, and the jägers at Cliff House swore their sharp ears possessed magical powers to make wind and weather subject to their wills.

Lian had never seen a Sidhari with his own eyes. The man's skin was as dark as the night itself, and his body as lean and powerful as a raptor's. His long black hair was braided in an intricate design, and his emerald eyes glowed even more brilliantly than kyrillian. The stranger was dressed in gray dragon leather, with knives hanging from his belt. Most startlingly, a pattern of jaggedly intersecting lines covered his face, concealing it in shadows.

"You don't want to mess with us," warned the watchman. "You still have a chance to turn and go your own way, and I suggest you take it." He pushed the gigantic stone creature forward, whose glowing ember-red eyes clashed peculiarly alongside the Sidhari's smoldering emerald gaze.

Though he stood before four men and a monster of living stone, the newcomer didn't flinch. "What wrong has he done?" he asked, nodding toward Lian.

"That doesn't concern you, green eye," Kort retorted gruffly.

"He murdered one of our own," Sorre said in loathing. "And he will be brought to justice."

"They threw my father off the cliff!" Lian cried. His eyes met the Sidhari's. "*They* are the murderers."

"Shut your trap!" barked one of the thugs, who struck Lian once more.

The Sidhari appeared to weigh the options. Finally, he said calmly, "Let him go."

Sorre looked at him in disbelief. "You want to die today, too, sharp ear? Fine. As you wish. Câchurt, Kort, finish him."

The stone giant confirmed the order with a chilling growl.

A faint smile appeared on the Sidhari's shadowed face. "So be it . . ."

In the next moment, the Sidhari sprang into action. Leaping forward, he pulled two knives—as long as short swords with slightly curved blades—from their sheaths at his belt. He ducked Kort's coming blow and rammed a blade into Kort's stomach. Releasing the handle, he spun around to face the man who held Lian, using his other blade to slit the man's throat. The victim fell gurgling to the ground, and Lian crashed down along with him.

Coughing, Lian raised his head just in time to witness the Sidhari begin his strange yet elegant and deadly dance. Ramming a blade into Sorre's side, he threw himself backward, rolled to avoid the stone giant's powerful yet delayed blows, and landed on his feet. Regaining his bearings, he leaped fluidly in front of the wounded henchman attempting escape. With the swift release of another dagger into the air, the man fell to the ground. Then, clutching his leather-covered chest and crouching to avoid Câchurt's blows, the Sidhari began to murmur words in an unknown tongue.

With a final powerful word, his murmuring ended. Raising his right hand, he sprang, lightning quick, toward the monster and struck him square in his broad black chest with a third short sword.

With a hollow thud, blue light gushed between hand and stone as if from an overripe fruit. The stone giant stiffened, his eyes stunned and frozen open. Their red glimmer slowly faded to a flicker. The Sidhari stepped back and glanced around. He glided from one enemy to the next, assessing his work swiftly and silently as he collected his weapons. As soon as the episode had begun, it was over.

Lian watched the Sidhari in utter disbelief; the man had just taken out four armed thugs and a seemingly invincible stone giant with the graceful lightness of a dancer. He could only stammer, "How . . . what . . ."

The Sidhari crouched down to wipe a blood-drenched blade on Sorre's shirt, then shoved it back into his belt. "But you just witnessed it yourself," he said with a note of chiding.

"Yes . . . right." Lian squinted to regain his vision as his head continued to spin. This night had been far too much for him to handle. He tried to separate confusion from coherent thought and feeling in order to speak. "Thank you. I . . . I . . . thank you. But tell me . . . why? Why did you do it?"

"Because it was the right thing to do," answered the Sidhari. "Because

I can tell a good man from a scoundrel. Because . . . I like to kill." The stranger regarded Lian intently. His eyes flickered with haunting madness. "Pick a reason."

Lian swallowed. *Have I traded disaster for catastrophe?* he wondered and attempted to pull himself up. *Did a murderer just spare my life?*

The Sidhari laughed again in his riddling way as though he knew exactly what Lian thought of him. Then he approached Casran's body and grasped the protruding wooden handle of Lian's spear. "I saved your life," he said, ripping the spear from the corpse with such force that he brought half the man's chest with it. The Sidhari shook bones and tissue off the spear's jagged blade.

Lian swallowed his queasiness. "Yes," he managed. "I am forever in your debt."

The Sidhari shook his head. "I'm not interested in debts. All I say is this: I cannot save you from Odan. If you stay in Skargakar, your life is doomed."

With new horror, Lian realized that the stranger was right. Casran, and all of his men, were dead. Odan, however, was still alive, and his hunger for revenge would be voracious. "But I don't know any other life," he murmured, more to himself than to his rescuer. "What should I do?"

"Go," said the Sidhari, handing the spear back to Lian. "Follow the only path a man can take when he has lust for the dragon hunt running through his veins."

With that, the Sidhari turned and went.

"Wait!" Lian begged. He limped toward the man until he stood just behind him. "But I don't know any . . ."

The fog grew thick around the stranger, until from one moment to the next, the plumes swallowed his figure. Lian frantically searched the white nothingness.

"Jägers," he whispered.

7

At a Crossroads

Thirteenth Day of the Fifth Moon, Year 841

What have I done?
   What should I do now?
   My life is over.
   I should leave Skargakar at once.
   Can I ever return?
These and many other thoughts whirled violently in the windstorm of Lian's head. He had taken the life of Casran, son of the most dangerous man in Skargakar. There was no evidence of the crime—the mysterious Sidhari had made sure of that—but there would surely be witnesses from the incident at Green Dragon. The line that began at the tavern, ran through the ravaged main room of Lian's house, and ended with the corpses at Kraghma's Jaws would easily lead straight to Lian.

There would be questions, though. How could a single young man have defeated five men and a stone giant? Such a riddle wouldn't prevent Odan from blaming Lian.

I should have thrown the bodies over the cliff, Lian thought as he limped aimlessly through the foggy alleys of Hafen, clutching his spear in his hand. He should have covered his tracks better after the Sidhari had vanished, but there were always people roaming the hills outside the city, even in the middle of the night. Fearing that someone would spot him at the scene of the crime, he had hurried away.

It would have been impossible to move Câchurt's massive stone form on his own, anyway. He could hardly believe that the Sidhari had really killed the giant. Maybe he wasn't dead, Lian considered. He could have been stunned into a deep sleep and could revive at any moment. If, or when, he did wake up, Lian hoped to be far away.

He had fled before getting rid of the bodies, bodies that would be discovered by dawn, at the latest. Lian wasn't worried about the village watch. They wouldn't rush to investigate the murders of a gang of cutthroats. Unless, that was, the captain owed a debt to Odan. Lian quickened his pace at the thought.

One way or another, the villain would begin the hunt for his son's murderer. Even if Odan wasn't aware that Lian was Lonjar's son, he would surely find out sooner or later. Plenty of people would talk for a few gems. So it was certain. Lian's time in Skargakar had run out.

Follow the only path a man can take when he has lust for the dragon hunt running through his veins, the Sidhari had advised. His meaning was clear: Lian should join a jäger ship and sail far away on the Cloudmere. If he waited many moons to return and took a new name, maybe the affair would blow over enough for him to live in Skargakar again—that is, if he ever even returned to Skargakar. He had heard of distant islands within the Cloudmere where humans and Nondurier lived peacefully. There were the Taijirin isles, of course. Some of those colonies were even said to be friendly toward strangers. Maybe Lian could find his luck there.

At least I'll live longer than if I stay here.

The plan had a catch, though. Aside from delivering a crystal frame to a ship once, Lian didn't know the first thing about life aboard one and even less about hunting dragons. Countless men in Skargakar vied for a place aboard a jäger ship. It wouldn't be easy to get the job, especially if he couldn't use his father's name to tip the scale in his favor. Doing so would be far too dangerous.

Captain Koos crossed his mind. Maybe his ship was still at harbor. *What was its name again?* As hard as he tried, Lian couldn't remember the vessel's name. So much had happened since their encounter at Waunar's workshop that the only thing swirling through Lian's mind now was gray haze that matched the fog filling the streets.

Maybe Waunar will tell me the ship's name, he thought.

He stumbled on a loose cobblestone and fell to the ground, just missing the low wall at his side. Pain from his injuries seared through his body. He clenched his teeth as dizziness overcame him. Before approaching any ships, he would need someone to look at his wounds. There wouldn't be any adventure if he died from an infection first.

Erene, he decided. Canzo's older brother, Hem, was married to a medic in Skargakar's infirmary. She and Hem, who earned his bread as a slaughterman alongside his brother, lived in a house with Canzo. Though Lian had only met Erene briefly, he hoped she wouldn't turn him away if he knocked at the door, even if Canzo wasn't home.

The two friends had parted ways near Cliff House, and Lian didn't think it out of the question that love-drunk Canzo had returned to test the prospect of a night alone with Anija.

As it happened, though, Canzo opened the door. From the look of his knee-length nightshirt and rumpled hair, Lian knew he had woken him. His friend's grogginess disappeared the moment he set eyes on Lian clutching his blood-splattered spear.

"What happened?" Canzo asked with widened eyes.

"I've had a rough evening," Lian replied weakly. Now that he was safe for the moment, his last reserves of strength faded like water into Sidhari sand. As his knees buckled, Canzo caught him before he hit the ground.

"Come in first," his friend said, helping him into the main room.

Hem, a bland man just a bit shorter than his brother, peered out from a hallway that led to the bedrooms. Wearing nothing except for brown wool trousers, he clutched a long-handled splitting ax. Apparently, he hadn't been sure what kind of midnight visit they were receiving.

"Lian?" Hem asked, his face matching Canzo's shock as he surveyed Lian's alarming condition. He leaned his ax against the wall. "Erene, come quickly!" he called over his shoulder. "And bring your tinctures. Lian is hurt."

As Canzo set Lian's spear on the table and helped him lie across a wooden bench, Hem approached. He studied Lian's wounds uneasily and eyed the weapon. "What in the world did you get yourself into? Were you in a fight?"

Lian nodded wearily. "I ran into some of Odan's henchmen. They wanted to kill me, but I got away."

"Odan Klingenhand?" Canzo's face paled, and lines of worry appeared across his forehead. Lian wondered if he felt concern for his family's safety, as well as for Lian's.

"I shouldn't say anything further about it. The more you know, the more danger you could be in."

"We're already in danger, one way or another," Hem answered. "If you've made Odan your enemy, that is." His gaze wandered once more to the spear. "*Did* you make him your enemy?"

Lian ran his tongue over his sore, cracked lips and nodded gravely.

Canzo groaned quietly, and Hem cursed under his breath.

"I shouldn't have come here," Lian said, trying to raise himself off the bench. "I'm sorry. I just didn't know—"

"Where do you think you're going, Lian?" a soft but determined voice interrupted.

Turning his head, Lian observed Erene. The plump young woman wore a nightgown and a patterned scarf around her head. Eyeing the spear, she unceremoniously approached her patient.

"You are injured and in desperate need of help," she began. "Nothing else is important right now. Hem, boil some water. And, Canzo, get your friend something to drink."

Without a word of argument, both men set to their tasks. Erene raised Lian's arms over his head, pulled off his shirt, and began to inspect his chest. The severity of his injuries was obvious; bruises and smeared blood covered his abdomen, and blood from his face and neck had streamed down his chest, the rivulets caked and dried.

With gentle hands, Erene began to treat Lian's wounds. Starting at his chest, she cleaned the cuts, applied a cooling salve, and bound his broken ribs.

Meanwhile, under pressure from Canzo and Hem, Lian began to tell what had happened. "But nothing you hear can leave these walls," he insisted. "If Odan finds out that you know anything, it will be a disaster. You know his reputation. If he finds out where I am, he won't show any mercy."

With heavy breaths, Canzo fell onto the bench across from Lian. "This is crazy," he mumbled. "I never would have thought that things would go this far."

"I'm sorry about your father," Hem said, taking the news noticeably better than his brother had. He set a broad hand on Lian's shoulder. "Casran was always a pig. I don't mourn his death in the slightest. Actually, you've relieved Skargakar from an enormous torment. And for that, I'll always admire you."

"If only I'd acted on actual courage and not pure stupidity," Lian replied, smiling uneasily.

"Call it what you will; it was a good deed. Even if you're forced to pay a steep price for it."

"What are you going to do?" Canzo asked. "Will you join a ship? Or go north to the realm beyond the wild forest?"

"It's too dangerous to flee across land. There are too many of Odan's men along the pathways through the forest, and it would be too.easy for him to track my route." Lian glanced at the floor. "No, I think I'll try my luck on the Cloudmere."

"Just as we always dreamed," murmured Canzo.

Lian raised his head to meet his friend's gaze. "Well, we sure never dreamed of it on these terms."

Erene fastened the final bandage at his side tightly. "Well, that's the last of it. You've been very lucky, Lian. None of your injuries seem life-threatening, but we'll have to wait until tomorrow to find out if you get any worse. You could have internal bleeding, but I'll have to wait awhile on that. I can only heal your wounds with Taijirin magic at the infirmary."

"In other words, you'll sleep here tonight," said Hem.

"No," Lian argued. "It's too dangerous. Someone might see me if I leave in the morning."

"So what?" Hem answered. "Nobody knows who you are on this street. And also, where else are you going to go? Going home is too dangerous. Odan's men are sure to be waiting there. But it will be difficult for them to track the way to our house. So you're safe here, for now."

Lian looked to Canzo. "Do you think so, too?"

His friend shrugged. "I guess so," he said uneasily. "I've only ever been to your house once or twice, and both times were in the middle of the night, so I doubt anyone saw me."

Lian remembered. On those drunken nights, when he'd been unable to walk straight, Canzo had helped him home.

"What I mean," Canzo continued, "is that nobody on your street could say anything about our friendship to Odan's men. You should be safe here, at least for a while."

"Aside from all that, you're exhausted and injured," Erene added.

Lian sighed and looked at the three gratefully. "I guess you're right. But I'll be gone before morning gray. I have to see Waunar one last time. He deserves to know why I'm leaving Skargakar. And maybe he can tell me where I'll have the best luck finding a ship to join."

"Well, that's settled, then," Hem said, satisfied. He motioned toward the stove at the far wall. "You can sleep by the fire. We've got extra blankets."

"I'll get them," Erene offered.

She disappeared briefly and returned holding two wool blankets and a sheepskin in her arms. Lian arranged the blankets near the stove, set his spear beside him on the stone floor, and resumed his place on the bench.

"Thank you," he said to his friends. "For everything."

The corners of Hem's mouth spread into a smile. "We few decent men in Skargakar have to stick together." With that, he and Erene returned to bed.

Canzo, who remained on his bench, raised the water pitcher from the table, filled two wooded cups, and pushed one across to Lian. "Not as good as the ale at Cliff House, but it's better than nothing."

"Water is just the thing," Lian answered. "My head is aching so much I wouldn't be able to swallow a single swig of anything else." He raised the cup to his lips.

Canzo scratched his head. "What a night . . ."

"You're telling me," answered Lian, and he set his cup back on the table. "Life can take a turn so quickly. Earlier tonight, our biggest concern was your future with Anija. And not that that's not still important . . . but now . . ."

He stopped midsentence as the memory of the stone giant flinging his father over the cliff flashed before him. Just before his death, Lonjar had tried to stop his son from getting involved in his mess. Drunk and broken as he was, he had tried to spare his son from a horrible fate.

There was no other option, Lian tried to convince himself. *Casran never would have let me go. He had practically already ordered my death.*

"I'm so sorry, Lian," Canzo said glumly. "I know that you and your father always had problems, but I never wished him such an end. I wouldn't wish that on anyone."

"Well, he shouldn't have gotten mixed up with Casran in the first place," Lian said, and he forced a smile. "It's crazy to think that he died trying to do something good after so many hopeless moons. He'd been trying to keep Casran from having his way with a girl. Pretty unbelievable . . ." He shook his head, unexpectedly exhausted, and blinked back tears that burned in his eyes. He emptied his glass and cleared his throat.

Canzo remained still.

"Anyway," Lian went on, "adventure in the Cloudmere has always been our greatest dream. Now I can finally find out if the jägers' tales are true." He thought again of his father, whose helplessness had always been the reason that Lian remained at home. Until now, his father had always needed him. Had all this happened because one of the Winds or some other of the many divinities called upon by the folk of Endar wanted to do Lian a favor? The idea that he could be responsible for his father's death filled him with dread. *Pull yourself together,* he told himself. *None of the Winds or gods are interested in you.*

Why should they be, anyway? Lian couldn't even remember the last time he had prayed.

"You know what?" Canzo asked then. "I'm coming with you."

"What?" Lian's eyes widened. "You would sail out to the Cloudmere?"

"Yes. I will with you."

"No, Canzo. Put the idea out of your head. You already have other plans. Just earlier tonight, you told me about how you're going to win Anija to be your wife."

"And you said that I shouldn't get too lost in that dream, remember?"

"I said that in jest," Lian answered. He knew that wasn't entirely true. He had his doubts about Anija's sincerity; however, he didn't want his friend to jump headlong into the decision to cast out to the Cloudmere if he might regret it later. "Of course you should ask Anija to be yours. You should have children, just as you imagined. When I return to Skargakar someday, I'll bring them scales from a fireblood and tail feathers from a Taijirin prince."

Canzo smiled at the thought, but his happiness quickly faded. "Sure, that would be something. Would it really happen that way? What if

Anija doesn't say yes? What if I'm nothing but a silly plaything to her, the dumb kid with the muscular arms?" he said, deflated.

Lian studied his friend. "Did something happen tonight? Why are you having doubts all of a sudden?"

Canzo blew air through his lips and stared into his cup. "I'm sure you remember how Anija told me to meet her after her shift."

"Of course. That's why I wasn't surprised when we parted ways outside Cliff House," Lian said, egging his friend on with a smile.

"Well, I went back inside and sat at a corner table. I waited for ages, but she never came. Instead, her father, Emman, came up to me and told me to give up. He said that Anija would never love a good-for-nothing like me. And he would never let his daughter marry a slaughterman who couldn't offer her a thing." He winced, remembering. "And then, he drove me out. I waited awhile behind the house, at the spot where Anija and I have met before, but she never came. Isn't that answer enough?"

Lian commiserated as he watched his friend, who sighed and forced a pitiful smile. "But my suffering is pathetic compared to yours! So a woman got the better of me. It wouldn't be the first time. I should just forget about her. I should . . ." He turned his cup in his hands. "I wish I could show Anija and her father that there's more to me than a lowly slaughterman. If I sail out to the Cloudmere with you and we catch a dragon, we'll be heroes. Maybe then I could change Anija's mind."

"Do you really want to give up your life for this?" Lian asked. "You aren't on anyone's death list. Nobody is forcing you to leave Skargakar."

Canzo leaned forward. "Lian, haven't we always wanted this? We haven't stayed in Skargakar all this time because our lives are so wonderful. You were worried about your father, and I was in love with Anija. Look at us now. Your father is gone, and Anija has cast me aside. Isn't fate hinting that our luck awaits us in the clouds? You say that I don't have to go, but I do. Otherwise, I'll have lost everything good in my life: the woman I love and the best friend I've ever had. So let me come with you."

Lian's heart warmed to his friend. "Faithful Canzo, how could I hold you back when it's so important to you? Believe me, I'd rather travel the Cloudmere with you than with anyone else. I'll admit, I'm afraid of what we'll find out there. But if we face it together, I know there's nothing to fear."

"Then let's seal it!" cried Canzo excitedly, springing to his feet. "This

night is the blackest of our entire lives. But glorious days await us ahead."
He stretched an arm out to Lian.

Lian shook on it, thankful and relieved—and winced as his wounds
smarted from the forceful movement.

"First thing tomorrow morning, I'll go to the slaughter yard to tell
them I'm leaving," Canzo said decidedly.

"And I'll visit Waunar. Maybe he'll know a tavern where I'll have the
best luck finding jägers," added Lian. "Before sunset, we'll cast off."

Overpowering optimism filled Lian. He knew he would never forget what had happened that night. His father's gruesome death and
Câchurt's terrifying blows would haunt him through countless sleepless
nights. In that moment, his terror faded just enough to make way for
new anticipation. Years of dreaming had finally opened into reality. Tomorrow, they would set out for the unknown.

8

The Dragon's Claw

Thirteenth Day of the Fifth Moon, Year 841

Before then, Lian had always found the early morning fog especially uncomfortable. Damp crept into his groggy limbs, and he shivered no matter what he wore. Today, though, he was grateful for the extra protection. Concealed from view by thick plumes of vapor, he reached Waunar's Crystal Carvers without meeting a soul.

The workshop was dark when Lian arrived—albeit earlier than usual. Admittedly, he hoped to speak to the old Nondurier before Jorun or Klaefften arrived at work; even though he trusted the others, he was all too aware how a few gems from Odan's bulging purse could loosen their tongues—that is, if he didn't use more violent ways of persuasion. No—it would be better for everyone if Lian kept his plans private.

Cautiously, Lian knocked at the wooden front door. Nothing happened. When he knocked a second time, more loudly, the wooden shutters above the workshop creaked open.

"We're closed," grumbled Waunar. "Come back later."

"Master, it's Lian," he called as softly as possible.

"Right, then," Waunar muttered, and the shutters clapped shut. Soon afterward, the front door clicked open to reveal a groggy Nondurier, still tying his apron around his waist.

"You're extra early this morning," Waunar grumbled.

"True, Master. But I must speak with you—alone."

Waunar's ears stood alert, and he stepped sideways to let Lian enter. "Then come in," he said, ushering the boy inside.

Waunar followed him into the workshop and took a seat at the table. Crossing his strong arms over his chest, he studied Lian, waiting.

At first, Lian began his story hesitantly, but as he described all that had happened, he grew braver. His description took on the emotions and colors of the events as they had occurred. He never doubted that he should tell the crystal carver about what had happened. The Nondurier may have been gruff—slightly odd, even—but Lian had always known him as an exceptionally decent and fair man. Perhaps, most importantly, Waunar loathed any kind of violence and intimidation and despised tyrants like Odan.

As Waunar listened, his expression darkened, and his short tail whipped back and forth against the edge of his stool. When Lian finished, a scornful growl rumbled from deep inside the Nondurier's throat. "Those crooks are an ulcer that throbs throughout all of Skargakar. I'd hoped that someone would do something about it, but the council and village guard are useless. I suppose it may as well have been you."

"That's why I came to you," Lian explained. "I have to disappear from here. No one can protect me from Odan. I needed to explain why I have to go. And . . . I need your help."

Waunar tilted his head. "How can I help? Do you need crystals?"

"No, it's not about money," Lian explained hurriedly. "I need your advice. Nobody knows more about jägers. Tell me, how can I find a place on a schooner?"

The man stood up and began to pace the room, stroking his hound-like snout thoughtfully. "You think too much of me," he said finally. "I merely prepare storage cases for their ships. I may be an ally to the jägers, but I wouldn't call myself their friend."

"But surely you can tell me something," Lian pressed. "Haven't you encountered all sorts of men in all your years—both good and bad?"

Waunar snorted the air from his snout. "Sure, but I've also received wind of how many of them died on the Cloudmere," he answered. "Dragon hunting isn't like other business." He turned to face Lian, now solemn. "The ships you're looking for—the ones that sail far away from Skargakar and venture deep into the Cloudmere to hunt and capture the greatest dragons—are also the vessels whose crews take the greatest risk. More have paid with their lives than can even be counted. I must make that very clear."

"If I stay in Skargakar or find work along the coast, my life will be over, anyway," Lian insisted. "I'd rather gamble my life at sea. At least aloft on the Cloudmere, there's a chance. Even dragons are more honorable than Odan."

"Yes, I'm sure you're right about that." Waunar sighed. "Well, if you want the most fearless jägers, I'll give you some advice. Go to the Dragon's Claw. That's where you'll find real jägers, not those pathetic coastal skippers at Cliff House who've hardly tested the wind into the Cloudmere." Waunar stepped closer to Lian. "But I must warn you. They're a raw bunch. You'd best be on your guard, and don't look too surprised. You'll never win their respect if they sense fear in you. Oh, and on the off chance that you run into Captain Shasta, send her my greetings—and remind her that she still owes me a barrel of beer." The Nondurier's jowls twitched with amusement.

Lian nodded. "Thank you, Master," he said.

Waunar gripped Lian's arm. "I'll be sorry to lose you," he said. "You've given decent work. May the Winds blow favorably upon you."

"Thanks," said Lian anxiously. "I'll do my best to survive."

The Nondurier grunted in agreement. "I wouldn't expect anything else. Now go. Quickly, before someone sees you."

Thus, Lian left the workshop. Even though Waunar had been a grumbling old hound most of the time, Lian felt a pang of regret as he stepped out the door.

By the time the sun had evaporated the last wisps of fog from Skargakar's streets, Lian was back inside Canzo's lodging. Both Hem and Erene had already left for the slaughter yard and infirmary, and Canzo still hadn't returned. Lian paced the house restlessly, uncertain what to do next. It wouldn't be safe to roam the streets before dark set in.

Eventually, he retrieved his father's spear, filled a bucket with water, and heaved it over to the table. Taking his place at the bench, he used a rag to remove the dried flecks of blood that covered the weapon's wooden handle and blade. Even though it was somehow fitting that Lonjar's weapon had been used to slay his killer, Lian couldn't bear the harrowing reminder of Casran's death.

As he rubbed, his eye wandered to the runes artfully etched into the blade's jagged edge. *What could they mean?* he wondered. Was it some sort of hunting blessing? Or the name of the first dragon his father ever captured, perhaps? Lian regretted never having asked his father. Studying the writing closer, he didn't recognize any symbols from the little Nondurish he knew. *Maybe it's some archaic form of Sidharese or Taijirish,* he considered.

A strange thought crossed Lian's mind. Could the spear be enchanted? He had heard countless stories of ancient magical weapons—blades that, with the right command, could unleash astonishing powers. He shook his head, smiling at his wild imagination. Why would his father have owned a magic spear? "And even if special powers happen to be lying dormant, how should I ever call them forth?" he muttered. Why had he thought such a silly thing?

He had just finished his work and set his rag aside, when the main room door opened, and Canzo burst into the room along with the afternoon sun. As he stepped forward, with a swing in his stride, a broad smile covered his face. "Lian, my friend. Are you ready for our adventure?"

"I've been ready all day," Lian answered, setting his spear onto the stone ground. "But tell me first, what happened to you?" He lifted himself from the bench. "You look like someone who just kissed a sprite."

"Not a sprite, exactly, but the woman I love comes close," Canzo replied dreamily, a sparkle in his eye.

Lian looked at his friend, surprised. "You met Anija?"

"Yes, but don't say it—I already know it was a stupid idea. I couldn't help it. I went back to Cliff House after leaving the slaughter yard. I had to see her for one last time before leaving Skargakar. And what luck that I did!" He stepped closer, rubbing his broad hands together excitedly.

Lian waited in suspense. Before he could ask why Anija had kissed him and why Canzo still wanted to set sail, his friend began. "Her father was busy in the village, so we met alone. She begged my forgiveness for disappearing last night. Her father had forbidden her to see me. He says

I'm not a good prospect because I don't earn enough gems, but she said that the truth is, she's in love with me."

"So I suppose you made up?" Lian said skeptically.

Canzo chuckled and his face reddened. "You could put it that way," he answered.

"But I don't understand, then. Why do you still want to leave?"

"That's obvious. Her father will never approve. He's right, too, when he says that a slaughterman's salary can't offer her much. If I were a jäger, it would be different. Once he sees me after our mission with my pockets overflowing with gems, he'll have to let me marry her."

"But aren't you worried that she'll find another lover while you're gone? We'll be away for ages—who knows when we'll return." Lian said hesitantly, though he knew his words were true.

His friend shook his head. "Lian, you don't understand the first thing about women. Once she's given you her heart, she'll be true to the end. Why else would Anija have given me a lock of her hair?" Canzo said, running a hand over his breast pocket.

Lian shrugged, giving in. "Maybe you're right. I hope so, anyway," he said. He wasn't convinced by the story, but he knew that Canzo would be better off venturing out on the Cloudmere with a lightened heart. It was possible he was wrong. In the immediate past, he'd experienced more than a few unbelievable occurrences.

"What did Waunar say?" Canzo asked as he opened the door to the nearby cupboard and pulled down a loaf of bread and parcel of cheese. "Did he tell you anything useful?"

They sat at the table and ate as Lian told Canzo his plan, but as with his suspicions about Anija, Lian decided it would be better to withhold the worst. So he left out the Nondurier's warnings of the dangers they risked at sea.

"Great," Canzo said through chews. "Let's gather our things and say farewell to Hem and Erene. Then we can set off."

Ever since the first time that Lian and Canzo had been in Cliff House, it had become their model for a true jäger's tavern. Sitting at those tables, during all the times they'd drunk herb ale and heard the talk from neighboring tables, the two had formed their dreams of life aloft the Cloudmere.

Now Lian recognized how far off Emman's tavern actually was from a true jäger's watering hole. He had always felt at home inside Cliff House's smoke-filled interior and the loud and puffed-up talk of its visitors. The large windows that opened out to the sea and the benches covered with brown leather cushions—not to mention Anija bustling from behind the counter—had all combined in an atmosphere that made Lian's imagination soar.

None of that atmosphere could be found at the Dragon's Claw, a dark cellar inside a dilapidated warehouse built into the cliff side at the end of a narrow alley at the west end of the harbor.

Before descending the steep and narrow stone staircase that led to the tavern, Lian noticed how the menacing guards below eyed him and Canzo with distrust. They waved the newcomers reluctantly past, probably because of the spear against Lian's shoulder. Canzo's scale armor, which he'd made himself during a break at the slaughter yard, must have also convinced them. The friends were lucky that the guards couldn't see the armor's makeshift and unskilled craftsmanship in the light of day. In the shadows, the armor appeared well used, an illusion emphasized by Canzo's large stature.

As they stepped inside the dusty room, Lian felt the distrustful eyes of the Dragon's Claw regulars fall upon him. After sizing up the newcomers, the jägers turned back to their drinks. Whatever they thought of Lian and Canzo, apparently they accepted them as members of their kind.

Lian leaned toward Canzo. "We should order a drink first. Then let's spread out."

His friend nodded in approval. He tried to look grim—an expression that would have appeared intimidating if not for his baby face and sparse chin whiskers.

As they passed through the long and dimly lit room toward the counter, Lian glanced around. It was difficult not to stare—the guests sitting at the tavern's tables were a decidedly striking group. These sort—humans and Nondurier who sported heavy scale armor decorated with dangling claws and teeth—would have stuck out in any other setting.

At the far end of the room, Lian spotted a group of Drak huddled closely together. With gray, leathery skin, clawlike fingers, and spined headdresses atop noseless, wrinkled heads, Drak were an unsettling combination of human and lizard. It was uncommon to meet one in the city—they usually lived in tribes out in the wilderness, and when spotted in cities were known for keeping to themselves.

Lian's eye fell on a woman with short hair, whose scar-covered left arm ended in a hooked blade. A tiny green dragon perched atop her shoulder and peered through black button eyes. When the lizardwing opened its mouth and let out a menacing hiss, Lian darted around to face the counter.

Without a doubt, a man standing at the bar was the most impressive sight of all. Two powerful, tan-colored wings sprouted from the bronze armor at his back, wings so large that they rose above his down-covered head and grazed the tavern ceiling. A black-tipped, brown feather head-dress poked out from his harness and fell in a half circle at the man's feet. When the man turned his head, Lian studied his face—humanlike, aside from round yellow eyes. Whistling to get the barkeep's attention, the Taijirin turned back to his neighbor, a broad-shouldered Nondurier who barely reached his chest.

"I'm not sure I'd go hunting with any of this lot," Canzo murmured as the two approached the counter. "They all give me the creeps."

"Maybe, but they're the only jägers around," Lian said softly. "Better get used to them now or forget about our plan altogether."

Lian waved the barkeep over, a bald-headed man with a potbelly, and ordered two herb ales. "To fearlessness," he said, holding up his mug.

"What kind of toast is that?" Canzo asked.

"That was Master Waunar's advice. Have no fear—or at least don't show it."

Canzo nodded, took a long swig of beer, and resumed his grimace as he set the mug on the counter. "I'll do my best," he said. He scanned the room. "How do we know who's a captain and who isn't?"

"I guess we'll have to ask," Lian answered. "Let's split up so we can find out sooner. We want to be on a ship by nightfall."

"Good idea," said Canzo. "Hem and Erene would be surprised if we show up again tomorrow morning." He chuckled quietly. "I'd like to spare us the humiliation."

"Enough dithering, then," said Lian, emptying his mug. "Night is approaching."

They moved along the tables, Lian in the front section of the room and Canzo in the back. With each new jäger, they tried to lead the conversation toward work aboard a schooner. But the task proved trickier than expected. A good number of the group turned away without a word, and none of the other jägers had a ship to call his own.

One Nondurier captain refused to hire workers as young as Lian. "I'd blame myself if you met death on your very first hunt," he said apologetically. "You've barely even lived."

Another human captain had less of a problem hiring young workers, but said that his ship was in the middle of a full repair. "We had a pretty bad run-in with a fireblood, and now we're stuck here for the next ten days, at least," he said impatiently. "But come back then if you're still in Skargakar. My ship is the *Damnation*. I can always use new sorts."

At the menacing look in the man's eye, Lian promised to keep the offer in mind and moved on as soon as he could.

With waning confidence, he pressed on until a hand on his arm caused him to look up. The short-haired huntress sat in her armchair, the tiny green lizardwing still perched on her shoulder. "I take it you're searching for a post aboard a schooner, little pet," she said in a dark and velvety voice as she looked Lian up and down.

"Uh, well, yes, that's right," he answered.

"I've got a ship," said the woman. "It isn't much, but it has everything one might need aloft in the Cloudmere."

"Is it a drachenjäger?" Lian asked, growing uneasy beneath her roving eyes.

"My people hunt anything that can be traded for money," the woman explained. "And a bit of young blood on board wouldn't hurt," she crooned. The tip of her tongue caressed her upper lip as she continued to eye him.

Lian stiffened, and she laughed softly. "Oh, don't fear, my boy. I'm quite gentle. Believe me, you'll have your share of fun, too. Plus, we split our wares evenly among everyone. It would be worth your while."

Lian thought the huntress might have a specific idea of fun in mind. Did she lust after a chamber boy to while away lonely nights on the Cloudmere? The glint of her blade-clad hand and the glimmer in her green eyes unnerved Lian. Not to mention she was at least twenty years his senior.

"I . . . uh . . . I'll run it by my comrade," Lian said, motioning over his shoulder to Canzo. His friend spoke animatedly to a man with shoulder-length silver hair and an eyepatch, who shook his head in refusal and turned away.

"Forget that meathead," the woman said. "I don't need him. You won't need him, either, aboard our ship. I can assure you."

Lian shook his head insistently. "Sorry, but we only come as a team."

She cast another glance at Canzo. "Well, my first mistress likes her boys meaty. Maybe he'll be good for her."

"Thank you, madam, but we'll keep searching."

The woman cast a last penetrating gaze over Lian and shrugged. "How you like, my pet. But you're missing out, believe me."

Shaken and dazed, Lian hastened away from the woman and joined Canzo at the counter, who already sat with a second beer to strengthen his resolve.

"Any luck?" his friend asked.

"No. You?" Lian asked, hopefully.

Canzo motioned toward the group of Drak in the far corner. "They'll take us, but we'd be the only two humans on board. I'm not sure that's such a good idea."

"Yes, well, I was presented with a similarly questionable proposition," Lian said.

Dispirited, Lian scowled. He'd imagined it would be easier to find work aboard a decent drachenjäger. When he realized that he'd forgotten to ask Waunar about Captain Koos, he grew even more dejected. The captain had seemed to like him. Hadn't he said that he would take him on board in a heartbeat? *Maybe I should go back to the workshop,* considered Lian. He worried that bothering the Dragon's Claw's customers about anything else might make them grow hostile.

At that moment, footsteps clattered down the stairs and into the Dragon's Claw. The newcomer wore a knee-length, midnight-blue tailcoat fastened down the front with metal buttons. A brimmed brown hat with a large feather plume covered his head, but the fine vestments were deceptive. Looking closer, Lian saw the clothes were ratty and dull and gave no sense of nobility paired with his unshaven chin, beady dark eyes, and gruff expression.

"Hear, hear, you death escorts and drunkards!" the man called unabashedly and slapped his hat down on the counter. "I need four men for a hunt, right away. We sail a ship that hunts only the most formidable drachen. Come and earn some real stones, for once."

To Lian's amazement, nobody raced off their stools to be first in line. Instead, only a few men and women even bothered to turn toward the man.

"When do you set sail, Mavron?" one jäger, who apparently knew the man, spoke up.

"Tomorrow at sunrise," he answered. "Captain stays at harbor for as little time as possible. As soon as all the wares from our last catch are sold and our stores of provisions restocked, we'll be off."

"How long will the mission last?" another asked.

"Six months, at least," said a voice from behind Mavron. The voice penetrated the whole room, though it remained quiet and calm.

Lian gasped. He could have picked that voice from a crowd a thousand deep. The Sidhari, the same who had saved his life the night before, stepped out of the stairway's shadow. The desert dweller's emerald-green eyes glowed eerily from his dark complexion.

"Lian, are you all right?" Canzo whispered. "You look like you've seen a ghost."

"That Sidhari," sputtered Lian, "is the man I met last night."

His friend's eyes widened. "The one who . . . shattered . . . Casran's brutes?" he asked.

"Yes . . . quiet!" Lian urged.

All around them, the crowd had taken up in murmurs. Some of the other jägers also recognized the Sidhari—and apparently didn't associate anything good with him.

"Hanon'ka, you're still serving aboard the *Carryola*?" a jäger seated near the stairs asked. It took a moment for Lian to grasp that Hanon'ka was the Sidhari's name and not some sort of peculiar jäger's greeting.

"Yes," the Sidhari answered plainly.

"And is Adaron still the captain of that ship?"

"Would it be anyone else?" returned the Sidhari.

"Surely not," the man scoffed. "And just as surely, I would never join that ship."

Hanon'ka took a step forward. "Do you care to insult Captain Adaron?"

The bearded man raised a hand in defense. "No, no, it's all right. I'm just not interested."

"And what of the rest of you?" the recruiter Mavron called. "Four spots are up for the taking. Experience on a ship is recommended but not required. The pay is good. You'll sail to places no jäger has ever ventured before. Not to mention, you'll be working aboard the most formidable jäger throughout the Cloudmere."

Lian nudged Canzo excitedly. "This is our chance! He said they set sail at dawn."

"But why isn't anyone else interested?" Canzo asked and nodded to the others, who quietly spoke among one another and exchanged darting glances.

Lian waved the concern away. "Forget them. None of them would take us on board, except a few who seem less than trustworthy, but I know this Hanon'ka. He defended my life against five other men. Any ship he serves can't be all bad."

Canzo stroked his sparse chin hairs in thought.

"What's wrong with all of you?" Mavron continued. "How often have you come to me in search of work? And now I have something, and you don't want it? Are you all afraid or what?"

Lian threw Canzo a final glance and, seeing his friend was too soft to decide for himself, spoke aloud. "Here!" he called. He stood tall and approached the two men. "My friend and I are searching for work aboard a ship," he said, trying to conceal the wobble in his voice.

The recruiter grinned to reveal foul, rotten teeth. "Ah, two young lads, untainted and hungry for adventure. Marvelous. What do you call yourselves?"

"I am Lian, and this is my friend Canzo," Lian answered.

Mavron joined them at the counter, and the rest of the crowd resumed their business. The recruiter had found two new victims, and the rest didn't interest them.

"And what do you know about the jäger life?" Mavron asked. Hanon'ka remained in the background, not letting on whether or not he recognized Lian. Even if the Sidhari hadn't intended to be discreet, Lian was grateful. He was just as happy to leave all talk of his run-in with Odan's son far away from this tavern.

"Only a little," Lian answered. "But we are ready to learn. And we have talents that would be useful on board a jäger ship. I'm trained in crystal carving, and Canzo is a slaughterman."

"Oh, that *does* sound promising," said Mavron, not hiding his satisfaction. His gaze fell onto the wrapped spear that hung across Lian's back. "Is that a jäger spear?" he asked.

"Yes," Lian answered. "My father left it to me."

"And do you know how to use it?"

"I can tell the front end from the back," Lian answered. His eyes darted toward Hanon'ka, whose emerald eyes flickered in recognition.

Mavron laughed. "That's a start. But do you really think you can kill a dragon with it?"

"With a little instruction I could."

The recruiter turned to Hanon'ka, beaming. "What fine specimens! Wouldn't they be an asset to our crew?" he asked.

The Sidhari eyed Lian and Canzo and remained silent for a long time. His expression revealed nothing. "Are you ready to venture out on the *Carryola*?" he asked finally as though the ship's name were enough explanation for all the wonders and dangers that awaited them.

"We are," Lian confirmed hurriedly.

"Yes, we want to sail out on the Cloudmere," added Canzo after a delay.

"Good," Hanon'ka said, and he turned back to Mavron. "Finish the formalities and give them their premiums. I'll wait outside. We're finished here. We've still got more taverns to get to tonight."

"Aye, Commander," Mavron said, nodding hastily.

Without another word, the Sidhari retreated, and the recruiter pulled out a scroll and unrolled the long parchment onto the table. Lian squinted in the tavern's dim lighting to read the contract's tiny slanted script.

"No need to read everything," said Mavron. "It merely states that you are bound to the *Carryola* for the duration of one mission and that you vow to serve your ship and captain in exchange for one one-hundredth of every catch."

"That doesn't sound like much," Canzo muttered.

"That depends on the worth of the catch. Think of the worth of a pearl from the heart of a fireblood, and then imagine your profit."

Canzo's eyes widened, and Mavron smiled, the deal closed.

Both Lian and Canzo inscribed their signatures at the bottom of the document—Lian's letters legible and Canzo's a rough approximation of what his name looked like, since he had never learned to read or write.

"Very nice," Mavron said as he rerolled the scroll and returned it to his tailcoat pocket. "Now here are your first week's salaries," he said, placing a handful of gems into each of their palms. Then, setting his feathered cap back onto his head, he turned to leave. "Report to the harbor at sunrise," he instructed. "The *Carryola* will be expecting you." Then he headed for the door.

"Wait! How will we recognize the ship?" Lian asked, holding him back.

The corner of Mavron's mouth twitched into a smirk. "Oh, believe me. You can't miss the *Carryola*."

9

The *Carryola*

Fourteenth Day of the Fifth Moon, Year 841

Lian and Canzo spent the night at a shabby boarding lodge on the outskirts of the harbor. They agreed it was best not to return to Hem and Erene. "Our adventure must begin here," insisted Lian. "From now forward, there's no going back."

Canzo agreed wholeheartedly.

There wasn't much chance of sleep in the brief time before morning light. First, they were well aware that they stood at a turning point, and the anticipation kept them wide awake. Furthermore, the one time Lian drifted off, a terrible nightmare plagued him—a black monster and its slobbering minions caught hold of him and threatened to throw him into a maelstrom that swirled in the clouds. Tossing and turning, and bathed in sweat, he decided it was better to stay awake than be tormented by his dreams.

Finally, when darkness gave way to a hazy, gray morning, Lian and Canzo made their way to the nearby pier. Besides the clothes on their backs, the filled waterskins at their waists, Lian's spear, and Canzo's breastplate, and the few gems. The streets were as good as empty, except for a few solitary figures huddled in doorways, clad in armor or cloaked beneath heavy coats, and a man who rolled a wheelbarrow slowly across their path.

As they reached the harbor, a seaward gust sent the fog scattering along the stony pier, whose wooden jetties stretched out like twisted fingers into the nothingness. The eastern sky glowed red as the sun pushed past the forest-covered mountain peaks that lined the coast.

Before them, ships' wooden hulls peeked out through the vapors. Most were modest in size, Cliff Clippers' schooners or coastal jägers' barges used for catching the tiny lizardwings that had become increasingly popular house pets in the village.

Other ships reached higher into the cool morning sky. Two or sometimes three masts held strong, albeit tethered sails. Rows of dragon-scale shields lined the railings. Carved figureheads, some painted and some simple polished wood, adorned their bows. Lian made out the usual forms of dragons but also saw horned horses, wildcats, and women of many folk, wearing little and gazing out into the distance, carrying the souls of the ships on which they were mounted. Especially impressive was an expertly carved Taijirin, whose wide and finely crafted wings stretched backward along the sides of their ship's hull.

"There are so many of them," said Canzo in awe. "How can we possibly know which one is the *Carryola*?"

Lian scanned the harbor. "Mavron said that we would surely recognize it." His gaze fell upon a silhouette docked at the farthest point down the wooden jetty still in his vision. He surveyed the nearby ships and then squinted back into the shadowed distance. His eyes widened when he grasped what he saw.

"Canzo . . ."

"Hm?"

"I think I found it." Lian pointed to the towering silhouette that loomed before them, now half-concealed behind a veil of fog.

Canzo looked beyond Lian's finger and raised his eyebrows in astonishment. "By all the Winds . . ."

"Let's go," Lian replied eagerly.

As they started, a hand closed abruptly around his arm. "Don't," a gruff voice whispered.

"What?" Lian asked, startled. He pulled himself free and stepped backward. Thoughts of Odan and his henchmen reeled in his mind, but this man, who had appeared beside them as though spat out of the nothingness, didn't seem like one of Odan's men. Instead, he seemed much more like any other sad, wasted, and outcast soul who roamed Skargakar's docks.

He was barefooted and cloaked in a tattered suit that must have been green once, fastened with a wide leather belt. A filthy leather pouch swung from a strap across his shoulder. Lian's gaze fell on the man's chest, where a darkly tarnished bronze amulet in the shape of a five-pointed star dangled from his neck by a strand of twine. The man leaned against a wooden walking stick with a carved knob reminiscent of a dragon skull. Pale-skinned and with a beardless and plump face, it was impossible to tell how old he was, and a gray scarf tied around his head fell over his eyes and concealed his expression.

He must be a former jäger down on his luck, Lian considered, and his thoughts turned to his father. Without Lian, he surely would have fallen into a similar destiny roaming Skargakar's streets.

"What did you say?" Canzo asked the man.

"I said, 'Don't do it,'" he replied and turned his head from Canzo to Lian. "Don't board that ship, young men. It will be your doom."

"How would *you* know, old man?" Canzo asked.

"I heard you talk of the *Carryola*," the man explained. He held a filthy arm out to them. "I implore you. That ship is cursed, and Captain Adaron is cursed. Mark my words. Death will befall any who answers the *Carryola*'s call."

"Stop telling such ghost stories," Lian snapped, now irritated. He wasn't about to let a naysayer dash his hopes before the sun had even risen. "Have you ever been on board the *Carryola*? Have you ever served Captain Adaron yourself?"

The old man shook his head. "No, but I didn't have to. I've heard all I need to know, and I've only heard grave things about that dark ship. No captain loathes dragons as much as Adaron, and he won't rest until he slays every last one of them."

"That's exactly why we're going," Lian argued. "We want to slay dragons, too. Which other mission could promise more adventure or riches than this?"

"Find your adventure somewhere else. I implore you. The *Carryola* will only bring you misery. I can feel it in my old bones." His fingers locked once more around Lian's arm, a startlingly familiar gesture.

"You've been drinking too much dragon blood!" Lian said, peeling the wrinkled hand off of his arm. "Now leave us in peace. If you really knew what you speak of, then you'd know just as well that there's no place left for us in Skargakar. Misery will befall us here far more quickly than aboard the *Carryola*, I assure you. Now go and spook someone else," he said and turned. "Come on, Canzo."

"Go, then, if you must," called the old man from behind them. "But beware! A shadow will cover you, larger than that cast by any other dragon of this world. Its body is violent and as black as the night through which it flies. Black as the fog from which it strikes. Black as the lightless chasm from whence it was born at the beginning of time. Flee if you encounter this shadow. For nothing can save you otherwise."

"Yes, all right," called Lian as he hurried on without looking back. "We'll look out."

"Who was that?" muttered Canzo once they had distanced themselves. "He really seemed like misery's prophet."

"Nobody special," Lian said with certainty. "Just another madman who thinks it's the end of the world every time he 'senses' a sign in the fog. I trust Hanon'ka far more than that zealot, that's for sure. I don't think a Sidhari would sail on a ship where death looms beside him."

"That may be," Canzo answered. "But who knows what motivates a Sidhari."

Lian stood still, his hands on his hips. "Are you having doubts, Canzo? Now—right before our departure? We signed a contract and accepted payment. We made a pact with each other."

"I know," Canzo said, nodding forcefully. "We're going. I'm sorry. I guess I let that old man get to me."

Grinning, Lian punched Canzo's shoulder. "Let's forget it. Skargakar and all its hardships will be far behind us soon. From now on, we have to look forward. Our new home is waiting out there," he said, pointing toward the large schooner's silhouette at the end of the jetty.

They walked to the start of the scaffolding that spanned into the distance. Studded with iron nails and wrapped with thick rope, the broad jetty's wooden beams loomed over the peer along with scores of others. No builder in the world could have managed to support this amount of weight on the mountain's surface with traditional construction. Lian's sharp eye noticed the gentle shimmer of kyrillian dispersed through-out the dock, which enabled these jetties to float over the Cloudmere's depths.

The wood sprang lightly beneath each footstep, a sensation that could make some souls squeamish, considering the endless nothingness at their feet. But Lian didn't give a second thought to how far the ground lay below his feet. He knew that the crystals could be depended upon to keep the dock afloat.

When they reached the ship, veils of mist surrounded them as though the ship's dark hull itself had released its foul breath into the air. Canzo gasped in awe. "What a monstrosity . . . ," he said, his eyes wide.

Lian nodded in agreement. The *Carryola*—for this must have been the ship—was the greatest vessel he had ever laid eyes on. From stern to bow, an armor of gray dragon scales covered the entire hull, which spanned at least forty paces long and ten paces wide—not counting its collapsed side sails. Two masts extended some twenty paces into the air, and Lian noticed structures at both ends of the ship that held smaller jäger kites, the more maneuverable chase boats, and harpoon ballistae.

Lian estimated how many kyrillian cases the *Carryola* would need to keep aloft. Surely, it would require twice as many as an average jäger ship, if not more, and Lian knew the cost of kyrillian well. *This captain must be enormously rich,* he thought.

Astonished, they walked the ship's length until they reached the bow. Lian noticed three rows of blackened metal spikes bolted to the armor, with kyrillian cases hanging from their bases. At first, he thought that the cases served merely to reinforce the ship's buoyancy, but he soon realized that they were meant to shield the hull itself. Dragons found a special sort of sport in ramming against the sides of jäger ships. Thanks to the spikes, at least an attacking beast wouldn't escape unscathed.

At the bow itself, they met a grim sight. Contrary to most other ships along the pier, the *Carryola* carried no carved wooden figurehead. Instead, the crew had nailed a polished dragon skull under the bowsprit. Long spikes from the dragon's headdress jutted out menacingly, and from inside its soundless jaw, a terrifying row of fangs threatened all who crossed the *Carryola*'s path.

"Is that the skull of a stormbringer?" Lian asked in awe.

Canzo, who had more experience identifying dragon skeletons, shook his head. "Too big for a bringer. If you ask me, it's a red. I can't believe it. A king would pay a sackful of gems for a skull like that, but instead, the captain nails it to the front of his ship, just like that. Who *is* this man?"

"Either he's so well off that riches no longer matter to him or this was a dragon he couldn't stand," Lian suggested.

"You can say that again," a voice answered from above.

Surprised, Lian looked up to find a stocky man leaning against the railing, a pipe between his teeth. Stringy white hair framed a round face browned by the sun, with water-blue eyes, a large nose, and a mouth curled into a sly grin. He wore a stained white robe with rolled-up sleeves and stood with his hairy forearms crossed against his chest. Perched on his left shoulder, a tiny red-orange lizardwing peered down through one eye at Lian and Canzo, its head tilted.

The man removed the pipe from his teeth and pointed it toward the dragon skull.

"That was Sancathos, the famous fireblood that attacked the Taijirin island Arsindair three years ago. He played cat-and-mouse with us for three weeks before we finally got him. We lost six men—and nearly lost the captain. And, well, such a special bond can never be forgotten. So the captain nailed Sancathos's skull to the *Carryola*'s bow. I find it hideous, but I see the advantage. Since then, no bandits have dared to tread more than five hundred paces toward our ship." He chuckled gleefully. "But tell me, lads, you're not the two newlings on board, are you?"

"We are," confirmed Lian introducing himself and Canzo.

"Well, come on board, then," said the man, ushering them with his pipe. "Hanon'ka is expecting you." He hobbled the length of the deck along the railing as Lian and Canzo followed from the jetty, until they met at the wooden gangplank.

As they stepped along the gangplank and onto the deck, Lian saw the reason for the man's limp. From his brown knee-length britches, a wooden leg extended to the floor. Lian wondered if a dragon was to blame.

"Welcome aboard," the man said, stretching out his arm in greeting. "They call me Smett. I swing the cooking spoon on this fine barge. I also pull teeth and brew a rum that will burn the tongue right out of your mouth—whereby the two go hand in hand, I must say. So if you need anything, or need to not need anything, don't hesitate to come to me."

"Thanks," said Lian, gulping. "I'll remember that. And that little man?" he asked, nodding toward the lizardwing.

"This is Flicc, and isn't a man, but a fine lady," Smett answered good-naturedly. "She makes sure that I behave and keeps me company in the galley—though I'm still not entirely sure if she likes my company or just my food."

The little dragon opened its tiny pointed jaws to reveal two rows of miniscule needle-sharp teeth and let out a squeaking hiss in response. Flicc didn't seem like any pet lizard-wing that Lian had ever seen before—that was for sure.

Lian surveyed the deck that now bustled with activity. The crew, all men from the look of it, busily passed provisions into the ship's belly, along with a host of other final preparations for their journey: coiling ropes and stacking spears. From what he could tell, mostly humans and Nondurier—but also a few brown-scaled Drak—made up the crew on Captain Adaron's ship. They went about their work with a hard seriousness. Lian could tell it would be wise not to cross them. There was also plenty of proof that these men had faced dragons: the skin on half of one man's face was a web of burn scars from a dragon's breath. He must have just escaped death. Two other men's arms ended in metal hooks, and Lian winced at the sight of two gaping talon wounds gouged into a stout Nondurier's head, the gashes so deep that Lian could hardly believe the man was still alive.

Just as with any other ship, the helm lay at the *Carryola*'s center between both masts, with steerage ropes running along a wheel-and-pulley system to access the kyrillian held in storage cases underneath the hull. Three men stood at the railing, speaking among themselves. One was the Sidhari, Hanon'ka. At his side stood a Nondurier who looked as though he could bend bows out of the metal spears that were stacked at the ship's bow and stern. A wide harness spanned his enormous hairy chest, and he wore a bright blue scarf knotted around his head. The third man was just as massive in stature, had rust-red hair, and wore tight-fitting brown leather garments adorned with intricate buckles.

"Is that Captain Adaron?" asked Lian.

"Him?" Smett said, chuckling. "Oh no, he's only Markaeth, the second navigator. He mans the deck at night watch or if Jaular—that's the Nondurier, our main helmsman—drinks too much yet again. But let me warn you now, never roll the dice with the ginger! His luck is notorious. He says it's the work of his lucky charm, the shriveled forefoot of a gold-scale hatchling. But if you ask me, he's swindling us somehow."

Lian wondered what kind of person would hang the foot of a freshly hatched dragon around his neck. Didn't they know the decree that only fully grown dragons could be hunted? Skargakar's inhabitants didn't want to risk exterminating the main source of their livelihood. Though when Markaeth turned, and when Lian saw his weaselly freckled face, he was certain that the second commander didn't give much stock to decrees.

"Where is the captain, then?" chimed Canzo. "Doesn't he want to meet us?"

"Oh, Adaron won't set foot on deck before we set off," answered Smett. "You should know that he's pretty eccentric. For one thing, he can't stand solid land. Some folk think he made an oath to never set foot on earth again until he's avenged the death of his bride."

Lian raised an eyebrow. "His bride?" he asked. "What does she have to do with anything?"

"Oh, that was years ago. Anyway, Ialrist can probably tell the story better than I can. He was there, after all." Smett paused and considered his words. "On the other hand, the flutter-man isn't very talkative these days, so you might not get much out of him. I just know this much: Many years ago, Adaron set out for the hunt with his young bride and a few crewmates. Along the way, they met a vicious jet-black dragon. All were killed, except Adaron and Ialrist, and among the dead, the captain mourned his bride most of all. Since then, he has sought revenge."

"Ialrist might be tight-lipped," said an unexpected voice, "but you talk too much, Smett."

As Lian turned his head, he spotted Hanon'ka. "Don't you have something to do, cook?" The first commander's words were less a question than a command.

The cheerfulness disappeared from Smett's face.

"Aye, sir," he answered, and he looked glumly to Lian and Canzo. "We'll see one another later," he added and hobbled away.

"Captain Adaron is a great man," said the Sidhari, his emerald eyes flickering. "And he is, without a doubt, the greatest of all drachenjägers. No skyship has caught and conquered more dragons than the *Carryola*. Her crew is courageous and loyal to the death. Her well-being is the captain's greatest concern—as important to him as food and his own heartbeat. Always remember that."

"Yes, uh . . . s-sir," Lian stammered.

"Commander," corrected Hanon'ka. "My status on board is first commander."

"Understood, Commander. Pardon me."

"Right, then." The glow in the Sidhari's eye eased, and his expression softened. "Welcome aboard. We'll be casting off soon. Now come. I'll give you the tour and introduce you to the men you'll be working with."

10

Entering the Cloudmere

Fourteenth Day of the Fifth Moon, Year 841

"Release the lines!" Hanon'ka ordered from his spot at the helm.

"Lines released!" came the calls from bow and stern as harbor workers unwound the heavy ropes mooring the *Carryola* to the jetty and tossed their lines to the men on board.

"Portside half-raised, light ascent ahead!"

From his position starboard, Lian awaited instruction as he stood by the sails that now fluttered freely. Glancing over his shoulder, the main helmsman, Jaular, pulled the knotted ropes that ran along the side of the hull, through the deck, and into the hold to access the kyrillian cases dispersed throughout the ship. He started with those below deck, then the few at the bow, and those along the stern and both sides of the ship—opening more cases portside. Lian noticed the crystals' force instantly when the ship lifted and bore to starboard. As Jaular continued to pull and release the lines, the *Carryola* drew away from the harbor, groaning as she leaned into a curve. By the time the ship's skull-studded bow faced the ether that stretched endlessly before them, a new day had begun to lighten the horizon.

It's really happening! Lian thought as excited anticipation surged over him. He glanced at Canzo, who stood at portside sail opposite him. His friend's ruddy cheeks were proof enough that he felt the same thrill.

To the horizon and beyond . . . What adventures awaited them? The possibilities had often occupied the friends' imaginations. Now Lian felt a new immediacy. He pictured islands full of Taijirin and a vast array of dragon sorts that would make anyone's head spin. Were there places beyond the Cloudmere even more extraordinary than he could conceive? Lian didn't know. He'd never heard of a schooner ever reaching the other end of the white expanse. What if they were the first!

One thing was certain; if any ship were capable of sailing to the end of the Cloudmere, then it had to be the *Carryola*. Lian couldn't understand why the jägers at the Dragon's Claw and the ragged soothsayer at the harbor had been so distrusting—or rather, so terrified—of this captain's ship. He was awed by the powerful vessel.

When Hanon'ka had explained the rules on board before castoff, Lian had been astonished how well conceived and well executed the design of the *Carryola* truly was.

There were crystals the size of his hand mounted into the floor of the upper deck, carved to illuminate the windowless rooms at middle deck below, where the crew's sleeping quarters and workshops were located.

In the stores, loaded by way of a crane structure at mizzenmast above deck, Hanon'ka had pointed out six more kyrillian cases, whose ropes disappeared through the ceiling and up to the deck. When the helmsman pulled the ropes from above, the Sidhari had described, the kyrillian reserve could keep the entire ship afloat.

"An emergency measure," he had explained. "In case we lose part of the hull in battle."

Canzo had turned slightly pale. "Could that really happen?"

"Anything can happen when we face these beasts," the Sidhari had answered, his eyes glimmering.

Back on deck, the crew now worked polishing artillery, sharpening spearheads, mending sails, coiling ropes, and scrubbing the deck. The men reacted to the newcomers' astonishment with a mixture of amusement and superiority. Most, like Lian and Canzo, had dark hair and tanned skin. A few, though, had surprisingly pale complexions and a blend of blond and copper hair. Lian had no idea which lands they came from, but he was sure they must be very far from home. Aside from Jaular, Lian spotted a few other Nondurier aboard. He also counted at least three Drak, who glared at the friends with sharp hostility. It was clear that they found it insulting to serve on a ship alongside such newlings. Lian, who had removed his spear from his back in the tight quarters below deck, clutched it tighter in front of his chest—to which Hanon'ka flashed a knowing smile before heading toward the helm. Captain Adaron remained nowhere in sight.

"Set the sails!" the Sidhari called. At the call, all on deck sprang into action.

Behind Lian, the crew set to work to complete Hanon'ka's orders, raising and lowering sails with strong ropes to hold them in place. Lian, too, turned toward the nearest side sail and took hold of a rope, and another mate ran to assist him. Together, they pulled and secured the rigging. When the sail opened up from its mast, its heavy gray canvas billowed with air. The *Carryola* picked up speed. Over the railing, mist quivered beneath the ship's hull.

The *Carryola* broke through the fog as it pushed away from the mainland. Gliding into the pale blue morning sky ahead, the sun rose in the east, bathing the distant clouds in orange light. Lian's heartbeat quickened. He inhaled deeply, smelled the fresh, clear air—void of the stink of slaughter yard, tanneries, and tavern kitchens—and let the cool wind blow against his cheeks.

A sudden shadow swept past, followed by a shrill cry—as though from the throat of a doomed and tortured soul. Lian steeled himself and forced his eyes open. "Man overboa—" he cried, but before he could finish the call, the figure's falling form broadened, and enormous wings unfolded from its back. With a powerful beat of its wings, the form set into an elegant gliding ascent to just above the ship's helm. *A Taijirin in flight!* Lian marveled. He had never seen a vogelfolk take flight before.

The men near Lian doubled over in laughter, and others standing farther off joined in. "He does that every time," said one man, chuckling and shaking his head, "and always manages to scare the pants off the newlings. Crazy flutter-man!"

"Who was that?" Lian asked with his eyes still glued to the sight. The Taijirin hovered just above the ship's bow, his tan wings flapping gently.

"That's Ialrist," answered Hanon'ka from his sudden position directly next to Lian. "One of our slayers and the captain's oldest crewmate. If you earn his respect, you'll have the most loyal comrade you could ever imagine. Make him your enemy, though, and it'll be your end."

"Ialrist," Lian murmured. He knew that jägers paid good money for one or two Taijirin among their ranks. No other folk were better suited to face dragons. A Taijirin was just as at home in the air as a Nondurier was at the helm of a ship. It shouldn't have surprised Lian that a vogelfolk served the *Carryola*, even if this was his first time seeing one in flight with his own eyes.

Hanon'ka's words raised another question. "Who are the other dragon slayers?" he asked. Lian knew dragon slayers were typically the most noticeable jägers of all. Only a specific sort possessed the level of brazen confidence to take on the insane task of battling a dragon to its death. Lian hadn't spotted anyone on board yet who quite fit that description.

"We have two on board," Hanon'ka answered, smiling mysteriously. "And don't worry. You won't miss the other one, either." His demeanor narrowed then, and he pointed toward the mast that towered above them. "Now take your place in the lookout. Someone needs to take over for Ialrist."

Lian obeyed and forced his queasiness aside as he climbed high up the mast's rigging to the crow's nest. He usually didn't have any problem with heights, but a sure-footed stance on Skargakar's solid docks to peer into the Cloudmere's depths was vastly different from clinging to a knotted rope ladder amid the clouds. To his relief, the *Carryola* didn't teeter or lurch as he'd heard ships afloat the Aquamere did—not that Lian had ever been on a watership before. Instead, the *Carryola* coasted over the clouds with majestic and steady calm.

Once he reached the top, Lian lowered himself into the lookout disguised in dragon scales. Above his head, a wooden beam ran from either side, resembling the perches for birds or lizardwings that Lian knew from the village. *Probably for Ialrist*, Lian thought. His enormous wings surely couldn't fit inside the close quarters of the crow's nest.

Lian gazed into the distance and scanned the clouds for any sign of dragons or other ships. The job didn't have any real significance until they drew farther away from Skargakar. Then it would be important to watch for dragons worth hunting. Encounters with other vessels would only be relevant after weeks aloft, when news from the mainland could be useful.

The only ship Lian saw now, which had set sail directly after the *Carryola* and now lay between them and the harbor, wasn't worth mentioning. The same went for a small swarm of greenscales, the green lizardwings that dove and spun among the clouds. Lian recognized the little dragons from lazy summer evenings of his youth, when he and Canzo would while away the time in the hillsides just outside the village. Looking up, they had watched the greenscales dip in and out of the clouds that had silently rolled past. Greenscales were comparably trustworthy creatures, likely because they weren't often hunted, Lian thought. Their meat tasted sour, and the rest of their parts didn't amount to much in the way of crystals.

Some jägers considered it a sign of good luck to spot greenscales at the onset of a journey. If they flew alongside a ship for a time, a plentiful catch was as good as certain.

From his vantage point, Lian noticed that these greenscales didn't approach the *Carryola*. After a while, he began to wonder if the creatures were wary of the dark ship in their midst. *Are they as mistrusting of Captain Adaron as the jägers in the Dragon's Claw were?* Lian wondered, but then he shrugged the thought aside. Dragons didn't swap horror stories about the shadowy ships that pursued them. They were only animals— albeit clever and dangerous ones.

As the greenscales disappeared starboard between two cloud mounds, Lian jumped when a scaly gray figure ripped through the mist and dove after them. The dragon was nearly ten times the size of the lizardwings, with a sinewy body, a skull covered in vicious spikes, and a thrashing tail. It let out a roar and struck a greenscale with its talons. The panic-stricken victim screeched as claws bore into its back.

"Dragon!" Lian cried in panic and pointed toward the scene.

The other greenscales darted frantically as the gray dragon sank his teeth into the lizardwing's throat. A powerful jerk of the beast's head tore the greenscale in two. Lian's stomach lurched, and he searched the deck below. "Dragon, starboard!" he called again.

But nobody seemed the least bit concerned, aside from Canzo, who raced along the railing to catch a glimpse of what was happening. "That's a grayback," he called up in awe. "Why is it so close to land?"

The dragon turned, revealing a back covered in horned plates. To Lian's amazement, a human figure sat among the spikes—a woman, by the look of her narrow shoulders and long brown hair. Leaning over the grayback's neck, she yelled a command in words that Lian couldn't understand. With a crack, her left hand fell onto the beast's flank.

The dragon leaned into a sharp curve, clutching both halves of its bloody catch in its front talons. With a few powerful beats of its wings, it headed straight for the *Carryola*. As though shook by thunder, Lian watched in shock.

As the dragon drew near, its rider became more recognizable. Hanon'ka had been right; there was no doubt that she was the other slayer. The huntress wore a tightly corseted leather dress and a leather harness armored with fine scales. Short swords hung from sheaths fastened at each hip, and from her upper arms, ankles, and back, Lian saw the flash of blades of various other weapons. Her collection mirrored Hanon'ka's, though in her case, no blade was shorter than her forearm.

By all the Winds, he thought. He had never seen a person more equipped to face a battle head-on. He feared the fate of any victim on the other end of her sword.

With a final flap of its leathery wings, the grayback landed on the *Carryola*'s bow, where Lian noticed a cleared area between the harpoon ballistae and foremast for this very purpose. The dragon released its catch with a wet splat onto the wooden planks and began to feast—with horrifying smacking, squelching, and crunching sounds.

Meanwhile, the slayer elegantly dismounted. Her face looked vaguely peculiar. It took Lian a few heartbeats to decipher the gruesome-looking red and blue symbols painted on her face. As she walked assuredly across the deck toward the helm, the crew in her wake stepped respectfully aside to let her pass.

A sound rang from behind, and a strong gust of wind seized Lian from inside his post. Stunned, he turned to find a man-sized shadow descending upon him with outspread wings. Lian let out a faint cry and ducked as the Taijirin, whom Lian had completely forgotten, landed on the perch above his head. Ialrist, as Hanon'ka had called him, folded his wings against his back, tipped his head forward, and regarded Lian with giant dark eyes.

"Wrong direction," said Ialrist calmly.

"What?" Lian asked in confusion. He'd never been so close to a vogel-folk before and found himself awed by the sight of the winged man. The shaggy, tan-colored down covering his face and arms grew in erratic patches and covered a slew of scars. For clothing, he wore soft, laced ankle boots, brick-red britches, and a sleeveless shirt covered by a matte-bronze armor over his chest. He held no weapon—which surprised Lian, who had come to expect the contrary after meeting the others belonging to Captain Adaron's crew.

"I said, 'You are looking in the wrong direction,'" said the slayer, who pointed toward the horizon. "Whoever mans the lookout has to look to the clouds, always. Dragons are spiteful. They'll hide behind cloud banks and attack out of nowhere. If you're careless, they'll attack before we're ready."

Lian kept silent. He considered objecting—to say that there was no real danger and that he *had* been looking out. In truth, he'd been dis-tracted by the sight of the other slayer and hadn't even noticed the vogel-folk until he was directly above him. If Ialrist had been a dragon any more malicious than a greenscale, that would have been the end of Lian's voyage.

"I understand," he answered. "Forgive me. I'll pay better attention from now on."

"Good," Ialrist said nodding toward the deck. "Now you can go down and get a better look at Corantha. I'll take over here."

"Corantha?" asked Lian. "Is that her name?"

"It is," Ialrist answered absently, focusing his gaze into the distance, just as he'd instructed Lian to do. "And her dragon is called Arax. But before you go near them, let me give you some advice." He glanced briefly at Lian. "Don't stare at them the way you're staring at me. They don't like it. And neither of them is as tolerant as I am."

Lian nodded uneasily. "I'll remember that," he said.

11

Adaron

Fifteenth Day of the Fifth Moon, Year 841

Lian awoke the next morning when the bronze bell on deck struck seven. Groaning, he wrestled his way out of his hammock. He had never spent a night in a hammock, and the experience wasn't terrible—more like floating inside a cocoon than he had expected. He would just have to get used to being constricted and unable to change position as he slept wrapped up in the rigging.

All around him, Canzo and the other six men with whom they shared their sleeping quarters rolled from their berths. There was Balen, the bald-headed helmsman and jäger kite pilot. There was also the ordinary crew: ancient old Aelfert, the two brothers Danark and Melvas—who, to Lian's eyes, seemed like the kind of men who would cut his throat without a second thought. Then there were the quiet Nondurier, Dunrir, and finally, a brown-scaled Drak, Gaaki, aide to the medic on board, whose mild gaze looked strange to Lian against his spike-covered lizard face. So far, Lian had counted five Drak aboard. From his observation, Gaaki seemed to be the loner.

Together, the eight men made up one group of three watches on board. From what Lian could tell, the watches rotated in three shifts: the day watch manned the deck from morning, when the sun hovered in the east, the night watch took over when the sky began to dim, and the early risers attended the thankless period before the sun appeared again. Every four days, the shifts rotated so that each group could sleep through the night for eight days in a row, before taking on the early-riser watch.

A fourth group aboard the ship busied themselves by day. Specialists like Smett, the cook, and Narso, the dark-skinned medic with thinning curly hair whose services might be needed at a moment's notice, were permitted to rest every night and were allowed their own sleeping quarters.

The only other members on board afforded the luxury of whole cabins to themselves and freedom from service duties were the captain, both dragon slayers, and Hanon'ka—though the first commander could often be found on deck; either he or the subcommander, Elrin, were always on board to make decisions. These privileged few slept in cabins at the bow, though Corantha usually slept on deck with her dragon, Arax, or so Lian had been told. She was far too restless to sleep anywhere other than beneath the open sky, Smett had said.

"Wake up, and move your tired bones!" called Balen, clapping his calloused hands as Lian and the others yawned and pulled on their shoes. Even though they slept with wool blankets, Lian understood quickly why they all, even Dunrir with his thick fur, slept in their clothes. It was freezing cold in the Cloudmere at night, and there was no stove in their chamber. The only open fire, aside from a few torches on deck, roared in Smett's galley and at the stern, where the large boiler used to process dragon innards was located.

As they left their sleeping quarters, Lian noticed the sleeping quarters across the hull remained empty. The early risers, manned by helmsman Markaeth, would only rest once Lian and the others took over. Nearing the ship's center, the men passed two more small cabins. Narso, the medic, walked out of his door, followed by the helmsman Jaular, who yawned, opening his hound's jaws wide, and straightened the weapon in its belt at his waist. Nothing stirred in the right-hand cabin. The commander of the late shift, the Nondurier Kurrn, and his watch would only rise to life at midday.

The scent of herbs and porridge lured Lian as he approached the mess, found almost directly at the ship's center underneath the helm. "You drink tea with breakfast?" he asked, sniffing into the air. Herb tea wasn't exactly a delicacy, but he was still surprised to find it on board. He had always assumed that crews drank beer and rum, which on second thought was absurd. Life as a jäger was dangerous enough even when fully sober.

"We have the medic to thank for that," answered Balen, who nodded toward Narso's slender figure. "Healing herbs are good for our health and our team. Narso here convinced the captain that they don't take up much space and barely cost any crystals at all." The man chuckled. "You should have seen the looks on the crew's faces when Smett set Scharmati tea on the table instead of ordinary water," he said, shaking his head.

"And in the evening, rum is replaced with kumja juice," added Dunrir with a growl as he took his place between Jaular and Narso in line, who each held an empty bowl for porridge and a cup for tea. The Nondurier scrunched up his snout in disgust, and his pointed ears flattened backward. "I can't stand kumja juice."

"And I can't stand it when people get sick when they're working outside all day because they don't take care of themselves," returned Narso as he shot an accusing glance over his shoulder. Then the medic noticed Lian and Canzo. "Oh, new faces. Did you step on board yesterday morning?" he asked.

"Yes," confirmed Lian, then introduced himself and Canzo.

"Fine, fine," said Narso. "Come to the infirmary tonight at the end of your watch for a full examination."

"But we're not sick," Lian argued.

The medic smiled with pursed lips and reached his bowl out to Smett, who ladled porridge from a large cauldron. "I'll be the judge of that," he said. Without another word, he made his way to the long table to sit with Jaular and two others Lian didn't recognize.

A wide grin spread across Smett's face as he pushed a hot bowl of mush and a cup of tea into Lian's hands. "Always worried, our good old medic." He chuckled.

"What is he afraid of?" asked Lian. "That we'll catch a cold?"

"Not that," answered Smett. "But you might have caught a parasite.

Or you could have carried white rot on board. Or maybe you've got the clap." The cook smiled wryly.

"Well, then, I feel much better now," Lian said nervously, and he carried his breakfast to Balen's table. As Hanon'ka had explained the previous morning, the crew organized themselves by watch group out of habit.

They ate mostly in silence. The mush was tasteless, but warm and filling. On the other hand, Lian struggled to swallow the extremely bitter Scharmati tea, scrunching his face in agony. "Now I see why you'd have rather gone on drinking water," he said. "This tastes no better than medicine."

Balen grumbled in agreement.

Between spoonfuls, Danark turned to Lian. "Say," he began. "That wrapped-up stick you brought on board—is it a jäger spear?"

Lian hesitated. He would have preferred not to discuss his past, but what could he do? He should have assumed that there would be questions. A weapon as large as a dragon spear was difficult to conceal. "It is," he answered finally. "Why do you ask?"

"Well, I was just wondering why you sleep with our lot if you're supposed to take over for Gaileon."

"Who's Gaileon?" Lian asked.

"He's the slayer who died during our last mission," Balen answered, now sinister. "He got too close to a chiselwing, and the scornful monster tore him apart. His cabin has been empty ever since."

"Well, I'm not a slayer," insisted Lian. "The spear is a memento from my father." He bit his lip. He'd already said more than he should have, but naturally, his words roused curiosity.

"Your father was a slayer?"

"Yes, but not one you'd know," Lian said, trying to cover his tracks. "He died recently, and his spear is the only thing he left behind. I don't know yet whether I'll follow in his footsteps or not. I have to get to know the Cloudmere first."

"You're smart to think of the dangers," Balen agreed.

Danark waved his cup in agitation. "I know a great many slayers, you know. Some were good men, and others were wretched bastards. Some died as old men surrounded by their riches, and others collapsed as drunkards in the gutter. Why, just a few nights ago in Skargakar, I met a fallen legend in a tavern. Lonjar Draksmasher . . . ever heard of him?"

"That's none of your business," snapped Lian.

Danark's lips pursed. "Just curious," he answered curtly, but his glare revealed a malicious hate.

But Lian shook his head. "I've only ever drunk my ale at Cliff House, and I've never encountered any Lonjar Draksmasher there."

It wasn't a lie. His father had never set foot in Cliff House. He had always preferred seedier establishments. Danark didn't seem convinced, though. "Are you sure about that?"

Lian stood up. "I really don't know what you want me to say. An interrogation is the last thing I signed up for," he said angrily. "Now if you'll excuse me, I'll be on deck."

"Oh, sit down, you hothead," Balen said, setting a hand on Lian's arm. "There's still a good while before the start of our watch. We wouldn't want to show up early and give the impression that we'd rather work longer, would we?"

Balen's objection was as convincing as his grip, and Lian wasn't interested in testing either on his second day on board. These men would be his companions by work, meals, and rest over the course of many moon cycles. It was better, he knew, to make nice with his comrades.

Lian sat again. "Fine. But let's talk about something else."

"I'd like to know when we'll finally see Captain Adaron," Canzo blurted good-naturedly. "He didn't even set foot on deck yesterday. I know Smett said he can't stand land, but there's no land in sight by now."

Balen exchanged darting glances with the others, negotiating how to answer wordlessly.

"The captain usually keeps to himself," he said finally, under his breath. "His soul wrestles with many demons."

"He's just a little off, that's all," Melvas added. "Doesn't set foot on land, never laughs or drinks, and hasn't touched a woman in years because of a vow he made to a woman who's been gone for ages." He snorted. "If he didn't lead the best hunting ship at sea, I'd have left this joyless boat a long time ago."

"Quiet, Melvas," Balen growled. "You're risking your neck with talk like that."

"Hey, I'm not the only one who thinks so," Melvas fired back. "But unlike those other cowards, at least I have the guts to speak my—" He stopped abruptly, with new fascination for the bowl of mush before him.

"What is it?" Balen asked, and he and Lian turned.

A man had entered the canteen from the stairway at the bow. Time had chiseled deep wrinkles into his scowling face, and his gaze was grave and distant. His well-crafted clothes—boots, trousers, and tailcoat— were as black as his hair, and aside from a dagger hanging from his leather belt, he carried neither weapons nor armor. Next to all the embellished and costumed jägers Lian had seen, the man's appearance was far from what he had expected, but this man needed no heavy armor, exotic weapons, or war paint to make an impression. His presence was more than sufficient to silence everyone.

This was Captain Adaron. Lian wondered if he had always been this grave or whether the loss of his former crew played a part.

Adaron inhaled and scanned the present company. Then, nodding in satisfaction, he turned to Hanon'ka, who stood in the entranceway behind him. "Call everyone to the deck, Commander," he said gruffly. "I'd like to have a word with the crew."

"Yes, Captain," answered Hanon'ka.

As Adaron disappeared up the stairs to the deck, the first commander approached the crew. "You heard the captain. Everyone on deck. Jaular, wake your watch. I'll deal with the rest."

The men in the canteen set into motion. A few grumbled and hungrily shoveled a few more spoonfuls of mush into their mouths, while the rest stood and headed for the stairs, their quiet mutterings adding to the commotion.

"Well, I guess that was Adaron," Canzo whispered to Lian. "I don't think I'd share a pint with him at Cliff House."

"I doubt he'd want that, either," replied Lian with a grin. "But a captain doesn't have to be friendly to lead a good ship."

"Hm, I guess not."

Above deck, they greeted the crisp morning air. Gleaming white as freshly washed linens, the Cloudmere enveloped the *Carryola,* its air damp and clear in Lian's nostrils. A small, squeaking swarm of blue lizardwings darted in the distance. Cold wind swept across the deck and puffed up the ship's sails as the *Carryola* picked up speed beneath their feet.

From his raised vantage at the helm, Adaron stood beside Elrin and surveyed the gathered crew. Once all had assembled, including Corantha and her dragon, Arax, he addressed the group.

"So once again our schooner has set sail amid the Cloudmere. After twelve missions, the *Carryola* is not the same vessel she was when she first departed from Skargakar's shores. And none of you—of us—are the same as the day we first hoisted her sails and loaded her harpoon ballistae for that first dragon hunt."

Adaron leaned forward and rested his arms on the railing before him. "More than one of us has been lost to eternal fog by these vicious beasts, and now new faces replace those who have left us. We have four new comrades aboard this mission, fearless young men who have answered the Cloudmere's call." Adaron cast a glance toward the newlings. "Greetings, Wil, Lian, Lannik, and Canzo," he said, and he locked eyes with each man in turn. "I offer you my respect." He continued, "The dragon hunt is not for the weak of body or spirit. You have agreed to a challenge that is not just the most noble but the most dangerous test of strength that exists between man and beast."

"And the most lucrative," one jokester called. Some among the crowd snorted, concealing chuckles.

The corners of Adaron's mouth twitched with the hint of a grin. "True. One can gain a few crystals aboard such a vessel. But the promise of riches isn't enough to call a drachenjäger. Anyone looking for this kind of adventure must possess only the strongest heart, most steadfast mind, and a fearless spirit. Men and women with that kind of virtue are few and far between. I am proud to stand in the presence of such brave souls."

The captain's face darkened as he continued to survey the crew. "The *Carryola* is not a ship for rounding up lap-dragons for gentlewomen, or riding-dragons for the state guard. We hunt the drachen—the most murderous monsters in Endar. Most would never dare to face them. Yet here you stand, ready to fight, when you could be cowering under the tables in Skargakar's taverns. For that, I offer you only my utmost respect. I couldn't dream of a better crew than all of you."

"Hear, hear!" Elrin called, and murmurs rippled among the group.

Adaron straightened up, and his expression hardened once more. "As I said, we are hunting beasts that no one else would dare to face, but there is one above all others that has frightened the crews of all other vessels. You know the name as well as I. He has prowled the *Carryola* since its very first time aloft. Gargantuan, the black demon, will one day be the pinnacle of our victories. Some say he's only a legend, a mere horror story to scare newlings, but I am certain that he is out there. I have stared into his murderous eye, as close as all of you stand to me now. On that day, all those years ago, Gargantuan ripped my heart from my chest, and since then, I have owed him the same courtesy."

Glancing around, Lian noticed the earnest and composed expressions of the crew. These men had heard their captain's call for revenge many times before, and his words stirred many of them. Corantha's glare, Lian noticed, smoldered with red-hot battle lust. Like Adaron, she seemed more than ready to face the beast.

Gargantuan . . . Lian had heard the name before, in a legend told by a jäger at Cliff House. He couldn't remember the details, only that Gargantuan was no ordinary dragon. He was one the Firstborn, a direct descendant of the Starborn—whatever that was supposed to mean. But from the way the hunter told the tale, Lian had been sure it wasn't true. Such a terrible creature couldn't possibly exist.

"Excuse me, Captain," Canzo called up from the crowd. "But what sort of dragon is Gargantuan? I've never heard of him before." Lian remembered that his friend hadn't been at Cliff House on the night he'd heard the legend.

The crew erupted in mutterings and shot mocking glances that made Canzo cower at the silliness of his question, but Adaron brought the men to silence with a decisive wave of his hand, gluing his gaze to Canzo.

"Gargantuan is nothing like any dragon you've ever seen," he began grimly. "He is one of the Firstborn, the oldest and greatest dragons of all. His body is powerful and black. Black as the fog from which he strikes. Black as the lightless chasm from whence he was born at the beginning of time."

Lian shuddered. These were the exact words that the prophet had spoken from the pier. How could two such different men give such an eerily precise description of the beast?

"Gargantuan is a monster of legends," Adaron continued. "Some even believe he fathered all the other drachen in existence. And still . . ." The captain paused and turned to the group once again. "And still, he is a beast of flesh and blood like any other. He can be injured, and killed, if we can muster the courage to face him. This ship will be his down-fall. That is why we sail the Cloudmere, to far beyond the Taijirin isles, where few have ever ventured before us. We shall find Gargantuan, kill him, and drag his lifeless carcass back to Skargakar. We will replace his legend with another: the tale of the *Carryola* and her fearless crew, who managed what no one else could fathom. I swear this to you all, as true as I stand here before you. Together, we shall decide that monster's miserable fate!"

12

The Bronzeneck

Twentieth Day of the Fifth Moon, Year 841

The following days rolled by with little change as Lian and Canzo accustomed themselves to daily life aboard the *Carryola*. They grew used to sleeping in hammocks, choking down bitter herbal tea without the experience spoiling their entire day, and never encouraging Smett at the beginning of a story—lest they become captive with no chance of escape.

The only dragons Lian spotted during this time were blue lizardwings, lured with scraps of food and then captured in nets and fried up by Smett for their evening dinner. While they may have lacked hunting opportunities, they had more work aboard than Lian thought possible. In the mornings, Hanon'ka oversaw the crew as they scrubbed the deck and rubbed down the dragon-scale shields covering the hull; since the damp of the Cloudmere crept into wood and skin, only constant care prevented moss from growing over the planks and breaking down the scales.

"As long as they're part of the dragon's body, the scales can't break down," explained Melvas as he and Lian oiled the scales along the ship's hull with rags as they clung to a net stretched across the hull. "But once the dragon is dead, they're an unbelievable amount of work."

"Why did the captain choose to cover the hull in scales, anyway?" Lian asked, pulling slightly on the strap around his waist that secured him against the net. "There are barely any fire-breathers on the Cloudmere. That's what I've heard, at least."

"One would be enough to take down a wooden ship with canvas sails," Melvas answered. "I suppose he could have covered the hull with burnished iron, but then the *Carryola* would be so heavy that she'd sink to the ground of the Cloudmere without a dragon's help." He shook his head. "No, there's nothing better than a good scale armor. And not to mention, they also shield against corrosion from spurts of a dragon's stomach acid."

"There are dragons that spray acid?" Lian asked in disbelief. "I've never heard that before."

"Then the rumors must be false. Either your father wasn't really a heroic dragon hunter, or he kept an awful lot from you."

Lian didn't want to talk about his father. Part of him longed to defend Lonjar Draksmasher's reputation, but he couldn't bear to admit how little his father had told about his past as a slayer.

"I'm sure that there's always much more to learn," he said flatly.

Melvas laughed. "That's good. That alone is the most important thing a jäger can know amid the Cloudmere."

"Hey!" a voice from above called. Simultaneously, a hand struck the railing. Tilting his head back, Lian saw Elrin glaring down at them. "You're not out there to chatter. Now polish the damn scales, you laggards, and if they're not glistening next time I come to inspect, you'll have to start all over again—"

"Dragon!" A call came from the lookout. "Giant bull—straight ahead!"

Elrin looked up and whipped around. "Captain?" he called and awaited the order.

"What kind?" Lian heard Adaron call back.

"A bronzeneck, sir," Wil called from the lookout.

Lian couldn't make out the captain's response, but after a moment, the subcommander yelled down to them once again. "You two come up and get a better look at the beast."

Lian clambered up the net and over the railing. On deck, the crew had set into motion, preparing for the hunt. They raised sails while men took their places at the harpoon ballistae at the bow and stern and hauled kyrillian buoys out from a trapdoor and carried them to the deck. Adaron stood beside the bowsprit, a telescope held to his right eye, and peered into the distance. Hanon'ka, with Ialrist and Corantha at his sides, waited a few steps behind the captain. When Adaron muttered a few words, the three nodded, and Corantha made her way to Arax, who snorted and stomped impatiently.

Adaron and Hanon'ka returned to their posts starboard. "The day watch will man the *Carryola*," announced Hanon'ka. "Balen, take a jäger kite. Melvas, Canzo, and Lian will go with you."

"Just one ship, Commander?" Balen asked. "And two newlings?"

"It's only a bronzeneck," Adaron answered sharply. "Do you doubt your own hunting abilities?"

Balen shook his head and frowned. "No, not that, Captain, but I can't steer the ship and kill the beast at the same time."

"You won't be alone," Hanon'ka said calmly. "Ialrist and Corantha will be in the air. And I'll meet you on board."

"Really?" Balen asked, surprised.

The Sidhari's emerald eyes glimmered. "I'll guide the novice jägers myself," he said, and his eyes fell on Lian. "Fetch your spear, Lian. It's time to see if your skills in the clouds are as good as they were on solid land."

Lian stood still as though struck by lightning. Had Danark been right? Was he supposed to be the *Carryola*'s third slayer? When Danark had spoken those words, Lian had thought the idea absurd and had wanted to object. He hadn't boarded the *Carryola* to be a slayer. And despite the weapon to his name and his confident words to Mavron at the Dragon's Claw, he wasn't sure he had the courage, but if Hanon'ka believed slaying was his calling, then Lian wasn't about to argue. The idea that he could be a warrior considered the equal to Ialrist and Corantha—that he could eat alongside them without feeling inferior—elated him.

"Just a moment," Lian said, and he ran under the deck and to his sleeping quarters. He grabbed the wrapped-up spear from his hammock and hurried back to the deck.

In the meantime, Hanon'ka, Balen, Melvas, and Canzo released one of the two small jäger kites from its place roped to the stern. Four small kyrillian cases lined the kite's sides, and there was room for six men on board—though three would have been enough to tend the sails, maneuver the ropes, and man the harpoon ballista at the bow.

As Balen carefully opened the storage cases to raise the kite above the *Carryola*'s support beams, Hanon'ka, Melvas, and Canzo jumped on board and grabbed the steerage ropes. Just before the kite rose out of his reach, Lian clutched his spear in one hand and clambered aboard.

"Good hunting!" called Adaron from below. Already behind them, Ialrist hopped onto the *Carryola*'s railing and stood tall. Spreading his wings wide, the clouds filled his feathers and lifted him into the air. With a rush of air, Arax took off from the bowsprit with Corantha astride his back. The huntress's wild smile revealed her fearlessness and joy at the prospect of facing an awaiting bronzeneck.

"Lian, come here," Hanon'ka called from the bow as Balen navigated the ship upward and sideways to gain distance from the *Carryola*. Canzo and Melvas set to carrying out the pilot's orders to hoist and set main and side sails.

The jäger kite quickly gained speed, and soon, they broke through the clouds and cast their eyes straight ahead toward the shimmering bronzeneck.

To Lian's surprise, the dragon showed no recognition of its pursuers, though it had surely spotted the *Carryola* below.

"Why doesn't he try to escape?" Lian asked.

"He doesn't seek cover because he doesn't know who we are," Hanon'ka answered. "Most dragons that fall victim to jägers simply disappear. Dragons don't travel in packs, especially large sorts, who live in solitude and seldom witness another attack, so the knowledge of the danger we pose never spreads far across the Cloudmere. Besides, only the cleverest dragons would find a way to warn their kind."

The Sidhari's face darkened. "And good thing. It would surely be difficult to face dragons if they knew of jägers. They would likely remember the threat and dive into the clouds. The hunt would be strenuous. Dragons avoid the clouds—that's why they always fly above the fleece, with a clear view—and we don't like it, either. It would be impossible to know where or when a beast would turn up. Most hunters turn back on such hunts. There are always other catches."

"There's another trick for sneaking up on a wary beast," Balen added.

"Tail him from just underneath, as we are now. Dragons are much less suspecting of threats from below than from things descending upon them. Also, they have blind spots. Their massive bodies block out a great span of sky behind them—even though their eyes face sideways—so they're clueless to what happens at their backs."

"True," Hanon'ka answered. "They tend to fly in loops when they're nervous, to keep track of what lies behind them, but this bronzeneck is young and inexperienced. We'll make sure he never has the chance to grow old and spread any warnings."

The Sidhari glanced over his shoulder, and Lian followed suit. The two slayers behind them followed closely at either side of the kite. Hanon'ka raised a hand, to which both nodded and disappeared into the cloud mounds that surrounded them.

"Get ready," Hanon'ka warned. "Unsheathe the spear." Bending forward, he opened a trapdoor in the floor and pulled out a harness made of two crossed straps and a wide leather belt with small metal cases fastened to each side. "And put this on," he instructed, handing the contraption to Lian.

"What is it?" Lian asked as he pulled his father's spear from its wool-blanket covering.

Without a word, the Sidhari clicked open one of the cases, and a violet light escaped. He gripped the harness tighter as it threatened to shoot upward out of his hands. Hurriedly, he clapped the box shut. "It's just a precaution," he explained. "If you fall off the dragon's back, we don't want to lose you in the clouds."

"The dragon's back?!" Lian asked with wide eyes. It became all too clear what was expected.

The glow kindled in the Sidhari's eyes. For a brief but agonizing moment, Lian imagined that a hideous demon stalked him from the Cloudmere's most horrible depths. Was this a waking nightmare?

"Drachen can be injured from a distance," began Hanon'ka. "But they can only be killed when faced head-on. Their scale armor is so hard and dense that only an expert marksman's arrow can penetrate it. However, every dragon has weak spots at their joints. It's easiest to pierce them with a spear from their backs. Thrust quickly, and you can take the monster down. Well, maybe *down* is the wrong word," he added. "Kyrillian buoys will keep him afloat so that we can tow him back to the schooner."

The Sidhari nodded toward a row of rolls that lay beneath a chain net. Thin but unbreakable ropes, made of twisted and carefully coiled rock-spider silk strands, ran from underneath the net and attached to the spears that stood ready to be loaded. These spears, when fired with the ballista at the bow, would pierce the dragon, and their buoys would keep the creature aloft.

While Lian fastened his harness, Hanon'ka approached the artillery at the bow and turned a crank. Creaking, the bowstring pulled back and locked into place, and the rope attached to the buoy tightened. Then Hanon'ka set a spear into the artillery, making sure that the rope was straight. If anything was knotted or tangled, or the buoys released from their metal netting too soon, they would shoot straight toward the sky, with spear and all. Since kyrillian lost its effect at a certain altitude, it wouldn't be impossible to retrieve the buoys, Lian knew. It was still tricky, because the ship could only ascend so high. Not to mention, freezing cold and dangerous altitude sickness awaited those who ventured too high.

Bit by bit, they stalked the bronzeneck until they reached shooting range. Hanon'ka huddled behind the harpoon, his eye glued to the spyglass attached to the weapon, following the dragon's form. Lian stood at his side, taut with excitement. The idea of jumping onto a dragon's back—which stretched twenty paces, at least—and ramming a spear into its neck filled him with dread, but there was no turning back. A part of him didn't want to, either. If he could pass this test, he knew, nothing else could ever frighten him again. *Well, maybe a fire-spitter,* he thought. *But at least I don't have to deal with one of them yet.* A bronzeneck was challenge enough.

"Lian," Canzo called from behind him, loud enough to carry over the wind.

Lian turned to his friend, who had gone pale. "Good luck," he said solemnly and forced a smile.

Lian nodded. "To us all," he answered.

"Hold on!" Hanon'ka called and nodded at Balen to give the order.

"Lower the sails!" came Balen's call. "From now on, kyrillian will steer us."

"What does he mean?" Lian asked quietly as Canzo and Melvas carried out the command. "The crystals can keep us afloat, but how can they propel us forward?"

The Sidhari's emerald eyes glowed. "Just hold on tightly," he answered.

As soon as Lian gripped the railing, his stomach dropped as Balen fully opened all the kyrillian cases on deck. The wooden hull groaned, and the side sails fluttered as the ship shot straight up.

There must be an extra row of crystals in the cases!

Lian understood kyrillian well enough to know that their speed was unusual. Once more, Adaron amazed him with the expense he put into his equipment.

The kite surged from its cover just behind the tip of the bronzeneck's tail. When the dragon turned its head and spotted them through the sideways slit of its eye, confusion clouded its gaze.

Although nearly twice as large as their vessel, the dragon launched away from its attackers with an upward whip of its tail and frantic beat of its giant leathery wings, plunging into the clouds.

Balen stood ready. When he pulled on the steering ropes, the ship tipped downward and plummeted into the clouds after the bronzeneck.

Hanon'ka pulled the ballista's trigger. With a sharp hiss, the bowstring released, and a metal spear shot straight toward its target. From underneath its netting, the finely spun silk rope unwound from its roll.

The harpoon sank into the bronzeneck's thinly armored hind leg with a crack. The beast thrashed its head and uttered a bellowing roar. To Lian, the sound seemed to express more fury than pain.

Balen tilted the kite and steered the ropes. At once, a kyrillian buoy ripped through its metal net and shot into the air, just past Lian's head.

"Next!" cried Hanon'ka, motioning toward the spears, and he hastily rewound his crank. Lian threw his own weapon to the deck and set another black metal spear into place.

The Sidhari turned toward Balen. "Second fire," he called.

"Too late," the driver answered, pointing over the railing. "He's gone into the fleece."

With a glance overboard, Lian saw what Balen meant. As the bronzeneck writhed below, its wings stirred up thick billows of fog that rose to their feet. A kyrillian buoy floated above the beast's back, a dancing ball of shimmering violet light.

"He won't last long now—not with that buoy attached to him,"

Hanon'ka said. "Keep your eyes open. He'll dive again soon, straight in line with the bow, if my eyes don't deceive me."

"Why straight?" asked Lian.

"Because he is young and inexperienced, as I said before," answered the Sidhari. "Fear propels him forward. It would never cross his mind to change direction to shake us off, and flying in circles wouldn't be logical, either, since he can't see through the clouds any better than we can, and just as well. We run the risk of hitting concealed peaks in the fleece, no matter how straight the course is."

"Over there!" Balen called, pointing ahead.

Some three hundred paces ahead, the bronzeneck emerged once more. Its wings flapped hectically as it made every effort to distance itself—in a straight line, no less—from their jäger kite.

"Hoist the sails!" the pilot called. "Hard toward the wind."

Canzo and Melvas did as instructed, and the kite sped forward. Hanon'ka loaded the harpoon once more. "If the second buoy strikes, we'll have him for sure," he explained. "Then he won't be able to dive away any longer."

The dragon made a sharp turn and struggled toward cover inside a mound of clouds on its left side. Before it could reach the spot, Arax's winged gray form shot from the cloud's depths and headed for the beast. The grayback let out a threatening roar, and the huntress howled a murderous cry into the mist.

The bronzeneck whipped around in surprise. With another dry snap, Hanon'ka fired once more, and the harpoon entered the dragon's body with a crack. Paired with the first, the second kyrillian buoy dragged the beast upward at an incline.

The dragon hissed and thrust its head backward in an effort to remove the spear with its jaws—but to no avail. "Now the third buoy," Hanon'ka said, "and then it's your turn. It has to end quickly now."

"Why the rush?" Lian asked as he handed another spear to the Sidhari. "He can't escape."

Hanon'ka glared at Lian. "A dragon should never suffer unnecessary pain. It is enough that he must die." He set the third spear into place. "Balen," he continued, "put us on the other side of the beast so we can get a better idea of his position. That way it will be easier for Lian to reach him."

"Aye, Commander," answered Balen. With Canzo's and Melvas's aid, he guided the ship around the dragon's flapping tail and made an elegant loop to reach its right flank.

The bronzeneck's movements grew labored. The kyrillian buoys, which suspended the dragon from its flank and near the base of its left wing, made it impossible for the beast to fly normally. Its wings beat frantically as it bucked its scaled body, talons clawing and neck strained, in a desperate attempt to break free. Perhaps such efforts would have been successful on solid land, but aloft, the bronzeneck's efforts were wasted.

For a brief moment, Lian pitied the doomed creature. He shoved his sympathy aside; jägers didn't hunt dragons out of malice. Their meat, skin, scales, and innards fed and clothed the folk of Skargakar. That was just the way of things. One creature killed the other to ensure the survival of his own kind.

With firm resolution, he gripped his spear. He wouldn't disappoint Canzo, Hanon'ka, or any of the others.

For the third time, Hanon'ka released the harpoon. When the harpoon penetrated the beast just behind its right wing, the Sidhari nodded with satisfaction.

"Outstanding shot," Balen complimented.

"It's only a bronzeneck," replied the Sidhari. "Not an especially difficult opponent." His glowing gaze fell on Lian. "Now, let's end it."

From the nearby clouds, Ialrist and Corantha descended from both sides. The bronzeneck snarled and whipped its tail with fury, but neither of the fighters cowered in its presence. Ialrist posed with his reaver and a spiked iron rod in his hands, and Corantha positioned a hunting bow and arrow. Neither of them attacked.

Balen attempted to steer the ship upward as the wind stirred by the dragon's frantic wings threatened to blow them off course. With the pilot's expert maneuvers and the help of the storage cases, their vessel remained on course.

The tortured beast's howls filled the air as their kit hovered above. Hanon'ka rushed past the others toward the stern. "Follow me!" he called to Lian.

At the far end of the railing, Hanon'ka picked up a roll of rope from the deck, its end attached to an iron hook bolted to the small deck. He threw the rope overboard. "Practiced slayers can slide down with one hand. Since this is your first time, I advise you to sling your spear over one shoulder and climb down with both hands." He motioned toward a leather band wrapped around the weapon's shaft, and for the first time, Lian understood it could be loosened to become a strap.

As he rushed to loosen it now, his heart thumped in his chest. His throat was dry and scratchy. He clenched his jaw and grabbed the rope. *Onward!* his spirit cried. *You can do this! You are Lonjar Draksmasher's son. There must be some good in that.*

Looking over his shoulder, Lian met Canzo's gaze, who forced a weak smile and raised his fist, his cheeks now feverish.

Beneath them, the bronzeneck roared.

"You have to get him in the neck, right where it meets the skull. There's a ring of horns on the crown of his head. The weakest point on the skull is right underneath them. Ram the spear right there, and he'll die quickly."

Lian nodded and threw a leg over the railing. "Right."

"And one more thing: if you slip, just let yourself fall. Don't grab hold of the dragon. If you get caught hanging on him sideways, you might run into his claws or teeth. Just let yourself fall into the clouds and then open the casings on your harness. The Cloudmere is vast and deep. You'll have plenty of time before you hit the ground."

Lian nodded without a word. His hands had cramped around the rope, and he worried that he wouldn't be able to let go, but when Hanon'ka clapped him on the shoulder, he shoved all doubt and fear away.

The bronzeneck howled once more, and Lian answered with a cry as he slid down the rope into the lofty depths. Wind blew through his hair and filled his nose with the stink of the monstrous chestnut-colored body that writhed and shimmered underneath him. The beast resembled a strange soldier clad in armor with the thick layer of scales covering its body. Giant horned plates ran along its back and grew smaller and sparser toward the tail. Powerful muscles rippled beneath its frantic wings, and beneath the dragon, cold fog curled and billowed, white and bottomless.

The rope ended four paces above the dragon's back. Without waiting for Balen to steer the boat lower, Lian let go.

He landed just between the dragon's wings. A shiver ran through its body and knocked Lian off balance. He grabbed for the nearest plate and squeezed his eyes shut as he fought for footing. The wind conjured by the beast's struggles rang in his ears. Up close, the stench was more than he could bear. *Not much better than the carcasses gutted at the slaughter yard. Canzo would feel right at home,* he thought. Fighting for balance, he reached a hand around his back and grasped the shaft of his spear.

Crouching low, he worked his way along the row of plates—for which he was all too thankful—toward the dragon's neck. The beast's strong shoulder muscles undulated as its thick neck thrashed wildly. At the base of its head, Lian spotted the horned headdress that Hanon'ka had described.

He pressed on, his gaze locked on the base of the beast's skull. It was time to finish this fight. Besides his target, he thought nothing and felt nothing. His spirit was numb, and the only sound in his ears was the rush of blood and wind.

Beneath the soles of his feet, the dragon's body trembled. A new sort of howl came from its throat, so primal and deafening that it penetrated Lian. He fell to his knees and grabbed the plate next to him. All the fear he had banished aboard the kite returned tenfold. *What am I doing? Am I crazy? I'm standing on a dragon's back and am supposed to kill him with this pathetic spear, and below me is this gaping abyss . . .* he thought as fog licked his back. He cursed the day that he'd ever indulged the maddening urge to venture into the Cloudmere and his father for ever getting mixed up with the greatest crook in Skargakar.

The winds shifted, whipping him from above. Through the gusts, a voice called his name.

With wide eyes, he turned. Not more than eight paces away, Ialrist hovered above him. The Taijirin's wings flapped powerfully against the dragon's windstorm as he pointed his iron spike resolutely toward the dragon's neck. "Do it!" he called. "Or I will!"

Lian stared dumbly at the vogelfolk. "Come, Lian," Ialrist encouraged. "Be a jäger!"

Be a jäger . . . The words echoed through Lian's mind. They could have come from his father's own mouth. Lian returned his gaze to the base of the bronzeneck's head. Finally, he sucked in a deep breath of cold air, pressed his lips together resolutely, and stood. His father's spear clutched in white knuckles, he made the final steps to the base of the bronzeneck's skull. Ialrist hovered behind him, and perhaps twenty strides farther back, Corantha flew atop Arax. High above them, the jäger kite floated and the *Carryola* just behind. Dozens of anticipating, speculating, and hopeful eyes awaited his action.

Lian took a wide-legged stance and released his hold on the dragon's spine. With his left hand grasping the shaft's middle and his right wrapped tightly around the base, he raised the spear. A shimmer ran across the runes as a ray of sun flashed across the blade—almost as though the weapon itself longed to taste dragon blood once more.

He brought the weapon down with a cry.

13

The Dark Heart

Twentieth Day of the Fifth Moon, Year 841

Herb ale foamed and sloshed as the wooden mugs knocked raucously together. In Lian's experience so far, drinking ale was a rare pleasure aboard. Adaron only permitted a few barrels of beer on board per journey, with strict instructions that they drink it on the most special occasions. The first successful catch was such an occasion.

"I thought you'd never make it," Melvas called across the din. "When you fell on your knees, I was sure you'd never stand again. You wouldn't be the first to blow your own horn on board, only to cower in failure when you met a dragon face-to-face."

"I never blew my own horn," Lian answered. "I never even considered slaying a dragon." His cheeks burned. "I came on board to experience life on the Cloudmere and to venture to places I'd only ever imagined."

"Spoken like a true landsman," a voice called from the second row, and laughter sounded through the crowd.

Aside from a few lookouts manning the deck, the crew's work was done for the day. Roped to the stern, kyrillian buoys still held the bronzeneck's body aloft. Early the next morning, Canzo and a few other slaughtermen would process the animal. Smaller sky vessels would dock at a floating island or mountain peak to carry out the work, but the *Carryola* had enough space to process the bronzeneck aboard. Thus, they could continue their mission without interruption.

Scales had to be removed and oiled; claws, teeth, and bones cleaned; and wings and skin tanned. Under the inspection of the medic, the innards would be sorted according to their worth, and Smett would set to work smoking and drying the meat. With plenty of work ahead, the *Carryola* would tack across the Cloudmere with lowered sails for the next few days.

For the moment, though, with the captain's permission, work could wait. Adaron, however, as well as Hanon'ka and the two slayers were nowhere in sight, but, as one helmsman explained to Lian, it would have been peculiar for them to join the men.

"When I first set out to sea," the old man, Aelfert, said, "I had the same desires as you. I longed to discover lands that had never before known the work of human hands." He leaned forward, and Lian saw laughter in his glimmering blue eyes. "I found those desires in the form of an enchanting Taijirin maiden far away in Raikvindar. Oh, how I found them."

The men roared.

"Don't forget the part where she abandoned you in her love nest," a voice called, "stuck on a mountain peak in the middle of nowhere like a fool!"

The mess hall exploded in laughter.

"Yes, a fool," Aelfert admitted, swallowing a swig of beer as he shrugged.

When the laughter had subsided, Balen, who sat beside Lian and Canzo, laid a broad hand on Lian's shoulder. "My boy, don't let these dimwits sully your dreams," he said earnestly. "In truth, we all feel as you do. No jäger would endure the hardships amid the clouds—the storms and cold, the hard work, and the abominable food . . ." Lian heard Smett grumble, but Balen held up a hand in defense and continued. "No jäger would endure it all if he didn't know the deep longing that you have named. I'm not speaking of crystals or glory. I mean the longing for wide-open freedom and for distant places that await us."

The pilot looked up and surveyed the crew, who sat silent. Their bearded faces, lit from the glow of the lanterns, all shared a look of inspired wonder as though just blessed by a priest.

"Speak, men," continued Balen. "Is there one among you who hasn't stood at the bow amid clear morning gray and watched the sun rise magnificently through the clouds? Who saw strands of white mist drenched in gold and wasn't enchanted at the sight? Or one who has seen the floating islands of Jarva, the crown colony Arsindair, or the mountains of Conyrhaidon, and didn't wonder if you had ever seen anything more beautiful?"

The snickering of the Drak huddled in the corner broke the silence. These four—Karnosk, Jarssas, Sheshac, and Srashi—all belonged to the second watch manned by Markaeth and mostly stayed together.

"Human sentimentality," Karnosk said with a grating voice. "Distance, sunrise, and landscape don't interest me. I sail the Cloudmere to hunt dragons and find a drachen pearl that will make me rich, and any of you who say otherwise are liars. Nobody becomes a dragon hunter out of longing. He does it because he hopes for riches."

"It's possible to wish for treasure and admire the clouds at the same time," Balen answered. "Not all of us are as corrupt as you, Karnosk."

The Drak let out a hissing laugh. "Remind me of that before our next wage day," he said. He beat his clawed fist against his chest. "I, for one, would rather be paid in crystals than in clouds and islands bathed in sunshine."

"Then you'll be disappointed," someone said. Turning, Lian saw Corantha descend the wooden stairs from the deck.

The huntress still sported red-and-blue war paint and wore a leather harness over a gray woolen shirt. Only a few daggers—her most essential weapons—dangled at her sides. She had rolled her sleeves up and wiped her blood-smeared hands on a rag.

"There was no pearl inside the bronzeneck," she began.

"How do you know?" asked Karnosk. "Did you already look for it?"

"Of course. I'm always curious," she answered. She tossed the blood-soaked towel in his direction, where it hit the table and fell to the deck.

"Anyway, we have other business here," Ialrist said from behind her, his wings pulled tightly to his back. "It is time for this," he said, lifting a silver bottle. A thin stream of white steam wandered into the air from its opening.

A few crew members winced, and the rest nodded in agreement.

The slayers turned to Lian. Reaching into a pouch at her belt, Corantha pulled out a pale, curved dragon fang, roughly the size of a dagger, which glinted in the lantern light.

"What is that for?" asked Lian.

"You get a mark so that all know and never forget how often you looked death in the eye," answered Corantha. She revealed her forearm, where a long row of tally mark scars ran from wrist to elbow. There must have been more than thirty. Now Lian understood why she had no trouble on a ship full of men. Nobody in his right mind would risk laying a hand on a woman who had taken the lives of thirty dragons—and Lian doubted that one got a victory mark for killing a greenscale. Awe for the slayer who had taken the lives of thirty dragons filled Lian.

"Choose which arm," Ialrist instructed.

Lian considered for a moment and set his right forearm decisively onto the table. With a dismissive wave, the Taijirin shoved Balen and Canzo out of the way, and he and Corantha took seats on either side of Lian.

Setting the silver flask onto the table, Ialrist placed his hands on Lian's arm.

"That's not necessary," Lian said as he resisted the man's iron hold. He was sure that other jägers would scoff at a weakling who would even think of pulling away during a marking ritual.

"Oh yes, it is," said Ialrist, "at least the first time, anyway."

Corantha and Ialrist exchanged knowing glances. Studying her face, Lian noticed that her war paint hadn't smudged at all during the fight. Up close, he realized that they were tattoos. The markings were similar to Hanon'ka's, only more striking. Hers was a war mask that she could never remove framed by wild brown hair. Lian was both shocked and fascinated, and he wondered if he would ever get to hear her story.

Corantha knocked the fang against the table to draw Lian out of his thoughts. "Are you ready?" she asked.

He braced himself and nodded.

Carefully, she dipped the fang's pointed end into the bottle and raised it before her eyes. Steam curled from its end up to the ceiling. "It'll only hurt a touch," she said.

"It's okay, I—" But his words were lost in a wave of searing pain. He'd assumed that Corantha would use the fang's point to cut a mark into his arm. Instead, she merely grazed the end along his skin. Far from comforting, it felt as though someone gently caressed him with a glowing poker pulled straight from the fire.

"From the body of the beast himself," said Corantha, nodding to the bottle. Whatever the liquid inside was, it burned fiercely and left a red and steaming trail behind seared on Lian's arm. As he clenched his fist to combat the pain, Ialrist's grip tightened.

A moment later, the procedure was over. Corantha removed the fang and dropped it into Canzo's half-empty mug of ale. Then, taking the mug next to it, she poured its contents over Lian's arm, and a new wave of pain washed over him. Finally, she clapped a hand over the wet and smarting burn, and he sucked in his breath sharply with the pain.

"Singed and spent," she said, laughing, and pulled Lian up to his feet as she stood. "To the newest drachenjäger!" she called, presenting his arm for all to see.

The crew raised their mugs and repeated the call.

"And to his first slay. May there be many more!" she called.

"And to how damned rich we'll all become!" called someone from the crowd.

Laughter broke out as the men knocked their mugs together in agreement. Corantha marched over to Smett, who manned the open barrel at the far side of the canteen. "Fill her up, man," she ordered thrusting her mug forward.

Lian grinned to Canzo, who sat smiling like a proud father. As he was about to take a seat, Ialrist returned to his side.

"Adaron is expecting you."

"The captain wants to speak to me?" Lian asked in surprise.

The Taijirin nodded absently. "You'll find him inside his cabin at the bow. Better hurry. He doesn't like to be kept waiting."

A few moments later, his arm still searing, Lian stood at the entrance to the captain's quarters, his heart pounding. As he raised his fist to knock, the door opened, and Hanon'ka emerged. The Sidhari's emerald eyes smoldered when he saw Lian.

"Ah, Lian. Just in time," he said. Then he brushed past Lian and disappeared up the stairs to the deck.

Beyond the door, a few lanterns suspended from the ceiling illuminated the dim room. A large table stood at the room's center, unrolled scrolls of parchment piled across its surface. Behind the table, the high back of a dark wooden chair towered in the shadows.

The room's far wall followed the curve of the ship's hull. To Lian's surprise, there were windows so that the captain could follow the ship's course. At the moment, nothing of note could be seen, save the moon's pale shine over the clouds.

Even so, the horizon seemed to occupy the captain's attentions. Turned away from the door, he stood upright, hands clasped behind his back. He gave no sign that he knew of Lian's presence, though Lian was sure he must have heard Hanon'ka greet him outside the door.

Lian remained rooted to his spot at the threshold, uncertain how to proceed. Glancing left and right, the size of the room surprised him. Despite its unusual shape, it spanned the width of the ship. To his right, a heavy curtain fell in front of what Lian assumed was a bed, and to his left stood a dresser full of tomes and scrolls, some of which appeared especially old, as well as a display of various bones and fangs. In the rear corner, Lian noticed a tall and narrow cabinet, with arched double glass doors ajar. From inside, a small dragon-oil lamp flickered across some object, though the red light was too faint for Lian to make out what lay atop a velvet box.

Is that a skeleton hand? he wondered. He tried to ignore the hairs rising on the back of his neck. At the sound of Adaron's voice, he jerked to attention.

"Step forward, Lian," the captain instructed. "Come closer."

"Captain," Lian answered. He cast a final glance on the strange shrine and followed the order.

When Lian reached the card table, Adaron turned halfway toward him and ushered him closer. "Come to the window."

Without a word, Lian stepped around the table and took his place at the older man's side. Adaron's presence was daunting, as though a shadow followed him. His eyes flickered menacingly, and his grave face looked like carved stone. Lian doubted that the room's dull light was the only reason for his sinister appearance.

"What do you see when you look out?" the captain asked.

Lian cleared his throat nervously. "I see clouds lit by the moon, Captain . . . and a few stars shining in the sky above."

"And do you like what you see?"

Lian stole a sideways glance, but the captain wasn't looking at him. "I . . . I don't know, really." He knew his answer was insufficient. The Cloudmere lay under a kind of spell at night. Unknown lands among a vast sea of towering pale white bluffs and deep black valleys stretched endlessly before the *Carryola*'s bow. In the distance, a tiny and unthreatening winged creature roved across the sliver of moon that hung low in the sky, and the stars sparkled like tiny drachen pearls in the distance. Lian had to keep himself from gasping at the scene's sublime beauty.

"Yes," said Lian finally. "I like it."

"Then I envy you," said Adaron. "I grew weary of that view long ago."

Lian dared to address the captain. "Why do you travel the Cloudmere, sir? Why not rest on land? You surely have enough riches by now."

Adaron turned away from the window and glared at Lian. "I'm not here because of the riches," he snapped.

Lian remembered what Smett had said when he and Canzo had arrived aboard. The captain sought revenge for the death of his bride and refused to set foot on land before that black dragon met its end. This ship wasn't the captain's home; it was his prison.

"I'm sure by now you've heard what they say about me," said Adaron. Lian nodded.

Adaron released a mirthless laugh. "They say I'm insane."

"No, Captain," Lian urged. "They say you're a man who takes his oath very seriously." *Almost too seriously,* he thought.

"Yes, I do take it seriously," Adaron replied. He turned away from the window and slowly walked to the table.

"It's the only way I *can* take it. Even when on some nights the clouds threaten to devour me and I can hardly bear to look outside." He stepped over to the cabinet in the corner and looked pensively at its contents.

Now closer to the cabinet, Lian noticed a sort of shrine, and within it, a skeleton hand lay propped atop of a black velvet stand. A chain hung from the bone fingers, and a medallion glittered beside it. The sight was morbid and deeply sad. Lian wondered, *Could the hand be the remains of the captain's lost bride?*

"I loved Enora more than any other in my life," Adaron began, promptly answering Lian's unspoken question. He lifted the hand, running his fingers over the pale bones and metal amulet. "When she was taken from me, I felt that my heart had been ripped from my chest. Now my heart has darkened. I no longer know laughter or joy. The only thing left is my scorn for the dragon, who not only took Enora but two of my oldest crewmates."

"How could that have happened, Captain?" Lian asked softly. "You're known as the greatest drachenjäger across the land."

"I wasn't then. Not yet. None of us had much idea what we were doing. We were careless and ended up paying the highest price." He turned away from the shrine to face Lian. "Have you ever known a woman who completely changed your life? Who filled the empty spot in your soul that you hadn't even known was there? And you would climb the highest mountain, dive the deepest depths, and face the greatest terrors just to see the shimmer of happiness in her eyes?"

Lian swallowed. "No, Captain," he answered.

"Then you're lucky to be spared such a fate."

Lian thought of Canzo. His friend's love for Anija wasn't necessarily the same, but it had still lured him to the Cloudmere. Canzo dreamed of his return to Skargakar, when the shimmer of happiness in Anija's eyes would greet him. Lian hoped that his friend wouldn't end up as broken as the captain. Anija wouldn't be devoured by a dragon, surely, but there were other kinds of deceits in Skargakar and other men to steal the heart of a young, hot-tempered barmaid.

"You must be wondering why I tell you all this," Adaron said.

"It did cross my mind, Captain."

The captain approached him. Though Adaron stood more than a half head taller, he didn't seem much stronger than Lian. Still, the fire in his eyes would have brought even Câchurt the stone demon to his knees.

"I saw you slay the bronzeneck," said Adaron. "You were brave, but you also hesitated."

Lian's cheeks grew hot. He struggled to find an excuse, but Adaron continued.

"Was your pause the result of fear? Or did you pity the living creature?" he asked.

"It . . . it was just a moment of weakness, Captain," Lian stammered. "I'd never ridden a dragon before. I was overwhelmed."

"Good," said Adaron. Lian's response seemed to be the answer he'd been looking for. "A jäger can learn grit with time, but Vazar himself bestows the willingness to kill."

Lian raised his eyebrows. "Vazar, Captain?"

"The eternal guardian and champion in the battle against evil," explained Adaron. "But I suppose the Three are unknown to you. To which gods do you confide your wishes and worries? The Four Winds? Crysostracha? Or do you just believe in yourself, like the self-sufficing Nondurier do?"

"I . . . uh . . . ," said Lian.

"It doesn't matter," said Adaron, waving Lian's answer away. "In all honesty, I'm as little interested in your faith as I am in your skin color or in which folk you belong to. I simply want to know if you are the man to handle a spear for me when we face the monster that I've been hunting, night after night ever since the first time I laid eyes on him. Hanon'ka believes that you have the stuff of a jäger. Do you?"

Lian summoned all the resolve he could muster and stood upright. This was not the time for reservations. "Captain, show me any dragon that I should slay in your name, and I will," he said.

Adaron leaned closer, his dark eyes drilling all the way to Lian's soul. "Gargantuan is no ordinary dragon," he said softly. "What I said at our journey's onset is truer than ever. He is the most formidable of all beasts, bigger and more dangerous than all the rest. Never, in all my days, have I seen another dragon that even compared. Many people say it was just a dream, but I *know* he is out there, lurking like a shadow of death, alone and concealed behind veils of mist, awaiting his next prey. When he strikes, ships and their crews vanish into the nothingness, never to be heard from again."

Lian tried to quell a wave of fear that crept within him. He balled his fists and glared at Adaron. "This ship will be his downfall, Captain. Gargantuan may be a dragon like no other, but as far as I can tell, the *Carryola* is a schooner with no other match. When we find this monster, we'll end his life."

For the first time that evening, a small but honest smile crept onto

Adaron's lips. "Yes, yes, so it shall be. Thank you for coming, Lian. You may go."

"Aye, Captain," Lian answered, and he turned to go.

"Oh, and one more thing," Adaron added.

Lian paused and turned back in the doorway. "Captain?"

"The words spoken within these walls were for your ears and your ears alone. I don't want to hear stories circulating among the men. So keep your mouth shut."

"I'll be as silent as the clouds," Lian promised, and he walked out the door.

Laughter from the canteen filled the walkway where the crew still celebrated. Instead of joining them, Lian walked up the steps to the deck. It would take some time alone, he knew, to process all that he'd heard.

14

Among the Taijirin

Twenty-Fifth Day of the Fifth Moon, Year 841

For two days, the crew performed the unpleasant work of processing the slain bronzeneck as the *Carryola* plowed toward the southwest. It was, as Lian had feared, bloody and strenuous work. The monster's stink attracted raptors, who screeched and hissed as they circled above the men's heads. The processed parts of the dragon were then stored in the hold, while they cut away the rest and threw it into the depths from the ship's stern. Raptors made certain that no bit, save for the most unappealing scraps of cartilage, disappeared beneath the fleece.

Once they completed their work, they hoisted the sails and picked up speed. Though the crew kept watch, no one spotted any dragons worth hunting. To supplement their provisions, men lured and caught a few light-gray lizardwings, called *screechers* for their penetratingly loud cries, but aside from that diversion, it was calm aboard. Lian and Canzo used the time after daily chores to learn all they could from the crew about the Cloudmere. By the third day, when Ialrist took off in front of the ship, they had learned enough to know that the *Carryola* neared Taijirin territory.

"He'll check the mood," Smett explained from his spot at the railing beside Lian and Canzo as they observed Ialrist in flight.

"Is the captain afraid we'll be unwelcome?" Canzo asked.

"It's impossible to tell with flutter-men," answered the cook. "Shiartris is one of the friendly isles. But if you ask me, the Taijirin are still bitter that they have to share the Cloudmere with the rest of us, even after so many moons. Before the Nondurier appeared with their skyships, the borders between our territories were clear. Now there are constant trespassers on Taijirin grounds—or they think so, at least."

"I always thought that the dangerous colonies lay much farther out, where barely anyone ever strays," said Lian.

"That's true," Smett answered. "More or less, at least. But the Taijirin leaders change even more frequently than our own. Every so often, there'll be some youngster who believes it his duty to convince his subjects that land dwellers are enemies. Since we haven't set foot on Shiartris for over a year, Adaron is wise to be cautious. A flock of angry Taijirin is the last thing we need. But we're lucky to have Ialrist with us. He always does his best to keep us in the winged ones' favor. I think there's only ever been one real conflict with the Taijirin—which is a wonder, when you consider how protective they are."

Hanon'ka interrupted the discussion, sharply asking Lian and Canzo if they didn't have something else they were supposed to be doing.

At midday, Ialrist returned to the ship. He reported directly to the captain, who looked satisfied by the Taijirin's news and held their course.

Anticipation surged through Lian. "Do you remember all the stories about the vogelfolk isles that we heard from the jägers at Cliff House?" he asked his friend as they scrubbed the deck. Slayers weren't normally required to do lower work, Lian knew, but Hanon'ka had insisted that he was still in training, despite his achievement. The captain alone would decide when Lian was ready to receive the same privileges as Corantha and Ialrist.

Canzo nodded. "I can't wait to see a Taijirin city with my own eyes. I wonder if they're really as splendid as they say and if they're that much brighter and more open than Skargakar."

"Why do you suppose we're docking so soon?" Lian asked. "The hold isn't remotely full yet. And don't the Taijirin hunt their own dragons? They won't want any of our wares."

His friend shrugged his broad shoulders. "The captain must have a reason."

"He's inquiring after Gargantuan," Melvas cut in from a few paces away. "Vogelfolk know the Cloudmere better than all others because they traverse the isles during their hunts. If the Black Leviathan shows up anywhere, the Taijirin will be the first to know."

That sounded plausible. There were undoubtedly ten or even twenty times more Taijirin than land dwellers under way in the clouds. During good moons, perhaps thirty ships departed from Skargakar's shores, and Lian couldn't believe that the number was much different at the other smaller cities along the coast.

"Does that mean the Taijirin have put you along the monster's tracks once before?" Canzo asked.

Melvas laughed. "Once? Ha! It's been at least a half dozen times in the five years since I've been on board."

"But you've never found him?" Lian probed.

"No. Whenever we've gotten close, the air had already gone cold." Melvas frowned. "The beast is fast. He races from one place to another and never stays anywhere for longer than a few days. Plus, I've heard that Gargantuan can see through the mist. Fog and gloom are his haven. That's why he can go so long without being spotted."

"I wonder how the captain will ever catch him," pondered Canzo aloud.

"With patience," another voice thundered.

Lian's friend winced, and as all three men looked up, they saw Adaron standing before them.

"With patience and brains," the captain continued calmly. "True, the Black Terror is fast and stealthy in nature, but he is still only an animal, and he follows patterns. He may not know it himself, but I am sure that he returns to certain places. I just need a few clues. If my suspicions are correct, I'll be able to tell where and when he'll show up next. And then"—Adaron's eyes narrowed—"we'll have him."

The sun had sunk below the horizon as the *Carryola* reached the isles of Shiartris. From afar, they merely looked like dark sunspots amid white clouds. As the spots grew, Lian noticed hovering lithos—smaller rock masses around a hundred paces high and fifty wide, and the largest peaks fifty times as large, at least.

From the rocks' undersides, Lian spotted the clearly recognizable violet glow of kyrillian, ensuring the enormous stone masses remained suspended. Along the rocks' faces, the Taijirin crown colony built the structures onto the cliff sides, jutting up into the air.

As the *Carryola* glided past the first cliff side, Lian's mouth fell open in astonishment. Shiartris was enormous! All around him, the rounded structures of Taijirin dwellings towered high into the sky with intricate curved arches and dome-shaped canopies. Bronze embellishments decorated their columns, glowing in the last light of the sun. The large windows and high entranceways gave the architecture an airy, open quality, one entirely different from the stout and solid houses that Lian knew in Skargakar.

Similar to nests in a birds' breeding colony, the Taijirin's houses were dispersed haphazardly across the rocks, with some smaller structures hanging dangerously low against the cliff side. There were no traditional streets, either. The few paths that ran along the slopes weren't much more than tiny trails. However, at various levels along the columns, bridges along the balconies and wooden platforms connected the structures. The Taijirin used giant cranes to transport heavy materials from one level of each structure to the next.

Everywhere, Taijirin flew—a wild and bustling confusion moving among the rock masses. While Ialrist had tan feathers, here Lian saw white, gray, and black, and to his amazement, some Taijirin had such strikingly colorful feathers that they reminded him of the birds found in the jungles far beyond his home.

"By the Winds," Canzo murmured from his post next to Lian. He threw his head back, taking in all the sights. "No story could have prepared me for this," he said, his eyes full of wonder.

Sharing Canzo's dreamy smile, Balen leaned against the railing next to them. "Wait until the night comes," he said. "A light glimmers inside every house, and the Taijirin zip through the air holding lanterns, like giant glowworms, while beneath the clouds glow violet with kyrillian. Such a show can never be forgotten."

The ship ascended to approach the largest island, its target a half-rounded plateau chiseled into the stone atop the rock face. One ship already moored there, a bulbous merchant ship that likely contained traders hoping to conduct business with the Taijirin Empire.

"Attention, all," Adaron said from the helm. "We'll dock in Shiartris shortly. All watches will continue as planned. I expect to see at least three men on deck at all times. The Taijirin may greet us as guests, but that doesn't mean there won't be prying eyes or skeptics who wish to harm our ship. So keep your eyes open, and don't allow anyone on board. If there's trouble, report to Hanon'ka, who will remain here. I will join Ialrist on the island."

Lian found it interesting that Adaron didn't consider the floating isles solid ground—which would go against his vow to never set foot there. *Well, the ground here isn't really solid,* he decided. If he chipped away enough kyrillian from the rocks' undersides, the whole mass would fall crashing to the Cloudmere's depths, far below the fleece. The thought sent shivers down his spine.

"Anyone else," Adaron continued, "is free to explore Shiartris. Enjoy the dancing, the music, and the exotic foods, but be on your best behavior. Stay away from drink, don't touch the women, and don't start any brawls. Our hosts have made it known that any crimes shall be punished according to Taijirin law, which is harsh and unforgiving. Do we understand one another?" He fiercely surveyed the gathered crew, who answered in a mumbling chorus of agreement.

"Good," the captain said finally. "Then go and enjoy yourselves."

The sky had already darkened when Lian and Canzo walked along the narrow path that stretched midway along the main isle of Shiartris. The *Carryola*, moored above them, was now out of view. Throughout the city, torches and oil lamps bathed the floating isle in flickering golden and red light.

The two friends walked with no specific goal. Instead, they meandered, taking in the unusual atmosphere with all its sounds, sights, and smells. Most of the Taijirin paid them no attention; for the most part, the folk seemed open to the presence of outsiders, contrary to Adaron's precautions. They did, though, catch a few hatchlings observing them shyly from the safety of raised balconies and platforms, with dark and round wide eyes—until, that is, a Taijirin in ceremonial robes ushered them inside. "Younglings," she called down, but the boys waved the apology away. They, too, stared in similar amazement at everything along their path.

Above all, the female Taijirin captured the young men's eyes. The few vogelfolk that Lian had encountered in Skargakar had always been men. Lian wondered if it were true that Taijirin men kept their women away from land dwellers for obscure cultural reasons, though no one was certain.

Taijirin women were breathtakingly and otherworldly beautiful, like creatures from a dream. No matter whether slight or round, young or old, each was exceptionally lovely. With large, expressive eyes and wings speckled with blue or red among gray and white feathers that spread wide in the breeze, Taijirin women seemed to Lian more like divine beings— like the good spirits from bedtime stories that mothers told their children. Taijirin men, Lian noticed, didn't possess the same unknowable, mythic air. They had tough and muscular bodies without softness or grace. In contrast to Ialrist's wide and thoughtful eyes, many of the men scowled through beady yellow eyes, filled with distrust and pride.

The path wound around a cliff side, where the friends discovered a group of two dozen houses that studded the rocks at various levels and faced a central square. Wooden bridges connected the structures to one another. From all the houses, white and colored lanterns bathed the scene in warm multicolored light.

On the edge of the square, a group of men and women gathered at tables and benches laughing, eating, and drinking together. A few hatchlings hopped among the benches, flapping their wings in attempted flight. From a corner, a band of musicians played various-sized pipes, while another tapped a complex rhythm on a drum.

"Canzo, look!" Lian marveled.

"They must be celebrating something," his friend remarked.

With a soft rustling sound, a woman landed beside them and folded her wings against her back. She carried a woven basket in her arms. Like the others in the group, she wore close-fitting clothing that didn't hinder her wings, and strips of decorative cloth were tied around her limbs, embellishments that looked formal as if part of some ritual.

"Greetings," she said, nodding to them both. She spoke the human tongue, with little hint of the unique melodious accent typical to Taijirin speech. "Did you arrive with the jäger ship?"

"Yes," Lian answered, and he introduced himself and Canzo. "Our captain gave us the evening free to explore your splendid city."

"It's our first time on a Taijirin island," Canzo added.

The Taijirin woman smiled warmly. "There are certainly larger and more impressive crown colonies, but I wouldn't choose to live anywhere but Shiartris."

"What are you celebrating?" Lian asked.

"The union of two nesting tribes," the Taijirin explained. "My nest-brother has chosen a bride from the neighboring family. The bond between our clans is now strengthened, and our voice on the council will be much louder." She beckoned them to follow her. "Come, join us. Soon the dancing will begin. If this is your first night among Taijirin, you'll surely enjoy that."

Lian held up a hand in objection. "Thank you, but we don't want to disturb you."

"Two humans can't disturb a group of fifty Taijirin," she answered airily.

"But will the bride and groom have the same opinion? We weren't invited."

The Taijirin laughed. "I'm the bridegroom's nest-sister. If I say you're not a disturbance, then it is so. Just find seats at the end of the table, get yourselves something to drink, and watch what happens. I know that jägers think we are proud and unapproachable, but they've never made the effort to get to know us better."

"Well, we'll have to do something about that," Lian said. He shot a sideways glance to Canzo. "What do you think, Canzo? Should we raise a mug to the union of two nesting tribes?"

"I wouldn't argue against a seat and a good swig of ale," his friend answered.

Their host chuckled. "Then follow me," she said. "You poor dears . . . always having to traverse the hard stone on foot to get anywhere." She shook her head.

Following her into the festivities, the friends found places at a bench near the musicians. The two vogelfolk at the table's other end, both with white and gray feathers, merely glanced at the young men and turned back to watch the drummer and pipe players. Before long, a Taijirin about their age brought mugs of something that smelled like fermented berries. With a powerful jump and a beat of his wings, he disappeared just as quickly as he'd come.

The friends raised their mugs to their hostess, who had joined the group of vogelfolk two tables over, near a couple dressed in especially festive garments. She raised her mug in return and smiled briefly, then turned to speak to the bridegroom beside her. Lian wondered if there were any differences between human and Taijirin siblings—not that he knew much about that. Canzo was the closest thing to a brother he had.

I know as good as nothing about the Taijirin, Lian thought, *except for stories from jägers and merchants.* Those stories, more often than not, dealt with conflict. He swore to himself to lift that misunderstanding however he could. Maybe he would start with convincing Ialrist to tell him more about his people.

The music shifted, now louder and livelier. Though Lian didn't recognize the melody, he could tell that it was time for the dancing.

The newlyweds stood, and half of the others joined them. Some gathered the small lanterns decorating the tables, and others lifted torches from their stands. Then they spread their wings in unison and lifted up over the plaza into the night sky. There above, under the star-studded firmament, the Taijirin began to dance.

It wasn't a dance in the usual sense, with specific movements set in time with the music. Instead, the Taijirin swept through the cool air, unbridled and free. They pivoted around one another, switched places, spiraled high into the air with powerful beats of their wings, and landed on the ground with an elegant skip. The folk swirled and reeled with joy as they held their lanterns before them, transforming the flames into glowing beams of light.

Like a swarm of fireflies on a balmy summer night, Lian marveled. Balen hadn't exaggerated.

"Amazing, isn't it?" Canzo marveled from beside Lian.

Lian looked at his friend and mirrored the blissful smile across his lips. "It is," he answered dreamily, and he raised his gaze back up to the sky.

The music changed again, this time to a slow melody that filled Lian with an overwhelming sense of longing. Most of the flying dancers stopped their heedless whirring and joined together. They formed a flowing wave that swelled back and forth, snaking and surging until it met in a circle—a display of such oneness that Lian's breath hitched in his chest.

"I wish Anija were here," Canzo murmured. "If only I could share this moment with her."

Lian looked over to his friend and laid a hand on his shoulder. "You can," he said softly. "Someday, when you return and you win her hand with your riches and tales of adventure, then she'll join you on another ship, and you can show her this place."

With glistening eyes, Canzo looked at him. "Do you really think it'll be like that?"

"Of course," Lian answered, and he forced a confident smile. "Just a few more kills, and the *Carryola*'s stores will be filled. Adaron will have to return to Skargakar then. Before this year is over, you'll be holding Anija in your arms."

That, or you'll find her in the arms of another man, thought Lian, but he didn't speak the thought aloud.

15

The Second Hunt

Twenty-Eighth Day of the Fifth Moon, Year 841

"There!" Danark called from the crow's nest on the morning of their second day aloft after departing from Shiartris. "Dragon, straight ahead!" All on deck directed their gazes to the clouds beyond the *Carryola*'s bow. On that morning, the mist not only billowed from beneath the ship's hull but also stretched high above them across the sky so that both layers of fleece joined together at the horizon in a dappled world of endless white.

Lian squinted far into the distance until he spotted the dark point darting in between the changing mountains of mist. He glanced over his shoulder and observed Adaron, who stood at the helm with a bronze spyglass held up to his eye. After searching for a moment, the captain's mouth curled with the hint of a smile. "A female swingblade," he declared. "Very good."

Lian took note. It was said that swingblades, comparable in size to bronzenecks, were especially cunning and aggressive. Their namesake, and most dangerous feature, was a razor-sharp "blade" at the end of its tail, resembling a broadsword. The blade was made of the same horn material as the plates along a bronzeneck's spine. The jägers warned that a single strike could slice a man in two or sever a ship's mast.

If carved properly, the end of a swingblade's tail could be fashioned into an excellent hand weapon that was easy to use and maintain. And above all, a weapon from such origins made an immense impression. In the right circles, the tail itself had the same worth as the finest jewelry. Lian wasn't surprised that the prospect of such a win lifted the captain's spirits.

"We'll send both jäger kites," Adaron said, turning to Hanon'ka. "I don't want this one to escape. Kurrn will steer the first, and Balen the second. Corantha will go with Kurrn, and Lian with Balen. Ialrist will accompany both and serve as a distraction."

The Sidhari glanced at Lian. "You heard the captain. Fetch your spear."

"Yes, Commander," answered Lian, hurrying off. Fear and excitement gripped him: fear of the beast, a much tougher opponent than the bronzeneck, and excitement at the chance to prove himself to the captain and Hanon'ka. He was ready to slay another beast—if Corantha didn't get to it first.

Once Lian returned to the deck, he climbed into the small jäger kite along with Balen, Melvas, Canzo, and Hanon'ka—their same arrangement from the last mission. Men from another watch boarded the other kite—Kurrn, Jakk, Wil, and Lannik—as well as Corantha, who bared her teeth in a wide and wild grin. "Let's see which of us will get the scar tonight," she sneered.

"It's not a tournament, Corantha," Hanon'ka warned.

"The hunt is always a tournament," she answered brazenly. "And the victor's reward is his life." Still smiling, she slapped the kite's side, and Kurrn steered the small boat into the air.

Balen followed with the second kite at a short distance. From the Carryola's bow, Ialrist took off into the clouds.

Since a siege from behind was too dangerous, Balen steered the kite away from the beast and toward the nearby cloud mountains that would shield them as they pursued the dragon. They would have to work together to avoid the monster's deadly tail, Hanon'ka explained. Ialrist would fly by the dragon as a distraction until the two kites broke from their cover in a simultaneous attack.

"We have to hit her with two kyrillian buoys before she can strike back," Hanon'ka explained while he and Lian loaded the harpoon at the kite's bow. "They'll have to sink into her hind flank so that she can no longer move her lower body. That's the only way to prevent the beast from knocking the buoys off with her tail."

"That would make things harder," Balen said. "But we should act quickly. She'll be angry, and if she manages to free herself, any further attack will be much more dangerous."

"I'm ready," Lian answered steadily. As the jäger kite ascended, he stood with his harness already fastened and his spear at the ready on the deck beside him.

"Why isn't Corantha riding Arax this time?" Canzo asked. He glanced backward toward the *Carryola*, where Arax perched on the bowsprit. They had already gained considerable distance from the vessel.

"Another dragon would just make a swingblade angrier," Hanon'ka answered. "And thus, more difficult to capture."

In front of them, the dragon let out a howl at the sight of Ialrist, who glided at a safe distance among the clouds, a tempting morsel for a hungry swingblade—or at least a distraction to spur its curiosity.

While Balen steered the kite closer, Lian got a better look at the dragon. The swingblade's body was less heavily armored than a bronzeneck's. Its greenish-gray scales looked smaller and softer, and the whole animal appeared quicker and more agile that what Lian had encountered before. Both the animal's swordlike tail and its long talons filled Lian with awe. He didn't envy Ialrist as he watched him tempt the beast so fearlessly.

Ialrist, too, felt it was time to end the game, and he let out a shrill battle cry.

"That's the sign," Hanon'ka said, and he began loading the harpoon. "Balen, lower the sails to attack!"

Balen repeated the order, and Canzo and Melvas set into motion tying in the main and side sails. Then Balen pulled the steering lines to close the foremost kyrillian cases. The jäger kite tipped forward, plowing toward the dragon.

Lian gripped his spear with one hand as he clung to the railing with the other. Wind whipped his face and fluttered through his hair. Across from them, the other schooner broke out of the clouds. Corantha stood proudly atop the harpoon ballista, laughing in the face of wind and danger, her tattooed face reminiscent of a crazed demon.

Another howl resounded through the clouds from below. Shocked, Lian glanced over the kite's side, and terror washed over him. A second swingblade barreled toward them—somewhat smaller than the first, though around the same size as their vessel.

"Look out!" he yelled.

Balen reacted immediately, tugging the steering lines to send the kite in a narrow left curve. Canzo let out a startled cry as the dragon rammed against the kite's side with a powerful blow. Though only a nudge, the vessel bucked and shied sideways.

With a cry, Lian dropped his spear and clung to the railing with both hands as the force of the blow threatened to rip him free. The beast's enormous scaled body passed so close that he could have reached out a hand to touch it.

"Down!" Hanon'ka yelled, and Lian ducked—not a heartbeat too soon.

With a whistle of air, the swingblade's tail sliced the air above Lian's head and passed over the length of the ship. Lian's heart stopped as the wind of the blade's wake rushed against his cheek. With a cracking sound, wood burst, and a man cried out. Then the dragon was gone.

Still crouching, Lian could barely believe how narrowly he had escaped death. Beside him, Hanon'ka pulled the ballista around and fired, but at that moment, the dragon changed course and avoided the shot. A single kyrillian buoy rose uselessly into the morning sky.

"Is that her mate?" Lian gasped as his gaze followed the second dragon.

Hanon'ka shook his head. "Swingblades are solitary creatures, and it's not mating season yet. It must be her son—though at that size, he should have separated from his mother a long time ago." The Sidhari scowled as though irritated with himself for not anticipating the turn of events, but how could he have?

Lian turned when he heard a groan. The kite lay half in wreckage. The top half of its mast was smashed and bent sideways, its sail dangling uselessly to the deck. From the helm, Balen heaved himself upright. Blood ran from a cut on his arm where a splinter had pierced him. Canzo and Melvas, too, pulled themselves to their feet. Aside from a few minor cuts and bruises, they appeared unharmed.

A swingblade roared and was answered by Ialrist's shrill battle cry.

With a quick glance over the railing, Lian's hopes sank. It didn't look as though either dragon would withdraw.

The other kite seemed to have fared better with the sudden turn of events. Corantha had successfully managed to sink a speared kyrillian buoy into the mother dragon's left flank, which, as the violet crystal buoy tugged upward, seemed to wildly enrage the beast. Flying in tight circles, the creature frantically tried to free itself from the annoying attachment.

Meanwhile, Ialrist darted back and forth to divert the other dragon's attention from Corantha's kite while she reloaded the harpoon. In the background, the *Carryola* approached with full sails to aid the crew's efforts. Though the schooner wasn't equipped to catch prey, it was a powerful weapon against opponents—even two swingblades. Lian watched as Arax took off from the bow to assist his companion.

"Melvas, take over the harpoon with Lian!" ordered Hanon'ka. "Canzo, remove the rubble as well as you can." The urgency in the Sidhari's green eyes belied his calm voice.

"Yes, Commander," Melvas answered, hurrying to the bow. Lian picked up his spear and slung the strap over his shoulder in case he lost his grip.

"Balen, can you still steer the ship?" the Sidhari asked.

"I should be able to," Balen growled, testing a rope. His face darkened as the ship set into a slow left turn. "The casing at the starboard bow is damaged. There won't be any kill for this kite today."

Hanon'ka nodded. "Then we'll just have to defend ourselves."

"Commander!" Melvas called. "The bull is heading back."

"Align the ballista!" commanded the Sidhari. "Balen, aim the bow straight toward him. We have to keep him from capsizing the ship."

"I'll try," Balen called, and he swore under his breath as he tugged the steering ropes.

Meanwhile, Lian and Melvas hurried to load the harpoon. A quick glance revealed that their vessel was on its own. The *Carryola* remained out of shooting range, and the mother dragon occupied the other slayers; they seemed to have decided to combine their strengths and remove one of the two beasts from the fight as quickly as possible.

Hopefully, that won't be a mistake, Lian thought. His throat tightened, and his tongue turned to sand inside his mouth.

The young swingblade swooped into view with a powerful beat of its wings and opened its jaws to reveal two rows of terrifying fangs. The beast's roar shook the sky, and Lian retched at its breath.

"Fire!" he urged.

"Not yet," Melvas answered. "Just a little closer . . ."

Beside him, Lian heard a string of quiet and unfamiliar words. As he looked to the side, he saw Hanon'ka sitting placidly on the deck with crossed legs and hands rested atop his thighs as though in meditation, his eyes fixed on the swingblade. With a calm but determined expression, he repeated an incantation in the Sidhari tongue again and again.

"Now," Melvas whispered, and he fired the second spear. The line sped forward, and the black metal arrow sank into the dragon's shoulder.

The swingblade roared with rage as a kyrillian buoy dragged it upward. It thrashed back and forth in an attempt to rip the spear from its flesh with its front claws. Lian watched in horror, terrified that the beast would succeed eventually. Surely, it was only a matter of time before the beast snatched them from their destroyed vessel. Lian prayed that the *Carryola* would get to them first.

A cool breeze began to blow, at first gently and then with increasing strength and speed. The dragon, too, seemed affected and flapped its wings frantically to stay aloft. A furious hiss sounded from its throat, and its eyes shone with bloodlust as the gust pushed it backward.

Lian looked back to Hanon'ka. The Sidhari remained still, his hands now stretched out toward the monster. *He is conjuring magic. Like he did in Skargakar, when he defeated the stone giant,* Lian thought. Ever since he'd boarded the *Carryola,* he'd wondered what the Sidhari's other powers were. He had heard plenty of stories of desert dwellers' secrets—that they could move wind and sands—but Hanon'ka hadn't shown any sign of his powers after the night at Kraghma's Jaws. Lian watched the mysterious dark-skinned man with fascination as his black hair fluttered in a storm conjured of his own volition.

A terrifying sound, somewhere between a roar and a shriek, penetrated the rushing in Lian's ears. Two kyrillian buoys held the struggling mother swingblade aloft while the second jäger kite and Arax circled it. As the dragon thrashed, Ialrist stood atop its back and raised his spiked reaver triumphantly to the sky. Hot blood rained from a gaping wound at the animal's neck into the white clouds below. The beast shook and shrieked a final time, and its powerful body went limp.

"One down!" Melvas called triumphantly, raising his fist.

A primal howl sounded from the sky. The swingblade bull, who flew just in front of them, shot upward, propelled by Hanon'ka's windstorm, gnashing his powerful jaws. The buoy suspending him shattered, and its remnants scattered into the wind.

Now free, the bull's fury multiplied. Hanon'ka's murmurs grew louder and more urgent, and he raised a hand toward the dragon. At a nudge from Melvas, Lian loaded a new spear into the ballista. The *Carryola* neared, along with Corantha, who now rode on Arax's back, eager to conquer the second dragon after Ialrist had handled the first.

The swingblade struggled amid Hanon'ka's windstorm, glaring at its opponents. Then, howling into the air, it pulled its wings close into its body and dove arrow-straight into the depths, swallowed into the clouds without a sound.

"What's he doing?" Canzo asked. Agitated, he looked around and ran from one side of the destroyed kite to the other.

The wind settled as quickly as it had raged. Hanon'ka, now silent, let his hands sink, squinting as he scanned the clouds. "Balen," he said finally. "Take us back to the *Carryola* as quick as you can."

"Aye, Commander," Balen answered, tugging the steering lines to lean the kite into a tight curve.

"Where is he now?" Melvas asked, turning the harpoon from left to right in a futile search. "He must be—"

He got no further. An enormous gray-green mass shot through the fleece next to the ship and sank its talons into the hull. The small vessel lurched upward, and Lian cried out as he was thrown into the air.

Time seemed to stop. Wide-eyed with shock, Lian watched the others—Melvas, Hanon'ka, Balen, and Canzo—as they were thrown from the deck. A kyrillian buoy released and lifted skyward in slow motion. The hanging sails filled with air and widened like a sheet on a washing line. In the background, Corantha neared astride Arax, both her face and his snout frozen in warriors' cries. The swingblade thrashed just in front of him. Its tail rose like a whip and came down brutally, full of pure loathing.

None of them would elude this deadly blade for long, Lian knew. The Four Winds alone would decide who would live and who would die. The beast's tail sliced past Melvas, just missing both Lian and Hanon'ka, but it lusted after blood—a life for a life—and it chose Canzo.

One moment, Lian's friend stood there, staring with terror at the approaching dragon, and the next, the beast's tail sliced through Canzo's body and sent him over the railing. A stream of blood glistened on the deck where he had stood, his handcrafted scale armor sliced by the blade as though it had been made of parchment paper.

The shock sent time spinning back to normal speed. Lian and the others cracked painfully back onto the deck. He dragged himself onto the railing. "No! Canzo!" he cried. Looking out, he watched his friend falling into the depths, a battered body severed in half and swallowed by the clouds.

"Canzo!" Lian called in agony. Looking up, he spotted the swingblade circling their kite once again, choosing its next victim.

Lian gripped the spear at his back and glared toward Balen with wild eyes. "Turn us around! Follow that dragon! Let me at him!" he cried.

Balen shook his head. "I can't. We—"

"Turn around!" Lian shrieked again. Hot tears blurred his sight. The swingblade howled from the clouds. Lian faced the clouds to answer its call.

"Come here, you monster! I'll kill you! I'll pierce your heart!" He raised his spear into the air and shook it.

He felt a strong hand against his shoulder. Turning around, he met Hanon'ka's glowing emerald gaze.

"Calm yourself, Lian," the Sidhari coaxed. "Our ship is damaged. We can't do anything more now. Leave the swingblade to Ialrist and Corantha."

Lian raised his spear again and grimaced. "No one has the right," he began, but then stopped abruptly. His fury transformed into wonder. "What in the . . . ?" he said, blinking at the runes that covered the spear's pointed end.

The peculiar symbols glowed with a golden fire, even more brightly than the Sidhari's own eyes. At that very moment, it was as though the tip came directly from the hot forge.

"What does that mean?" Lian wondered aloud.

A look of grim distrust came over Hanon'ka's expression. "I'd like to know that, too," he answered. "I've never seen such a thing before. It seems like the weapon shares the same desire to kill the dragon as you do."

A shadow fell over them as they neared the *Carryola*. Ballistae cracked as their deadly weapons flew toward the dragon still thirsty for blood.

Lian and Hanon'ka continued to study the spear. Eventually, the glowing runes faded until not a trace of their glimmer remained.

Lian faltered and, if not for Hanon'ka's support, would have fallen. He had never felt so weak or empty. His rage had sapped all the energy from his body. He barely heard the shots that entered the swingblade's flanks or registered Corantha's cry as her quick and unflinching hand brought the bull to death. He didn't notice when Balen steered their kite to just above and beside the *Carryola* and landed on her deck. His spirit was gone.

A deep pain spread from inside him and swelled into overwhelming mourning. *Canzo . . .* , Lian thought in disbelief. *Canzo is dead.*

16

The Hardest Juncture

Twenty-Eighth Day of the Fifth Moon, Year 841

The darkness of their sleeping quarters below deck matched the darkness inside of Lian's heart. A weak light irked him from a small oil lamp next to the door. Lian would have preferred to blow it out, but it wasn't up to him. He wanted to see nothing, hear nothing, and feel nothing—nothing whatsoever.

While the captain never permitted anyone to extinguish the lights—it was too dangerous to trip through the *Carryola*'s belly in the pitch-blackness of night—the light of Lian's spirit had gone out, and neither the mercy of indifference nor the ability to forget soothed him.

Instead, he relived his friend's horrible final moments over and over, while lying in his hammock and staring unblinking at the ceiling—how the swingblade's tail struck his friend's chest and threw him overboard and into the depths. Before his very eyes, Lian saw the pale and terror-stricken face of the man he'd known since childhood. He saw the stream of crimson blood, strangely harrowing yet beautiful, and he saw the disturbing image of his friend's body cut in two, falling toward the depths and vanishing under the fleece. Lian didn't think he'd ever be able to forget that image.

Canzo, he thought. *First my father, and now Canzo . . .*

Lian wondered what he had done, or which missteps he had made, to call forth the icy Northern Wind. The Northern Wind, which stemmed from the Cloudmere itself, gusted in the winter moons. Many in Skargakar believed that it carried sickness and death on its currents. Fearing it as the harbinger of misery, they attempted to shield themselves from its cold grip through rituals—prayers, charms, and sacrifices.

Lian had never been very religious, although he prayed to the Four Winds out of habit whenever he felt confused or afraid like most others he knew. Now he asked himself if the Winds were punishing him for his neglect.

No! he thought. The Winds hadn't taken his father. Odan's horrible son had, and the Winds hadn't taken Canzo's life, either. A dragon of flesh and blood was to blame. Lian had avenged his father's death when he'd bored a spear into Casran's heart. The battle against the swingblade had denied him his revenge—a reality that seemed to infuriate Lian's weapon as much as it did himself.

He ran a finger along the wooden shaft of his spear. He couldn't bear to let go of the weapon; it was the lifeline to his own sanity, which could unravel at any moment.

Still baffled, he studied the runes again. The strange symbols shimmered faintly in the light from the oil lamp, but not as brilliantly as they had during the hunt. "What could you mean?" he whispered. He wished his father had told him about the spear, but the weapon's origin remained a riddle, as did the glowing symbols etched into its handle.

A cautious knock at the doorframe pulled Lian from his thoughts. As he looked down from his hammock, Smett pushed the curtain aside and peered into the room. Sympathy covered his wrinkled cheeks. "Can I come in?" he whispered.

Lian nodded without a word. He couldn't speak, but the cook was—gossiping tongue aside—a good soul. Now that Canzo was gone, Lian had no real friends aboard. Hanon'ka didn't count, he knew; the Sidhari was more of a mentor than a friend—not to mention, he was also the first commander, Lian's superior. As far as the others on board went, Lian shared little more than a common goal with the crew.

Smett's wooden leg tapped against the deck as he slowly approached Lian's hammock. He pulled a stool over and lowered himself onto it with a groan. Lian, too, swung his legs out of his hammock to sit upright. The two men faced each other in silence for a long time.

"Today, you experienced what many consider a jäger's most difficult trial," Smett began. He paused, waiting for an objection. When none came, he continued. "But it is not a trial that you must endure alone. Almost every one of us has endured this pain you feel, myself included. That is why . . . that is why I can understand what you are feeling now." He sighed and shook his head. "We've all lost comrades to the Cloudmere. Sometimes eternal, true companions. Life as a jäger is dangerous, more dangerous than any adventure tale you'll ever hear from half-drunken men in Skargakar's taverns. Illness, storm, pirates, Taijirin, and of course the dragons—they can all be our ends. Or it could even be another man's knife that kills you, from the man sitting next to you at the dining table, because he doesn't like your face or wants the medallion around your neck for his own."

"You speak a strange sort of comfort," Lian muttered.

"I'm not offering comfort," answered Smett. "You should mourn. You should be angry. It is your right to do so. The death of your friend is tragic. He was a good man, as far as I could tell, and he surely didn't deserve to be slashed by a damned swingblade, but dragons don't decide which of us are good or evil. If there are really such things as gods—which I doubt more with each mission—it sometimes seems that they protect the scoundrels over the honest among us."

Lian pursed his lips and looked away. "You know the worst thing? It's my fault that he's dead," he said quietly without looking at Smett. "My dream to sail on the Cloudmere was always stronger than his. When my father was murdered, it was my decision to leave Skargakar. Canzo just decided to come along because he was a good friend. And maybe because he wanted to impress his future wife, I guess."

"He had a bride?" Smett asked dully.

"Yes, a barmaid, but . . ." Lian glanced toward the cook and forced a smile. "It's a sad story. He always loved her more than she loved him." Lian wondered if Anija would even shed a tear when she heard of Canzo's death. Still, he vowed to let her know when he returned home.

"Anyway, he didn't decide whether to take the journey until the very last moment," Lian continued. "Because of me, he was convinced that glory and riches would bring him honor back home. But the only thing awaiting him in the end was a dragon. I was careless to let him come."

In truth, he was glad that Canzo had decided to come. He had been afraid to venture alone into the unknown. *My own cowardace cost him his life,* he thought now in sorrow.

"Do you know what the captain would say to that?" asked Smett.

Lian shook his head.

"A dragon awaits every jäger. The only question is which will kill the other." Smett stood then. "And now it's time. Will you join me?"

"Where?" asked Lian.

The cook nodded toward the ceiling. "On deck. Captain Adaron wishes to bestow your friend the final honor and present the man closest to him with a part of the beast that killed him. So is the custom among drachenjägers." His face softened into a smile. "Cheer up," he continued. "You'll be part of a small circle of jägers to receive a shard of a swing-blade's tail. It might not be enough for a sword, but you'll probably get a dagger out of it, at least. That'll be a valuable memento—even if it won't bring your friend back." He placed a firm hand on Lian's shoulder and then hobbled toward the entranceway.

With a sigh, Lian lowered himself from his hammock and followed Smett out of the room, still clutching his spear.

"Oh, one more thing," Smett added, pausing in the doorway. "Did Canzo leave behind anything dear to him on board? An amulet? Or something to remember his family or his bride, perhaps?"

Lian studied the cook as he tried to make sense of the question. "Uh, yes," he said finally. "He kept a lock of Anija's hair inside his pillowcase, if I'm not mistaken."

"Better take that along," Smett said.

"Why?"

"As an offering to the dead."

Lian leaned over Canzo's hammock and retrieved the lock of Anija's silky black hair from the pillowcase—the only proof that his friend and Anija were bound in true love. Stuffing the strands into his pocket, he followed Smett onto the deck.

Most of the crew had already assembled. The men stood somberly, and a few nodded to him or patted his shoulder. Lian was thankful for the unexpected sympathy, though he doubted that their sorrow was genuine. The crew had only known Canzo for a matter of days. Lian considered perhaps they were reminded of their own friends who had been lost. Maybe they knew what Hanon'ka and Elrin, who looked down on them from the helm, expected of them.

Lian passed the poop deck, where the slaughtermen had already secured the dragon so that they could begin their grisly work. Corantha, Ialrist, and Adaron stood watching the men as they exchanged quiet words. Then they approached the rest of the crew.

Hanon'ka surveyed the men assembled before him. Then he calmly lifted a hand to the bell fastened to the helm's railing, sounding it once. The few whispers that traveled through the crowd went silent.

Adaron stepped up to the helm and looked upon Lian and the others. His dark eyes burned with a suffering that mirrored Lian's own grief. This man, who had slain dragons for years to rid his heart of the pain of losing his beloved, to no avail, mourned the loss of every crew member aboard his ship. With every casualty, a dark veil of pain draped anew across his soul.

"The Cloudmere gives, and the Cloudmere takes away," Adaron said into the stillness. He surveyed the men as though imploring each to meet his eyes. "It bestows riches and gives us dragons both great and small to slay for sustenance, clothing, and prosperity—if we're lucky. But it also robs us of our friends and comrades. It feasts on them with gnashing jaws, shreds them with sharp talons, and slings them with whipping wings and tails into the nothingness."

Around Lian, the crew nodded.

"*Today, I lost the best man I ever knew.* There is likely no one on board the *Carryola* who doesn't know that thought or who never uttered those words," Adaron continued. "Every loss must be mourned. Every death pierces our hearts anew, but not only that. Each death must also be a new incentive. Great Drachen are dangerous opponents, perhaps the most dangerous in existence." He placed his hands on the railing before him and leaned closer. His voice surged with passion. "If we want to conquer them without losing lives, then we must improve. We must become masters of the hunt—quick, alert, and prepared for every surprise. Perhaps then, the next monster we encounter won't cost us yet another man. We won't allow another dragon to win the next battle against us! Never! They have taken far too much from us already."

Mutters of agreement answered the captain's words.

As he listened to the captain, Lian realized that he had been mistaken. It wasn't just the death of another man that affected Adaron. It was the fact that a dragon had caused it. The captain's loathing for dragons seemed to mount as the moments passed.

Adaron stood upright and turned to Lian. "There is a tradition among the drachenjägers," he began. "If a life is taken by a dragon and the monster is slain, then a piece of the beast goes to the person nearest the victim—a tooth from the jaws that mauled or a claw from the foot that tore. This fragment shall remain a remembrance, a warning, and an incentive. We honor the dead with a memento so that they are never forgotten."

Lian wondered if he had wrongly understood the meaning of a jäger's decorations. If a jäger adorned his armor with teeth and claws, maybe it wasn't just to show how many dragons he had slain—or at least not always. Maybe the tokens were also symbols for the price of his kill. That would turn those who wore them into living memorials, to warn others of the dangers at sea. Lian remembered how braggarts at Cliff House had gone silent whenever a jäger brandishing claws and teeth entered their midst. He had mistaken the action as respect for the warrior himself. From now on, he would know better.

"You were nearest to Canzo," Adaron continued. "So you will receive a shard from his killer's tail. Ialrist," he said, glancing toward the Taijirin who stood together with Corantha at the edge of the helm.

Ialrist stepped forward slowly, balancing in his hands a shard of the horn-plated blade that had torn Canzo in half. For a horrible moment, Lian thought he still saw the blood of his friend glistening on the blade, but the shard had been wiped clean.

Lian wondered how the slaughtermen had managed to sever the plate. From what he knew, the horn plate was as good as unbreakable. That was why the blade was such a valuable weapon. *Canzo could have answered the question,* he thought mournfully.

A lump grew in his throat, and he coughed in an effort to clear it away. "Thank you, sir," he said, taking the shard in his hands. It was astonishingly light and, if his eyes didn't deceive him, extraordinarily sharp. An expert weapon smith could turn it into an excellent dagger.

That would have to wait until they reached a city. Carefully, Lian stuck the fragment into his belt.

Nodding in satisfaction, the captain addressed Lian. "I have been informed that your friend prayed to the Four Winds. Is that true?"

"Yes," Lian answered. "But he believed in their power more than I."

"I know that it is custom of those faithful to the Winds to offer the ashes of their dead to the air. We rarely have a body to burn or ashes to scatter. Therefore, it is our tradition to throw an item dear to the deceased into the clouds instead, in hopes that our offering shall please him in eternity. Is there anything that you would like to offer?"

"Yes. A lock of hair given to him as token from the woman he loved." He pulled the strands from his pocket. "I think he'll like it," he added softly.

"Good. Take it to the railing while we call forth the Four Winds," Adaron instructed.

Hanon'ka tolled the bell.

"We call forth the Western Wind, bringer of the new," chanted Adaron, "who from far shores blows change and awakens knowledge."

"We call forth the Western Wind," repeated any crew members who shared Canzo's faith. Lian, too, mouthed the ritual words as he slowly made his way through the crowd toward the railing at portside, the strands of Anija's hair held tightly in his hand.

"We call forth the Southern Wind, bringer of life," continued the captain as the bell tolled again, "whose warmth makes the world bloom and fills all who wander her currents with happiness."

"We call forth the Southern Wind," answered Lian in unison with the others. He stepped up to the wooden railing that separated him from the wide and fathomless depths of the Cloudmere. Looking down, he searched into the deep, where somewhere Canzo's body lay destroyed on the ground.

Once again, the bell tolled for his friend into the soundless sky. "We call forth the Eastern Wind, who urges us home. Whose eye over house and hearth grounds us and honors our hard work."

Lian spoke the ritual response. Then he raised the strands of hair and stretched out his arm. The strands fluttered in the whipping wind, but Lian couldn't release them.

The bell tolled a fourth time.

"We call forth the Northern Wind, lord to the cold." Adaron spoke the fourth words of the call spoken for generations. "Whose icy tinge chills heart and soul, and who teaches us meekness before the power of creation."

The Northern Wind, thought Lian in sorrow, *who carried Canzo's soul away with him. Hopefully to a better place.*

"We call forth all Four Winds," Adaron's voice boomed, "to guide Canzo into eternity."

"So it shall be," answered Lian softly. Then he let go of the strands, which dropped a few paces before a gust broke them apart and sent them scattering into the clouds, where they disappeared from view. *Farewell, my friend, until we meet again on the other side.*

With a deep breath, Lian returned to Smett's side. Looking up to the captain, he nodded his thanks.

Hanon'ka sounded the bell a final time to signal the end of the ceremony. No one moved or uttered a sound. Instead, they waited somberly.

"There is another tradition," Adaron announced as he descended the steps from helm to deck. Then he began to unbutton his black tailcoat. "Or, *I* have a tradition, to be exact."

The captain removed his tailcoat and handed it to Ialrist, then pulled off his dark shirt. The crew stepped back to make room. Adaron stepped in the center, followed by Hanon'ka, who held a leather strap in his hands.

"What's that for?" Lian asked Smett, growing nervous.

"See for yourself," answered the cook in monotone.

Adaron handed his shirt to Ialrist, whose frown was sign enough that what was to come was nothing good. That didn't seem to make any difference to the captain. His naked skin, though pale as a nobleman's, was anything but soft. Hard, sinewy muscles bulged from his arms and shoulders, and old scars covered his entire chest.

Adaron looked upon all present in grim silence. Then he turned and positioned himself before the helm, gripping the railing from above, his arms stretched and back slightly hunched. Filled with horror, Lian saw the gruesome scars covering his skin.

"Ten lashes!" Adaron ordered.

"Aye, Captain," Hanon'ka answered through tight lips, and he raised the belt. Then he struck, not with the brutality of a tyrant but without holding back, either. The strap fell onto the captain's naked skin with a clap, leaving a smarting red welt in its stead. The captain groaned when the leather met his skin.

"Why is he doing this?" whispered Lian, aghast. "Why has he ordered his own flogging?"

"Because he lost a battle with a dragon," Smett answered quietly. "And blames himself. He wants the defeat to burn on his back as it does on his soul." The cook shook his head gravely. "Sometimes I wonder where his mania will lead us and if this will all end in disaster."

Silently, Lian watched Hanon'ka beat the captain, stroke for stroke, until blood ran down Adaron's back. He understood the old man's worry. His own heart hung heavy with sorrow, but that feeling, he hoped, would pass eventually with time. It seemed that the shadow burdening the captain would only ever darken.

17

The Storm

Fifth Day of the Sixth Moon, Year 841

Over the days that followed, the *Carryola* eased without sail toward the southwest, while her crew set to work to process the two swingblades. All hands were needed to preserve the meat of both dragons before it went off. Thus, Lian had little time to mourn the loss of his friend. Only at night, when the others collapsed exhausted into their hammocks, did he feel the emptiness of the hammock beside his own and consider how alone he was in the world.

Smett proved a true soul during those days. Not only did he sneak Lian a few extra morsels from the galley, but he also offered a friendly ear in case Lian wanted to talk, though Lian never took the offer.

On the evening of the fifth day, as Lian sat at the crow's nest gazing into the darkening horizon, Ialrist landed, just as before, onto his perch. The Taijirin peered down at Lian from above.

"Ialrist, what brings you here?" Lian asked. As usual, the Taijirin's presence unsettled him. The man was somehow aloof yet scrutinizing, as though he searched Lian's soul to discern his innermost secrets.

"I saw what happened during the battle against the swingblades," Ialrist began. For a moment, Lian was sure that the Taijirin would mention Canzo and the monster that killed him. Resentment boiled inside of him; Ialrist had made no other effort to show sympathy or compassion for his loss. Ialrist pressed on.

"I saw what happened to your spear—how the runes began to glow."

Astonished, Lian studied the Taijirin. "Was it really so bright?" he asked. Ialrist had been more than a hundred paces away at the time. Plus, it had been the middle of the day.

"The glow was bright enough for my eyes to notice," Ialrist answered. Lian remembered that vogelfolk's vision went far beyond the abilities and limitations of human sight. Ialrist had sharper eyes than all others aboard the *Carryola*.

The slayer leaned forward. "Your weapon . . . is special. Where did you get it?"

"What's it to you?" Lian asked in defense.

"I'm just curious," Ialrist answered. "I come from far away, from a land beyond the forests, deserts, water oceans, and the plains. I traversed Endar with Adaron for ages before the Cloudmere put an end to our wandering, and never before have I seen a weapon such as yours. Sure, I have heard of such spears, but in the stories, ordinary men or women never handled these weapons."

Lian tore his gaze away from the horizon and turned to Ialrist. "Do you know more about this spear?" Even though it would have interested Lian just as much to hear of the Taijirin's adventures beyond the Cloudmere, his curiosity about the weapon was more pressing.

Ialrist nodded. "A bit, yes, if my mind doesn't deceive me."

"Please, tell me anything you can," Lian implored. "I inherited the spear from my father, but he never told me where he got it. I never even saw the runes glow until you did." Though he was skeptical, it was easiest to assume that the flash had merely been a reflection of sun on the runes.

"It happens in moments when you are filled with wrath, doesn't it?" Ialrist asked. "After the death of your friend, you were filled with loathing for the swingblade and with the need for revenge."

"Yes, that's right," Lian answered.

"Then it *is* possible that one of the six drachen spears belonging to the Theurgs of Fundur could still be in existence," the Taijirin said in awe.

Lian stared at Ialrist, confused. "Who are the . . . Theurgs? And what do you know about their spears?" he asked.

Ialrist cocked his head. "I've only been told of them once, when we found signs of their existence among the ruins of Fundur. That was many years ago, when everything was . . . better." He went silent.

"Please, go on," Lian coaxed.

"No, I shall not speak of Adaron and myself or the others. It only causes pain to remember the past." He ruffled his wings as though to shake off the thoughts his words had awakened. Then he looked at Lian. "But I'll tell you what we learned. Centuries ago, the realm beyond the deserts broke out in war. Drachen fought against sorcerers who called themselves Theurgs. Their home was the city Fundur in the realm Quanish. As the tide of blood turned against the Theurgs and the dragons threatened to obliterate their kingdom, the soldiers made an unholy pact and forged six new drachen spears. Six unparalleled warriors took them up. Their scorn for dragons flowed into the spears and transformed them into the most powerful weapons to ever taste dragon's blood."

The Taijirin's gaze wandered to the distance. "Horrible slaughter followed . . . but in the end, Fundur fell, and the spears were erased from history along with the warriors who wielded them. They still tell the legends in the region that was once Quanish, and many still search for the spears. As far as I know, nothing has ever been found."

Breathless, Lian stared at Ialrist. "And you believe that my father left such a spear to me?"

"I don't know," Ialrist admitted. "What happened during the battle against the swingblade, however, was no accident. An ancient power stirs within your weapon, to be sure. Whether it is truly one of the spears invincible against dragons, only time will tell."

Ialrist leaned farther forward. "Many jägers would kill for such a weapon. Lucky for you, the legend of the drachen spears from Fundur is unknown in Skargakar. Only a very few who have traveled far enough will have heard the tale. If you want my advice, don't speak with anyone on board about it. They're all a bunch of cutthroats and crooks. You'd do best to not trust any of them—not about something so precious."

"What about you, sir?" Lian dared to ask. "You know the legend, and you saw the runes glow—although I think that you and Hanon'ka are the only ones." He didn't believe that Melvas or Balen had noticed. Or they didn't speak of it later, at least. "How do I know I can trust you?" he asked.

Ialrist's lips curled into a sly smile. "You don't have much other choice. I suppose you could kill me so I can't divulge your secret—but you are no murderer. At least not one with corrupt motives."

Lian remembered his run-in with Casran. Nothing but pure revenge had driven his spear then. "You don't know me as well as you think you do," he said.

Ialrist thrust his head forward and eyed Lian with his raptor's gaze. "Or you don't know yourself as well as *you* think," he responded cryptically. Then he straightened up. "Either way, you can relax. My quest for riches lies far behind me. Your spear doesn't interest me—or if it does, it's only as an artifact from a past time. I would like to study the runes more closely at some point, with your permission."

Lian nodded. It wouldn't hurt to allow the Taijirin the small favor. Plus, he would win more than he would lose. "We could meet tonight," he offered.

"I doubt that," said Ialrist. "We'll all have our hands full tonight."

Lian raised his eyebrows. "Why is that?" he asked.

The Taijirin pointed past Lian toward the horizon. "Because a storm is coming that we won't be able to evade."

Later that evening, the *Carryola* reached the sinister cloud front that separated them from the violent storm awaiting them.

Lian had already experienced a few storms in his lifetime. Living on the coast, in direct contact with the Cloudmere, a yearly winter storm was commonplace. Lian was acquainted with how the elements surged in a storm—the roar of wind, pelting rain, crashing thunder, and blinding lightning. Until now, he had always experienced their wrath behind four walls with a roof over his head and wooden shutters shut tight against the wind and rain.

Today, there was no barrier or shelter to protect him. Lian and Melvas pushed through the rain across the wet deck to secure any loose cargo so that it wouldn't go overboard. His soaked clothes clung to his body.

Colored flecks danced before his eyes—an aftereffect of the bolts of lightning that ripped through the darkness.

At the foremast, a few cases came loose from their holds and slid across the deck. Lian hurried away from the bow and past Arax's sleeping area. Corantha and her dragon, however, were nowhere in sight. Turning toward the sky, Lian spotted them in flight behind the ship. The dragon, Melvas explained, felt more at ease in the air.

Above their heads, sailors clambered up the rigging to haul in the sails. Orders were called, and men cried out their responses from dizzying heights as they weathered the storm. From the helm, Adaron and Jaular struggled to keep the *Carryola* on course, a task that required extra skill; with each gust of wind that threw the ship sideways, the lines to the kyrillian cases had to be maneuvered to bring the ship back on course. If the captain and the Nondurier erred in response to any change in the air currents, the vessel would capsize—a deadly prospect for them all.

"Where is the commander?" Jaular bellowed. "We could use his help."

"Over here," Hanon'ka called from the deck. His hair and garments fluttered in the wind as he entered the deck from the canteen. Lightning flashed and thunder cracked as though the storm warned the Sidhari not to interfere.

Hanon'ka seemed unconcerned as he ran past Lian. When he reached the stern, he stood still. Then he raised his hands to the black sky and offered himself to the furious storm before him as though conjuring a spell.

"What's he doing?" Lian called to Melvas, yelling over the raging wind. "Is he working his magic again?"

"Yes!" cried Melvas back to him. "Do you remember the wind he unleashed to fend off the swingblade?"

"Of course!"

"This is the same, but in reverse. He's trying to weaken the wind."

"Can he do that?" Lian asked in doubt. The cyclone against the dragon had been astonishing enough, but taming the furious elements that raged now seemed unthinkable.

"He is a Sidhari," Melvas answered as though that were explanation enough.

Lian strained to hear Hanon'ka's bellowing words over the roaring wind. Then a powerful gust from starboard threw the *Carryola* to the side, and he stumbled. He caught hold of a rope attached to the foremast and held tightly. *He'll never manage it. Nobody can control such a storm.*

A horn's sudden blare sounded three times from above. Lian looked up to the crow's nest to see Danark—manning a post that Lian didn't envy for anything in the world at that moment—sound the alarm.

"The Winds have it in for us." Melvas swore beside him.

Three sounds of the horn meant floating lithos ahead. Normally, it was easy enough to sail around the rock masses, but in a storm like this, Lian knew that the obstacles could be deadly, no matter if they tried to circumvent them or sail overhead.

"Hanon'ka!" Jaular called from the helm.

"Leave him!" Adaron called sharply. "He's doing his part."

"I have to see this," Lian called to Melvas, running to the railing. Leaning into the air, he stared into the night.

At first, nothing happened. It was too dark, and the streaming rain blurred his view. Then a flash of lightning ripped through the darkness and lit up the clouds. Lian's stomach turned. "By all the Winds," he murmured.

Before them, not just a few lithos appeared out of the clouds, but an entire mountain range loomed before them. As far as his gaze reached— which wasn't very far—dark masses hung amid the clouds, their steep and towering formations sharp and menacing. As they appeared, some rocks were barely two hundred paces apart. In calm weather, an expert navigator might steer a schooner through such a mountain range with ease, but in such a storm, to enter would be a death wish.

Adaron seemed to share Lian's opinion. "Hard starboard!" he bellowed. "Keep us away from those mountains, Jaular!"

"I'm trying, Captain!" the Nondurier answered. "But the wind is forcing us toward them. We need—"

He stopped short and looked to Hanon'ka as the storm let up from one moment to the next. The Sidhari stood tall on the *Carryola*'s deck, arms raised and fingers outstretched. His voice carried more clearly to them now, and Lian made out words.

Beyond the ship's edge, the storm carried on with unaltered fury behind a sheet of rain that acted like a wall between their ship and the air before them. Lian could hear the wind's deafening roar, but the distant gust was a stark contrast to the gentle breeze that wafted against his cheek on board.

"He's imposed his own will on the storm," Melvas explained from beside him, his voice filled with awe. "I'm sure I've seen him tame the elements at least a dozen times, but his magic always amazes me. So much power . . ."

Jaular smiled, now relieved. "He did it! Now we just need to turn the ship."

"No," Adaron called. "Keep her where she is. If we turn now, the direction of the wind will change, and Hanon'ka might lose focus."

"But we're still heading toward the lithos."

Adaron nodded. "Then we'll make do. Steer us to one of the larger rocks. We'll find shelter from the wind and sit the storm out."

"That's dangerous, Captain," Jaular argued. "In such a dense grouping of mountains, there is no true shelter from the gale. The wind howls unbridled across the treacherous mountain walls. If Hanon'ka loses strength, the wind would throw us straight into the rock wall, mark my words."

Adaron's eyes narrowed as he gazed into the darkness. Lightning flared above, and the looming masses flashed before the bow. "Maybe you're right," the captain said. "We'll—"

The horn sounded once more, this time in two sets of double blares, in quick succession.

An icy grip clawed Lian's heart. He, like the others on board, knew the meaning of Danark's signal.

"Not now," moaned Melvas.

"Dragon," Lian murmured.

Danark sounded the double tone, and Melvas and Lian exchanged panicked glances.

"A whole swarm?" Lian asked.

From the helm, Jaular swore in Nondurish. Adaron approached the bell. "Alarm!" he cried, tolling the bell wildly. "All men to their weapons. Take your places at the ballistae!"

Balen, who had been working at the bow, bellowed to the men, "Move, you lazy hounds! Gaaki, Aelfert, to the stern. Melvas, you and I to starboard. Lian, fetch your spear. You'll back us up."

A shrill screech rang from the darkness, and Lian made out the shadowed forms that sped toward them as he raced below deck.

"What is it?" Smett asked as Lian ran past the galley.

"Dragon attack," Lian called over his shoulder. "A whole swarm."

The cook swore as Lian raced away.

When he returned to the deck with his weapon in hand, the single cry through the darkness had swelled into a shrieking chorus. The shadows had grown into massive figures that now circled the *Carryola* at the edge of the light from lanterns and torches that the men had carried to the deck to see their enemies more clearly. There wasn't much chance to see through the unabating rain, but every hand's breadth made a difference.

A screech sounded from above as the first giant gray body descended upon them. Lian braced himself before realizing that the form was Arax, with Corantha astride his back.

"What are they?" Jaular cried, the urgency in his voice revealing his fear.

"Raptors!" Corantha called through the storm. "We'll attack."

"Be careful!" Adaron called.

"Always!" She laughed, and as she released a howling battle cry, her dragon echoed the call.

The raptors didn't falter. If anything, the slayer's cry seemed to spur them on. With ear-splitting shrieks, they neared the ship.

Lian hurried past Markaeth and the Drak, who crouched behind the railing, holding crossbows and staring into the clouds. Lian raised his spear and took his place behind the two harpoons at the bow. Looking upward into the storm, he scanned the ship's perimeter.

Melvas spotted the first assailants. "Here they come," he called, swiveling his weapon around. He fired, but his first shot proved that the bulky weapon wasn't built for shooting dragons the same size and speed as horses. It was impossible to keep them in view.

The nearest raptor screamed as it swerved sideways and sailed straight over the *Carryola*'s bow. Lian ducked as the beast's gray body and scythe-shaped wings whooshed just overhead. The raptors closed in on the men from all sides amid the roaring storm as lightning and thunder mixed with the dragons' shrieks and men's own cries of warning.

Balen, Melvas, Gaaki, and Aelfert attempted to keep the attackers at bay, though they barely sank a single shot with the ballistae. The raptors were simply too fast. Balen eventually managed to shoot one in the chest, sending it flapping into the depths.

The crew holding crossbows fared little better. Their weapons were best for attacks in proximity. From afar, the wind merely tossed the weapons' lightweight bolts off course. Lian knew that waiting to get close was dangerous. He watched in suspense as one man shot a raptor in the throat, which then fell onto him in a deadly mass of flesh, bones, and claws.

Lian took a gamble and ran from portside to starboard, brandishing his spear at any dragon that attempted to land. When a bull headed toward him with outstretched claws, he rammed the spear's end into the beast's chest. The thrust cast the dragon over the railing, where it vanished into the murk. When another approached, Lian pierced both its wings before Urdin sliced the raging animal's head from its long neck with a powerful strike of his ax.

The runes on the end of Lian's spear only flickered weakly during the battle. Either the weapon didn't consider raptors worthy enough opponents, or Lian's panic left no room for rage.

Another raptor sprang onto the bowsprit and snapped its pointed jaws just above Melvas's head. As he raced for cover, Lian jumped forward and thrust his spear into the beast's throat. The bull threw its head back in pain, threatening to rip the weapon from Lian's hands, but Lian pulled back quickly. Blood spurted from the monster's mouth as it gurgled, continuing to shriek. Then Balen, with a shot from his ballista, sent the beast into the nothingness over the edge of the bowsprit.

"Thanks," Melvas gasped, pulling himself to his feet.

"Next time, it'll be you saving my life," Lian said. "That's how we—"

The storm descended abruptly upon the ship. Thrown off his feet, Lian cried out, overcome by confusion. In a flash, he understood. *Hanon'ka!* The Sidhari no longer controlled the storm. Had the battle cost him his concentration, or could the commander be . . . *No! I can't even think of such a thing.*

"Lian!" Balen bellowed. "Behind you!"

Lian spun around, ducking as he turned, and raised his spear. He was too slow. A shadow fell upon him, and his shoulders flared with searing pain as powerful talons sank into his flesh. Then he felt the strange sensation of complete weightlessness as the raptor lifted him from his feet and carried him into the air. Without thinking, he dropped his spear onto the deck and gripped at the claws. He treaded the air as he struggled to free himself from his hold.

By then, the deck lay far behind him as the raptor carried him into the storm-whipped clouds. If he fell now, his life would be over. He clung to the raptor's talons. Wherever the dragon took him would be better than the ground his feet would find if he were released into the black void.

The raptor let out a shrill cry and tensed its body. Lian also cried out as he struggled to keep hold as the beast frantically flapped its wings. He tilted his head back to glimpse what had happened. When he spotted a spear now burrowed into the beast's underside, he grew ice cold.

Lightning flashed, and thunder shook the sky.

The raptor writhed in panic and began to plummet downward—with Lian still trapped in its claws.

18

The Cloudmere Floor

Fifth Day of the Sixth Moon, year 841

The fall into the abyss seemed to last forever. Through storm, rain, and darkness, they dropped deeper and deeper. At first, Lian cried out along with the panicked raptor. Then both went silent. Lian began to pray to the Winds, with desperate hope that one of the four would mercifully send a miracle to a lost soul like him, who rarely paid deference. The animal, now close to death, tenaciously flapped its wings as though all would be well if only it could find its way back to the comfort of its den.

Lian knew that the creature's hopes were foolish. He knew what the spear burrowed into the dragon's belly meant. The dragon would perish, and Lian along with it as soon as it realized the fruitlessness of its fight and ceased its struggle.

Why am I deceiving myself? Lian thought. One way or another, he was done for. Nothing ever returned once it met the Cloudmere floor.

Lian wondered if the Winds' powers reached as far as the depths. Could the Southern Wind carry him to the warm place where his father and Canzo awaited him? The idea of meeting his friend so soon was a bitter comfort. Lian wished he could change his fate to live out a long life in Skargakar, on solid land, with his friend at his side, but it was too late for that now.

What if the Winds never found him? Maybe his would be just another damned soul lost to eternal cold and damp darkness. Perhaps he was destined to roam the abyss, a pale, restless phantom among the fog, for all eternity.

Was there even a bottom to the Cloudmere's depths? The folk of Skargakar assumed so. But if no one had ever returned from its depths, how could they be certain? Lian could just as easily continue to fall, farther and farther, until he died from hunger and thirst.

His mind raced. Completely powerless, his fate now dangled in the raptor's talons. Staring into the darkness, he couldn't make out any forms. High above them, lightning lit the sky, and muffled thunder rumbled in the distance. Even in these flashes of light, Lian saw only thick and endless clouds as he rushed downward.

The rain lessened as the storm abated somewhat farther down, though it was impossible to tell whether thick clouds shielded Lian or if the storm lost strength with the increasing depths. The lightning dimly lit the all-encompassing fog, which began to dissipate around him. Indiscernibly at first, Lian realized complete darkness no longer surrounded him. He spotted a weak, sickly, green fleck of light beneath him—a peculiar light that rapidly grew larger as they neared.

For a moment, Lian forgot his fear. There was something below them. Could it be the Cloudmere floor? Was it possible that there was life there after all, as foreign or unhallowed as it might be?

I'll never find out, thought Lian. *When I hit the ground, I'll die instantly.* Sorrow overcame him. He wasn't ready to die. He had still hardly even lived. "Fly!" he cried up to the raptor. "Fly for me!"

The faint light increased in size until it had expanded into an entire field. Both Lian and the raptor cried out as they broke through the mist. For a fraction of a heartbeat, he made out the unfamiliar forms of giant bulbous structures.

The dying dragon lost hold of its prey. Falling through the air, Lian slammed into a rubbery surface, bounced once, and landed in something soft with a wet squelching sound. Though he could barely believe it—he was still alive!

For a long while, Lian didn't dare to move. He feared that his body would realize that he was supposed to be dead and would correct its error. While his heart hammered, he lay still and stared into the fog above. His back was wet—he hoped not from his own blood, but the wetness drenching his clothes was cold as though from water or whichever other liquid the surface under him secreted.

Carefully turning his head, he scanned his surroundings. Before him, fat and fleshy stalks—like tree trunks but with smooth surfaces—rose into the mist, higher than two paces, and ended in large and round caps. The light green glow Lian had spotted emanated from these domes, and from their undersides, a collection of gills crowded closely together. *Mushrooms,* he thought. *I've landed in a field of giant mushrooms.*

Lian carefully tested his limbs. He could move both arms and legs without much pain. His shoulders seared from the gashes inflicted by the raptor, and his ribs smarted from the fall, but under the circumstances, he considered himself lucky. Before taking his post at the crow's nest just before the storm, he had pulled a thick jacket over his shirt. This protection from wind and cold had also protected him from worse damage in the raptor's deadly grip.

Relieved he wasn't badly injured despite the odds, Lian rolled over with a groan. It was now nauseatingly clear that the liquid beneath him wasn't water but a kind of slime that covered the surface of the mushrooms. In fact, it wasn't the plants themselves that glowed but this putrid green muck, stinking of rot, that now covered his back.

Despite his revulsion, Lian sank into the yielding surface, grateful that the fungus had saved his life. He pulled himself across until he reached the plant's domed edge. It was impossible to gauge how high above ground he was, and after escaping death once, he hoped to avoid breaking his neck with his very first steps.

He had no reason for concern. Glancing down, Lian saw that barely a man's height separated him from the marshy ground. He wished that he could test the ground's solidity, but he had nothing besides the clothes on his body and the ordinary dagger in his belt. He considered how difficult it would be to climb his way across the mushroom caps toward the edge of the field. As it appeared, the climb would be too arduous. The mushrooms varied too much in height.

Instead, the decision was made for him. As he rolled onto his knees to pull himself to his feet and get a better look at his surroundings, he broke through the mushroom's top and landed with a squelch into the mud.

Lian gasped and swore as he pulled himself to his feet. Wiping mud from his face and hair, he looked around. As far as he could see, glowing fungi surrounded him. Mist threaded around the trunk-like stalks and collected into an impenetrable shroud of fog above Lian's head. Raising his gaze, he noticed a weak flash of light high above him, followed by distant thunder. How deep had he fallen? A thousand paces? Two thousand? Or even more? It was impossible to know.

Besides occasional echoes of thunder, he heard nothing; his immediate surroundings were as quiet and motionless as a grave. Lian wondered what had become of the raptor that had tumbled with him. Had the impact killed it? Lian doubted that the dragon still posed a threat, but he thought it best to be cautious.

Then Lian laughed uneasily. What was the point of caution now? He had reached the Cloudmere floor and was many days' journey away from land. A swift death by a raptor may have been a more merciful end than what likely awaited him here, where he would probably wander until he starved or collapsed from exhaustion. Even if he, through some miracle, found a mountain to lead him back above the fleece, he would be stranded, alone and without a chance of being saved. He would become little more than an appetizing tidbit for the next dragon that flew by.

"Stop!" he scolded himself under his breath. "You're not dead yet. You survived a fall to the Cloudmere floor and have lived to tell the tale. Is that not a sign from the Winds that it's not your time yet? So might as well prove yourself worthy and fight for your life!"

Slowly, he inched his way through the mushroom forest. He was desperate for food and something to drink. *Water must be in ample supply in such a damp place as this,* he assumed. If he could find something less slimy than the mushroom skin, it might just be drinkable. As for food . . . maybe it wouldn't be so bad to find the raptor again, he thought. Raw dragon meat was edible for at least two or three days before it went bad. He would rather have a stomachache from eating old meat than starve to death.

Lian would need the Winds' help to find the raptor, though. By now, he had lost track of where he had landed, and one mushroom looked just like the next. Since he couldn't have strayed far from the place into which he'd fallen, it made the most sense to search for the raptor by moving in concentric circles and marking notches into the mushroom stalks with his dagger as he fanned out with each revolution to keep track—which, thanks to the soft skin of their trunks, wasn't difficult.

He had already marked about twenty mushrooms when a weak flapping caught his eye farther ahead. Holding his dagger loosely, he approached the form until he came upon the raptor crumpled on the ground atop a patch of glowing moss. One of the creature's wings was raised, its bony spokes broken and twisted, and the spear stuck out from its underside, splintered in half. Though the swamp underneath the dragon's body was colored red, the creature was still alive. As Lian stepped closer, it turned its fearsome head toward him and fixed its yellow eyes on his face. Recognizing Lian's figure, the dragon began to thrash frantically as though to collect itself, either to flee or to attack.

"Not so fast," Lian said aloud, sinking his blade into the beast's throat. He stepped back to avoid being scratched in the leg or having his hand bitten off. He leaned against a mushroom and waited.

Before long, the creature's twitching began to subside.

Even though the dragon had transported Lian to his unfortunate location, he felt a pang of remorse. He was truly alone now. He shoved the thought aside.

Using his knife, he set to work cutting meat from the dragon's flank. Using the dragon's leathery wing, he wrapped meat chunks into a bundle, which he fastened shut with two claws. Then he bound a thighbone and lower jawbone together with sinew, fashioning a makeshift battle-ax. Now, if he encountered any other creatures, at least he would have another way to defend himself besides his blade. The jawbone was as least as long as a sword and made much more of a harrowing impression than the broken end of the spear that pierced the raptor's belly.

Once he had collected all he could, Lian set off. He wasn't sure where to go or what he expected to find, but he wouldn't stand still in the swamp next to a dragon's remains to await his own end—that much was certain.

The mushroom forest illuminated his way. After a while, they thinned out into scattered groups, until he spotted only single domes amid the fog that barely reached his shoulder. In place of the bizarre growths, impenetrable blackness surrounded him.

Lian rubbed his makeshift ax across the top of a smaller mushroom, but the green film glowed too weakly to give off much light. He would have to wait until morning, with the hope that the sun's rays might light the fog enough to keep him from encountering danger.

Sighing, Lian found a half-dry spot underneath a mushroom and sat down to wait. High above, the storm gradually subsided, and silence sank over the landscape. Though it was uncomfortably cold and damp, exhaustion overcame Lian. The storm, the battle against the swarm of raptors, the fall, and his wanderings down here had all taken their toll. At first, he fought the urge to sleep. An unknown enemy might discover or attack him, but eventually, his eyelids fell.

When he jerked awake, it was impossible to tell how long he'd slept. A fair span of time had surely passed, because his surroundings had changed remarkably. The darkness had lightened into a murky dawn, and fog draped its gray veil across everything.

Mumbling a curse to himself, he rubbed his eyes. He'd been stupid to leave himself so defenseless, in plain sight. The thought of being attacked sent shivers down his spine. Still, he felt relief; his body had needed rest, and luckily, nothing had eaten him in his sleep.

Groaning, he pulled himself to his feet. While his limbs were stiff and sore from lying in such an awkward position for so long in the damp, his shoulder didn't feel any worse than it had earlier. He took that as a good sign.

He rubbed his battered and frozen limbs back to life. Then he unwrapped the bundle of dragon meat and cut a piece away. Even though it looked fresh, he had to force himself to chew and swallow the raw flesh.

"I never liked your mush in the morning, Smett," he murmured, wincing, cutting himself another piece. "But I'd give anything for a bowl now." The thought of standing in the *Carryola*'s canteen and taking a steaming bowl from the jolly grinning cook was almost more than he could bear.

After choking down another chunk, he wrapped up the rest and picked up his ax. The daylight would be useful as long as it lasted. The faster he pressed forward, the sooner he would arrive . . . well, where? He had no idea what he was searching for. *But anywhere is better than here,* he reasoned. His situation could only improve.

Silently, he stepped through the perpetual fog that now filled the

Cloudmere floor. At first, he waded knee deep through mud, but after a while, the ground began to harden. Lian recognized what looked like pale green grass growing on its surface, but with much wider blades and a revolting fishy odor.

As he pressed forward, Lian spotted even more unfamiliar growths, resembling mustard-yellow boulders. He placed a hand on one. Its surface was deceptively soft, and when he pressed against it, clear water flowed out from the pillowy stone. He drank for a long time to quench his desperate thirst. Then he cut a few head-sized pieces away, to save for later.

Lian noticed other plants along his way. He recognized ferns from the wild forest near Skargakar, though these rose at least two paces into the air. Pale green moss covered the surfaces of boulders. He encountered another forest of bizarre mushrooms, which he stayed away from because the growths seemed filled with an eerie life of their own. They swayed back and forth as though stirred in a breeze—only no breeze stirred them.

He saw no animals or any other intelligent forms of life. On one hand, he was relieved, for he was constantly aware of his lack of shield. On the other, he doubted that any creatures living in this dreary land would be friendly.

Hunger returned with time, and Lian choked down a few more chunks of dragon meat. He wondered if the mushrooms or other plants were edible, but he wasn't prepared to toy with his health to find out.

Over time, his legs began to ache. He wasn't used to such long journeys on foot. Most of his time in Skargakar had been spent seated, either at his workbench or in taverns like Cliff House. Besides that, the ground he walked was either slick with slime or rocky and uneven, both of which made speed impossible. He forced himself onward as fast as he dared.

Wisps of fog began to darken as the Cloudmere floor nodded toward the end of day. He hoped to find a moss field or group of mushrooms to provide light before the ground sank into complete darkness. The idea of spending another night in pitch-black nothingness filled him with dread.

He wandered until completely exhausted and collapsed beside a pillowy water stone, whose glowing, mossy surface lit a few paces into the night, but not much sleep was possible. First, fear of the terrors that lurked in the night kept him awake, then pangs of hunger gnawed at him, and finally, shivers of cold set in. Once his eyes finally fell shut, frantic dreams startled him awake again, plagued anew by the terrors of fear, hunger, and cold.

Eventually, dawn cast its pale light. Lian choked down the rest of his dragon meat and drank from the rest of his stones. Then, cutting a few more fragments away from the stone he'd rested against, he continued onward.

Farther and farther, he pressed through the fog. He stepped through mud and over wet grass as he passed nightmarish plants and sharp rock formations. After a while—he couldn't tell how long—a canyon made it impossible to pass and forced him to change direction. Sometime later, he was forced to take another detour to avoid entering a forest of grotesquely bloated trees, whose trunks were smeared with thick drippings that fell from their yellowish-green leaves.

His stomach, now a gaping hole of hunger, grumbled. He wished he could fill it with bowls of stew—or even better, a whole roasted screecher. Here in the depths, nothing so appetizing appeared. When he passed another set of mushrooms, he gave in to his hunger. Wiping away the green slime as best he could, he bit into the morsel, but it was so bitter that he spat it out again instantly. For the rest of that day, he felt ill.

When the third day dawned, Lian was ready to admit defeat. He was so hungry and tired that he couldn't pull himself away from his uncomfortable nook made of hard stone. *Where am I even going?* he wondered. *I'll starve—that's how this will end. Why bother anymore? This spot is just as good as any to die.*

His thoughts turned to his father and Canzo, who had both died fighting—more or less, anyway. Lonjar Draksmasher had fought Casran's men until the end. And Canzo had given his best at the jäger kite's sails to defeat the swingblade. Both men had taken their lives into their own hands. They hadn't just lain down to await death.

You're not dead yet, Lian reminded himself with his last shred of survival instinct. *So get up and keep going!* With a groan, he pulled himself to his feet.

Moving forward became increasingly difficult, though there was no longer knee-deep mud to wade through. Eventually, he recognized that not only did his weakened limbs slow his pace but the ground itself rose almost imperceptibly beneath his feet at an incline. *Maybe I'm approaching a mountain!* he realized. The thought quickened his pace.

Instead of a mountain, the incline turned out to be a chain of small hills that disappeared into the darkness. Lian walked along their edge, hoping that the hills would become larger mountains. He tried to eat a few mushrooms, which were smaller and tasteless this time and not covered in as much slime. When his stomach didn't rebel, he plucked all that he could find and stored them in his wing-skin bundle. They wouldn't last long, he knew, but were better than nothing. With renewed strength, he pressed on.

The trail continued for another half day until Lian realized that he was going the wrong way. The hills now grew flatter and eventually began to decline. If the hills led to mountains, he was going in the wrong direction to find them. He cursed under his breath and looked around, uncertain whether he should turn around or continue. It would take another half day alone to reach his starting point, and the way into the fully unknown stretched on before him.

"Come on, Winds," he muttered. "You didn't have me survive the fall into these depths just to let me meet a miserable death while I was there, did you? Give me a sign. Tell me what to do." He walked a few paces in a random direction.

About fifty paces before him, a silhouette appeared in the darkness (it was rare to see beyond that distance, he had learned). An enormous and grotesque figure loomed before him. Struck with fright, Lian dropped to the ground for cover. After a while, it became clear that the figure, though at least as large as a bronzeneck, wasn't moving. Since he couldn't hear breathing or any other sound, he assumed that whatever monster lay before him must already be dead.

Could it be a dragon? Not all dragons met their ends at the hands of jägers, he knew. There were other reasons for their deaths amid the clouds, whether from battles between their kind or from sickness or old age. Their lifeless bodies inevitably fell into the depths, to decompose into the earth.

Lian supposed it was also possible that a monster had made the depths its home. Indeed, he had heard countless stories about horrible creatures that lurked in the depths of the Cloudmere. Perhaps there could be a spark of truth in the tales. Hadn't a jäger brought a puffy gray monster back to Skargakar once? Nobody had been able to say what it was or where it had come from. Lian's stomach lurched at the thought.

The smartest thing would be to retreat and evade the dark figure without disturbing it. On the other hand, he was almost more afraid of his own imagination than the thing itself. Maybe it would be better to know what it was for sure. He didn't have much more to lose.

Lian took a deep breath and stepped toward the massive figure. After a brief inspection, he knew what it was without a doubt. His eyes widened, and his heart thumped in his chest.

A half-destroyed ship sprawled before him in the shadows behind wisps of mist.

19

From the Depths

Eighth Day of the Sixth Moon, Year 841

The ship was smaller than the *Carryola*. It measured about thirty paces from bow to stern, and one of its two masts was splintered and toppled. From the other, sails hung in scorched tatters—the main reason for its terrifying silhouette in the fog.

On closer inspection, the whole ship was in bad shape. The vessel must have crashed onto the ground at full force. The hull was broken in two, scoured with burn marks, and sunken halfway into the mud. As it appeared, the unlucky sailors must have encountered a fireblood, and since they must have been traders or adventurers instead of jägers—the ship had no harpoons or structures to fasten a captured dragon to the hull—the encounter apparently cost them their lives.

The ship must have crashed only recently, Lian thought. Barely any moss grew on its hull, and he saw no wood rot. Excitement surged in his chest. Maybe there would be something real to eat aboard! There could even still be people living in the wreck!

His first instinct was to call out and run forward, waving, but he urged himself to remain cautious. There was no use in carelessness. Just because he hadn't seen any other life-forms besides the eerie swaying mushrooms didn't mean that dangers weren't lurking in the depths.

"Hello?" he called softly.

No answer came.

"Hello?" he repeated. "Is anyone there?" Slowly, he approached the ship's bow, hoping to find a way onto the deck without having to struggle over the slime-covered hull.

When he saw the crew's safety net, used for scrubbing the ship's hull, he felt light-headed with relief. He set his weapon and rations on the ground beside him and tested the net's stability with both hands. Once satisfied that the ropes would hold his weight, he climbed up the ship's side to the railing. With each movement of his arms, he winced at the pain of his shoulder wounds.

Carefully, Lian peered over the railing and onto the steep sloping deck. Eyeing the black scorch marks along the wood, he pitied the crew as he imagined their awful end. There was no injustice greater than being taken by an opponent without a chance for survival.

Lian pulled himself over the ledge and found a stable grip on the damp wood. Then he began to search the ship. The slanted deck slowed his pace, but he managed. He started at the stern, where the captain's quarters usually lay—Adaron's lodgings at the bow were an exception—and after a few moments, he found something on the captain's desk that quickened his heartbeat: a small lantern and a box of matches.

He hurried to light the lantern. As the cabin filled with golden light, a healing warmth rose in Lian's blood as though he sat at that very moment with Canzo beside the hearth at Cliff House on a cold winter's night, listening to a ballad sung by a wandering bard. "A tiny flicker of hope in this dark world," he whispered.

Gripping the lantern's handle in one hand and his blade in the other, Lian continued to search the wreckage. His hunt yielded further reward: he found extra oil for the lantern, a woolen blanket, and a thick coat, which he pulled on instantly. He also spotted a set of fine garments in the captain's quarters, along with a hold half full with bales of cloth, which confirmed Lian's assumption that the ship had been a merchant vessel.

He found none of the crew, neither their corpses nor their living forms.

This confused Lian. Their departure couldn't have been organized. The crew had abandoned too many useful wares, like warm clothing and tools, which would have been too precious to leave behind when navigating the desolate Cloudmere floor.

The only thing missing was nourishment. That, too, was strange. Lian couldn't find even a moldy piece of bread. Not a single crumb remained aboard. The galley and canteen were clear, with boxes and bottles smashed on the floor planks and emptied of their contents. *Someone has already been very thorough.*

He sighed and sank onto one of the boxes. His search hadn't been a complete failure, but he had hoped for better. *At least I'm not as cold anymore—and I won't have to sit in the pitch-blackness when night falls.*

He peered through a crack in the ship's side. The light of day, which had colored the mist gray around the wreckage, had started to dim. It wouldn't be long before nightfall. "I should stay here tonight," Lian said aloud. He could even sleep in a bunk, albeit a slanted one. *It might be better to hang a hammock from a piece of sail,* he considered.

Just then, his eye caught a mellow violet glow through the crack in the hull. At first he stared, bewildered. When the realization hit him, he jumped to his feet. *Kyrillian!*

Filled with sudden excitement, Lian ran back to the deck and hurried down the net to the ground below. He ran around the wreckage until he found the spot he had viewed from the deck. Setting his lamp into the mud at his side, he knelt. A feeling of unimaginable joy charged through him. Before him, chipped and battered, a kyrillian case lay next to the ship. Lian hadn't noticed it on first inspection because it was almost completely covered in mud.

Hastily, Lian dug the case free and carefully inspected its contents. "Yes!" he exclaimed. A load as heavy as a mountain lifted from his shoulders when he saw that at least half the violet kyrillian crystals shimmered, unharmed, in their casings. Of course, a case this size couldn't raise the entire ship into the sky. *But it might be able to lift a single man.* If he fastened the crystals to a few planks, he might be able to escape this deathly damp grave after all!

Lian raised his gaze toward the mist-veiled sky and lifted his arms into the air. "Oh, Winds, I thank you!" he called. "Thank you!"

He began to formulate a plan with fervent enthusiasm. Though he wasn't a ship carpenter, he had enough experience with the mechanics of kyrillian frames and the woodwork aboard a ship to build a safety raft and distribute crystals to keep it from capsizing. Returning to the wrecked ship, he found an ax to chop a few planks away. As he passed the open entrance to the storeroom, his gaze fell on the knocked-over barrels on the floor, and he had another thought.

"That would be even easier," he said aloud. "And probably safer."

Lian rolled three of the largest barrels to the deck. Each was big enough for a man his size to crouch inside. As he imagined it, he could connect all three, fit inside one, and use the others to store wares that would prolong his survival. He didn't worry about the kyrillian; there were surely enough crystals inside the storage frame to raise three barrels filled with cargo.

Using a rope cut away from the mast, he lowered the barrels to the ground. With every motion, pain ripped through his shoulders as his scabs tore open. Lian didn't look. He would tend to his injuries as soon as he reached safety.

Once all three barrels had reached the ground beside the ship, Lian climbed down and organized them into a triangle, with their openings upright. Using a gimlet he'd found in the carpenter's workshop, he drilled holes into the barrels' sides and threaded rope through the holes, which he knotted tightly to fashion a raft. A skilled craftsman wouldn't have bothered with the holes, but Lian wanted to make sure that his raft wouldn't fall to pieces in the clouds.

Darkness had descended in the meantime. To continue his work, Lian returned to the ship and collected any source of light he could find. He was surrounded by a circle of light from lanterns, torches, candles, and oil lamps—some with red flames, some with yellow. It was a waste, he knew, but he wasn't concerned about that. All he wanted was to complete the small vessel that would transport him to safety on the other side of the fleece.

Just as he finished tying a triangle-shaped piece of canvas across the barrels' openings to fill with kyrillian from underneath to raise his raft into the air, a movement beyond his circle of light caught his attention. Lian peered warily into the shadows, pulled the last knots tight, and picked up his jaw ax from the mud next to him.

A squishing sound of bare feet trekking through mud surrounded him. He noticed movement from behind him at the wreck's bow. From the stern, he heard a ghostly howl and, darting to face it, raised his weapon. "Who's there?" he called into the seething mist.

The howling returned, answered by a similar sound from the opposite side of Lian's circle of light. Eyes came in sight—large, sallow, glowing circles, always two together, and at least a dozen pairs. As the bodies materialized through the fog, the hairs raised on Lian's neck and a hard knot of terror grew in his gut.

The monsters were only distantly similar to humans. Their grayish skin was hard and gnarled. Their hands and feet seemed too large for their bodies, or rather, their arms and legs too thin. Sparse shreds of what looked like moss covered their emaciated bodies, and grotesque growths covered their hairless skulls. Their large, lifeless eyes had no pupils and stared blindly through Lian.

Howls poured out of wide mouths filled with rotted and smashed teeth. Whether the noise was a way of speaking or mere wordless craving, Lian couldn't say, and he preferred not to know. These creatures didn't appear to have surfaced to welcome him into their midst. They seemed hungry, and the only edible thing—aside from a few measly mushrooms—was himself.

In panic, he dropped his ax and grabbed his dagger, but not to attack the newcomers. Racing to the storage frames, he fell to his knees in the mud and began to rip the kyrillian crystals from their casings. Catching the crystals as they flew upward, he threw them underneath the triangle-shaped sail attached to the barrels. With the first few crystals, he barely noticed a difference, but with the fourth or fifth, the sail began to lift into the air.

The ghouls loomed closer. Their creeping steps squelched through the slime, and their howls multiplied into a chorus of damned souls.

"Get back!" Lian cried. "Be gone!"

His words achieved nothing. The creatures weren't deterred, but they didn't rush toward him, either. They seemed, instead, to have all the time in the world. By now, Lian was surrounded with no chance of escape. When they reached the candles and lanterns, Lian spotted naked gray feet ending in claws. Feet trampled the flames and extinguished their light, sending wisps of smoke into the air above the muck. Blackness fell around Lian.

Terror overcame him. He would never make it. So close to a return to the other side of the fleece, and he was done for. He'd never be able to fend off these ghouls and free the crystals at the same time. As he loosened the next crystal from its holder, his knife slipped and sliced into his hand. He cried out at the pain. Cursing, he shook out his injured hand, caught the crystal that shot into the air, spun around, and tossed it in with the others.

The sail continued to lift silently above the barrels. He had to be careful now. He would have to be on board himself before he could load the last three or four crystals; otherwise, his lifeboat would lift off without him. With flying fingers, he ripped the next crystal free and stuck it into his jacket pocket, praying that it wouldn't rip through the fabric toward the sky. Almost there—but time sped by. Only a few steps separated Lian from the monsters, who now reached out toward him, staring with sallow eyes and opening their howling mouths eagerly.

"No!" Lian yelled, changing from his knife back to the jaw ax, which he raised against the opponents as they closed in on him.

The first let out an anguished yowl as the tooth-lined blade of the raptor's jaw slashed its side. The ax sank into a second monster's throat. Dark blood spurted, and the ghoul fell gurgling backward, but the third beast caught the weapon's dull blade and held on tightly. Rather than be pulled forward, Lian let go of the handle.

An uneasy thought crossed his mind. It was risky, but Lian chose to gamble. His life would be over, anyway, if he did nothing. Leaning forward, he groped for the storage case and slammed the lid shut. Then he thrust whole case in front of himself.

His shoulders smarted as though stabbed by two hot spears, and his cut hand burned with pain. Lian cried out and thrust the case twice more against his opponents. Then, raising it over his head, he rammed the case between the ropes and into the inflated sail.

"Four Winds, stand with me!" he prayed. Backing toward the raft, he swung a leg over the barrel's edge, gripped the nearest rope with his good hand, and pushed open the case's gills with his injured hand.

Without a weight to carry, the case shot into the air as though fired from a catapult. It hit the sail above and picked up the three barrels along with Lian into the air.

Lian cried out once more as the force jolted through his body. A hand clawed at his jacket and nearly pulled him away from the rising barrels, but Lian clutched the barrel's edge and tried to shake himself free from his opponent still clawing toward him.

Moans carried from below as the ghouls watched their prey escape. The cries quickly faded as the raft sped into the fog. A cold hand closed around Lian's throat and tried to pull him backward. Coughing and gasping for breath, Lian threw his whole weight forward and fell into the barrel.

The kyrillian's violet glow from above lit Lian's otherwise dark surroundings. In the glow, he spotted the gimlet he'd used to drill the holes lying inside with him. As he stretched out his hand, a monster clawed at his clothes and hair to pull him out of the barrel. Hot breath blew against Lian's neck.

His hand closed around the gimlet. Groaning, Lian turned toward the monster until its hideous face was no more than a hand's width away from his own. Giant pallid eyes, now illuminated by the kyrillian's violet glow, stared through him. In the violet light, the gray face seemed to glow with a cursed magic.

The monster opened its fanged mouth and charged toward Lian, who rammed the gimlet's metal point into its cheek just in time.

The creature shrieked and pulled backward. Lian used its own momentum to send it flying over the barrel's edge. Howling, the gruesome creature disappeared into the darkness.

Lian sank back and gasped for breath. For a long while, he lay half inside the barrel, nearly paralyzed, with one hand cramped around the rope and the other draped powerlessly over the barrel's edge. A black veil pushed at the corner of his eye, threatening to send him into full unconsciousness. *No!* Lian fought the urge and shook his head forcefully. He refused to submit to weakness now. He couldn't give in—not when he still faced such danger.

Reaching up toward the sail, he adjusted the position of the casing and closed the flaps halfway to slow the raft's ascent. He couldn't believe his luck. The pull of the case could just as easily have ripped the sail away and sent his only chance of escape flying into the clouds. Not that he would have lived with the disappointment for long; the gray ghouls would surely have ripped him apart in a matter of moments.

"Thank you," he murmured weakly into the nothingness. "Thank you, Winds." From the chasm at the bottom of the Cloudmere, he rose into the air. He had survived a fate that all lore insisted no person could survive. From now on, he would think differently of the powers that guarded the destinies of mortals. If he received any riches from this journey, he would sacrifice most to the merciful spirits who had spared his life. He swore this oath in silence.

Then he laughed at his thoughts. "My riches . . . ha! I'm not even saved yet." He had no food or water and no shelter from storm. He was just as likely to encounter a dragon in the cloud expanse before he met a ship. This raft, as sure as it had rescued him from death, could just as well become his grave.

The world around him transformed unexpectedly. The impenetrable dark fog dissipated, and Lian's small vessel rose into a cool and clear night sky. Silver moonlight bathed his face, and a magnificently starry, cloudless sky stretched powerful and glittering above him.

Unfathomable relief overcame Lian. He had never seen anything more beautiful. For a moment, he forgot all pain, hunger, exhaustion, and worry of what might come. He had escaped the depths of the Cloudmere and fled the grasp of eternal stillness and endless misery. Now he reentered the kingdom of the living! Lian threw his head back and laughed aloud with joy into the silent night that surrounded him.

20

From Bad to Worse

Ninth Day of the Sixth Moon, Year 841

Sleep eventually took hold, and something hard eventually prodded Lian, startling him awake from jumbled dreams.

Lian squinted in the bright daylight at the feathered faces of three Taijirin. One man clung to Lian's raft while the other two hovered in the air just behind him. Their wings flapped loudly to keep them afloat, a sound that Lian was surprised hadn't woken him. He must have been truly exhausted.

He was *still* exhausted, even though he must have slept for at least half a day. A night spent crammed into a barrel explained the anguish he felt in his neck and back, on top of which his shoulder wounds throbbed, and the cut on his hand smarted terribly. It took a moment for Lian to realize that he'd been woken with the blunt end of a club, and the Taijirin staring down at him with dark eyes seemed less concerned than benumbed as they tested whether their discovery was alive or dead.

The Taijirin who perched atop Lian's raft now raised his head and spoke to his comrades in the Taijirish tongue without looking back at him.

"Please," Lian said rawly through a parched throat. "Do you have any water?"

All three fell silent and stared at him.

"Can you understand me?" he asked. He wasn't sure whether they could speak the language of land dwellers. As he struggled to lift himself out of the barrel, the Taijirin on board pointed his weapon at Lian's chest and spoke harsh words that were surely an order.

"Stay down," translated another gruffly.

Lian obeyed reluctantly. He didn't like the way the Taijirin looked at him. Had he just been plunged into even worse danger than he had escaped?

The vogelfolk who had spoken Lian's tongue wore a bronze breastplate, arm and leg armor, decorated boots, and close-fitting clothing. Since his attendants wore simple leather harnesses, it seemed he was the leader of their small group. His armor and weapons indicated that these weren't just any Taijirin fighters but soldiers of an island kingdom.

The leader gave his attendant an order, and the man loosened the waterskin from his belt and tossed it to Lian. Gratefully, Lian held the pouch to his cracked lips. The water tasted so cool and refreshing that Lian would have been happy to empty the whole thing, but he was well aware of the soldiers' weapons and grim demeanors. He drank only three swigs, then handed the pouch back, but the Taijirin who had thrown it to him only shook his head and said something sounding like a refusal.

Lian didn't dispute the offer. He quickly swallowed a few more gulps before closing the pouch and laying it on his lap.

After his experience in Shiartris, Lian was elated at the idea of visiting another crown colony, especially if it meant an end to his uncomfortable raft journey. However, he also was reminded of all the stories of hostile Taijirin that he'd heard in Skargakar.

"Forgive me," Lian said, and he turned toward the leader in bronze armor. "Are you here to rescue me, or for another reason?"

"Others will decide that," the Taijirin replied. "We will take you to Vindirion. The council will decide your fate."

"I'm a castaway from a drachenjäger ship, the *Carryola*," Lian pressed. "Please, allow me the chance to search for my ship."

"You don't make requests," answered the Taijirin. At a brief order, the man nearest to Lian jumped off the barrels with a beat of his wings. He and the second soldier gripped the ropes that connected the barrels to the sail filled with loose kyrillian and began to pull the vessel.

Resigned, Lian's head sank against the wall of his barrel. There was no other choice but to wait. He couldn't escape the Taijirin and remain atop his raft. If he tried to jump ship and somehow managed to grab some kyrillian, he risked the possibility that the men would decide to kill him on the spot.

By the time they reached Vindirion, the sun had passed well over its zenith. Unlike Shiartris, the Taijirin had not built the city atop lithos but rather on top of the inhospitable summits of three massive mountains, with jagged peaks jutting through the clouds. This city was also considerably larger. Lian's gaze fell on a splendid array of stone structures, with balconies and archways, and an especially forbidding tower dominating their center. Here, the soldiers protected their city from all enemies, whether dragon, pirates, or hostile members of their own folk.

Surprisingly, Lian also recognized street traffic. Either residents moved through this colony on foot more frequently, or they accommodated advantageous trade deals more often than one would think. As Lian's raft drew closer and observers turned their gazes toward him, he saw that the answer lay somewhere in the middle. The city not only contained Taijirin moving as expected between the structures from all levels but also numerous skyships moored to the jetties underneath the lookout towers.

Lian's eyes widened promptly when he saw a ship he recognized. "The *Carryola*!" he called and pointed toward the imposing jäger schooner roped some distance away. "My ship! Please, take me to Captain Adaron. You'll surely be rewarded for your help."

"Silence!" the Taijirin leader snapped. "No more orders from you, plucked bird. We are taking you to the tower, where the council will decide the rest."

"But you can't," begged Lian. "That is my ship! The *Carryola*! . . .

Hey!" He waved his arms in an effort to catch his crew's attention, but the ship was too far away for the men to notice him.

One of the soldiers pointed the scythe on the other end of his club at Lian's throat. He spat a threat that Lian could not understand, though its meaning was very clear.

Furious, Lian went silent and sank back into the barrel. He continued to watch the *Carryola*, the only home he knew. The men, tiny from such a distance, climbed along the rigging amid tattered sails. The storm and battle against the raptors had clearly shaken Adaron's pride, likely the reason why the captain had docked again so shortly after their visit to Shiartris.

The fortress proved to be a massive collection of walls and towers that stood along the rock wall just below the peak of the highest and steepest mountainside. Atop the mountain itself, another imposing building stretched upward, its rounded balconies decorated by pillars. *This must be the court center of Vindirion*, Lian assumed—where they would decide his fate.

He hoped he could return to the *Carryola*. Why would the Taijirin want to hold him prisoner?

His hopes sank when he saw a large group of chained captives, both Nondurier and human, led by more Taijirin along a street toward the tower. Dragging tools at their sides, the prisoners looked completely exhausted. *Slaves! The Taijirin use slaves*, he realized.

He wouldn't end up that way. He couldn't. He hadn't battled his way back from the depths of the Cloudmere to live out the rest of his life as a captive. Frantically, he racked his brain to come up with an escape plan, resisting the urge to lunge for the crystal casing and jump overboard.

Not so fast, he reminded himself. His future still wasn't decided. Maybe Captain Adaron could still save him. Sure, the captain wouldn't have any reason to do so—he thought that Lian had been killed in the storm. *I have to get a message to him somehow.*

They landed on the flat roof of the main building, surrounded by stone peaks. Large ballistae lined the roof's sides, aimed toward the empty sky to fend off dragon attacks, most likely. The weapons wouldn't be much help against attack from ships or hostile Taijirin.

"Out," the deputy ordered, and when Lian didn't move quickly enough, a soldier helped with a gruff swing of his hand, knocking the dagger from

Lian's belt and into the barrel. The other soldier clapped the case shut, and it fell to the ground. He then removed a few loose crystals from the sail and positioned the rest to anchor the raft.

The soldiers led Lian across the tower's roof and along a defense wall until they reached an entranceway. A long staircase descended deep into the bowels of the fortress, where high, wide corridors differed from the cramped hallways in the lodgings that Lian knew. *The extravagant architecture must allow for the Taijirin's wingspan.* Even in a fortress, usually a completely secure structure, large windows and open areas granted access to the sky above. Since Lian saw nothing but dizzyingly steep rock faces below, he thought twice before jumping for freedom.

They reached a heavy iron gate that opened into another passageway. The corridor ended in darkness. Was this the dungeon? Or the slaves' sleeping quarters? Either way, Lian didn't want to stay any longer than necessary. The soldiers pushed him into a small entranceway behind the gate and past the unattended table and stool for the guard. Across the room, small cells with barred gates lined both sides of the sloping walkway.

Nothing stirred, though Lian's eyes hadn't yet adjusted to the darkness. It was difficult to make out what might lurk in the dark corners of the chambers.

A man approached—a Nondurier, to Lian's surprise. He wore coarse leather clothing and a leather patch that concealed his left eye. A whip and a large set of keys hung from the belt at his waist.

"A new one?" he growled, surveying Lian with his good eye.

"Yes," the deputy answered. "Lock him up until the council decides what should happen to him."

The guard nodded and unlocked the nearest cell. The soldiers flung Lian inside, where he fell to the ground, crying out as he landed on his injured shoulder. Turning over, he glared at his tormentors.

The Taijirin gave him a final snide glance and turned to leave.

"Wait!" Lian called. "The *Carryola*! Please, tell Captain Adaron that I'm here. He'll buy my freedom, I'm sure of it. Please!"

The Taijirin had already forgotten him. The Nondurier, too, only glanced briefly through the bars as he locked the gate, paying no more mind to Lian's pleading than the Taijirin had.

He slouched, defeated, and cursed under his breath. If the Taijirin tried to enslave him or eat him—he'd heard stories in Skargakar's taverns—his situation would be just as bad as if he'd stayed on the Cloudmere floor. He had to escape. But how?

He scanned the cell—empty. Not even any straw or dried corn husks were stacked on the floor, probably because field wares were a luxury here in the mountains and not something to waste on prisoners.

A sliver of daylight fell through a small opening near the ceiling, just below the roof. The hole, a poor excuse for a window, allowed a merciful stream of fresh air and warmth into the cold stone room. On the floor near the far wall, Lian spotted a hole where he could relieve himself when needed, but as escapes, both the piss hole and window were too small. The locked gate offered the only chance at freedom, but it didn't give the impression that it would bend if he rattled the bars. *I'm stuck here,* he confirmed gloomily.

Above his head, the weak shimmering of a single floating kyrillian crystal caught his eye. At first, he wondered what the carved stone could be doing there, but then he remembered that he had stuffed a crystal into his jacket pocket as he'd fended off the monsters at the bottom of the Cloudmere. Lian patted his sides and confirmed that his pockets were empty. The crystal must have flown out when the guards threw him into the cell.

He looked up at the magic stone resentfully. A handful of them might help him escape, assuming he managed to break through the gate and found a larger window, but a single stone was useless.

He heard steps in the hallway. A bedraggled human boy appeared before the gate. He was thin—smaller than Lian—with short, straggly brown hair. His old, knee-length shirt and britches were ripped and covered in filth. The lad couldn't have been much older than thirteen or fourteen to Lian's eye. The tray the boy carried, however, was far more interesting to Lian than the boy himself, for atop the tray, the boy balanced a jug of water and a small bowl of what smelled like roasted dragon meat.

"I'm to bring you food and drink," the boy said timidly.

Lian stood and approached the gate. The boy eyed him shyly, then lifted the jug from the tray and handed it through the bars. Crouching down, he pushed the tray with the bowl underneath the gate. Lian's stomach grumbled, and he dropped to his knees and began to eat. The meat was strangely spiced, but it tasted wonderful. At least the Taijirin saw the worth in keeping their slaves from starving.

The boy remained at the door and watched Lian curiously. *Maybe he can help me,* Lian considered. "What's your name?" he asked through a full mouth.

"Kris," the boy answered.

"Do you live here of your own accord, or are you a . . ." Lian lowered his voice. "Are you a slave?"

Kris nodded, appearing to consider how to answer. "The Taijirin took me a year ago. I was with my father aboard a merchant ship when pirates attacked us. They killed everyone—except for me, because I hid. Then the pirates set fire to the ship. I would have died, but some Taijirin found and saved me." His expression turned dark as he remembered his horrible past.

Lian lowered his next piece of meat. "By the Winds . . . I'm sorry."

Kris shrugged his narrow shoulders and looked at the floor. "Nothing to do about it now," he said softly.

For a moment, both remained silent. Even though Lian was hungry, he thought it insensitive to continue eating, so he set his bowl to the side and approached the gate, ushering Kris closer. "Tell me, are you able to move freely through the city?"

The boy nodded but then shook his head. "I can go to the market and the trading quarter, but not to the harbor. If the soldiers find me there, they'll . . . punish me. And there are a lot of soldiers there."

Lian cursed under his breath. He'd been afraid of that. The Taijirin kept close watch over their slaves.

"Why?" Kris asked.

"There's a ship at the pier, the *Carryola,* a giant jäger ship. You'd know it if you saw it."

"Yes, I saw it as it approached. It looked like it had been through a storm."

"That's right. I'm part of its crew. I went overboard in that storm."

"Overboard?" Kris's eyes widened in disbelief. "How are you still alive?"

"That's a long story that will have to wait. Right now, this is more important: Captain Adaron and the others don't know that I'm still alive or that I'm here. Do you think you could get a message to them somehow?"

Kris eyed Lian unsurely. "I don't know. Why should I risk my neck for you?"

Lian didn't have a decent answer to that very reasonable question. He didn't know what Kris would consider a good enough reason. The only thing he could offer was a chance—a chance with an outcome he couldn't guarantee. *But I have no other choice*, he decided.

"If you pass on my message, you can come with me when I get out of here."

Kris looked at him in disbelief. "How would you manage that?"

Lian looked at the boy earnestly. "I'm a dragon jäger, one of the most important members of the crew. When Captain Adaron comes to my aid, I'll make sure that both you and I are freed."

Kris's expression lit up, which sent a pang through Lian's gut. He saw the boy's doubtful longing to leave his prison, mixed with the fear of being disappointed and left behind by Lian.

I swear to you that I'll try to save you, Lian promised the boy silently.

"All right, then," Kris said finally, after considering for a long while. "I'll do it. What message should I give?"

21

Held Hostage

Tenth Day of the Sixth Moon, Year 841

The wait was long. The following morning, the one-eyed Nondurier returned, accompanied by a Taijirin soldier, and unlocked the gate to Lian's cell. "Follow him," the Nondurier growled and nodded toward the silent warrior.

"Where to?" Lian asked as though he had any say in the matter.

"Does it look like they would tell me anything?" sulked the Nondurier. "You might try asking him, but I doubt he'll answer. He can't speak your tongue."

The soldier tapped the watchman's shoulder and spat either a reproach or a demand, to which the Nondurier bowed his head and stepped aside. Impatiently, the winged man waved Lian toward him while his other hand gripped the handle of his dagger.

Lian obeyed the order. The Nondurier stood in front of him and pulled a pair of metal shackles from his belt. "A minor precaution," he explained as he closed the shackles around Lian's wrists. "We wouldn't want you to have the foolish idea to attack anyone. They throw humans into the depths from the mountaintop as penalty."

"I'd rather avoid that," Lian answered. "I've just returned from the Cloudmere floor."

The watchman's baffled face lightened considerably as he stepped aside, and the soldier led Lian along the passageway.

A second solder awaited them at the dungeon's exit, and together, the three of them crossed the length of the dungeon. Lian tried to ask his new escort where they were headed, but the soldier was no more talkative than the first. Not for the first time during his journey, Lian regretted never having learned at least a little Taijirish. If he ever made it back to the *Carryola,* he would make sure to pick up some phrases from Ialrist. *Not that he's a man of many words, either,* Lian thought.

Outside, they crossed a narrow courtyard and entered the main structure, its entrance decorated in elaborate crests of various vultures and dragons. They ascended a wide stairway until they reached a massive door, where two watchmen in bronze armor stood at attention. Lian's second escort instructed him to stand still, and he gripped Lian's shoulder harshly. Glaring through hateful yellow eyes, he hissed, "You'll show respect when you stand before the commander, plucked bird. Otherwise, you'll regret it."

Lian's heart rate quickened. Captain Adaron must have spoken to the leaders of the city if they were bringing him before the commander. Would he be set free? He could barely dare to hope.

"Understood?" the soldier asked impatiently.

"Yes," Lian answered hurriedly.

His escort nodded, then approached the door and knocked. The watchmen barely acknowledged him.

"Enter!" a voice called from inside.

The soldier pushed the door open and dragged Lian across the threshold with the help of his comrade. An enormous Taijirin sat behind a heavy wooden table stacked with scrolls of parchment. He wore golden armor, with a wide red sash across his breast.

Two visitors already stood before the table, one dressed all in black and the other another Taijirin.

"Captain!" Lian cried. "Ialrist! It's so good to see you both!"

"Respect, I said," hissed the soldier behind him, striking the back of Lian's head.

Lian stood rigid and raised his glance to the giant Taijirin before bowing humbly. "Commander," he said.

The man behind the table snorted under his breath and turned toward Adaron.

"Is this your man, Captain?"

"Yes, Commander Shiraik," Adaron confirmed. He glanced at Lian, and an odd perplexity passed across his somber face. "Though I can barely think it possible that anyone abducted by a raptor in a storm could ever return."

"If only you knew what it took—" Lian answered.

"That's nice, and you can tell it all when you're back on board your ship," Commander Shiraik cut in.

Pleasantly surprised, Lian turned to face the Taijirin. "Am I released, then?"

"You can go." Shiraik's mouth curled into a sinister grin. "Once your captain pays a ransom in the amount of six hundred kyrillian crystals."

"What?" Lian asked, startled. The amount was downright outlandish. Six hundred crystals made up a small fortune.

Adaron and Ialrist seemed to share Lian's opinion. "Why not just ask for a drachen pearl or two," said Ialrist. "It would be just as bold."

Shiraik's expression hardened. "Vindirion Taijirin rescued him adrift the Cloudmere. His death was certain, and thus his life belongs to us. He is young and strong and could work off his debt to us for years to come. And most of all, if he is blessed by the Illuminated Wings with the ability to defy storm and beast, he is especially valuable to us."

"You know full well that no captain would pay that number of crystals for one man," Adaron growled. "Why did you even bother to grant us an audience? Have you nothing better to do than feast on others' pain?"

"Maybe not," answered Shiraik. "But I assumed his freedom would be worth any sum to you. Anyway, you're the one who begged for an audience. You wouldn't make that effort with just any jäger, would you, Captain?"

"What are you implying?" Adaron asked angrily.

"Oh, your reputation precedes you. Captain Adaron—the man on the hunt for Gargantuan, at any sacrifice. Tell me, how many men has your hunt already cost? Has it been worth it?"

"You know nothing about me," spat the captain. He stepped forward, and the two guards at Lian's sides stood alert.

Shiraik held up a hand and smiled fearlessly at Adaron. "I know a great deal about what happens on the Cloudmere, but I do wonder one thing." His vulture eyes narrowed as he studied Lian. "How did you know that your man was here if you thought he was dead? Who gave him away?"

"No one," Ialrist answered hurriedly. "I saw when he arrived and informed the captain. My eyesight is sharp—as you should surely know."

Shiraik shook his head. "All respect, Prince Ialrist, but I don't believe you. If you had spotted his arrival, you wouldn't have waited an entire night before contacting me. You couldn't have known which fate he would endure. No, someone told you. But who? That would interest me greatly, because it means that either I can't trust one of my own soldiers or that a slave dared to enter the harbor, which is strictly forbidden."

"I don't see the reason to divulge anything more than necessary," answered Adaron.

"How about a trade?" asked Shiraik. "Your man for the life of the traitor."

The captain raised an eyebrow. "That would be a shockingly reasonable price, Commander. You were right about one thing. I'm prepared to make sacrifices to reach a goal."

"No!" Lian cried. It cost him all his strength to reject an offer for his freedom, but he refused to throw Kris onto the chopping block. The boy had risked everything for him. He couldn't stab him in the back now.

"Don't tell the commander anything, Captain," Lian pleaded. "I've already watched one friend die during this journey. There can't be another brought to death on my account."

Shiraik sighed with contentment. "Ah, such a gentle soul. Offers his life for someone he's only known for one day." He raised an admonishing finger. "Believe me, Captain. For this young man, six hundred kyrillian crystals is by no means too high of a price."

"I won't be gouged by you," Adaron answered quietly. "Not like this." He turned to Lian. "I'm sorry, but I can't put up a sum that high. I'll leave the decision to you. You can buy your freedom with the life of a stranger. If you decide against it, we'll leave you here. I'm sorry to lose you—you could become a great slayer—but *I* won't make another attempt to free you. That must be clear."

Lian couldn't think how to respond. His thoughts rushed like winter winds through his head. He longed to leave Vindirion and wanted to escape his fate as a slave under the wings of the Taijirin as readily as a hare looked to escape an eagle. However, betraying Kris would be a betrayal to himself, too. He would never sleep again without remembering the nightmare of a weedy boy gutted by a cackling Shiraik.

With a long inhale, Lian stood straight. "Forgive me, Captain, for the unnecessary fortress visit. I cannot buy my own life with the life of another. I will remain captive to the Taijirin." He shot a scowl toward Shiraik. "For now."

The commander nodded in satisfaction. "A speech fit for a hero. Very good. I almost wish that you were one of us. Your selflessness and your will to combat would make you a splendid soldier." His expression hardened, and he looked to the guards. "Take him away."

"Captain!" Lian called as the guard dragged him away by the arms. "Give Ialrist my spear. And tell Hanon'ka that I'm sorry I had to end the life that he fought to save in this way."

Adaron and Ialrist regarded him in silence. The captain's expression didn't stir, though his eyes burned with a fiery scorn. Whether he was angry because Shiraik had humiliated him or because he considered Lian's decision foolish, Lian couldn't say. Ialrist, on the other hand, seethed with fury as though not far off from initiating a fight with Shiraik and his guards, but he controlled himself.

The commander had called him *prince*, Lian remembered. He would have loved to know why.

I'll never find out now, he thought with remorse as the two soldiers dragged him out of the room and the heavy door banged shut behind him.

Soon after, the gate to his cell locked behind him, too. Lian sank defeated to the floor against the far wall. He leaned his head against the cool stone and sighed. "Am I a hero or a fool?" he murmured, but the walls didn't respond.

The day dragged on. The Taijirin apparently didn't intend to let Lian out of his cell to do any sort of labor while the *Carryola* still docked at harbor. The danger was too great that he would try to flee. Instead, he sat on the floor and watched the light wander over the stone as the sun passed across the sky.

Every so often, the Nondurier guard brought food and fresh water. "As I see it, your morning outing didn't much improve your situation," he said flatly.

"No," Lian answered, dejected. "But I don't know if that was ever possible." He took his tray from underneath the gate. "These Taijirin are spiteful. How can you work for them?"

The Nondurier smiled weakly. "My life was a lot worse before," he said, and he left.

Shortly after, he returned with a Taijirin soldier—and Kris. The gate opened, and the soldier threw the boy into the cell with Lian. "There, go to your friend," growled the Taijirin. "He'll keep you company until the commander decides what to do with you."

"Ow!" Kris cried as he fell. He struggled to his feet and glared at his tormentor. "I'm innocent! I've done nothing wrong."

"Tell it to the commander, not to me," the soldier spat. "But I doubt he'll listen." He laughed as the gate slammed shut once more, and both men disappeared down the hallway.

Kris knelt, propped his elbows onto his bent knees, and buried his face into his arms. Lian heard a faint sniffling from his side of the cell.

Slowly, Lian approached him. "Are you okay?" he asked quietly.

For a moment, there came no answer. Then Kris raised his head. His eyes were red, and his cheeks were slick with tears. He wiped a hand across his face. "No, of course not. What a stupid question."

"You're right. I'm sorry." Lian crouched beside the boy and set a hand on his narrow shoulder.

Kris shook the hand away. "Leave me alone."

Lian raised his hands in defense. "Whatever you say," he said. He returned to his place at the wall, where he lowered himself down and watched the boy, who stared at the barred door as tears of despair continued to fall down his cheeks.

He felt truly sorry for Kris. The boy had risked his life for Lian and, as it appeared, had lost the gamble. Lian had sacrificed his own life to protect Kris. Not only would he live out the rest of his days as a slave to the Taijirin, his noble act had also been for nothing. He wondered if the commander had known of Kris's guilt even before the meeting that morning and if he had only held the hearing to watch the outsiders squirm. *What a deceitful bastard!*

After a long silence, Lian turned to Kris. "What went wrong? How did they discover you?"

"Nothing went wrong," the boy answered, his tears now dried. "I was a shadow in the night." He looked at Lian resentfully. "But nobody except for Gunjal and I ever visited you. Nobody except for us and a few soldiers even knew you were here."

"Gunjal is the Nondurier?"

Kris nodded. "Gunjal would never do anything for a prisoner. He is happy, even though he sits in this dungeon just like the rest of us, just on the other side of the gate."

"So the commander blamed you."

Kris nodded again. "I guess so. Did your captain have to run to the commander right away? He could have at least thought of a decent excuse for why he knew about your arrival."

"They had one that actually wasn't too bad," answered Lian. "But I think that Shiraik already knew by then. He was toying with us. Maybe that's even why he assigned you to bring me food in the first place."

"Who knows?" Kris's head sank onto his arms. "I just hope that he doesn't dangle me into the clouds again."

"Is that the punishment?"

Kris nodded. "The last time I tried to escape, I was locked in a cage for three days and lowered at least three hundred paces into the clouds. I nearly froze. There are . . . things . . . out there in the fog. I don't exactly know what, but something flew around the cage for the whole second night. I heard the rustle of wings and felt strong gusts of wind from something gigantic passing by. It was terrifying."

"I believe it," Lian said, but he didn't tell of his own horrible encounters. Instead, he asked, "Do the Taijirin ever kill slaves for misdeeds?"

"I've never heard of that happening," Kris said, looking up. "Not for attempted escape, at least; otherwise, I'd already have been killed three times, but if you attack or kill a Taijirin, you could be thrown from the cliff side."

"I don't plan on that," said Lian. "I just want one thing: to get out of here." He feared that many winds would blow across the Cloudmere before that time came.

For now, he was trapped. Adaron had made it clear that he wasn't ready to incite the Taijirin's anger by helping him escape. Even if he wasn't happy about it, Lian could understand the captain's position. Lian was only one man. The captain had to think of the entire crew—not to mention, he needed Taijirin favor to continue receiving notice of Black Leviathan sightings. With a heavy sigh, Lian sank his head onto the cold, hard stone floor and closed his eyes. He was completely and utterly at the Taijirin's mercy.

22

Unexpected Help

Eleventh Day of the Sixth Moon, Year 841

Lian and Kris spent the next two days in their cell and received food and water three times a day. On the evening of the second day, a new person appeared to remove their trays. The slave, who was raggedly dressed and silent, carried a pail of water. Lian used the opportunity to clean the wounds on his shoulders. To his relief, they seemed to be healing relatively well. They weren't infected, at least, and only smarted when touched directly.

Kris glanced agog at the strange gashes on Lian's bare upper body as he rinsed his own face and hands. "What kind of cuts are those?" he asked. "They look like claw marks."

"I had an encounter with a raptor," Lian answered.

"And? Did you kill it?"

"No, it carried me away from my ship."

Kris's eyes widened. "A raptor . . . snatched you?"

"Yep, that's how I went overboard."

"The *Carryola*," Kris said, nodding. "You said you would tell me the story."

Lian pulled his shirt back over his head and brushed dripping hair away from his forehead. "Right. It's a long story, but I suppose we have time for it now." He found a dry spot on the floor and sat down next to Kris. Then he began to describe the inconceivable experiences that had led him to Vindirion.

Kris listened with growing astonishment—and increasing skepticism. Once Lian had finished, the boy shook his head. "Giant mushrooms, wet stones that you can squeeze with a hand, and monsters worse than living death . . . that's unbelievable."

"And yet it's all true," Lian answered. "Why should I lie? We're not competing jägers spinning tales in a tavern over pints of herb ale."

"You're right," Kris said, shivering. "But I get a chill just thinking about it. I would have died from fear."

Lian grinned. "Believe me, I was sure my life was over. It's still a wonder to me that I escaped." He looked around the cell and sighed. "But a mocking Western Wind blew me from one terror straight into the next, and I don't dare to hope for a second miracle to free us this time."

Just then, a cloth bundle fell through the small opening above their heads and landed with a thud onto the floor. Lian looked up but only saw a shadow move away from the window and disappear into the twilight. "What in the . . . ?" he said, startled.

Kris arrived at the bundle first and, crouching, shoved its contents into the shadows. Glancing furtively at the gate, he placed a finger over his lips.

Lian understood the cue and nodded. They couldn't raise any suspicions. He stood cautiously and moved to the bars separating them from the passageway. Nothing stirred. Whatever Gunjal was doing, he paid no attention to his prisoners for the moment.

He turned back to Kris. "What is it?" he whispered.

Kris pulled the bundle forward and, after a moment's hesitation, untied the strand of twine that fastened it. As he unwrapped the cloth, Lian recognized the thick weave of sail canvas. *That could be from the* Carryola. Had Ialrist been their secret visitor? Lian glanced once more toward the cell window. Nobody besides a Taijirin could reach it from the outside.

Inside the bundle, they discovered Lian's crumpled harness and a thin metal wand, ending on one side in a bunch of keys and on the other in various hooks and prongs. "What is it?" Kris breathed, first eyeing the harness.

Excitement gripped Lian. "A harness from the *Carryola*," he whispered. He pointed to the metal cases hanging from both sides of the wide leather belt underneath two crossed straps. "You can fly with it."

"Fly?" Kris repeated in disbelief.

"Yes. There's kyrillian inside the cases." Lian showed him carefully. With a smile, he ran a hand over the harness. "If we can just get to a mountain peak or roof, we can use it to lift up into the sky."

"And to get out of this cell, we have this," Kris said, and he held up the metal wand. "It's a locksmith's tools, isn't it?"

"I think so," Lian answered. "We should be able to unlock the gate with it—with the right skill."

"And do you have that skill?" Kris asked, eyeing Lian.

"I don't know," he admitted. "I worked as a crystal carver before joining the *Carryola*. We used similar tools. I guess my crewmates think I can figure this out, too."

As he pushed the harness away, Lian noticed a gray-green shard of horn underneath—the piece of the swingblade's tail that Adaron had given him. Someone had wound a piece of rope around a leather strap into a sort of handle. *A makeshift dagger,* he realized. *Light, easy to hide, and fatally sharp.*

Finally, Lian noticed a piece of parchment folded within the scrap of canvas. Unfolding it, he read the message: WE SAIL AT DAWN. IF YOU'RE ON BOARD THEN, WE'LL TAKE YOU WITH US. H.

"Hanon'ka," murmured Lian.

"What does that mean?" asked Kris.

Lian turned to the boy. "It means that two of the most important men on board the *Carryola* are helping us break out of here." He remembered how Adaron had formulated his parting words. *I'm sorry to lose you—you could become a great slayer—but I won't make another attempt to free you.* Had he purposely said *I* instead of *we* to give the crew an opportunity to free Lian? Or was Adaron unaware of the Sidhari's and the Taijirin's mission?

"We?" asked Kris hopefully. "Does that mean that you'll really take me with you?"

Lian hesitated, thinking carefully. The message only referred to him. Neither Hanon'ka nor Ialrist knew about his cell mate. On the other hand, he'd promised to do everything possible to take Kris along. Adaron might very well be unwelcoming to a new passenger, but he wouldn't throw him overboard, either—at least not until they reached the next port. Lian hoped so, at least.

"Yes," he said finally. "We'll go together. Neither of us could make it alone. I can get us out of this cell and on board the *Carryola*, but you know the way out of the fortress. We need each other."

Kris beamed. "That's fine," he said, then turned quickly away as though the sudden show of joy made him uncomfortable.

He seems so young, Lian thought. Maybe it was just because he had all too recently lost his best friend, but a protective instinct surged in him unlike anything he'd ever felt before. *You will live and be free,* he promised Kris silently. *I'll make sure of it.*

They waited until night fell over Vindirion. Gunjal made his final rounds and left the dungeon, his considerable jaws opening in a wide yawn. As Kris described, a Taijirin soldier would take his place at the entranceway, and another would replace him at midnight. Since he had been captured, Lian hadn't seen the night guards, who didn't pass the front section of the dungeon and never bothered to go to the trouble of making rounds.

"No one suspects a breakout," Kris whispered. "This part of the dungeon only holds foreigners—humans, Drak, or Nondurier. There are almost never any escapes. Where could they even go without wings?"

"It's fine by me if they don't pay any attention to us," Lian answered. "It will make our escape easier."

"But how can we get past the watchman?" Kris asked, scanning the passageway. "If he sounds the alarm, we won't even make it a hundred paces."

Lian considered their options. "Maybe there's some sort of trick," he said finally.

His plan wasn't perfect, but they had no other choice but to risk it. He outlined the details hurriedly, and when the boy didn't have any better ideas, they set to work.

Soon after, a piercing cry sounded into the shadowed hallway. The cry came from Kris, who writhed and whimpered on the floor.

"Hey!" Lian called from the gate. "Watchman, come here! This boy is sick."

He made the call a second time before footsteps neared their cell, and a Taijirin solider peered through the bars in the flickering light of an oil lamp that hung nearby.

Lian backed up a few steps. "Look," he said, pointing toward Kris. "The dragon meat must have been rancid this evening. He needs a healer."

The soldier neared the bars, disinterested. "You don't actually believe I'll fall for this trick," he said with his singsong accent. "You just want me to open the gate, so that you—"

Just then, Lian slammed against the gate, which he had unlocked earlier, and the door flew open and bashed into the Taijirin's face. The man stumbled backward, crashing into the opposite wall, while Lian slipped past him and turned to face his opponent. He grabbed the man's collar and held the point of his swingblade dagger against the Taijirin's throat. "Nice and calm," he hissed to the winged man. "I don't want to hear a peep out of you, understood? If so, you're dead."

The soldier eyed the jagged blade in Lian's hand warily. "You'll regret this, plucked bird!" he sputtered.

"Maybe so. But you won't enjoy the moment for long if you don't stay quiet."

Kris darted to Lian's side and scanned the entranceway to make sure nothing stirred. Then Lian pulled the Taijirin into their cell while Kris seized his weapons. "See if you can find any chains or rope to secure him," Lian said.

"Right," Kris answered, and he hurried away.

"What are you trying to achieve?" the soldier asked. "You're crazy if you think you'll ever make it out of this fortress."

"That's *my* worry, not yours," answered Lian. "One thing is clear. Accepting a life in captivity is far crazier, and you're about to find out exactly how that feels."

Kris returned with a few sets of shackles, and together they bound the Taijirin and stuck a torn-off piece of his shirt into his mouth so that he couldn't cry for help. Then Lian stuffed the swingblade shard and lock pick into his bag and fastened his harness so that he had both hands free.

Finally, he stuffed the soldier's short sword and ring of keys into his belt. The Taijirin observed him in silent scorn.

"Don't worry," he said to the soldier as he and Kris backed out of the cell. "You'll be freed soon enough." With these final words, the gate fell shut.

When Lian turned, he saw the shriveled face of a Drak who had watched the whole thing in silence from his cell. The key ring at Lian's side held the attention of his dark eyes. He reached a clawed hand longingly through the bars, and two more Drak appeared from the shadows behind him.

Lian nodded slowly. "Give us a bit of headway," he said. "It's better if we all stay on our own."

The Drak nodded his spike-covered head.

Lian turned to Kris. "Do you know which key opens the gate at the entrance?"

The boy pointed to a large key in the bunch. "That one," he said.

"Okay, then." Quickly, Lian removed the single key from the ring and reached the rest of the keys through the bars to the awaiting Drak. "Good luck," he said, and he turned back toward Kris. "Come on."

They slipped forward to the guard table, which—to Lian's relief—was unoccupied, with no second guard to complicate their escape. Lian carefully unlocked the dungeon gate, and he and Kris hurried down the pathway until they reached a larger passage. "Now you take over," he whispered to Kris. "We have to make it out of here without being noticed. It would be best to find a place where the building juts into the sky so that we can fall into the air and not slam straight into the mountainside."

Kris nodded. "I think I know just the place. It's a bit . . . uncomfortable, but it's not far." Huddling low, the boy set off to the right and down a wide corridor, and Lian followed. Luckily, it was so late that no one else appeared. After only a few paces, they reached a wide circular staircase leading upward. "This way," Kris whispered.

Once again, the size and grandeur of the fortress astonished Lian. Even the most inconsequential staircase—Lian doubted that Kris was leading them into the commander's receiving chamber—had a spaciousness that would make any "plucked bird" gasp at its extravagance. Along

the walls, paintings hung at regular intervals, depicting Taijirin-like figures whose wings seemed made of pure light and whose bodies were
illuminated as though from the sun's rays. Kneeling at the feet of these
holy beings were ordinary Taijirin, who raised up chalices, swords, and
axes as though in sacrifice.

"What is this?" Lian asked. "A temple?

The boy glanced over his shoulder, confused. "What makes you think
that?" he asked.

"The pictures," Lian explained, motioning toward the walls.

"Oh," Kris said, and he grimaced. "Not quite. The pictures show
how the Illuminated Wings govern the mortals. They are meant to remind
the condemned that their true judgment awaits them after death."

"Death?"

"Yes, we're going to the execution chamber."

Now Lian looked uneasy. "Not exactly encouraging . . ."

"Hey, you wanted somewhere to fall freely into the sky," hissed
Kris. "The execution chamber leads directly into the clouds."

Lian wondered why the Taijirin would condemn a criminal to the air
when most prisoners were able to fly. He received his gruesome answer
once they passed through a door and stepped onto a stone landing at the
edge of the fortress wall. Jagged stone crenellations lined the landing. A
few dozen paces away, two watchmen stood, their attention directed out-
ward to the city, as one man pointed out something to the other that happened far below. At the far end of the small plateau, Lian spotted a stone
pedestal extending beyond the edge to jut into the gaping sky. Beside the
pedestal, he saw what resembled a narrow wooden butcher's block on a
balcony. While the torches lining the stone wall didn't reveal much, Lian
thought he saw dark stains spattering the wood as they passed by.

"Do they chop off criminals' wings before throwing them into the
depths?" he whispered.

"Not all of them," answered Kris. "Most of them are just tied up. They
only take wings for the most heinous crimes. Those souls will spend eternity with the disgrace of stumps on their backs, unable to fly in the afterlife."

Lian cringed. The justice of the Taijirin seemed barbaric to him. *On
the other hand, it's no worse than what we humans do,* he thought. *We also
let the guilty fall, and sometimes even the innocent.*

They hid behind the platform and scanned the guards' walkway and fortress towers. It didn't appear that anyone kept an eye on the execution chamber. Lian wasn't surprised—who would choose to be reminded of such a gruesome place?

Carefully, he tested the harness across his chest, which raised him into the air, exactly as it should. "Climb onto my back," he then instructed Kris. "We'll try it together now. Better hook your arms under the belt so that I can't lose you."

"Okay," Kris said, and he climbed onto Lian's back with a quiet groan. When they heard cries from below, followed by quick steps, the two soldiers took off into the sky above.

"Damn!" Lian swore, ducking. "They found the watchman." Luckily, the fortress gate held the soldiers' attention. It didn't seem to occur to any of the Taijirin that runaways might jump over the wall.

Quickly, Lian opened the kyrillian cases. He and Kris rose from the floor slowly. Then he clapped the cases shut. "And now let's go! Just hold on tight."

"You can be sure of that," Kris answered, his voice shuddering with fear.

Lian crawled on all fours onto the stone platform. At his feet, he saw only deep darkness. Even the fog that seethed silently below them was indecipherable. He prayed that Kris wasn't wrong. If there were rock fragments underneath them, as there were at Kraghma's Jaws, their fall would be brief.

A Taijirin battle cry startled Lian. Without looking around, he sent a prayer to the Four Winds and stepped over the platform edge.

23

Escape from Vindirion

Eleventh Day of the Sixth Moon, Year 841

They fell like a stone into the depths. Lian gritted his teeth to keep from screaming while Kris clung to his back, first whimpering softly and then going silent. Lian squeezed his eyes shut and counted silently to five. They must have broken through the fleece by then. Then he clicked the cases open, at first just a crack and then, once they had slowed down, the rest of the way. They stopped short in the air. Surrounded by pitch-black nothingness, they hovered between the chasm that gaped underneath them and the Taijirin who hunted them from above.

Lian's heart hammered, and the blood rushed loudly in his ears. Fear washed over him. His stomach cramped as he recalled falling toward his death while the raptor's talons bored through his shoulders, and he gasped softly.

"Lian," Kris whispered. "Is everything okay?"

He shook his head and shoved the fear away. Then he began to feel the harness slowly tug them upward. He wasn't in the raptor's talons anymore. They wouldn't fall into the depths. This time, he was in control of their fate.

"Lian," Kris repeated. His voice squeaked with panic.

"I'm fine," Lian answered softly. "Really. What about you?"

"I'm . . . I'm all right. Please, just get us to the ship quickly."

"I'll do my best," he answered. "Hold on."

With all Lian had learned about kyrillian, it was relatively simple to navigate their ascent. Before long, they broke through the murky fleece and into the open sky. The lanterns of Vindirion lit the clouds as Lian struggled to find his bearings. "Help me, Kris," he said. "Point me toward the harbor."

"Over there," the boy answered. "See the high building with three red fires burning? The harbor is just to the right."

After a short search, Lian found the spot. "Good. Then we just have a little ways to go." He tested whether or not the cases at his sides would propel them forward if he tilted their position. The harness, however, was more flexible than a ship's hull, and they continued to travel upward. At this rate, they would never reach the pier.

Lian cursed under his breath. They would have to try the second, more dangerous option. Treading the air, they drifted back to the edge of the fortress wall and sank down until almost completely concealed by fog. With Kris's weight on his back, he climbed along the stones, trying to avoid using his injured hand. The rush of flapping wings and calls of soldiers sounded from above, but no one came for them.

Slowly, they made their way along the length of the fortress wall and around the side of the mountain toward the harbor below. The work was exhausting. The harness dug into Lian's sides, and Kris's weight pressed against his back. His arm muscles trembled, his hand and shoulder wounds burned, and he shivered in the chilled air as sweat coated his body. Every so often, he used the cases to raise their altitude. Eventually, the soldiers' cries began to fade behind them, until they finally caught sight of the harbor.

"Good thing we didn't wait until after midnight," Lian groaned. "I don't know if I could have handled the sight of the *Carryola* casting off while we were stuck on this mountain."

"Mm," Kris answered weakly.

"Everything all right?" Lian asked.

"I can barely feel my arm, but otherwise . . . ," Kris said through gritted teeth.

"Hold on. We're almost there," Lian coaxed, and he began lowering them to the ground. *I hope so, anyway,* he added to himself.

Finally, they reached the ground. Lian raced past the tethered ships, grateful that the night watchmen were too preoccupied with activity in the air to notice movement on the ground. Dragons and pirates tended to attack from above, and the non-winged prisoners of Vindirion tended not to initiate raids—from what Kris had said.

Lian's heartbeat quickened when he spotted the *Carryola* up ahead, black and forbidding with its heavily armored sides and threatening dragon-skull figurehead. He led them around the ship, careful to remain out of sight from the watchtower. He climbed up the netting at the ship's side and triumphantly grabbed hold of the railing. A dark hand offered itself from the other side, and when he grasped it, Lian and Kris were hauled on board.

"Welcome back," Hanon'ka said. The glimmer of his emerald eyes matched the smile across his lips. "We've been expecting you." He motioned toward Ialrist, who now lowered himself from a rope at the foremast. The Taijirin had tracked their process after all.

"Thanks," gasped Lian. He flipped the cases at his sides shut and sank to the deck, exhausted. Kris loosened himself free and fell moaning onto the planks beside him.

"I see you brought a guest," said Hanon'ka then.

"I did. This is Kris, a slave from the fortress. He helped me escape, and I promised to take him on board."

"That'll be for the captain to decide, but first, we should go below deck. It would be unpleasant for us all if they find you now."

Hanon'ka and Ialrist pulled them to their feet and helped them down the stairs to the canteen. They passed Markaeth, Karnosk, and a young boatman named Cabbyr, who kept watch on deck. All three men stared in amazement. "How is it possible?" Cabbyr murmured. "You went overboard in the midst of a storm. A raptor carried you away into the clouds. Nobody can survive something like that."

"I was lucky," answered Lian.

Markaeth slapped a hand onto Lian's shoulder and grinned. "Don't take it personally. It's a miracle you've returned, but how did you manage it? Did you talk that bloody animal into carrying you back or what?"

"Not exactly," said Lian, grinning.

"You can tell the story later," Hanon'ka said sternly. "First, you have to hide. And you," he said, glancing at the watchmen. "Keep your eyes open in case the Taijirin give us any trouble."

"Aye, Commander," Markaeth said, nodding.

Downstairs, they greeted Smett in the empty canteen. He sat at a table with a mug of ale, busily whittling something that looked like a sort of whistle. Flicc, his bright red lizardwing, accompanied him. At the other side of the table, Lian spotted another mug and an empty wooden bowl.

"I can barely believe it!" the cook said, grinning, and he stood. Flicc squawked and flapped onto the table. "He has returned! You must be favored by the Southern Wind!"

"I really must." Lian laughed. He was relieved to see a friendly face and introduced Kris.

"Ha! Well, then, I'll fetch another bowl and the kettle with the rest of tonight's stew," said the cook. "You must both be hungry."

"I could eat half a dragon," Lian admitted.

Smett chuckled. "There's not very much left, but it should be enough to fill your bellies." He whistled to Flicc, who hopped onto his shoulder, and they disappeared into the galley.

"I'll take back the harness and tools," said Ialrist, "and stow them. Then I'll tell the captain that you've returned."

"Maybe you should wait until we've cast off," Hanon'ka suggested. "He might be angry when he finds out."

The sides of the Taijirin's mouth twitched, then broke into a smile. "Adaron knows exactly what we planned. He isn't oblivious. He doesn't owe a thing to a crook like Shiraik, especially if he can't keep track of his own prisoners."

"How did you manage it?" Lian asked. He pulled the bundle from his coat pocket and set it onto the table.

"You have the commander to thank for that," said Ialrist. "He said it would be a waste to leave you in Vindirion."

"But it was Ialrist who wanted to help you in the first place," corrected Hanon'ka.

Surprised, Lian looked at the Taijirin. He wasn't shocked that Hanon'ka would help him—the Sidhari had already stepped forward more than once on his behalf—but he had always thought Ialrist was indifferent to him.

The slayer shrugged his wings. "I'd just rather see you carry your father's spear yourself. I couldn't use it if I knew you lived in slavery, and I know we'll need the weapon again before this is all over." His heavy gaze conveyed a message that Lian couldn't understand.

"I place myself in your debt," Lian told the man. "I hope that someday I can return the favor."

"I'd rather it didn't come to that," Ialrist said. Then he turned and left the room.

"So now we eat," announced Smett, returning with steaming bowls full of stew. The scent of dragon meat wafted through the room, and Lian's stomach growled with anticipation.

"Eat," ordered Smett with high spirits.

Lian and Kris hurriedly picked up their spoons and ate eagerly. Amid mouthfuls of strongly spiced stew, Lian nearly forgot his exhaustion and the pains in his arms and back. Smett, who sat across from them, grinned as he watched.

Kris, full after only a few bites, studied Flicc. "Is she friendly?" he asked. "She's a shimmercomb, isn't she?"

The cook's bushy eyebrows rose in surprise. "You know your dragons well, my boy. And you're right, yes. This here is Flicc."

"I like dragons," Kris said, and he reached a chunk of meat toward the lizardwing, who stretched her thin neck out to receive the morsel. With a quick snap of her tiny jaws, Flicc snatched the meat out of the boy's fingers.

Smett exchanged a glance with Hanon'ka, who still leaned against the nearby wall and watched them with crossed arms. "You like dragons, eh?" Smett asked.

Kris nodded. "I do. They're so majestic and beautiful." He sighed.

"Well, then, you're on the wrong ship," said the cook. "The *Carryola* is a drachenjäger."

"I know," Kris said, and he scowled, shrugging. "I'm not a dreamer, you know. I understand that our food and clothing, leather, scale armor, and all has to come from somewhere, but that doesn't mean I can't be amazed or have respect for dragons, does it?"

"You speak remarkably wisely for your age," said Hanon'ka.

The boy looked away bashfully. "I don't know. I'm just rambling." He held another piece of meat out to Flicc, and the lizardwing swallowed it with pleasure.

"Don't give her too much, or she won't eat what I put in front of her," Smett grumbled. "The little lady can be a right beast," he said, scratching his stubbled chin. "But she clearly likes you." Flicc took two steps across the table and reached her neck out to Kris, who tickled the spot under the dragon's leathery chin.

"She can tell that I like her, too," the boy said, smiling.

Smett chuckled softly. Then his expression darkened. Lian noticed that Hanon'ka, too, stood rigid. Turning, he watched the captain stride into the room.

Adaron scanned the men silently. He acknowledged Lian with a faint nod, the nearest to a welcome greeting that Lian could expect. When his gaze fell on Kris, the boy shivered at his first sight of the grave man.

"Who is this?" Adaron asked. He studied Kris with a mixture of curiosity and dismissal—as a nobleman would look upon an interesting but unwanted beetle that had crept into his chambers.

When Lian introduced the boy, Adaron turned to Hanon'ka. "Send him off the gangplank. We can't use a child on board."

"No!" Kris cried out.

"Captain—" Lian started, but Adaron's menacing glare stopped his pleadings.

"Do you have something to say?" the captain snarled.

It took all Lian's courage to pull himself to his feet. "Yes, sir," he said, trying his hardest to sound calm and collected. "This boy risked his life to get a message to you, and he helped me escape by guiding me through the fortress. I promised him freedom and a passage to a new life."

"I am not bound by your promises," Adaron answered gruffly.

"Of course not," continued Lian. "But can't my survival, and the part that Kris played in getting me back to the *Carryola,* soften your heart?"

"There's no room for the boy. The *Carryola* doesn't have any use for him."

"Please, sir. What if he bunked in my quarters? The hammock . . ." Lian stopped and swallowed. "The hammock next to mine has been free ever since Canzo left."

"And, Captain," Smett added, "I could use the extra hands in the galley. Ever since the raptors took Kylion and Markol, I've stood alone at the kettles. If the boy can peel potatoes and wash turnips, he'd be welcome. You can manage that, can't you, lad?" He looked at Kris.

"I can even cook," Kris answered softly, his arms crossed defensively across his narrow chest.

"You hear that?" said Smett. "A true prodigy, and Flicc even likes him. She has a nose for scalawags and charlatans, as you know, Captain."

Lian watched as Adaron's wall of refusal began to crumble. He considered appealing to the captain's sympathies once more, but he held back. Adaron was no man for excessive pleading. Lian and Smett had said their pieces. This decision now belonged to the man who held the fates of all those on board in his hands.

Adaron looked toward Hanon'ka, whose expression was as hard to read as ever. Finally, the Sidhari nodded.

"Fine, then," said Adaron. "As you wish. The boy will sleep with you, Lian, and earn his bread with you, Smett. But if there's trouble"—he glared at Lian—"then you'll take the responsibility. Understood?"

Lian pursed his lips tightly. "Yes, Captain. I promise you that Kris won't make any trouble, and he'll be on his way as soon as we reach the next harbor."

"We'll see," growled the captain, turning to leave. "We'll see."

Soon after—still long before dawn—the *Carryola* pushed away from Vindirion. Nobody tried to stop them or came on board in search of Lian or Kris. Whether or not the commander knew of their escape and chose to avoid conflict with Adaron, Lian couldn't say. He was simply relieved to have an end to his unpleasant excursion. He was finally back on board—the place where he belonged.

24

Blood and the Desert

Twenty-Fourth Day of the Sixth Moon, Year 841

The *Carryola* sailed westward during the following days. It seemed that the Vindirion Taijirin had seen and told enough of the giant black dragon's movements for Adaron to glean a pattern. After studying sightings of the beast on a map, he finally arrived at a goal—or at least an area within the limitless Cloudmere where Gargantuan appeared during the summer moons.

The rest of the crew learned of Kris's presence. A few men, including Danark, poked fun at the boy, while the Drak on board—Karnosk especially—treated him with open contempt. Smett made it clear, however, that Kris stood under his wing, and anyone who treated him badly could expect unpleasant surprises in their soup bowls, so the men left the boy alone. The little fun they found in tormenting a newling wasn't worth the risk of swallowing unknown remains in their stews or soapy water in their mugs.

Thus, Kris became the newest member of the *Carryola*. At night, he tossed in his hammock at Lian's side, and during the day, he disappeared into the galley. Most of the time in between he spent with Lian, who was grateful for the new friend—even if that friend was practically a child. After his first kill, part of him had hoped that Hanon'ka, Ialrist, or Corantha might have become a friend.

They encountered two more dragons—first another bronzeneck and then, two days later, a heavily armored obsidianscale. The first attack came at night while Lian and his comrades slept, and the next while his group held watch, though Ialrist and Corantha reached the beast first. Hanon'ka didn't hold Lian's inaction against him. He still hadn't regained his full strength, the Sidhari explained, and wasn't yet ready for battle.

The Sidhari's assessment wasn't entirely wrong. Lian's wounds still needed time to heal and cease their constant ache—even under the medic Narso's care. Memories of his nightmarish journey left Lian with a constant fear of being hunted. Night terrors plagued him—a flapping raptor clawed his back as he fell into nothingness, where ravenous, sallow-eyed banshees fought over his body. When he would finally wake, breathless and bathed in sweat, Kris's sympathetic gaze greeted him from his neighboring hammock. For some reason, he always felt better then.

Talking about it didn't help soothe his terrors. The crew was eager to hear of Lian's adventure on the Cloudmere floor. His tales chilled and astounded them, though no one could truly understand what he had been through. Only Ialrist regarded him with strange, knowing looks as Lian told the story, but Lian had no chance to ask why.

At midday on the twenty-fourth day of the sixth moon, the *Carryola* passed the last of the Cloudmere isles, leaving the area where not only most Taijirin lived but most dragons kept their nests or dens. As they left jäger territory, they kept a narrow course—a ship could be lost here if a captain misread the maps, but Adaron seemed certain of their route.

"He always does this," Hanon'ka explained as they stood at the bow and looked out into the clouds at dawn. Lian had just asked the Sidhari why the captain led their ship through an area known for its lack of dragons and whether the crew disputed his choice.

"Adaron likes to make decisions that are strange to the rest of us, and yet we return from every mission with great bounty. So the crew follows him, no matter his route."

Hanon'ka looked toward the horizon, where the first silver of a new day lit up the sky. "He knows more about the Cloudmere and its inhabitants than anyone else on board, myself included, and I've been traveling these white widths for almost two decades."

"Have you served Adaron the whole time?" Lian asked.

Hanon'ka glanced toward Lian as he considered. "No," he answered finally. "I came to the *Carryola* nine years ago. Before that, I sailed on three other ships. When I heard about Captain Adaron and his hunt for Gargantuan, I looked for his ship in every harbor we docked. When I finally found him, I begged him to take me on board."

"Why did you want to hunt Gargantuan so badly? Did he . . ." Lian halted, realizing that his question might be too personal.

"Is my beloved also on that monster's conscience?" The Sidhari's emerald eyes flickered with laughter. "No. I've never seen the Firstborn before, but I hope to meet him one day. He is worthy enough to take my life."

Lian looked at Hanon'ka in astonishment. "Take your life? You want to die?"

"I want him to show me a good fight. If I die from it, I will fulfill my fate."

Lian was reminded of what he had said to Canzo on the day of their departure: Lian couldn't believe that a Sidhari would serve on board the *Carryola* if he believed death steered the vessel. Or did he misjudge Hanon'ka terribly?

"But . . . why would you wish to end your life?" Lian asked. "Why endure a nine-year journey instead of falling on your blade like other men who long for death?"

The commander studied him somberly. "I have a heavy burden from my past. I carry a guilt for which death would be a small price, and I won't commit suicide, because that is not the way of the Sidhari. A death of one's own free will must have meaning. Only then will Shaom grant favor on the warrior's soul. And that's all I'll tell you about it."

Lian nodded. "Forgive me if I was too bold."

"You're not too bold. Too bold is the man who only sees knowledge within power or crystals."

"Then allow me one more thing." Lian longed for an answer to something he'd wondered for ages.

"I'll permit one more," said Hanon'ka, and the sides of his mouth curled into a smile. "But don't let me change my mind."

"It's nothing too personal," Lian assured, and the Sidhari ushered him to continue.

"How did you gain the power to control the wind like you did in the battle against the swingblade and again during the storm?" Lian asked.

Once again, the Sidhari considered a long time before answering. "This skill belongs to all Sidhari," he said finally. "Some more than others. It's nothing more for us than tasting the desert air of Shaom or reading the colors of its sands. For thousands of years, my folk have held a deep connection with our land. It's different for people who wander the world with no home of their own and who settle on land without knowing its trees or understanding the streams that flow through its rocks. Our ties to the desert Shaom allow us to control its elements. No, that's not right. That sounds as if we rule them. It's more correct to say that we ask Shaom's waters, sands, and winds to be of service to us. That is how we can call forth water where the ground is dry or why the dunes part to let us pass. It's how the wind carries our words to distant friends."

"But this isn't desert," Lian objected. "We're aloft the Cloudmere, many days'—even weeks'—journey from the great deserts. The winds that blow here are not the desert winds of your home."

An odd smile passed over the Sidhari's lips. "Does the desert end within me just because I can no longer see sands? Is the wind bound by chains? Don't you even say in your prayers that the warmth of the Southern Wind makes the world bloom and the Northern Wind carries the souls of the dead to a warmer place? Where do you think that warmth comes from?"

Lian had never considered this before. The ritual lines had always just been words to him, passed down through generations. It had never occurred to him that the winds' properties could come from an earthly origin.

Hanon'ka nodded knowingly at Lian's surprise. "As long as I can sense Shaom and can hear her eternal whisper in my ear, my abilities will never dry up. Any wind that fills our sails has blown through the Dunemere of Shaom at some point and carries a bit of sand and dust from my home. This distant echo accompanies me on my journey—and always will."

Lian looked out, deep in thought. The eastern sky lightened slowly. Soon the sun would rise. "I envy your powers," he said finally.

The Sidhari's eyes glowed. "You're not the first to say that," he answered. "I can only tell you what I told them: we live in a world full of magic. Your great talents are a straight shot with a drachen spear and an extraordinary intuition for kyrillian crystals. Who knows how your fate will unfold. You have fallen to the Cloudmere floor and found your way back. Most on board call that a miracle. Some say luck itself protects you or that the Winds have something special in store for you. Maybe it's superstition, but maybe not."

Later that morning, Lian joined Balen, Melvas, and the rest of their watch in the canteen before beginning their chores. As Lian passed the galley, Smett called out his name.

"Your young friend is missing," whispered the cook when Lian came near. "He was supposed to fetch a sack of flour from the hold and hasn't returned. Could you look for him? I can't get away, and none of the others give a damn."

"Sure," Lian said. "I'll see what's kept him."

He took a lantern and headed for the stairs that led into the *Carryola*'s belly, toward the hold. Without deck prisms installed in the ceiling for the sun to shine through, it was much darker in the lower deck than middle deck, and there were no lamps besides the one in Lian's hand. The unpleasant stench of brined dragon meat and oiled scales burned Lian's nostrils from the open room at the stern, sectioned off by a waist-high wooden gate.

Supplies were stored toward the bow. Lian ducked to avoid the low ceiling and reached his lantern in front of him. "Kris?" he called. "Kris, are you down here?"

There was no answer. He looked around and struggled to make sense of the chaotic rolls of rope, bolts of sail, wooden planks, casings, barrels, and sacks surrounding him—let alone decipher a person who could be hiding, or even unconscious, among the mess.

Worry began to claw its icy hand inside his chest. Was it possible that someone on board who was resentful of Kris's presence could have done something to the boy? Maybe Danark or Karnosk?

"Kris?" Lian called again. His lantern swung in his hand as his movements grew more panicked. "Where are you?" he called.

When he heard a hollow rattle, he held his breath to listen. The sound came from the left corner near some barrels of ale. Had the boy drunk himself into a stupor? The thought seemed absurd.

Lian edged closer and tiptoed around the barrels. His lantern light revealed two bare legs before Kris jumped behind a stack of barrels and out of sight. When Lian spotted a pail filled with water, colored red like thinned-out blood, a wave of worry overcame him.

He hurried around the barrels. "Kris!" he cried. "What have those pigs done to you? I'll kill—" He stopped midsentence, and his eyes widened from horror and shock.

Before him, in the shine of the lantern, Kris huddled behind the barrels. The boy was barefoot and held his damp trousers balled in a clump against his chest. A few bloodied strips of linen lay on the floor at his side, wet with a few dark clots. He looked at Lian with a fear that bordered on panic.

"Please," he whispered. "Don't tell anyone on board. Don't tell."

"Kris," Lian breathed. "What happened?" He set his lantern to the side and tentatively began to step forward. "Who did this to you?"

The boy shook his head. Tears of doubt collected in his eyes.

Lian carefully touched his shoulder. "Where are you hurt?"

Kris jerked away, closer to the wall. "Don't touch me. Please, don't touch me."

At that moment, Lian noticed a small amount of blood that had collected where the boy had been sitting. A hard lump grew in his gut, and he grew cold. Scornful rage sparked in his chest, and his heart rate quickened into a thundering inferno of hate. "Who?!" he sputtered. "Tell me who did this."

Kris shook his head. "Nobody," he whimpered. "No one has done anything. It's . . ." He squeezed his eyes closed, and a tear rolled down his dirt-smeared cheek. "It's perfectly natural, Lian. My body bleeds because it has to. For years now, moon after moon, the old bleeds away to make way for the new."

Lian stared at Kris, dumbfounded. "What do you mean? Why do you bleed every . . ." A shocking idea struck him. As he looked at Kris— really looked, for the first time—his eyes widened. "You're . . ." His words hung in the air.

"Not a boy," whispered Kris.

"But how? And why?" Lian went from hot to cold as thoughts swirled in his mind. His reason couldn't accept that he had mistaken Kris for a boy the entire time. He had been sure that he—she—was a boy of maybe seventeen summers old, but now the truth was as plain as day. The slight body, soft features, and large—though currently horrified— eyes. Kris was a young woman disguised behind short hair and boyish clothing.

"Just let me finish here," she pleaded. "It won't take long, and then I'll answer all your questions. Just, please, Lian, in the name of our friendship, don't reveal my secret."

Overwhelmed, Lian backed up a few steps. "Yes, uh, sure. I'll . . . I'll be sure to keep quiet, but we have to hurry. Smett has sent me. He, uh, requires your presence—"

"No!" she begged, now glaring at him. "Please don't act like we don't know each other. Please keep treating me like the boy you thought I was. I know it's strange, but if you still care about my life, please think of me as the Kris that helped you escape Vindirion."

Lian inhaled deeply. Knowing Kris was a woman felt strange. They had always spoken familiarly, like family or close friends, as he and Canzo used to do. *Don't think about that now,* he told himself. *It was just a part of her disguise. It didn't mean anything.*

"All right, fine," he muttered. He walked away from Kris's hiding place and sat with his back against a barrel while Kris washed and dressed. For a while, neither said a word. The only sounds were the soft slosh of water and rustle of clothing, and the muffled laughs and calls of men from middle deck.

"Will you tell me your real name?" Lian asked.

After a pause, she answered. "Krisiana. My name is Krisiana."

"And how old are you really?"

"I'm not sure," she admitted. "Older than I look, probably. But young enough to still pass for a boy."

"Hm," Lian mumbled. "And the story you told me. Is it true?"

"Most of it." Kris appeared next to him, her trousers still damp. "But we should discuss it later. Smett is waiting for me."

"How will we explain where you were and that there?" Lian asked, motioning toward her wet clothes.

"The flour sack caught on a nail and ripped open. Flour scattered everywhere, and I wanted to wash it all away so that I wouldn't get into trouble. So I got wet."

"That's a pretty good story, I have to admit."

Kris shrugged. "I have years of practice finding excuses."

"Won't Smett beat you with the cooking spoon for losing the flour?" Lian asked.

"He'll be angry, to be sure, but every time he sees me with Flicc, his heart softens. I doubt I'll get much more than a mild scolding." Kris smiled impishly. "But let's not lose any more time. If Smett sends some-one else to look for *you*, we'll both be in for it."

They grabbed a sack of flour, and Lian used his swingblade dagger to tear it open. Then they scattered some of its contents onto the planks and rinsed it away with water. After pouring the rest through a refuse hold in the floor, they made their way upstairs.

The canteen bustled as both Lian's watch and the night watch, who had just woken up, took their meals. It was easy for Lian and Kris to make their ways unnoticed through the commotion. Once in the galley, they handed Smett the sack of flour. "Your lost assistant returns," Lian an-nounced. "He had a mishap, but he can tell you about it himself. I'm go-ing to get something to eat." He turned to Kris. "See you tonight, right? You always said you wanted to hear how I came on board the *Carryola*."

Kris nodded eagerly, falling fully into her role as an inquisitive boy. "Yes! We'll talk later." She looked shyly at Smett. "If Smett allows it."

"We'll see," grumbled the cook, his hands propped on his hips as he scowled at the torn sack of flour. "But if you don't have a damned good excuse for this here, you'll be chopping turnips until your fingers fall off."

Lian grinned. "Go easy, Smett. The whole thing is very unpleasant for him. He really wants to please you. He thinks very highly of you, you know."

"Is that so?" Smett said, and his scowl softened around the edges.

Kris looked at the floor bashfully as Smett broke out in hearty laughter.

25

The Island

Second Day of the Seventh Moon, Year 841

That night, Lian and Kris never had the chance to continue their discussion. In fact, during the following days, they were constantly surrounded by other crew members, and couldn't exchange more than a few words. The days were a struggle for Lian. He kept his word and forced himself to give no hint, through word or deed, of Kris's secret, even though his head reeled not only with questions that remained unanswered but with how to act around the new Kris. When he'd thought she was a boy, Lian would not have thought twice before teasing him or clapping a hand on his shoulder. Now he felt trapped.

It was less Kris's fault than his own. She played the part of the fun-loving boy with the expertise of someone who had grown into a false identity over the course of many moons. The only thing the most discerning observer might notice, was her easy familiarity toward Lian, but nobody would have been able to deduce that the two shared a secret. "The lad is beginning to trust you, eh?" was the sole mention of it—from Smett's tongue.

Lian answered with a detached mumble, at which the cook laughed.

Lian, however, remained uneasy about his new intimacy with Kris, which he first realized when lying in his hammock one night. All the things that he had felt in Kris's presence—the unexpected instinct to protect her in the Taijirin dungeon or the comfort he felt when he woke from a nightmare and felt Kris's presence soothe him—had until then seemed like signs of a bond between an older and younger brother. In truth—and he only grasped this now—he had felt the pangs of an even more intimate bond. A part of him must have known all along that Kris was concealing her true self. Now that he knew the truth, his new feelings made him nervous—especially in his current surroundings aboard a drachenjäger. He felt pulled in opposite directions. Kris, too, noticed the change, and began to respond with confusion of her own.

Luckily, the crew took his restraint for no more than piqued tenseness. It had been almost a week since they had spotted any dragons worth hunting. The men were restless and longed for a change—any change. Only their fear of Adaron and trust in Hanon'ka's navigation seemed to keep them from jumping ship.

On the second day of the seventh moon, a distraction at midday abruptly appeared at the horizon.

When the call sounded, Lian was busy at the ship's side with Melvas, once again oiling the ship's scale armor.

"Land ahead!" Cabbyr called from the crow's nest. "A lithos, straight ahead! By the Winds, she's huge!"

Lian squinted toward the horizon and spotted the dark mass that hovered among the clouds.

"It can't be," murmured Melvas.

Above them on deck, men raced to the bow and spoke in agitated confusion.

"What's wrong?" Lian asked. "What's so exciting about sailing past a floating island?"

"What's so exciting?" Melvas said, shaking his head. "Do you know nothing about the Cloudmere?"

Lian looked at him blankly.

"No, of course you don't," said the man. "How would you? You're still wet behind the ears." He leaned forward and motioned toward the island. "We're excited because there aren't supposed to be any islands

in these parts—at least none of that size. Any map you study will show
the stretch beyond Vindirion completely empty. A boulder here, a crag
there, maybe, but surely not any island the size of a village. There are
only a few lithos that size in existence."

Lian wrinkled his brow. "Then the maps must be wrong. The island
is right there."

Melvas grinned. "Right. And what does that mean?"

"That the maps are inaccurate and not worth the crystals paid for them?"

"Wrong! That this island appeared so recently out of the clouds that
nobody has ever discovered and reported it. It can only have been aloft
for a half year at the most. So if we set anchor, we'd be setting foot on
untrodden territory."

Lian remembered a solemn word of instruction that Waunar had offered at the start of his training. Floating isles didn't just appear like
magic in the Cloudmere overnight. The current, and more likely, theory
of scholars was that a network of kyrillian veins covered the entire floor
of the Cloudmere. Over decades, the veins multiplied until their pull
was so strong that sections from the ground broke into the air. Kyrillian
masses could take years to rise into the ether, and over time, wind and
weather marred their outside layers. By the time the lithos broke free of
the clouds, they looked nothing like their origins anymore.

This was all assumption, though. There wasn't much account about
the treasures that flourished in the Cloudmere's depths. Maybe now
Lian would be able to confirm the theory. On the Taijirin colony Shiartris, he hadn't seen any glowing moss or giant fungi, but if he was about
to tread upon a freshly risen lithos, who knew what he would find.

No one was surprised when Adaron changed course toward the un-
named island. The chance for the crew to explore and collect provisions
seemed worth the half day's extra journey.

Lian and Melvas had just finished their work along the hull when the
Carryola reached her target. Adaron steered the ship upward and circled
the island once to get an idea of the landscape. The island was oval
shaped, with a wide core of jagged gray mountains that ran from north
to south, and whose highest peaks reached a good two hundred paces
into the sky. They found no flowing water, but Lian, who peered over the
railing along with the others, spotted a few standing pools among thick
high-climbing ferns and young leafy trees.

They anchored atop a free area at the southern slope of the highest peak. The spot occupied the almost exact middle of the island, with direct access to an easily spotted landmark, to simplify both their mission and their return to the ship.

Adaron gathered the crew on deck. "You will all explore the island," he announced, "aside from Jaular and four men from the day watch. The early watch may decide whether to explore or to stay behind. You must all return on board at the start of the night watch." He turned to Hanon'ka. "Divide the men into groups and assign their duties. Speak to Narso, Smett, Garon, and Urdin, and assign men accordingly. Anyone remaining will search for supplies and keep an eye out for anything of interest."

"Aye, Captain," answered the Sidhari.

"Then good luck," said the captain, and Hanon'ka turned to the medic, cook, crystal carver, and carpenter. Ialrist and Corantha, astride Arax, set off to keep watch from above and to warn the others of possible dangers. The rest of the crew awaited instruction.

Then the commander began to organize the men into groups. Narso set off with his assistants, Cabbyr and Gaaki, to search for healing plants, while Garon gathered six men to chop wood for repairs aboard the ship and jäger kites.

When Hanon'ka approached Lian, Smett and Kris stepped aside.

"Commander?" Lian asked.

"Smett wants you to go with Kris to search for herbs for the kitchen. The boy knows what's needed, and you're the best to keep watch over him. So fetch your spear and make your way."

Lian glanced suspiciously from Smett to Kris and then nodded. "I'll be right back," he said.

Before long, Lian walked beside Kris through the ferns at the foot of the mountain. Kris carried a large satchel slung across her shoulder, and Lian held his spear. If the island had recently surfaced through the clouds, their most likely threat was something with wings—raptors not least of all—and a spear would be their best chance of defense.

Lian grew uneasy as he was reminded of the eerie ghouls he'd encountered on the Cloudmere floor. He prayed that nothing similar lurked here in the mountains when the kyrillian broke from the ground.

"You're so quiet," Kris said. She studied him for a moment. "Does it bother you that I talked old Smett into letting us out together? I thought we'd finally have a chance to talk."

"No, it's not that," answered Lian. "I was reminded that it hasn't been very long since I walked on ground like this—only it was thousands of leagues beneath the clouds. It looks so different, but strangely familiar." It wasn't exactly true, but he didn't want to worry Kris by speaking of sallow-eyed and deformed human-eating terrors.

"Would you have rather stayed on board?" Kris asked.

"By all the Winds, no." Lian smiled. "I'm glad that we can finally speak uninterrupted. There *are* herbs, though, aren't there?"

"I don't have the faintest idea," she answered, smiling back. "But Smett seemed to buy it. Otherwise, he never would have let us go."

"I'm not so sure about that," Lian said, glancing back toward the ship that grew smaller in their wake.

"What do you mean?"

"Smett always seems cheerful and carefree, but he's actually very observant and perceptive." Lian thought back to his conversation with Smett just after Canzo's death. "I think he knows much more about what happens on board than he ever lets on."

"You think he's seen through me and is protecting me from the rest of the crew?" Kris asked.

"Is it unthinkable? You're safer in his galley than anywhere else on board."

"Why do you care so much about my safety? I'm just a scrappy newling," Kris answered, reminding Lian of the rules. "Don't forget."

Lian glanced once more over his shoulder. The ship was now out of sight behind the mountain, and no men from the other groups crossed their path. Among the giant ferns and scattered trees, they were completely alone.

Lian stood still and faced Kris. "I can't forget for a moment," he said heatedly. "But you're not a newling, and it's hard for me to treat you like one. I . . . it . . . it just feels strange . . . like we . . . you know."

"Like we're destined for each other? I know, I feel it, too. But you need to treat me as before; we've discussed that already. If you care about me at all, if you really want to help me, then set your anxiety aside and look at this like a game. I'm a boy, and you rescued me from captivity—someone I look up to. We're playing roles, both of us, and the *Carryola's* crew is our audience."

"But we don't have to play roles here," Lian answered. "Not while we're alone."

"We're not alone on this island," Kris responded.

Lian spread his arms wide. "Look around," he said. "No one can see us, and no one can hear us."

"You don't know that. There could always be someone lurking nearby."

"You're—" Lian stopped before saying something that he might later regret. "Oh, damn it, whatever you say." He turned around angrily and continued on his way.

Kris grabbed his arm to stop him. "Lian, please. Let me explain."

Silently, he turned to her.

She ran a nervous hand through her shaggy short hair. "I've been living in disguise for almost three years, ever since I was separated from my parents. First, I found shelter on the streets of Skargakar, but my cover was blown. I paid for that bitterly. I ran again, this time to a trading ship. Most of the crew, to my relief, were Nondurier, but there were a few humans, too. I had to be constantly vigilant or risk discovery. With the Taijirin, I learned how to keep my wits about me. They sit on roofs and ledges where you'd never expect them. Their eyesight is so sharp they can spot almost anything. I couldn't let myself forget my role. Not ever—even when I wanted to."

"But if—" Lian began, but a wave of her hand silenced him.

"I don't want to argue," she continued. "Ever since my time in Skargakar, I've never trusted anyone, and nobody has ever stood up for me. I've practically forgotten what it means to have someone there for me and to be there for someone." She hesitated and looked away. "Call me what you want," she said softly. "But please don't forget that you hold my fate in your hands." She searched his eyes briefly as though looking for confirmation that he understood. Then she stamped through the ferns, hurrying onward.

In a daze, Lian watched her walk away. He hadn't expected such an explanation. Joy battled with fear inside his chest, until uncertainty won the fight. Quietly, Lian hurried to follow her. *It would be so much easier if she were a boy*, he thought begrudgingly.

Lian wondered if he should tell Kris this last thought, but he decided against it. It would only make him sound like a rebellious child. Since Kris also didn't seem eager to speak any further, the two slipped through the wilderness in silence.

The island was extraordinarily quiet. Not a single creature rustled through the brush, and few birds sang, which supported the theory that the land was young and untouched. Once, Lian thought he had heard the screech of a lizardwing, but when he looked up to the sky, he saw nothing but clouds.

To Lian's surprise, Kris discovered some edible herbs growing in the sunny patches of ground between the ferns. Winds had either blown the seeds across the wide expanse of the Cloudmere, or they existed in a time before the fog set in. Lian had heard that the Cloudmere stemmed from unnatural origins, but knew nothing of what magical influence created it, or when.

Eventually, Lian broke their silence. "There's something I don't understand."

Kris looked at him and waited for him to continue.

"If you've been so careful for so long, how did you find yourself in the . . . difficult situation that I found you in? What was different from all the other moons?"

Kris hesitated before answering. Any word about her true sex seemed one too many. When she spoke, she answered cautiously. "I was unlucky. In Skargakar, there was always a way for me to hide away for a few days. Plus, I had a friend who looked out for me."

"Your friend knew?"

Kris nodded. "He was like you—but he disappeared. A band of Cliff Clippers threw him into the clouds when he couldn't pay the crystals he owed."

Lian winced. "I'm sorry."

"It feels like a lifetime ago now," Kris said, shrugging.

"And later?" Lian asked.

"The crew of the trading ship was inattentive, and there weren't rotating watches like there are on the *Carryola*. They stayed on deck during the day, got drunk in the evenings, and slept off the drink at night. It's a wonder they weren't attacked by pirates sooner, if you ask me, but it meant that it was easy to sneak away. With the Taijirin, it wasn't much different. Vogelfolk eyes spot many things, but their pride and arrogance make them overlook just as much. I was a wingless one—not to mention a child to them."

"I see," said Lian. "And then you boarded a ship full of people, where eyes are always watching."

Kris nodded. "Don't get me wrong. I'm eternally grateful to you for saving me, but you haven't made my life on board the *Carryola* easier. Except . . ." She hesitated. "That time, the blood was just heavier. It happens sometimes, and I wasn't prepared. Ultimately, it's my own fault that I was discovered, but at least it was you who found me."

"I promise that I'll do everything I can to protect your secret," Lian confirmed. "I don't want anything to happen to you. That was true when we met in the dungeon, and that's even truer now."

A relieved grin spread across Kris's cheeks. "Thanks, Lian. You're a good friend," she said.

A tinge of embarrassment overcame him as he returned her smile. "I try," he said. He wished he could come up with something wittier to say, but the words stuck in his throat.

As they continued, he noticed something in the rock face, half concealed between two green plants nearby.

"Look!" he said, pointing toward the rock. "Is that an entrance into the mountain?"

Kris looked forward, and her eyes widened. "Maybe. Let's take a look."

They carefully approached the rock face until they made out an ancient and weather-beaten portal, almost completely overgrown by ferns and vines. Columns and a round archway reached a good four paces high and two wide, expertly carved from the stone. Strange patterns and runes, barely decipherable, covered the surface, and a few steps led up to the entrance without a door.

"What is this?" Lian asked in wonder. "It's too fine to be the entrance to a mine."

"Maybe a tomb?" Kris suggested. "Or a temple?"

Lian squinted into the entrance but saw only a plain stone passageway that disappeared into the darkness. "I can't tell how far down it goes," he said. "I wish I had a lantern."

"I can't do anything about a lantern, but I have a torch," Kris said, smiling as she reached a hand into her satchel.

Lian stared at her in surprise. "You packed a torch?"

"Smett thought it would be a good idea," she explained. "He said that the darkness in these parts can come so quickly that it's easy to be caught off guard. And he wanted to keep us from stumbling all the way back through the forest."

"How considerate of our cook," Lian said, still wondering how much the old man knew about his and Kris's secret or how much he thought he knew.

They lit the torch and stepped into the passage.

"What do you think?" Lian asked. "Should we look around a bit? Maybe we'll find a king's abandoned treasure. That would certainly make an impression on the captain," he said.

Kris's eyes sparkled with the lust for adventure. "Lead the way," she said. "I'm right behind you."

26

The Magic Spring

Second Day of the Seventh Moon, Year 841

Gradually, Lian and Kris pressed farther into the darkness. The smooth stone of the passageway remained unchanged. As they walked side by side, no further embellishments, junctions, or entranceways appeared. The wet and slippery stone under their feet sloped slightly downward so that each step required care. The air tasted metallic, though Lian couldn't tell why.

"How far does this go?" Kris wondered aloud after they'd gone about fifty paces.

The only sounds were the crunches of pebbles under their feet and their quiet breathing.

"I have no idea," Lian answered, a slight echo emphasizing his point. "It seems like it continues like this for a while."

"It smells strange," Kris pointed out.

"I noticed, too. It's as if you held a cold sword blade under your nose," Lian said.

"That's a strange comparison," she said, and she sniffed the air. "But not inaccurate. I wonder if it's coming from the stone." She turned to the wall and sniffed again but then shook her head. "No, it just smells like cold stone."

"Let's keep going," Lian suggested. "Maybe we'll find an explanation."

A few paces onward, they noticed a weak light before them.

"What's that?" Lian murmured.

Part of the ceiling had caved in, and debris blocked the way, save for a thin gap just wide enough for a person to squeeze through. Lian peered through to the shimmering silver light on the other side.

"Something is in there," he whispered, turning to Kris. "It'll only fit one at a time. Hold on to the torch and wait here." He handed her the light.

"Be careful," she said softly.

"Don't worry. If anything lived there, it already would have made itself known." Still, he pulled his spear from his shoulder and clutched it with both hands. Despite his fear, his curiosity urged him forward.

He stepped to the top of the stone pile and looked through the crack. A few paces ahead, he saw a rock wall covered in—if he wasn't mistaken—glittering crystal veins. "It looks like a chamber," he said over his shoulder. "I'm going to get a better look. If it's safe, I'll call for you." Carefully, he pushed his way through the narrow gap.

Once on the other side, he found himself in a cavernous room, almost perfectly round and about fifteen paces wide with a high, domed ceiling. White veins of glimmering crystal covered the stone surfaces, which sparkled like stars and sent light rippling across the walls. The light itself—a mellow white glow that brightened and dimmed as Lian looked into it—emanated from a group of crystal pillars in the center of the room, reaching powerfully from the ground to the ceiling.

Surrounding the pillars, a pool took up most of the room, the water shimmering in the light of the crystals. Lian sank to his knees at its edge and stared into the depths. As he gazed, he realized that the substance wasn't water but something viscous—like melted silver. The metallic scent was much stronger. The pool didn't seem to have any drain or spout or any way for the water to flow in or out.

"What is this place?" Lian whispered as he scanned the room in astonishment. This was certainly unlike any temple he had ever seen before.

"Lian?" Kris called from the other side of the barrier. "Is everything all right?"

"Yes," he called back. "Come here! You have to see this!"

He heard rustling as Kris pushed her way through the gap. Once through to the other side, she gasped. "By the Winds!"

"I know," Lian said, and he stood. "It's amazing, isn't it?"

Kris walked to his side and absorbed the sight with reverence. "I always wondered if there was magic in the world beyond floating kyrillian or Sidhari weather tricks. This is all the answer I need."

Her words struck a chord deep within him. She was right. This place was made of pure magic—or was a spring from which magic flowed. *Maybe it's a place where sorcerers once gathered to conduct their rituals,* Lian considered.

He motioned toward the pillars at the chamber's center. He'd never seen such large, bright crystals before. "Their light shines much brighter than kyrillian. I wonder what powers they contain," he said. "I wish I could get a closer look."

He searched the room again but didn't find any stepping-stones or a bridge to cross the silver pool. Raising his spear from the ground, he pointed its end toward the liquid and then hesitated. "You don't happen to know anything about magic, do you?" he asked.

"Sorry," she said, shaking her head. "Why do you ask?"

"My father's spear contains some sort of power," Lian explained. "It glows when I'm fighting dragons. I'd like to test if the pool is shallow enough to wade through, but what if the water is enchanted, too? Could two opposing kinds of enchantment cause a reaction?"

Kris shook her head. "I can't say for sure, but the spear didn't react when we entered the chamber. Its magic must not conflict with whatever is at work here. You could test the water with the blunt end, just to be safe."

"Good idea," Lian said, rotating the weapon in his hands. Then he crouched and held the spear over the pool. No flash occurred between the wood and the silver, and nothing else out of the ordinary occurred. Gingerly, he dipped the spear's handle into the liquid.

The shaft sank soundlessly into the silver water until it met hard stone. The pool was about knee deep—at least near the bank. Lian stood up.

"I'm going to wade across," he said determinedly. As he pulled the handle out of the silver water, thick beads dripped off the spear's end and fell into the pool without leaving a trace.

"Isn't it dangerous?" Kris asked. "What if there's a sudden drop? Can you swim?"

Lian shook his head. No one from Skargakar knew how to swim. There weren't any lakes nearby where he could have learned. The only bodies of water at all were a few streams at the edge of the village, which were all too shallow to do more than wet his feet. "I'll be careful," he promised.

He considered removing his boots and rolling up his pant legs to prevent them from absorbing the liquid but decided against it; scraping a foot on a jagged crystal wouldn't get him anywhere. He also felt uneasy about stepping into liquid so opaque. If any creatures lurked underneath, he didn't want to tempt them with bare toes.

As Kris stood at the bank, looking worried, Lian stepped into the water. The liquid was surprisingly pleasant—room temperature and, strangely, not particularly wet. If it weren't for the splash as his spear handle entered the liquid with each step, he would have wondered if the pool was just an illusion or a trick to keep curious hands away from the crystals.

After he had traveled halfway, he confirmed that the pool's depth was even all the way across. Lian turned to Kris and grinned. "See? It's not even—"

He slipped on something underfoot and lost his balance. Crying out in surprise, arms flailing, he fell backward into the liquid silver.

"Lian!" Kris cried.

Thick liquid filled his mouth and nose as it closed over his head. He emerged again instantly, coughing and sputtering, and shook himself off. "I'm fine," he said. "Really. I'm just—"

Then the visions appeared.

A ship aloft on a cloudy sea.
A shadow as dark as the night.
The sun eclipsed by giant black wings.
Before fire consumes the sky.

Shrieks of men, who burn like torches.
Giant eyes seethe with flickering hate.
A woman ripped to pieces by relentless claws.
And a snapping jaw lined with fangs.

A Nondurier grimaces, gutted and doomed.
A Sidhari as good as dead.
Two black giants plunge to their bitter ends.
And madness itself steers onward.

Lian cried out as the images flashed before his eyes. Gasping with terror, he watched the chaotic pictures of battle and death descend upon him, leaving nothing but darkness in their wake.

At least, he thought so at first.

Then he noticed a glimmer above as a white glow slowly brightened. Blinking, he found himself back in the crystal chamber, knee deep in liquid silver. *No*, he thought. *Something isn't right.*

Lian looked around. The room seemed larger—much larger. The ceiling arched high above, the walls stretched farther away, and the brightly glowing crystals towered high above him. Though this place looked similar to the chamber where he had stood with Kris, it felt more like a powerful shrine. The silver spring had transformed into a wide sea that came up to Lian's chest, and Kris was nowhere in sight.

The realization brought him to his feet. *Kris?* He slipped and almost fell again. The light warped into blurred streaks as he moved his head, as though he'd drunk an entire barrel of ale or had been drugged.

He gazed into the silver pool slowly lapping against his wavering arms.

What's wrong with me? he wondered. *Where am I? Where is Kris?*

She is still there, a gentle yet powerful voice said from behind him, or rather, from within him. The words sounded in his mind. *She's saving you because she believes you are drowning.*

I don't understand. Lian turned around, and his eyes widened in confusion. The crystals reached far above him toward the distant ceiling, and a cluster of spears the length of towers stood at their bases. The weapons had sharp ends and smooth, shining surfaces that glowed white, green, and violet. Though the crystals' glow paled in comparison to the spears' magnificence, their light brightened and dimmed in the same way. It seemed as though the shrine—if it was a shrine—glowed to the pulse of a slowly beating heart.

What is this place? Lian whispered—or did he just think it? Words and thoughts fused together.

This place has no name, because it only exists within you, the gentle voice explained. *Your body remains in the small cave that you discovered underneath the mountain, but your soul is with me—just as I'd hoped.*

A figure materialized as though stepping forth from the crystal itself. Lian's vision remained blurry, and any movement of his head cast veils of light over the scene. The form approached slowly.

Overwhelmed by the strangeness of it all, Lian looked at the figure standing at the edge of the silver spring a few steps away from him. The slender woman wore a silver-white robe that cascaded to the floor. Her face was human, but when Lian looked closely, he noticed a fine layer of scales scattered across the snow-white skin along her temples and cheeks, shimmering in the light of the glowing crystals. Long, silver hair cascaded past her shoulders, and her eyes glowed with a silver-white fire.

It was impossible to tell how old the woman was. A supernatural aura of power and majesty that contained no age emanated from her.

Who are you? he asked. *And what does this all mean? Why am I here? Am I hallucinating?*

The woman shook her head. *There's no time to answer questions, Lian. You won't be here for long. I have called you here to warn you. You are going the wrong way, but you can still be saved. If you decide correctly, your whole life can change.*

Something tugged at him, and the streams of light brightened. Frozen to the spot, he willed himself to remember what it felt like to move.

I don't understand, he said, now worried. *Which way? What am I supposed to decide?*

You'll understand soon enough, trust me, the woman answered. *Follow your instincts instead of heeding the warning cries of others. You alone can decide what is right and what is wrong. We shouldn't be foes.*

Something pulled at him once again, and he tried to shake off the force. He wasn't ready to leave this place. He still had so many questions.

Why do you speak in riddles? he called to the woman of white. *Who are you, and what do you want? Why would we be foes? I don't even know who you are.*

You carry the weapon of a great man, but brandish it like an enemy, said the woman. She raised a slender hand with crystalline fingernails and pointed to the spot beside Lian. His spear lay powerless in the silver, and the runes on its end glowed lustily for dragon blood.

His surroundings distorted and bent in a kaleidoscope of color and light, and an invisible force took hold of him. *No!* he cried and shook his head. *Not yet!* The ghostly shrine and its occupant returned into focus. *What do you know about this weapon?* he asked the woman of white.

Many generations ago, a man carried it alongside five comrades who fought against evil itself to protect the innocent. He brandished it to save lives, not to kill. He followed kindness and mercy, not lust and hate. The enchanted weapon obeys the one who wields it, but the wielder must decide his motive. You're treading the way of heroes, Lian, but you have to decide for yourself if you want to become one. And now . . .

The stone shrine shook fiercely, and an unearthly howl filled the space. An unknown force threw Lian from his feet, and he landed with a splash in the silver liquid.

Farewell. The woman raised a parting hand.

No! Lian called as his surroundings began to dissolve. *I still have so many questions!*

Another day.

Lian squeezed his eyes shut and tried to focus all his energy on the figure within the dazzling swirl of light. The woman of white had become little more than a wisp of mist with, strangely, more dimension than it should have had. *Will we meet again?*

Who can tell?

The shrine shook again, and Lian gasped for breath as the silver rose around him. He reached out a hand. *Please! At least tell your name!*

The mist took on a new form that, just for a moment, looked like a ghostly dragon, with a crown of heavy shield-like plates that ended in six spikes.

Kesrondaia . . .

"*Lian!*" a voice thundered in his ear. "Lian, come back!"

Gasping, he blinked his eyes open and found himself back in the original chamber. He recognized Kris, kneeling next to him as she struggled to revive him.

When she called out again, he raised a hand. "It's okay," he groaned, struggling to pull himself up. "I'm . . . I'm here again." He rubbed his smarting cheeks, which she had slapped hard in her efforts.

"Oh, thank the Southern Wind!" She threw her arms around his neck and rested her head on his cheek, her role as a boy abandoned. "I was afraid I'd lost you."

Lian wheezed as he struggled to support both their weights with his arms. "I'm fine. What happened?"

Kris lingered before letting go and then glanced toward the silver pool. "You . . . you tried to wade to the island and almost made it. But you lost your footing and fell into the silver."

"I remember all that," Lian said. "But then I came up again, right away."

"Yes . . . but you barely finished your sentence before your eyes rolled back in your head and you fell back again, and that time, you didn't come up." She searched his face. "I ran to you, to pull you out before you drowned. Thank the Winds the pool isn't very deep. I dragged you back to the bank and shook you, but you wouldn't wake. You convulsed and murmured nonsense as though you were caught in a nightmare."

"A nightmare," Lian said, nodding. "It really was." He turned and looked upon the silver liquid and the crystals glowing at its center. "It must be some sort of drug. I only swallowed a mouthful and had the most terrible visions. I saw a black dragon, the *Carryola*, and so much death and destruction . . . It was awful." He didn't know why he refrained from telling her about Kesrondaia, but he didn't feel ready to speak about it, so he kept it to himself.

"Well, it's over now," Kris said. She smiled and laid a hand on his shoulder. "As long as you don't enter the pool again."

Lian frowned. "I have to. My spear is still there."

"I took it when I pulled you out," Kris said, handing him his father's weapon. The blade glinted in the light from the crystals and the torch on the ground beside them, but the runes didn't stir. There was no trace of the silver liquid on the spear or on Lian's own body, he noticed. He wasn't wet, and his clothes weren't tinted silver—as though he'd never fallen into the pool in the first place.

"Thanks," Lian said, taking the spear. "That was brave of you." They pulled themselves to their feet and stood facing each other. "I'm not sure if you saved my life," he said then, "but thank you, anyway, for what you risked to save me."

Kris smiled shyly. "You would have done the same for me."

"True," he admitted.

For a moment, they looked at each other in silence. Lian didn't know if it was the fault of the crystals, but the shine in Kris's eyes seemed to reflect exactly what he felt at that moment—an unexpectedly strong yearning for closeness, warmth, and her. He longed to drop the spear, take her in his arms, and forget all about the terrible events. If he wasn't mistaken, she seemed to hope for the same.

Then she dropped her gaze and turned. "We should get back to the ship. The others are surely waiting for us by now."

"Oh, uh, you're right." Lian cleared his throat. He slung his spear over his shoulder, and Kris picked up her torch.

"You go first," he said. With a nod, she climbed the stone mound and disappeared through the gap. Lian remained for a moment, looking at the pool of water and the crystal island at its center one last time. *I have called you here to warn you,* the voice of the silver-white woman, Kesrondaia, had spoken within his mind. *You are going the wrong way, but you can still be saved. If you decide correctly, your whole life can change.*

"So many questions," Lian murmured. His hand fell onto the waterskin hanging from his belt. After a pause, he pulled out its cork, drank two gulps of the water inside, and shook the rest onto the stone ground. Then he crouched down and filled the pouch with the silver liquid. *Maybe I'll be able to see her again this way.*

"Lian?" Kris's concerned voice spoke through the other side of the gap.

"Coming!" he called, and he recorked the skin. Then he left the secret place of enchantment, doubtful that he would ever return.

27

Nock Nock

Second Day of the Seventh Moon, Year 841

"Just promise me one thing," Lian said to Kris as they emerged from the stone entrance back into the sunlight to continue their search for herbs. "Don't tell anyone on board about that place."

Kris looked at him suspiciously. "You want to keep our discovery secret from the captain and the others," she said slowly, her words less a question than an observation.

"That's right. I . . . I don't know why, but I have the feeling that chamber was meant just for us. I wouldn't want the others to get the idea to fill their barrels with the silver water in order to sell it when we return to Skargakar."

"Or to break the crystals from the walls in hope that they'd be of some worth," Kris suggested.

"Right. That would be like desecrating a holy city—or harming the magic that resides there." Lian looked toward Kris. "Do you know what I mean?"

She nodded. "I feel the same way. It was . . . wonderful and terrifying. We should keep it to ourselves." The corners of her mouth curled into a smile. "I know we've only shared secrets for a few days, but if this keeps up, we'll be as close as warriors who've fought alongside each other for years."

Lian smiled. "As far as I'm concerned, that would be fine," he said. He was well aware that he ran dangerously close to falling out of the role he had agreed to play, but at that moment, he didn't care.

The events inside the cave had changed him considerably. Even though the encounter with Kesrondaia bewildered him, there seemed a sudden and inexplicable clarity between him and Kris. Her bravery at the silver pool and, most of all, how she'd looked at him afterward, melted his uncertainty. She had feelings for him, no more doubt about it, and the knowledge only strengthened Lian's own.

He did begin to fear Adaron's actions if he ever found out that Kris was actually a woman. *We just can't give ourselves away,* he thought.

"Careful," Kris warned. "Anyone could read that smile on your face." She lifted a twig from the ground and used it to jab Lian in the side.

"Hey!" he cried, feigning anger. Then his voice lowered. "You won't even allow a little chance."

"How much chance do you want?" she asked. "You already survived the Cloudmere floor and Taijirin imprisonment."

He was about to answer when Kris directed her branch to a pile of leaves growing in the shade at the base of a tree. "Look there, minaka weed! Smett will be thrilled. It tastes excellent paired with dragon meat," she said excitedly. Tossing the branch aside, she hurried over and knelt beside the shrub. "Help me. We'll dig the whole thing up with its roots. Then Smett can plant it in a pot and keep it alive. The cool galley will be the perfect conditions for it to flourish."

Lian sighed and joined her. As he began to dig, she grabbed his hands. "Very gently, understand," she said softly, "or we'll damage the roots, and we don't want the minaka to die, do we?"

Lian's heartbeat quickened. His throat had gone dry. "No," he whispered rawly. "We wouldn't want that."

"Good," she said, looking deep into his eyes, her own glistening brightly. This time, he couldn't blame the torch or the magic crystals. Her fingers gently grazed his own as she led his hands into the earth.

She leaned closer. "I'll allow you all the chance in the world," she said, barely audibly. "But we have to stay strong until the *Carryola* reaches harbor."

Lian leaned forward. He could feel her warm breath against his lips. "I'm so strong that even dragons quake before me," he said softly.

"But there aren't any dragons around," she said.

"Well, that's a relief."

They heard a prolonged cry—half howl and half roar.

Kris sat upright. "Oh," she said. "Maybe there *are* dragons on this island." She pulled away and jumped to her feet—the magical moment gone as quickly as it had appeared. "Come on!" she called. "Let's find out what it is."

"Are you crazy?" Lian said, and he struggled to his feet as he cradled the minaka plant. "If it's a dragon, then we should make a run for it!"

She grinned. "What was it you said before? You're so strong that even dragons quake before you?"

"That was just a joke," Lian said. "By the way, what should I do with this?" he asked, holding out the plant.

"Put it in my bag." Kris held open her satchel, and Lian laid the minaka plant carefully next to the others. Then he pulled his spear from his back and gripped it with both hands, just to be safe.

Another howl rang through the woods, filled with menace and pain, though the cry lacked a vicious dragon's intensity. Lian assumed the creature couldn't be larger than the raptor that had snatched him from the deck during the storm.

Lian ran to keep up with Kris, who raced ahead through the underbrush. *What is she hoping to find?* he wondered, shaking his head. She wasn't a slayer. She'd even said herself that she loved and admired the creatures, but most were far too dangerous to get close to. He prayed that she wasn't running into harm's way.

Ahead of them, beyond a thick row of ferns, they heard a squawk and a screech—and, to Lian's surprise, a high-pitched cackle. They didn't seem to be the first to have reached the dragon. Lian heard a man's voice, though he couldn't understand the words, followed by a muffled beating sound and another howl.

What was that? Lian wondered. He tried to warn Kris to take care as she pushed her way forward. But before he could speak, she cried out in disgust and tore through the ferns. "Hey! What are you doing, you bastards?"

Lian cursed under his breath and followed. When he saw what was taking place in the small, concealed cove lined with rocks, his stomach turned.

Before him, Karnosk and Srashi stood at a dragon's nest. The hatchlings were around the size of a sheepdog's pups, with muted-green scales that shimmered blue at the edges. The mother lay beside its nest with broken wings, blood streaming from multiple stab wounds across its body.

Lian counted six hatchlings, none old enough to fly. They must have been waiting for their mother to return with food when the jägers arrived. The two Drak seemed to have found sick sport in impaling the hatchlings with their cutlasses. Four of the hatchlings already lay motionless in a pool of their own blood. The other two hopped and frantically flapped their tiny wings, unsure whether they hoped to fly or stay by their injured mother.

Kris stood before the Drak, her eyes burning with scorn. "What is wrong with you?" she shouted. "Killing hatchlings is forbidden; that's the law! Stop it now, you filthy slaughtermen!"

Karnosk and Srashi laughed. Lian sensed they were drunk, though he couldn't imagine how they'd found the means. Smett and Hanon'ka kept strict watch over any alcohol aboard.

"Well, well, if it isn't the newling," Karnosk growled, still chuckling. "What are you doing here?"

"We were gathering herbs for Smett," Lian said as he clutched his spear tightly. "And his question is fully justified. What by the Winds are you doing here? Shouldn't you be keeping watch on board?"

"Markaeth only needed four men," Srashi spat. "We drew lots, and the two of us were lucky. Now we're enjoying the merits of this fine island." He pulled a red fruit from the pouch at his belt. "Want one? They're fantastic." He laughed.

"Ugh, no," Kris said, wincing at the smell of fermented juice. "You're drunk."

Both Drak cackled. "And what of it?" Karnosk replied. "The captain and commander are far off. We should have a little fun. This is the only land we've set foot on in weeks."

"You call this fun?" Lian asked, motioning toward the butchered dragons. "This has nothing to do with hunting. Slaughtering hatchlings is cruel, not to mention forbidden."

"Bah," said the Drak, waving his cutlass. "And who's going to stop us? You two?" His eyes seethed with reproach. "Just try." He raised his blade and moved toward the hatchlings.

"No!" Kris cried, but as she moved to intervene, Srashi grabbed her shirt collar and yanked her sideways. Karnosk lifted a hatchling by its tail and sliced its head off its writhing body.

With a desperate cry, the mother attempted to pull itself up. Srashi walked to its side and sank his blade into its flesh once more.

Nausea overcame Lian. Though he was accustomed to dragon hunting, this level of savagery was more than he could bear. *You are going the wrong way, but you can still be saved. If you decide correctly, your whole life can change.*

He stepped forward and raised his spear. "Stop!" he called as Karnosk turned to the last dragon. "If you raise your blade one more time, you'll regret it!"

The Drak turned to him, his eyes glaring with evil. "Oh, really? What will you do? Stab me? Kill us both?"

"Careful. You don't want to test how far I'll go," Lian growled.

Karnosk charged toward him and raised his blade. "You wouldn't dare," he snarled.

I've seen this all before, Lian thought. The cliff at the edge of the fog, a victim beaten half to death by vicious men, and a leader who believed himself immortal because no man dared to face him. Casran had paid for such hubris with his life.

Lian's eyes narrowed. "The last man to believe that is dead now," he said flatly, and he raised his spear. "And he was a lot more intimidating than you two."

"Karnosk," Srashi sputtered. "Look! His spear!"

A flash of uncertainty passed across Karnosk's face. "What is that? The runes . . ."

To Lian's amazement, the strange symbols flickered with an ominous fire-red light. Apparently, Drak blood was sufficient to kindle the weapon's lust. Even though it gave away his secret, Lian took charge.

"Yes, look carefully," he spat. He used all of his loathing to stoke the smoldering runes. "If you hurt that hatchling, this will be the last thing you'll ever see. Ancients forged this weapon to kill the greatest drachen of all. Your life will just be incidental."

Srashi stifled a whimper. "Let's go, Karnosk. It's not worth it. We've had our fun. Let's return to the ship now."

The other Drak stood still, with murder in his eyes.

"Well?" Lian asked. "How do you want this to end? Either you go your way, or I'll mix your blood into the hatchling pool. It makes no difference to me either way."

After a moment, Karnosk backed up slowly and pointed his blade toward Lian. "This isn't over, human. At some point, you won't have your spear in your hand. Whenever that moment comes, I'll be there."

"Take care what you say," answered Lian. "If the captain gets wind of such talk, you'll be off the ship before we reach the next harbor."

Srashi set a clawed hand onto his comrade's shoulder. "Come, Karnosk," he pleaded.

Karnosk brushed the hand away. "We'll see," he said. With a sideways glance, he hissed at Kris, who jerked back in surprise. Then both Drak shoved their blades into their belts and disappeared among the ferns.

Lian waited to be sure that they wouldn't decide to return, then he lowered his spear, and the glowing runes paled. For the first time, he noticed how his heart hammered in his chest. He had risked a great deal. Not only did he now have an enemy on board, but he'd also revealed the secret of his father's weapon. Life on board the *Carryola* wouldn't become any easier, he worried. *I have to warn Ialrist and Hanon'ka*, he thought.

A hand rested on his arm. "You were brave," Kris said gratefully.

"Brave or stupid," he answered. "Who knows." He looked toward the dragons. "And for what? We didn't accomplish anything. She'll die for sure," he said, nodding toward the mother. "And the hatchling will starve."

"We don't know that," Kris answered. "Let's take a look."

Lian shook his head. "It won't help, Kris. Look at her. She's lost too much blood. We can't save her." He stepped closer and surveyed the gruesome scene, his stomach turning as he absorbed how badly the Drak had maimed the creatures.

"I'm sorry," he said to the dragon as he inspected its wounds. "I wish we could heal you. But that would take a miracle."

The grayish-green-scaled creature shrugged its broken limbs and let out a miserable cry. A few steps away, the last hatchling squawked. *This can't be true,* he thought, overcome with sorrow. *No creature deserves such brutality.*

The dragon mother spasmed and reached its neck forward with a choking sound. Lian could barely watch as its death approached.

The dragon gagged again and spat a stream of whitish slime onto Lian's chest and face. With a cry, he fell backward. "Oh, you Winds!" he swore, dropping his spear to wipe away the slime. "That's vile!" he cried, worried that the dragon's saliva could be poisonous or corrosive.

The dragon mother closed its eyes, and its body went motionless.

"Thanks for the parting gift," Lian growled. "Oh, Winds, it stinks!" Full of revulsion, he scrunched up his nose and attempted to wipe the spit from his jacket. At least the liquid didn't burn his skin, he realized with relief.

"Wait!" Kris cried. "Don't wipe it away!"

"What?" Lian asked in confusion. "You want me to keep the slime on my jacket? It'll never wash out once it dries."

"You don't understand," Kris continued. "She did it on purpose. She knew that she had to die, so she spat on you to carry on her scent. That way the hatchling will accept you as its new mother."

"As what?" Lian stared at her in disbelief.

"As its new mother. Look." Kris motioned toward the dragon baby that clumsily crept toward Lian.

"No," Lian said, and he shook his head. "No, that's impossible. I can't carry a dragon aboard the *Carryola.* The captain would never allow it."

"Smett has Flicc," Kris said. "And maybe we can keep it in the galley. Just for a few days, until we leave the ship." Her eyes begged. "Please, Lian. We can't abandon it. If we trade shirts, it will attach to me. Then I can take care of it."

"I . . . ," Lian began, but then he looked down at the baby dragon. Staring up at him with round eyes, the creature let out a faint squawk. Lian sighed, crouched down, and lifted the animal's small and surprisingly warm body into his arms. "We'll regret this," he muttered as he stood and unbuttoned his shirt with his other hand. "I'm sure of that."

"Not today," said Kris, who stood on her tiptoes and planted a kiss on his cheek.

"Don't you get used to this," said Smett with mild reproach as he eyed the hatchling that Lian set onto the table in the galley. "You can't return from every land venture with a new friend. The *Carryola* is a drachenjäger, not a rescue boat for the Good Sons of the Four Winds."

"I know," Lian answered flatly. They had smuggled the animal on board once darkness had fallen and had gone directly to Smett. If anyone on board the *Carryola* understood Lian's reasoning, Smett did.

The hatchling perched on the table, hungrily snapping down a few morsels of bread. Flicc eyed the new guest jealously as the hatchling ate, its long nose knocking against the wooden table in its excitement.

"But it really wasn't my fault this time," Lian urged. "The barbarians Karnosk and Srashi are responsible." He had already roughly informed Smett about the massacre they had encountered.

The cook scratched his head. "Yes, we do have to watch out for those two. I never trusted them myself, but they're good slaughtermen and fearless fighters. For Adaron, that's good enough."

"We can worry more about Karnosk and Srashi later," Lian said. "Right now, I'm only concerned about this little guy. So will you help us?"

"Please," cut in Kris, who had stood silently next to Lian until then. "I'll make sure that he doesn't eat anything he's not supposed to."

"Hm." Smett sighed, and he eyed Flicc. "What do you think, my pretty?"

The rust-colored lizardwing screeched and shook her head.

"She's not convinced." Smett smiled.

"She's just jealous," Kris said as she approached the older dragon and scratched underneath her leathery chin. "Come now, Flicc. Be polite."

Flic closed her eyes and purred softly.

Smett sighed in surrender. "Fine, then. I'll put in a good word about our new guest with the captain." Shaking his head, he looked at the hatchling. "This galley is turning into a safe haven for all the lost souls on the Cloudmere."

Lian smiled. "You're a good man, Smett, and I place myself in your debt."

"You're already in my debt because of this fellow here," Smett said, nodding toward Kris.

"Then I'm doubly indebted," Lian corrected himself.

The cook raised a finger in warning. "And someday, I'll come to collect. You can be sure of that, my son." His frown softened at the edges. "But there's still some time. What should we call the little lad?"

The hatchling snapped the last piece of bread in its tiny jaws and swallowed it down. Then it squawked and rapped its beak onto the countertop as if requesting more.

A smile spread across Lian's cheeks. "Let's call him Nock Nock." He wagged a finger at the little dragon. "What do you think of that, hm? Nock Nock?"

A violet tongue shot from the hatchling's mouth and licked a crumb off Lian's finger. A strange sensation washed over Lian as though, without even trying, he had made an important choice about his destiny.

28

The Fireblood

Seventh Day of the Seventh Moon, Year 841

"He's not here!" the captain shouted angrily, lowering his bronze spyglass. "Why isn't he here? How are my maps wrong?"

Lian, who scrubbed the deck with a few others, exchanged looks with Melvas. Apparently, the captain had reached the inevitable moment when he realized that all his efforts over the past moons might once again be for naught.

After a good half-moon of sailing undisturbed, the *Carryola* had entered an area of the Cloudmere known as the Sea of a Thousand Fangs two days earlier. Adaron had determined that Gargantuan would appear there at some point between the end of the sixth moon and start of the seventh.

The place had earned its name from a long stretch of mountains through the clouds, where an abundance of dangerous ridges and peaks jutted through the fleece. If a man went overboard here, he would likely be a smear on the hard stone before he could ever bemoan his fate. Only those weary of life would risk raising sails in a place where a rock could easily tear apart a ship's hull.

The *Carryola* hovered at a safe distance from the peaks. Adaron had instructed Jaular to rise two hundred paces above the clouds so that they would have a better view. Four men kept watch—one in each direction—and Ialrist, and Corantha atop Arax, had set out to search the area in flight, but thus far, none of their efforts had been successful.

"Ialrist," Adaron bellowed, more noticeably agitated than usual. The Taijirin now stood beside him at the bow. "What have I missed? All the announcements from the isles and all the reports from drachenjägers and merchant ships have pointed to this spot. Why isn't he here?"

"I can't answer that, Adaron," his old friend said. Ialrist's sharp eyes searched the horizon before them. "Maybe he was held up by something. Life cannot follow a calendar or map. He could have been injured in battle or found an especially plentiful prey somewhere. Maybe he's even taken a mate and is protecting a brood instead of traversing the clouds."

"Gargantuan protecting a brood?" Adaron grimaced. "I don't know whether to laugh or shudder at the thought."

"Dragon!" cried the young watchman Wil from his post. "A burst of flame starboard!"

Excitement gripped Lian as he exchanged another glance with Melvas. Fire could only mean the greatest and most dangerous dragon type. All men on deck hurried toward the railing and peered into the clouds. Lian, too, stood and stared into the sky.

"Well?" Karnosk asked, his sinister lizard face already sparked with anticipation. "Is it Gargantuan?"

"No," answered Ialrist, squinting into the distance. "It's a red."

The men grew excited at his words. Firebloods, known as reds for short, were some of the most dangerous, and most profitable, catches that a jäger could make. Only the bravest and most experienced crews would risk getting close to a fire-breather. They were simply too clever and too careful.

"Captain?" Markaeth said. "Should we set up the jäger kites?"

Adaron stared into the distance lit from a burst of flame. "It isn't Gargantuan," he murmured.

"But it's a red," Ialrist reminded him. The Taijirin muttered something then to his old comrade and rested a hand on his shoulder.

At first reluctantly, but then with increasing resolution, the captain nodded. "Ialrist is right. Avoiding an opportunity such as this will only weaken our favor with the gods." His voice grew louder. "Let's prove to them, and to the world, that the *Carryola* can take on any dragon! We'll show them all that we won't be deterred by anything. Tonight, I shall hold a drachen pearl in my hands. What say you?"

The men's zealous roars were answer enough.

"Markaeth, have your men secure the sails and clear the deck, then take your positions at the artillery. Balen and Kurrn, choose four men each, and go with the jäger kites. Ialrist and Corantha, tail the monster and lure him toward us."

Corantha bared her teeth in a wide grin. "Finally, a challenge!"

"All men to their posts!" ordered Hanon'ka, who took over for Adaron.

They all hurried into motion, toward bow or stern and up into the rigging. Ialrist and Corantha disappeared below deck and returned with their weapons. Balen and Kurrn chose their men. "Lian," called Balen. "Fetch your weapon. Today you'll learn the true meaning of 'trial by fire.'"

"Hopefully not too fiery," Lian murmured as he raced down the stairs to his sleeping quarters. As his hand closed around his spear, he paused. Kesrondaia's words floated into his consciousness. *You carry the weapon of a great man, but brandish it like an enemy.* He'd thought he'd seen the flash of a dragon before his departure, at the place where the woman of white had stood. Was it possible that she was a protector of dragons and that his own hunt for drachen was the work of a foe?

He shook his head in frustration. He had saved Nock Nock and would never think to kill a dragon out of pure lust or viciousness. But this was different! This was a hunt, an endeavor in the name of the folk of the foggy coast. Anyway, a fireblood was hardly a defenseless victim. Lian's comrades trusted that he would do his best to protect their lives. As one of Adaron's slayers, he was expected to face the beast. *Though Corantha will probably beat me to it,* he thought. She fought with a wild fervor that neither he nor Ialrist could match. This thought relieved his dilemma somewhat.

Lian returned down the hallway, where he met Kris just outside the galley.

"Lian," she said. "I heard they spotted a fireblood."

"It was just sighted."

Kris looked at him, her face pained with worry. He could tell that she longed to hug him, but couldn't risk blowing her cover. "Take care of yourself," she said, and she touched his arm quickly.

He grinned confidently, as he would to any young apprentice. "Don't worry. It's just a fire-breather. It'll be good practice for the battle against Gargantuan." He winked and then ran past her along the hallway and up the stairs. Only after he was far enough away did he allow his true emotions to show: excitement and a touch of fear. He was about to face a monster far more dangerous than the bronzeneck or swingblade he'd fought before.

"Hurry! Get aboard!" Balen called when Lian returned to the deck. He clambered onto the jäger kite to join Dunrir, Melvas, and Danark. The other kite that held Kurrn's group had already taken flight, and both Ialrist and Corantha, with Arax, were already under way. "Good luck!" Hanon'ka called after them. "Remember everything you've learned until now, and you'll live through this fight."

"Thanks for the encouragement," Lian called back, and he raised his spear. Then he looked ahead, where Balen prepared the kyrillian buoys and Danark loaded the harpoon. Melvas hoisted the main and side sails, and the kite lifted into the air.

At the center of the deck, Lian noticed a stack of five large shields that he'd never seen before, made of thick dragon scales. "What are those?" he asked.

"A last resort, in case we have the misfortune to fly in front of the red's jaws," Balen explained gravely. "They're fire shields. If you see the beast's jaws start to glow, duck behind a shield and pray to the Winds that it holds up against the inferno."

Lian glanced uneasily toward the monster that flew among the clouds, clad in red-scaled armor, eyeing the comparatively tiny shield. He hoped he'd never have to find out if it worked.

As he pulled his harness over his chest, Lian wondered why their jäger kite coasted among the clouds instead of charging for the dragon. Both slayers in the air sought cover as well. "What's going on?" he asked Balen. "Aren't we going to attack?"

Balen shook his head. "A red can't be killed that easily," he explained.

"We might be able to sink a few buoys into his back, but he'll either just escape into the clouds or scorch our kite with us inside of it."

"Then what are we going to do?"

"We have to wait until he takes notice of the *Carryola*. Firebloods are easily agitated, especially when they think a rival has entered their territory. While he's preoccupied with the ship, we'll sneak up on him and unleash the slayers onto his back. It'll be their job to pierce the two main tendons that connect his wings. That way, his flight will be impaired. If we can hold him above the clouds with buoys and jäger kites, we'll be able to reach the spot at his neck to puncture his aorta. That will kill him for sure."

Behind them, Lian heard a sudden unearthly drone.

"What is *that*?" Lian asked. The sound was like a dragon roar, but distorted. He looked behind them, confused. The *Carryola* coasted freely through the open air between mounds of cloud and the fireblood. The crew pulled in her sails, and at the railing near the bow, they positioned more fire shields at the ready. The drone blared once more. When Lian squinted, he thought he noticed Elrin, the subcommander, blowing into a strange curved horn.

"Our drachen horn," Balen explained, grinning. "Captain Adaron is provoking the beast."

A roar shook the clouds as the monster threw itself toward them, its wings beating powerfully. "Winds, stand by us," Lian murmured, eyeing the beast's thick red scales, hardened coal-black underside, long spikes along its wings and back, and terrifying claws. The red opened its jaws, tilted its head back, and shot a stream of flame into the sky.

Behind Lian, Melvas began to pray.

"Bite your tongue," Dunrir growled from the helm. "No Wind or god can help you now. We alone will decide whether we live or die." The Nondurier steered the ship to the edge of the clouds. Ialrist, Corantha, and the second kite followed suit. Meanwhile, the crew aboard the *Carryola* busily distracted the dragon. When a burst of flame met the scale-armored hull, Lian wondered if their approach was normal. Did other jägers take such dangerous measures to kill a red?

There was no time to wonder. The *Carryola*'s ballistae cracked as their deadly projectiles shot toward the dragon. A spear hit against the thick armor of scales at the beast's flank, while the other sank into its belly. The beast roared ferociously and spat another stream of fire toward the bow.

Ialrist and Corantha swooped down, taking care to stay behind the colossal dragon. Kurrn, too, steered the second kite downward. "Go!" Balen cried from the ballista, taking aim.

Lian gripped the railing tightly as Dunrir tilted their kite forward, steering them in a steep curve that brought them to the red's tail. "Get ready, Lian!" Balen called. "When I say go, throw down your rope and climb down."

"Aye!" Lian confirmed. He slung his spear across his back and tested his harness. Then, gripping the rope at the railing, he awaited the order.

Up ahead, Ialrist circled the beast like a vulture inspecting its prey. The Taijirin landed at the center of the monster's back, his reaver gripped tightly in his hand. Then Corantha appeared, and Lian gasped as she threw herself from Arax's back without a rope. Just before landing, the huntress opened the cases on her harness and gracefully landed on her feet, aided by the kyrillian.

Dunrir maneuvered the kite just above the dragon's back. "Go!" Balen cried, and Lian didn't hesitate. He slung his rope over the kite's ledge, gripped its end, sent a parting prayer to the Winds, and lowered himself into the depths.

He fell far too quickly and tried to grip the rope tighter to slow himself. Gasping in pain from the force that ran through his arms and shoulders, he feared his zeal would be his end.

He landed beside the other two slayers. Corantha grinned at him wildly. "There's nothing better than riding on the back of a red!" she shouted against the roar of the wind.

"No talking. Just do it," Ialrist instructed. "Lian, get yourself to his neck, and lunge as soon as the kite is positioned. Corantha, you take the left wing, and I'll take the right."

"Aye, my friend," Corantha called confidently, and she pulled a long-handled ax from behind her back. Lian had never seen her carry the weapon before. "There's a proper weapon for every dragon," she answered when she noticed his questioning glance.

Lian nodded and headed for the beast's thickly scaled neck. Then the ground underneath his feet tilted—or rather reared up from underneath, farther and farther, until the dragon's back seemed to reach straight into the sky. Caught unprepared, the wind gathered under Ialrist's wings, ripping him backward and throwing him clear of the dragon. Corantha swore loudly as her ax flew from her hand and vanished in the clouds. Both she and Lian clung to the horn plates along the dragon's back as the beast, with violently flapping wings, rose higher into the sky.

"It caught onto our plan," Corantha called. "Cursed lizard!"

As the fireblood's body tried to shake the remaining pests from its back, Lian cried out in inarticulate panic. With sheer will alone, he managed to wedge his feet between the plates to keep himself from falling.

The dragon turned sharply to the left, and the *Carryola*, along with both jäger kites, appeared in view. The three vessels approached from below. Jaular, Dunrir, and Kurrn must have opened all kyrillian cases to reach the dragon's altitude. As long as the dragon flew above them, it had the upper hand.

Apparently, the red knew that, too. As a rumble ran through its enormous body, it stretched its neck forward and spat a burst of flame at its attackers below. The blaze scorched the *Carryola*'s deck, spread toward the right, and set fire to one of the kites—which one, Lian couldn't say. At the sight of his comrades running frantically on deck—tiny burning figures from his altitude—he grew nauseous.

A fist against his shoulder caught his attention. Corantha had struggled to his side by climbing along the nearby plates. "We have to do something quickly!" she cried.

"How are we supposed to slay this beast?" Lian yelled. "We only have my—" But the rest of his words transformed into a cry as the red took off in a nosedive. With its wings pulled in tightly, it shot like an arrow into the depths and plummeted straight between the burning ships, falling with the fury of a god's fist. As it fell, the red bucked on its own axis, a movement sufficient to shake both Lian and Corantha off its back.

29

On Life and Death

Seventh Day of the Seventh Moon, Year 841

The sky and the other slayers whirled above as Lian floundered through the air. From the corner of his eye, he saw the red, below him among the clouds, spread its wings wide and sail upward.

As the clouds drew nearer, Lian fumbled with the metal cases at his sides. With frantic fingers, he managed to open them. Gasping and with a racing heart, he jolted to a stop in the air. Corantha, too, hung suspended not far off from him. She scowled at the fireblood as the beast prepared its next attack.

"He must be old!" she called to Lian. "He's already survived a few slayers before us. That's the only way to explain his tactics."

Arax swooped to Corantha's side, and she climbed onto his back. Lian looked toward Ialrist. Without help, he would continue to lift helplessly into the air, barely able to move right or left, but the Taijirin was busy transporting buckets of water to the burning jäger kites. Even amid screams and cries of confusion, the *Carryola* turned once more to face the enemy.

With a swish, Corantha appeared at his side. Lian cried out as Arax's jaws grabbed his collar and swung him onto his back behind the huntress.

"Thanks," Lian gasped, fumbling unsteadily for a hold on the dragon's smooth back.

Corantha turned to him. "Goddess, stand by me," she said, and she rolled her eyes. "Grab hold of my belt, then, if you're about to fall off."

"Oh, okay. Thanks," Lian said, and he did as he was told.

"Just don't get used to it," she warned haughtily.

"Don't worry," he answered. "What now?"

"What do you think?" Corantha laughed. "We're going to charge."

She leaned forward and instructed Arax in words that Lian didn't know. With a roar, the grayback rose into the clouds.

Above them, the battle between the *Carryola* and the fireblood was under way. One of the jäger kites, too, had returned to the fray. Two kyrillian buoys extended from the dragon's flank, though the beast barely acknowledged their pull. Instead, it let out another deafening roar and sent another stream of flame against the hull of Adaron's ship. If dragon scales hadn't covered the *Carryola,* it would have been a burning wreck plummeting groundward by now.

A thunderous ball of blue light shot past Lian from the ship's bow and exploded against the fire dragon's head. The beast roared in pain.

"Finally!" Corantha cried. "Why did Janosthir wait so long to use his thunder launcher?"

Lian knew Janosthir to be a strange man, though he hadn't had much to do with him thus far. Stocky and muscular like a Nondurier, but human, he identified himself as a Settlander and served as defense aboard the *Carryola.* Lian had only ever seen him man the harpoons during battle. Apparently, he had other tricks up his sleeve.

"Look!" Corantha called to Lian. "The dragon is stunned. This is our chance. Arax, quick!"

With a few powerful beats of his wings, the grayback pulled them upward.

"What's your plan?" Lian asked.

"That depends," she said, glancing over her shoulder. "Is your spear really as powerful as they say?"

"How do you know about that?" He hadn't spoken about his weapon to anyone since his run-in with Karnosk and Srashi on the island.

"I overheard the Drak," Corantha answered. "So? Can your weapon really slay the greatest dragons?"

"That's what I've been told," Lian answered. "But I don't know for sure."

"Well, we're about to find out," she said. Arax pressed against the wind stirred from the dragon's massive wings as he continued to raise them toward their goal. "Give me the spear!" she yelled, reaching out her hand.

"No chance!" Lian shouted, filled with sudden ambition. "I'll handle it myself."

"Fine. When you land, get yourself to the monster's head and ram the spear into its brain." Corantha looked toward him once, and her tattooed face curled into a grotesque mocking grin. "Ready to jump?"

Lian swallowed. He'd be damned if he would give in to his fear. His pressed his lips together decisively. "Just get me close enough," he said.

"Ha!" Corantha called. Apparently, she hadn't expected his answer. "You're crazy! I think I'm beginning to like you after all." She gave Arax another order, and the grayback pulled them farther upward.

"Swing your leg over Arax's back so that you can slide behind his wings," Corantha said. "Then give me your hand. I'll hold on until we're right over the monster's head."

"Got it," Lian said. Another explosion thundered above him, and he clenched his jaw. He hoped that Janosthir's zeal wouldn't fling him off the red's head.

The red howled in rage and pain and jerked to the side. Arax leaned into a tight curve to approach the beast from the side. Lian hurried to grab Corantha's outstretched arm. Her grip was like iron, and her sinewy muscles pulled taut against his weight.

He looked below to the heaving red mass of scales and horns beneath him. The stink of charred meat penetrated his nostrils. A row of spikes along the monster's spine broadened into a menacing horned headdress at the back of its head.

"Now!" cried Corantha.

Lian steeled himself and released his fingers, and Corantha let go.

He fell all of two paces before landing just behind the monster's head. Panting, he fell to his knees, grabbed hold of a nearby spike, and took the spear from his back.

The red thrashed its head indignantly, and Lian clung to the bony growths on its back for dear life. From the side, he caught sight of the men aboard the *Carryola*, whose cries and waves showed their horror and astonishment. Elrin, who stood at the railing, covered in soot, grinned and raised his horn to his lips, sounding once more the droning challenge of the drachenjäger.

As the sound diverted the red's attention, Lian took his chance. Steadying himself, he raised his spear into the air and aimed downward.

You carry the weapon of a great man, but brandish it like an enemy.

The voice spoke within his mind.

No! No! he thought. *Not now.*

Let your instinct guide you instead of following the orders of others. Then you'll understand the difference between right and wrong.

Lian winced as he stared at his spear, unable to attack. *I have to!* he screamed to the voice in his head. *This beast will kill us all if I don't!*

We shouldn't be foes.

I'm sorry.

With all his strength, Lian brought the spear down.

The point knocked against the hardened scales on the red's head.

"No," Lian murmured in disbelief. "No, it can't be true." He stared at the weapon and raised it once more, but the runes didn't stir. This time, Lian was unable to unleash the weapon's powers.

Ialrist landed beside Lian from above with a rustling beat of his wings. "You have to want it!" he cried, and he tore the spear out of Lian's hand. "You have to hate the beast!" He took aim. "Die, you monster!" he roared.

With an explosion of light, the runes fired to life, their gleam as bright as the midday sun. As Ialrist brought the spear down, the point bore into the beast's hard scale armor and pierced through the thick skull bone with a crack, sinking halfway into the fireblood's head.

The dragon tilted its head back and released a terrible howl that shook the sky and nearly stole Lian's wits. Then its wings went limp, and its head slumped lifelessly, held just barely aloft by the kyrillian buoys.

Harpoon ballistae cracked as the *Carryola* and her kites bound their ropes to the titan's body to keep it from falling into the depths. Lian knelt at the dragon's head and closed his eyes. They had prevailed. But at what cost?

"Kurrn, Jakk, Lannik, and Aelfert," said Adaron, his expression grim as the crew assembled on the charred deck later that afternoon. "You were all good men, and none of you deserved to die in flames. But life as a drachenjäger is a dance along a knife's blade: magnificent, as long as it lasts, but deadly if you lose your footing."

Lian struggled to listen as the captain continued his liturgy. As he stood amid the group between Smett and Kris, his gaze focused on the red's powerful body, now bound to the *Carryola*'s side while Hanon'ka and Kettler, the chief slaughterman, assessed it. He couldn't get over his failure. He hadn't been able to summon the deadly runes on his father's weapon. *You have to want it!* Ialrist had insisted. Lian *had* really wanted it. Hadn't he?

After the fight and their return to the *Carryola*, Ialrist had pulled Lian aside and had asked what had happened. "I don't know," was all Lian could answer. "The weapon refused to obey."

The Taijirin had studied him with piercing eyes. "Was it the weapon that refused, or was it you? You should decide before we meet the next dragon." With those words, the Taijirin had left him standing.

There was no denying it: his mystical encounter with Kesrondaia and the run-in with Karnosk and Srashi, who found sport in slaughtering dragon hatchlings, had changed something in Lian. He had begun to doubt. At least the doubt was still faint, and he could ignore it if he tried hard enough. Still, it was there and spoke with the voice of the mysterious woman of white, urging him to turn from a course that would sully a legacy that reached back for generations.

Lian wondered if his father had known of the spear's power. Had Kesrondaia also appeared to him and urged him to turn away from the hunt? Could all of it—his terrible injury and the end of his life as the hailed jäger Lonjar Draksmasher—have been caused during a decisive moment of doubt where he, too, had been unable to kill? Had he become a drunk because he could never decide whether he had acted rightly or not?

Lian knew he would never receive the answers to these questions, but the answers didn't matter, really. The only important thing now was how he would proceed. He stood at a crossroads, the second since Casran's death. The decision was his: either follow the path of his fate as a slayer—as he had done when leaving Skargakar—or swear off the hunt and step into the unknown, toward the voice of a shimmering woman of white with the ghostly spirit of a powerful dragon within her.

The captain ended his eulogy, and the remains of the dead went overboard into the clouds. Then the mementos were distributed. Balen received a fang to commemorate Aelfert's death, and Dunrir another, as the oldest confidant of his landsman Kurrn. Jakk and Lannik hadn't had any real friends on board, so Adaron ordered both their fangs to be mounted to the ship's hull in their memory. Then he took his flogging from Elrin, that grisly retribution for breaking his oath to prevent any more victims from their crew.

The crew watched the grim ritual in silence, but Lian sensed an underlying unrest among them, and he had some idea why. No dead souls or whipping interested them as much as a rumor that had started to spread among them after the battle. They longed to see the drachen pearl with their own eyes, that great treasure that only a jäger could rip from the body of a dragon. Sure, none of them would ever hold one. Adaron would surely protect such a prize for himself, and turn it into a sack of crystals at the next possible trading port—or at the latest when they returned to Skargakar. Lian, too, hoped to see the sight with his own eyes someday. It was an experience, he'd heard among jägers, that was practically holy.

Gasping, Adaron broke away from the helm railing, where he had clung during the beating. "Medic," he moaned weakly.

Narso appeared from the crowd, not hiding his disapproval for having to tend to these senseless wounds yet again. He led Adaron up to the helm and lowered him onto a cushion. With a practiced hand, he cleaned and bandaged the wounds, then helped the captain back into his shirt and jacket. Meanwhile, Hanon'ka and Kettler joined them. Kettler held a round object wrapped inside a blanket, about the size of a human head. The group on deck waited in suspense.

Adaron took a moment to catch his breath and faced the men at the railing.

"And now," he began, "we celebrate the siege of a great beast, of one of the most terrible creatures in all the Cloudmere! Allow me to present a prize coveted by every jäger. Kettler!" he summoned.

At the captain's invitation, the slaughterman handed him the cloth-bound object. Adaron moved the blanket corners aside and let the fabric fall to the deck. Then he held the object high into the air.

"They call it a drachen pearl, the heart of a Great Drachen," he called. Murmurs moved through the crowd, and Lian, too, held his breath.

"By all Winds," whispered Kris next to him. "It's beautiful . . ."

Lian could only agree. The pearl was magnificent. It gleamed like a reddish-gold star, wrapped in mist and trapped inside a crystal ball. Lian noticed that his gaze gravitated toward the pearl's center. He felt the fleeting but fierce sensation of the great power at its core. The majesty of the beast and the pearl it harbored—the deep and ancient magic contained within its spirit—filled him with awe. He wondered what that magic could create or destroy if unleashed.

The reverent moment ended abruptly when Adaron held out a hand. Kettler bowed hastily and handed the blanket back to him, and the captain wrapped the pearl out of view. The captain did not allow anyone to touch the prize, though Lian read in many of their faces that they longed to hold the trophy, if only for a moment.

There was also another longing that Karnosk—of all people—put into words. "Captain," said the Drak. "Will we go home now?"

"Back to Skargakar?" The question shocked Adaron. "No. Why would we?"

The Drak folded his arms across his chest. "With your permission, Captain, we've gained a pearl and a great bounty from the red, not to mention all the profits we've gathered from our previous kills. The *Carryola*'s hold is filled to the brim. I don't think we should risk our riches by continuing to cross the clouds. We should turn them into crystals."

"He's not wrong, Captain," Markaeth dared to add. "We've been aloft a good two moons and haven't met a soul besides dragons and Taijirin. I, for one, would pay a great price to see the curves of a human woman again. Here on board, there's nothing to compare to that kind of pleasure. No offense, Corantha."

Lian felt Kris inch closer to him as though trying to disappear from the freckled man's view.

"Your view of my curves would be brief," Corantha answered. "About as long as it would take me to gouge out your eyes."

Markaeth snorted and turned away.

"The men aren't wrong," said Elrin. "Our haul is plentiful, and the last crowded port lies far behind us. We've also lost seven men. If we met Gargantuan, would we even be equipped to face him? We don't even know where to find him. Why don't we continue our search after a few days in Skargakar or—"

"That's enough!" Adaron bellowed. Though he had listened silently, his anger had magnified as the men spoke. "We are closer to Gargantuan than ever before. I can feel it! And I won't give the order to turn home. The *Carryola* is greater than any other jäger ship—and so is its crew. I regret losing our dead, yes, but we won't miss them when we fight the Black Leviathan. This ship is more than equipped to face Gargantuan. So stop your insubordination!"

He scanned the men until his gaze landed on Markaeth and Karnosk. "You shouldn't be lying on plush tits in your dreams, but on hard dragon scales. Your heart shouldn't burn with lust for glittering crystals, but for bathing in Gargantuan's blood! You consider a drachen pearl the greatest prize?" With flashing eyes, he ripped the blanket away and revealed the glowing jewel. "It's nothing! I could throw it overboard and wouldn't even think twice. Maybe I should. And while I'm at it, I'll cut the red from the ship so that our hold isn't too full."

He made a sweeping gesture, and cries sounded through the crew. Hanon'ka gripped the captain's shoulder and whispered into his ear. Although Adaron continued to scowl, the Sidhari's words seemed to have an effect. The captain handed the pearl back to Kettler, who hurried to cover it before Adaron changed his mind.

Adaron leaned forward and braced his hands on the railing. "I assumed it was already clear to everyone on board, but perhaps I should repeat myself so that we all understand one another. The goal of the *Carryola* is to find and kill Gargantuan. Any other dragons we happen to capture only serve to improve our battle skills and strengthen our ship. We shall not die fat and satisfied in our beds before we slay the ultimate beast! The reward—and this I assure you—will be greater triumph than anything you can imagine. Our riches will know no limits, and our names will echo through eternity. Bards will sing ballads of our deeds into the farthest corners of the known world, and the name of every person standing at my side on that glorious day will be breathed as the name of the greatest hero: those fearless souls who slew the Firstborn and brought Gargantuan to his end."

The captain straightened up, black and forbidding—unbending in body and spirit—and glared at them. "Nothing besides our siege of the Black Leviathan will turn this ship toward home. Nothing! His time has come. And now, I'll say no more about it. Go!"

Grumbling, the men exchanged glances. The captain's fiery words had clearly intimidated them, but no one seemed convinced.

Hanon'ka stepped forward. "You heard the captain," he called, and the fire in his eyes burned almost as brightly as the pearl's core. "Get to work! There's a red to be slaughtered and a ship to keep afloat. Hop to!"

Next to Lian, Smett sighed. "That wasn't the celebration I'd hoped for," he said. He clapped Kris on her narrow shoulder. "Come, my boy. We're needed in the galley. I've got a hankering for the warmth of the stove and for Flicc. It's gotten very cold out here, don't you think?"

Kris nodded and smiled nervously. Before leaving, she turned to Lian. "See you later," she said.

"Yes, later." He returned her smile.

A chill blew against his back, and he shuddered. Smett was right. A cold wind had descended over the deck, and it came from the north.

30

The Water of Vision

Ninth Day of the Seventh Moon, Year 841

Shrieks of men, who burn like torches.
Giant eyes seethe with flickering hate.
A woman ripped to pieces by relentless claws.
And a snapping jaw lined with fangs.

Panting, Lian knelt among the boxes in the hold. Sweat drenched his face, and his heart raced. As the effect from the silver water slowly faded, so, too, did the terrible images. A quarter moon had passed since he'd filled the skin inside the mysterious cave on the lithos with no name.

The battle against the fireblood and his own hesitation to kill disturbed him. Most of all, though, he longed for answers and guidance. He had begun to drink the silver water in hopes of making contact with Kesrondaia. He had tried three times in the last few nights—and had failed with each attempt. Aside from the garbled and disturbing images, which revealed a doomed battle between the *Carryola* and a shadowy black monster, the silver water left only a hollow feeling of fear afterward.

Lian wondered what to make of the visions. Were they nightmares reflecting his own fear of Gargantuan, a fear fanned by Adaron's fiery words? Or were the images premonitions of what lay before him? Could the water be warning that the *Carryola* was sailing toward its doom?

I have to speak to someone, Lian thought. His hands shook as he picked up the waterskin and studied it. *I have to know whether I'm going crazy or if we're approaching real danger.* Maybe he should speak to Hanon'ka. If anyone knew about magic, it was the tattooed Sidhari. Or maybe Smett was the better choice. The cook had seen much in his life—and wasn't the ship's first commander. *If Smett can't help me, there's still a chance I can confide in Hanon'ka.*

Lian pulled himself up and left his hiding place. Just before midnight, the whole ship was quiet. The day watch slept soundly, while the late watch stood guard. The early morning watch, which Lian would join before long, dozed in their hammocks.

Smett, however, was likely still awake. The cook usually only took rest after distributing a small midnight meal to the early and late watches. Then he slept until dawn in order to be standing in the galley before breakfast.

To Lian's surprise, Smett wasn't alone. Leaning against the wall of the canteen, Ialrist stood with his arms crossed over his armored chest as he watched the cook stirring his infamous kettle of mush.

"Lian," Ialrist said in surprise when he entered the room.

Flicc and Nock Nock, who perched together on a cabinet—they'd become one heart and soul—looked up sleepily and uttered quiet squawks in greeting.

"Forgive me," Lian said. "Am I intruding?"

Smett turned from the steaming cauldron. "No, come in, Lian," he invited jovially. "We're not telling any great secrets. Or do you see it differently?" he asked the Taijirin with a sideways glance.

The Taijirin waited before answering. "I think Lian is trustworthy enough."

Now curious, Lian looked from one man to the other. For the moment, he'd forgotten his own worry. "What is it?" he asked.

"We're pondering how Ialrist can convince Adaron to turn the *Carryola* toward harbor," answered Smett, testing the brew with his spoon.

Lian turned to Ialrist, astonished. "You agree that we should call off the hunt? From your performance against the red, I took you for an un-wavering advocate of a battle against Gargantuan."

"Then I fooled you, just as your spear did," Ialrist answered calmly.

"What do you mean?"

"Your weapon is awakened by strong urges," explained the slayer. "It's enough to call those urges in a moment of battle. It's true; I carry an old grudge against these monsters. I can never forgive the loss of my com-rades. *But* I am *not* Adaron. I won't be consumed by my emotions. Many years have passed and enough blood has been spilled to even the score. I kill because it's my job aboard this ship. It's what I can do better than anyone on board, except for Corantha, maybe. That doesn't mean I don't know how to awaken hunting lust or a warrior's rage when it's necessary. When scorn and hate are needed to fuel an enchanted weapon, I'm more than capable."

Lian studied the Taijirin in amazement. "You surprise me again."

The corners of Ialrist's mouth twitched. "That isn't difficult. We've only sailed together for two moons. You barely know me."

"That's true. It also explains why I didn't know that you two are friends," Lian said, looking from Ialrist to Smett.

"Friends? Me, with the flutter-man?" the cook scoffed. "Let's not ex-aggerate." He grinned and winked.

Ialrist wasn't deterred. "Smett was the first to board the *Carryola* when Adaron and I set out," he explained. "He's a good man, and he's not just tougher than he looks. He's also far wiser. I've never been too proud to take his advice when it's offered."

The cook brandished his spoon like a weapon. "Stop it," he said. "If you keep embarrassing me, you'll make me over-salt the brew."

"So what have you decided?" Lian asked, changing the subject. "How can you convince the captain to turn around?"

"We don't have an answer yet," Ialrist admitted. "We're closer to Gar-gantuan today than we've been in moons, maybe than ever before. That's what Adaron wants to believe, at least. He has to believe it; otherwise, he'll be forced to wonder if the whole mission has been for nothing." Ialrist's expression darkened. "Adaron's need for vengeance clouds his perspective and judgment. I'm not sure if I can convince him that it would be smarter to save crew and ship instead of tossing them into battle."

"I can only say this," offered Smett. "The crew's mood isn't at its best. The battle against the red did them in. Many are wounded, even if only with scrapes. They long for hard ground under their feet, if only for a few days and nights. Adaron may well try to ignore it . . ." He sighed. "But what about you, Lian? Did hunger drag you out of your hammock early? Or is something on your mind?"

"I . . ." Lian hesitated and glanced at Ialrist.

The Taijirin pushed away from the wall. "Then I'll leave you alone now."

"No!" Lian rushed to say. "It's good that you're here. You have traveled far, as you've told me yourself. Maybe you can help." He pulled the waterskin from his side, took an empty bowl from the shelf, and filled it with the silver water. He reached the bowl out to Smett and Ialrist. "Do you know what this is?" he asked.

Smett raised his bushy eyebrows. "By my soul, I've never seen anything like it. Cold, liquid silver?"

"Give me the bowl," Ialrist demanded, unusually agitated. When Lian handed it to him, the Taijirin studied its contents carefully, sniffed deeply, and dipped a finger into the liquid.

"Be careful!" Lian cried as Ialrist raised the fingertip to his lips, but when the Taijirin went stiff and his face darkened, he knew it was too late.

The vision seemed to only last for the blink of an eye, most likely because Ialrist had only swallowed a small amount. "It calls forth nightmares and visions," Lian explained once the Taijirin's eyes had cleared.

"Yes," Ialrist answered. "As I'd thought." He eyed Lian sharply. "Where did you get this?"

"You know about silver water?" Lian asked. He was as stunned as he was hopeful.

The Taijirin nodded. "I wouldn't bet my life on it, but it's similar to a liquid that we call the Water of Vision. It is said that a person can gaze into distant places and see coming events. I never drank it myself, but I've seen others use it."

"To see coming events?" Lian's heart hammered in his chest. "Then the visions tell the future?"

"A distorted, possible future," Ialrist elaborated. "Nothing can predict the future with certainty, not even the Water of Vision. Too many choices inform each moment. It may very well be, though, that the water shows what may happen. It doesn't show everything, however, or rather, it alters the facts, so I've heard. One can't rely on the visions alone. I'll ask you again: *Where did you get this?* This water can only be found in enchanted places that are all kept under close secret."

Lian described the cave on the nameless lithos and told of what had happened there. He refrained, though, from telling of his encounter with Kesrondaia. As much as he longed to know more about her, he still wasn't ready to reveal his secret.

When he ended his tale, he waited for the reprimand to come. He knew he shouldn't have withheld information from the captain. To his surprise, the Taijirin nodded. "You were right not to tell anyone. The Water of Vision is dangerous and highly addictive. Men lose sight of the present and become consumed by terrifying visions of the future. A person can go insane. I shudder to think what would happen if Adaron caught wind of it." His voice carried a deep somberness.

"How often have you drunk the water since we set sail?"

Lian swallowed. "Once," he lied.

Ialrist's piercing gaze bore into Lian's mind. "Tell the truth. Your life could depend on it."

Ashamed, Lian looked to the floor. "Fine. Three times. I swear." He raised his head and fixed his eyes on Ialrist. "Three times."

The Taijirin nodded slowly. "Good. Then your dependence will only be slight, but you should stop right away. This form of magic isn't for the inexperienced." He held out a hand. "Give me the waterskin, and I'll throw it overboard."

"I . . . I can do it myself," Lian answered. "Or, can't I keep it, if I promise not to drink any more of it? Who knows when it might be useful?"

Ialrist shook his head. "It's never useful. It's only a danger. You'll break every promise you make—maybe not today or tomorrow, but sooner or later. The water's lure is too great." He reached his hand toward Lian. "Give it to me."

"You just want to keep it for yourself!" Lian argued.

Smett inhaled sharply. "Be careful what you say, lad."

Surprised, Lian braced himself. He expected the Taijirin to challenge him to a fight for insulting his honor.

Ialrist dropped his hand. "I can only advise you if you'll let me," he said softly. "But if you'd rather fall into ruin, go ahead. You wouldn't be the first I couldn't hold back."

Shattered, Lian glanced at the waterskin in his hand. He knew that the Taijirin was right. He could already feel the urge to drink the liquid again. He longed to learn everything he could from the vision so that he could prevent it from occurring. How many gulps did the skin hold? Surely only a dozen or a few more at best. At least he'd be able to use those few opportunities for good.

No! his mind urged. *It's no good. The water has control of me. And if I give in . . . ?*

A person can go insane—Ialrist's words returned.

"Ialrist," he said to the Taijirin, who had turned away and stood near Smett. Lian held the waterskin out to him. "Take it, please. And forgive me for speaking so thoughtlessly. I guess I'm not myself."

The Taijirin took the skin. "Then I won't lose any time," he said, and he stepped toward the door. "We'll speak more later, Smett."

"You know where to find me," the cook answered. "Perhaps the light of a new day will reveal how to make Adaron see reason."

Lian watched Ialrist leave, and he joined the cook at his kettle. "He really is a great man, isn't he?" he said, nodding toward the door.

Smett nodded. "The greatest on board, without a doubt—the truest friend and a gallant soul. The only other one who comes close is Hanon'ka, but there's a shadow hanging over our Sidhari."

"I know." A question burned on Lian's tongue. Why did Hanon'ka have a death wish? But he didn't know if the Sidhari had ever spoken to Smett in confidence, so he remained silent. Instead, he asked another question that had bothered him for a long time. "Tell me, Smett, if you've known Ialrist since the *Carryola*'s first days, do you happen to know about his past?"

Smett glanced at Lian. "What do you mean, exactly?"

"While we were in Vindirion, something extraordinary happened. Ialrist and Adaron snuck into the fortress to free me. The Taijirin commander, Shiraik, addressed Ialrist as a prince. Is that true? Is Ialrist royalty? And if so, for which kingdom?"

The cook chuckled. "He doesn't sound it from the rooftops, but our good winged man happens to be a nobleman of the highest blood—at least among the Taijirin. Why do you think we always send him first when we're approaching the isles?"

"I thought he was scouting the territory," Lian admitted.

"That's what everyone is supposed to think," said Smett. "And he does that, too, but he also establishes himself as a prince in exile, which seems to make quite an impression. So far, the Taijirin have never caused trouble, and we have Ialrist to thank."

"But you don't know which kingdom he hails from?"

Smett shrugged. "Oh, what does a name even mean when it's not bound to thoughts and feelings? Ialrist comes from far away, I know that much, and he's descended from a distinguished line of rulers. They say his ancestors were heroes. The only story that he ever told me himself was so fantastic I could barely believe it. From the mouth of any other man, I would have taken it for a jäger's fable. He mentioned armies of dead, dragons made from crystal, and an order of knights who brandished enchanted weapons. Simply unbelievable." Chuckling softly, the cook shook his head.

Lian pressed him. "Tell me more. It's been a long time since I heard a good hero's tale." With a pang of sorrow, he remembered evenings at Cliff House with Canzo, where traveling bards had woven songs of knights, sorcerers, and captive princesses.

Smett looked at him jovially. "You really want to hear that old—"

A cry, followed by commotion, interrupted him. Lian heard commands roared in a foreign tongue, along with clinking weapons and the clatter of steps.

"By all bones and skulls—" started Smett.

Sheshac's appearance at the doorway, holding a long knife in both hands, cut his thought short.

"Easy now," the Drak hissed, his yellow lizard eyes seething. "Stay where you are. If you don't make trouble, nothing will happen to you."

31

Drak Scorn

Tenth Day of the Seventh Moon, Year 841

"Mutiny!" Smett yelled in anger. Before Sheshac could react, the cook dug his spoon deep into the kettle and sent a load of hot brew catapulting toward their attacker.

The Drak jerked backward, giving Smett the time he needed. He grabbed a large iron griddle from its hook on the wall, gripped its handle with both hands, and swung it before him like a club. The pan resounded like a gong against Sheshac's brown-scaled face with a crunch. The Drak let out a moan and fell down, unconscious.

Flicc and Nock Nock now stood alert and hopped excitedly back and forth on the cabinet shelf. The hatchling, especially, darted its head frantically and squawked with worry.

"There, there," Lian calmed. "The man is gone." *At least one of them,* he thought.

"I can't believe the Drak staged a mutiny," Smett growled, setting the pan against his shoulder without looking at the nervous dragons. "Karnosk and the others have always been troublemakers. They've only ever been interested in crystals and other loot. I suppose they've set their eyes on the drachen pearl. Damned traitors." He stepped toward the door and peered into the hallway. "Are you coming?" he said over his shoulder.

Lian pulled a meat cleaver from the wall, but then shook his head. "You save the captain," he said. "I have to check on Kris."

The cook grinned. "That boy has really done a number on you." He chuckled.

"His life is more important to me than Adaron's," Lian explained.

Smett nodded and gripped his pan. Then he set out toward the cries and clanks of blades coming from Adaron's, Hanon'ka's, and the slayers' sleeping quarters. Lian looked sharply toward Flicc and Nock Nock. "Stay here," he instructed, and he set out in the other direction as an uneasy feeling built in his gut.

After a few steps, he came upon Srashi and—to his surprise—Danark, who held the men of the day and early morning watches hostage. Srashi brandished his blade—the same he'd used to skewer the hatchlings— while Danark pointed Lian's own spear at Melvas, Gaaki, Kris, and Dunrir, the new leader of their group after Hanon'ka had assigned Balen to Kurrn's old room following his death.

"Lian!" Srashi exclaimed. To Lian's secret pleasure, the Drak sounded nervous.

"What's going on here?" Lian asked fiercely. "Have you gone mad? To turn against your own comrades? Against your own brother?"

"Shut up," Danark snarled. "We're doing what's best for everyone. We're forcing the captain and first commander to dock at the next harbor so that the booty in the hold can finally be turned into crystals. We want to get paid and go our ways, before we have to fight the Firstborn."

"Are you cowards?" Lian asked. "We all knew what we signed up for when we boarded the *Carryola*. Or didn't Hanon'ka ask if you were ready to accept the challenge?"

"Of course he did," Srashi hissed. "I'm not afraid of any dragon, but the captain won't see reason. This ship is full of loot. Why have we fought and suffered over the last moons if not to sell our bounty and piss away our shares however we choose? We've earned it!"

"Not like this," Lian implored. "Speak with the first and second commanders, and let them work on Adaron. A riot will only set us back. How many are you? Five? Six?"

"Enough," growled Danark. "And the second commander sees things our way, too—just so you know."

Lian's uneasiness grew. Six crewmen staging a rash attack on Adaron was serious. He shook his head. "What about Corantha, Ialrist, and Hanon'ka? What about the men in these rooms? These are your comrades."

"Listen to Lian, Danark," Melvas said from the back room. "Don't make yourself regret this, brother. Your attack is already going wrong. You'll never win."

"We'll see about that." In Danark's eye, Lian spotted a sinister glimmer. "You have no idea what I've got in my hand, Melvas," Danark said through bared teeth. "But I do, and so does Lian. This weapon makes its attacker invincible—if he knows how to use it." He clutched the spear tighter. For a moment, Lian's heart stopped as he saw a shimmer of light flicker near the spear's end.

Then he realized that the glimmer was merely a reflection of the lantern light, and a sneer spread across his face. "Invincible?" he spat. "Who told you that fairy tale?"

"I saw how you conjured the runes on the weapon," the Drak answered.

"So what? Have I ever claimed I was invincible?" Lian shook his head. "This spear slays dragons. Its magic doesn't go beyond that."

"Oh, this spear will slay humans perfectly well, too, mark my words," Danark jeered. "And in your case, it'll even be worth it."

Lian's beating heart threatened to jump out of his chest. "What is that supposed to mean?" he asked. He tried to keep Danark talking while he considered how to retrieve his spear.

"Do you remember the story I told you when you arrived?" Danark asked. "About the time I saw the drunkard Lonjar Draksmasher in a tavern?"

"Forgive me for not remembering your every word," snapped Lian.

"I think you remember well," Danark continued. "Anyway, that wasn't the whole story. On that night, Lonjar confronted Casran, the son of Odan Klingenhand. Not a good idea, if you ask me."

"What are you getting at?"

"Only that I knew the old man was done for—and then sure thing, just before we set sail, I learned of his death. What do you know? Another man wound up dead: Odan's son. That means that Draksmasher's kin must have sought revenge, and I'm sure that Odan would pay a pretty sum for that man's head."

"What does all that have to do with me?" asked Lian furiously.

"Well, that was unclear to me for a long time," Danark answered. "Then I ran into a certain Captain Koos from the *Draconia* while we were docked in Vindirion. Not only did he know about Lonjar Draksmasher, he also gave quite the description of his son. I'd say you're the spitting image!"

Lian cursed his bad luck. Only a few people in Skargakar even knew that Lonjar was his father. Danark had met exactly one aloft the Cloudmere. Sometimes the wind blew the strangest course.

With a deep inhale, Lian stood tall. "It's good of you to expose me. I am Lian, son of Lonjar Draksmasher. Yes, I killed Casran, Odan's son, as retribution for my father's blood, but if you really believe you'll get a ransom for my head, then you're sorely mistaken. Not after I end this foolish riot! If I don't kill you myself, then Ialrist or Hanon'ka certainly will."

"Or I will," said a quiet voice with a dangerous tinge of excitement. From the shadows behind Danark, a hand appeared, holding an enormous blade against Danark's throat. At his shoulder, a demonic face appeared, its mouth spread into a wide grin. "Drop the spear, Danark," Corantha breathed into his ear. "Or I'll cut off your head and drink your blood dry."

Srashi's body went rigid. In the blink of an eye, Balen sprang forward and slammed him into the wall. "Got him!" he gasped. "Lian! His weapon!"

Without hesitating, Lian dropped his cleaver and grabbed the Drak's trapped arm. He twisted it and brought the scaled wrist down on his knee. With a pained hiss, Srashi released his blade, which fell clanging to the deck.

"I'll finish you, filthy lizard!" Balen growled, and his large fist fell onto Srashi's head.

"Srashi!" Danark yelled, tensing his body.

"Didn't I tell you to drop your weapon?" Corantha reminded him, pressing her blade against his neck until a thin stream of blood trickled onto his shirt.

Danark swore under his breath and let the spear fall.

Balen landed another punch. Soft scales broke apart under the man's knuckles, and Lian saw the shine of Drak blood.

"Have mercy!" whimpered Srashi. "I only followed Karnosk's orders!"

Lian pitied him, despite himself. "I think he understands," he told Balen. "That's enough."

The man eyed Lian indignantly but then nodded. "Right. The captain will decide what to do with mutineers."

Janosthir, Wil, Dunrir, and Melvas emerged half-dressed from the sleeping chamber, and Gaaki peered out from the doorframe. Balen shoved the stunned Srashi into Lian's arms. "Wil, Melvas, Gaaki, stay with Lian, and keep an eye on these two traitors. Take them to the canteen. The rest of you, come with me."

"Take good care of your brother," Corantha taunted Melvas as she handed Danark over and stepped back into the shadows.

Balen and the others picked up their weapons and ran toward the bow.

"You're such a damned idiot!" snapped Melvas as he and Gaaki took hold of Danark.

Lian shoved the now jabbering Srashi toward Wil, pushed past the brothers, and retrieved his spear. Then he looked into the room. "Kris?" he called.

"I'm here," she called from her hammock, where she sat—somewhat pale, but unharmed.

"Are you all right?" Lian crouched down and rested a hand on her knee—the most intimate gesture that he dared among the other men.

"Of course."

Lian studied her face, and she returned a small but trusting smile.

"I don't understand what got into him and the others," he said angrily. "Mutiny is insane! The captain might be a fanatic, but he's not a slave driver. There's no need to rise against him. It's absurd. Did they really think they had a chance against Hanon'ka and the slayers?"

"Who knows what they were thinking," Kris answered. "They've always made me nervous." She shuddered, pulling herself to her feet. "Is it true what Danark said?" she asked, studying him. "Did you really kill Casran?"

Lian pursed his lips. "It wasn't exactly planned, but I have no regrets. Casran killed my father, after my father beat him for trying to take advantage of a girl at the tavern earlier that night. It was one of Lonjar Draksmasher's very few valiant acts—and he paid for it with his life. I couldn't let his death go unavenged."

"Then I owe you even more thanks," Kris said softly.

Lian raised his brow. "What do you mean?" he asked.

"My friend from Skargakar was also killed at Casran's order," she explained. "You remember: the debt of crystals and the Cliff Clippers' throw . . ."

"Casran was a real bastard," Lian confirmed.

Kris nodded.

"Hey, Lian!" Smett called from the hallway. "What's going on in there?"

Lian left the room and met Smett, who stood with Melvas and others in the hall, still holding his pan, now streaked with blood. "We're fine," he answered. "What happened?"

"The mutiny is over. The resistance went out as quickly as fire in wet straw," Smett scoffed. "Damned traitors. They wanted to capture the drachen pearl and run off with a kite."

"Run off?" cut in Danark. "No! We wanted Adaron to stand down and to take the *Carryola* home!"

"Well, my friend, it seems that Karnosk and Jarssas had other ideas," said Smett. "We found them by the jäger kites after they'd convinced the poor fools they'd recruited to help untie them."

Danark swore again.

"What about the pearl?" Wil asked nervously.

"That is still in safekeeping," answered the cook.

"How many were they?" asked Lian.

"All in all, nearly ten, I'd say," Smett answered grimly. "That's no good. No good at all. I only ever experienced anything like this once before, years ago. The captain erred by taking too many new men on board at once, and they rose against him. Thank the Winds they failed."

"What happened to them?"

"Adaron threw them all overboard," answered Hanon'ka as he stepped forward between Balen and Dunrir. "Then we sailed home, because our crew was too small to hunt anymore."

Balen nudged Srashi's arm. "Go on, traitors. To the deck."

"Have mercy!" the Drak cried. "I didn't want this. Karnosk forced me."

"Please," Melvas begged Hanon'ka as Danark stood silently next to him. "Karnosk deceived my brother, too."

"Don't tell me," the Sidhari answered solemnly. "Tell the captain."

Some moments later, the whole crew stood assembled on deck under the heavy night sky. Torches and lanterns illuminated the ship and the nearby clouds.

Adaron stood at the wheel, his left arm bound in a blood-soaked bandage. A second bandage protected his forehead. Narso had stitched a few smaller slash wounds on his chest, but as Ialrist and Kettler brought the final criminals forward, the captain motioned the medic to step down. With an unbuttoned shirt and a scowl that made the cloudy night sky seem cheery, he stomped down to the deck.

The captain stood before the men at the bow and waited in punishing silence. Three men lay dead at his feet: the subcommander Elrin and a haggard man named Leachim—both part of the mutiny—and the sailmaker Bellem, an old Nondurier who must have gotten in the way when the criminals tried to escape. The other seven mutineers—Karnosk and Jarssas, Sheshac, Srashi, Danark, Markaeth, and Urdin—stood in a row, bound in ropes, each guarded by a crew member. They were all injured, Urdin so badly that he swayed on his feet, his face ghostly pale. Lian doubted he would survive more than a few days, even if Adaron spared his life.

Lian joined Smett and Kris along with the others who faced the captives. It worried him that so many men had risen against the captain, not only because it showed how bad morale was on board but also because the captain could well call for a mass execution. He didn't want to witness such a thing and couldn't bear that Kris would have to, either.

"Markaeth, Karnosk, and you, Urdin . . ." Adaron spat the names as he passed each man, his expression bewildered and full of scorn. "What were you thinking? How did you concoct the idiotic plan to take my life and my ship? No one, if not Gargantuan himself, will ever conquer me or my ship! Understood?"

Srashi, Danark, and Sheshac murmured in agreement, while the rest remained silent.

Adaron breathed deeply and lifted his arms in frustration. "What should I do with you? What do I do with men who can no longer be trusted? Who have shamefully deceived me? Should I lock you up? We don't have room on board. Should I leave you at the nearest port? I don't see any islands among this darkness. Should I kill you?" He pulled a dagger from his belt and stepped toward Srashi, who whimpered in fear. "I could murder every last one of you! What do you think?" The blade shone bloodred in the light of the nearby dragon-oil lamp.

"Have pity," pleaded Srashi in a wavering whisper. "I was deceived. If you grant me mercy, I'll be true from here forward."

"Coward," snarled Karnosk.

"Coward, you say?" Danark demanded. "It was you who tried to get away with Jarssas, while we did your dirty work."

"Silence!" Balen ordered.

The captain turned to the two Drak farthest on the left. "Karnosk and Jarssas, your crimes are the greatest, without a doubt. Not only did you raise blades against me, but you betrayed your comrades. For this, there's only one worthy sentence: death."

Karnosk thrashed and spat, but Dunrir held him steady.

"It was Karnosk's idea!" Jarssas called.

"I know," answered Adaron. "That's why your death will be quicker." He nodded to Hanon'ka and Ialrist. "Throw him overboard."

"No!" shrieked the Drak as the two men dragged him toward the railing. "I'll do anything you say! I'll . . ."

Ialrist exchanged glances with the captain and gripped Jarssas tightly at the waist. When the nod came, he pushed off into the air with a powerful beat of his wings. Once he'd flown a few paces into the darkness, he let go of the Drak. The man's drawn-out cry quickly faded as he fell into the clouds.

Srashi whimpered and shook his head.

"And now for you," Adaron said, turning toward Karnosk. "Do you have any last words?"

"You are a sick man who has long forgotten what is good for his ship and his crew," Karnosk spat. "I might die today, but I can assure you"—he raised his voice—"I guarantee you'll all follow me eventually. And on that day, when the captain brings death on each one of you, you'll wish I'd been successful!"

"Successful in stealing a drachen pearl?" said Smett. "Hardly." He spat onto the deck.

"Thank you for those candid words," Adaron said, and he faced the

Drak. "I can respect a man who shows no fear. Too bad you won't live to see the last and most glorious battle yet." He turned to Hanon'ka. "Bind and gag him, then string him fifty paces into the fog. The dragons can feast on his flesh."

"Aye, Captain," came Hanon'ka's reply.

"Captain!" called Ialrist as he landed on deck with a beat of his wings. "I've spotted a ship, sailing without light or leader, some two hundred paces in front of us. The masts are broken but not burned."

"Not burned?" Adaron raised an eyebrow and considered for a moment. "We'll take a look. But first . . ." Lightning quick, Adaron thrust his dagger into Karnosk's throat. "I thought it would end differently," he told the man. "But I don't have any more time to waste on your death."

The Drak twitched and gurgled as his eyes widened. He tried to step forward, but Dunrir held him tightly. Kris muffled a gasp and took a step backward. Lian watched in horror as Karnosk died. It only took a few breaths before the blood-drenched man fell to the deck. Then Adaron pulled his blade from the dead man's throat, wiped it clean on his torn shirt, and returned it to his belt.

"Throw all the dead overboard—except for Bellem. We'll hold a special ceremony for our sailmaker. Take him below deck in the meantime, along with the other mutineers. Lock them all up together in a room. Maybe they'll come in handy at some point. Janosthir, you keep watch. All men with injuries, report to the canteen. The medic will take care of you. The rest, prepare yourselves. We're going to get a better look at this ghost ship."

32

The Crewless Ship

Tenth Day of the Seventh Moon, Year 841

The abandoned ship was around thirty paces long, with three masts—a tall mainmast and two smaller on either side. Harpoon ballistae were mounted at the bow and stern, and rows of metal shields strengthened the railing. Even the deck structures appeared robust, as though built to withstand any destruction a dragon could impose.

None of this, though, could diminish the devastating power the ship must have encountered. From his post at the *Carryola*'s bow, Lian struggled to make out the damage. Despite the lanterns and torches on board, it was too dark to see much. Clouds clogged the sky above them, and the light from the nearly full moon shone through only a chink in the fleece. Additional wisps of mist hung in the air and blurred any view. For all Lian knew, the silent and shadowed wreck headed straight toward lithos territory.

There was no doubt that the ship was dead. Two of the three masts were broken, and the stern was half-smashed, rammed by an unknown enormous force. When Balen—whom Adaron had named subcommander after Elrin's execution—sent a call into the mist, there came no answer in return.

"It must have been a dragon," said the captain, who stood with Hanon'ka at the bow and peered through his bronze spyglass. Lian doubted that the lens made much difference on such a night. "I see claw gashes in the wood that could only come from a monster at least the size of a red, but there don't seem to be any burn marks." Lian heard the excitement build in Adaron's voice. "Could it be . . . ?" The captain stopped short and exchanged looks with the first commander.

"I'll send a kite to get a better look," suggested Hanon'ka.

Adaron nodded. "I'll go myself."

"Are you sure? We don't know if there's any life on board."

"We'll be cautious," said Adaron. "I am—apart from Ialrist—the only one who can tell if Gargantuan took the lives of those luckless souls. I'm going, so no more arguments."

"As you wish, Captain," the Sidhari answered. Then he turned and walked away, circumventing Corantha and Arax, who perched before the mast and watched the crewless ship with only mild interest. As Hanon'ka neared Lian and Melvas, he waved them over. "Arm yourselves and meet me at the stern. You'll assist the captain, along with Balen and Ialrist."

"Aye, Commander," confirmed Lian, but Hanon'ka had already moved on.

"Everything is upside down," Melvas said as they made their way below deck. "Our watch is supposed to begin soon, but between the battle with the red and the mutiny, we don't have enough men. I wonder if Adaron will finally turn around. Our sailmaker is dead, and the carpenter is badly injured. We barely have enough crew for two watches."

"The captain might be consumed with revenge, but he's no fool," said Lian. "If he doesn't pardon the prisoners and assign Garon, Kettler, Narso, and Smett to the watch, then he'll have to turn home. You'll see; tomorrow morning, Hanon'ka will instruct us to sail to the next harbor."

"I wish he would," said Melvas. "We've sailed so far out that I'm starting to grow nervous. And now this doomed ship . . . It's not a good omen." He shivered as they entered their sleeping chamber and picked up their weapons.

"You're not superstitious all of a sudden, are you?" Lian asked, and he grinned.

"I'm just cautious," answered Melvas. "It never hurt, in all my time on the Cloudmere."

They hurried back to deck. Balen stood ready at the steerage ropes aboard the single undamaged jäger kite. He had filled the boat with lanterns, and from a bowl at the bow, a flame burned bright. "You two, stand ready at the sails," he instructed, and Lian and Melvas climbed on board and took their positions.

Shortly after, Ialrist and Adaron boarded the vessel. The captain had changed clothes, so his injuries were no longer visible. He had tied a black handkerchief around his bandaged forehead. Only his grimace of pain, and the fact that his left arm hung limply at his side, gave away that he should have been recovering in bed, but none dared to speak the thought.

"Let's go," said Adaron, and Balen lifted the kite up and off the deck.

Slowly, they neared the lifeless wreck veiled by chilling fog. As their kite drifted toward the listing ship, Lian heard the groan of ropes, and somewhere, two metal parts rapped against each other. The unsettling odor of death gave a hint to the unpleasantness they might find.

"This battle wasn't long ago," whispered Ialrist as he struggled not to retch from the stink of fresh decay.

"No," answered Adaron fiercely. "Good for us."

Lian wondered what could be good for them about a recent battle, but he was relieved he hadn't yet eaten his midnight meal.

At Balen's signal, Lian and Melvas pulled in the sails, and the kite stopped short with a dull thud against the wreck's hull. Ialrist took off from the railing. While Balen secured the steerage lines, Lian threw a rope to the Taijirin, who secured their vessel to the larger ship.

"You stay on board and stand alert," Adaron instructed Balen. Then he turned to Lian and Melvas. "You two, come with me."

First, they passed lanterns onto the wreck. Adaron handed one to Ialrist and pulled out his weapon—a short broadsword. "Spread out. And report anything you see," he said. With a nod, Ialrist made his way toward the stern.

Lian set his lantern atop a tipped crate. "You hold the light, and I'll lead," he suggested to Melvas, who raised his lantern in answer. The man clenched his other hand around the handle of his short ax, his face as pale as the fog that enveloped them.

Lian clutched his spear with both hands and scanned the deck. In the light of the lanterns and torches, the sheer scope of the destruction on board stole his breath. Debris covered the deck: ripped sails, broken splinters of mast, and burst crates and barrels. In one place, the railing had collapsed as though from the crash of an unfathomably heavy body. Bashed planks reminded Lian of giant claws that must have dug into the ship's side as the demonic creature had attempted to cling to the hull.

All around them, a brown liquid covered the wood. When Melvas held his lantern closer, Lian noted that it was dried blood, which must have rained down in sickening sprays to drench the deck, sails, and railing in such a way.

Before long, they reached the source of the horrible stench. Pieces of corpses littered the deck, revealing the horribly violent deaths the crew had endured. Giant fangs had ripped open the head or chest on some of the bodies, which provided a strange comfort when compared to a bearded man Lian spotted, whose left side was shredded into a sickening jumble of blood, flesh, and torn clothing from shoulder to leg. Lian retched at the sight of the man's crusted face frozen into a shriek of unthinkable terror. For the first time, he knew the full extent of the danger they faced.

"No sign of fire," Melvas said flatly, "or acid. What kind of monster could do such damage without any flame or bile?"

"Gargantuan," Adaron answered stonily from the helm as he scanned the corpses. "It had to be. Sure, he can spit fire, but he would rather destroy his opponents through pure strength. He must have caught them completely off guard, the poor devils." The captain gazed into the fog. "Where are you, monster?" he said into the night. "You're somewhere out there, aren't you? I know it. I can feel it. But if you think you can gorge yourself on the *Carryola*'s men as you have these luckless souls, then you are sorely mistaken. We are prepared for battle and will dole the same death that you have brought upon so many good men and women."

Behind them, a door swung open, and Lian whipped around in surprise, but only Ialrist looked out from the stairway that led below deck. "Adaron," he called. "I found something."

The captain turned away from the towering clouds and moved toward

Ialrist. Since there was no more to see on deck besides more rubble, limbs, and entrails, Lian and Melvas followed.

The stink dissipated below deck, thankfully. The ship's captain must have ordered everyone topside to fight. Although there were no corpses, there was still terrible chaos. The dragon had rammed its full weight into the hull. Not a single plate in the galley remained on its shelf, and every stool in the canteen was toppled and smashed. Huge holes punctured the hull in many places, and tattered hammocks dangled into nothingness as a cold wind blew through the rooms.

"Back here," said Ialrist, leading the way. "In the captain's chambers." Lian and Melvas remained in the doorway as the captain and Ialrist entered the room. The chamber was considerably smaller than the *Carryola*'s, but this captain evidently had a zeal for hunting dragons that rivaled Adaron's. Claws, fangs, and bones decorated the walls, and skulls of small dragons stared out from their mounts. Spears of various forms and eras hung at the wall above the bed, and on the wall next to the desk, Lian saw a detailed drawing of a man standing at a ship's bow, raising a spear against a winged beast. Lian wondered if the image was a portrait of the captain himself: an immortalization of the hero he longed to see within himself.

That captain sat at his chair with his back to Lian, a sunken shell of grayed flesh with shaggy black hair wearing blood-encrusted clothing.

Adaron paced to the other side of the chair and winced as he studied the man's wounds.

"Here," Ialrist said, pointing to the open log at the captain's desk. "He was writing as he took his last breaths. Look here. He describes his encounter with the monster. The handwriting is bad and gets worse from line to line. But look at this, here."

Adaron leaned forward and squinted in the dim lantern light. "Gargantuan," he murmured. "It was the black demon." His studied the corpse. "You knew your opponent, but you couldn't slay him. Your ship was too weak, but you heard the legends." He paused. "Tell me, what do you know?" he continued. "What does he look like today? How does he fight? And where did you find him? I must know."

Melvas cleared his throat. "Captain—"

Adaron tensed. "Everyone out!" he bellowed. "Melvas, Lian, return to the deck—or to Balen at the kite. Ialrist, wait at the door. Nobody is to bother me until I set foot out of this room. Let's see"—he glared from the dead man to the log and back again—"what secrets I can draw out of our friend here."

Ialrist frowned, a strange mixture of defeat and worry. For a moment, it seemed he might argue. Then he set a hand on the captain's shoulder. "Be careful, Adaron. You know that everything has its price."

Lian shuddered when he saw Adaron's frozen stare. "The time for care is over, my friend. We are so close to our goal. I won't relent until I get my revenge—even before the master of the depths himself."

With a sigh, Ialrist nodded and walked out the door. "Why are you still standing there?" he snapped at Lian and Melvas. "Didn't you hear the captain?"

"Yes, sir," Melvas answered hurriedly, and Lian nodded. Then they rushed back to the deck and toward the jäger kite, where Balen looked into the murky darkness that separated them from the nearby *Carryola*.

"What is he planning?" Lian asked Melvas nervously. He hardly believed that Adaron would spend his time lounging on the captain's bed and studying a log. The exchange between Adaron and Ialrist had implied something far more sinister.

"I don't know," Melvas hedged, avoiding Lian's gaze.

"Melvas!" Lian urged. "You know something. Tell me!"

"What happened?" Balen asked, looking toward the wreck. "Where are they?"

Lian told him about the dead captain in his chamber and Adaron's strange behavior.

"By the Winds," Balen said while his fingers made a complex sign of protection. "That doesn't sound good."

"Just tell me," pleaded Lian. "What is it?"

A strange guttural melody carried from the hull. Lian couldn't understand the words, for the ritual sounds didn't belong to any language he knew. He was reminded of when Hanon'ka had called the elements into his control, but Adaron's call alluded to something much darker.

"Men tell stories on board," Balen said softly, though no one else was listening. "Some years ago, we docked at a cloister high on a mountain peak above the fog, on the far eastern coast. They say that the men there were sorcerers . . . of the dark arts. Adaron and Hanon'ka went to meet them. The first commander returned shortly afterward and only said that the captain would remain."

Balen scowled as he remembered. "We anchored in the shade of that hallowed place for two whole weeks. No one went in, and no one came out. The men on board came close to mutiny, but Hanon'ka ordered us to stay. When Adaron finally returned, something had . . . changed him. On the outside, nothing was different, but something in his eyes had altered. His soul had darkened. They say he learned . . . how to speak to the dead."

Lian was skeptical. "That's nothing more than a horror tale. No one can speak to the dead! That kind of magic only exists in stories."

"Well, I've witnessed the captain shut himself in a room with the dead three times since then," Balen described. "The first time, I was close enough to listen."

"I saw a green light shine underneath the cabin door," Melvas added quietly. "It looked wrong. I ran away as fast as I could, even though the second commander had sent me to call the captain. Nothing good comes when Adaron shares a room with the dead."

Lian glanced uneasily back toward the door and listened to the strange sounds that continued. He thought he saw a green light shine from the torn hull, but it must have been his imagination. The captain's chamber was undamaged, and its two windows pointed toward the stern and not toward their kite.

Lian couldn't say how long he endured the uneasy silence. The moon disappeared completely behind the clouds. It was still just as dark as when they'd first set foot on the doomed ship, perhaps even darker, when Adaron and Ialrist finally returned. Both men boarded the kite in silence. The captain seemed exhausted but satisfied. Ialrist, however, was as cold and distant as sharp cliffs on a rainy fall morning.

"Find anything interesting, Captain?" Balen dared to ask.

Adaron turned, and a thin yet triumphant smile appeared across his pale face. "Oh yes, Balen, I did. Arm yourselves, men. I have found the way to Gargantuan's den."

33

Lair of Evil

Eleventh Day of the Seventh Moon, Year 841

On the following day, a strange mood loomed over *Carryola*. Lian sensed an odd mixture of anticipation and fear. Many were suspicious because Adaron had pardoned some of the mutineers. Sheshac and Srashi had convinced him that their remorse was genuine, and the captain took them back into service after ten lashes each.

Markaeth and Danark, however, remained captive. Lian, who had warned Hanon'ka that Danark plotted to collect a ransom for his head, was relieved when Danark wasn't released. Though Melvas acted embittered over his brother's captivity, he directed the majority of his scorn at Danark for being an utter fool. Urdin, gravely injured after the uprising, hadn't survived the night and was tossed along with Bellem into the clouds. They now lacked the two most important craftsmen on board if any need for repairs arose in the future.

The *Carryola* did not sail homeward, as so many wished, but farther north into the realm of the Thousand Fangs. To make better time and avoid the danger of crashing into peaks concealed by fog, Adaron

ordered an ascent a hundred paces above the fleece. Their clear surroundings, however, meant that their ship flew in plain sight of nearby
predators. Still, Adaron would hear no reason. As they steered onward
at full sail, he cared only about the Black Leviathan, Gargantuan, who
lay in wait within his den.

At around midday, they spotted the Thousand Fangs below. The
name suited the islands of sharp and rugged lithos, tiny from their distance, where hardly a blade of grass grew. Lian peered over the railing
along with the rest of the nervous crew. To him, the peaks looked like
spear ends jutting up toward the heavens, awaiting the next unsuspecting adventurer to fall onto them.

The captain's gaze had pointed straight ahead ever since they had
sailed away from the crewless ship and pushed their lonely way through
the clouds. The rest of the crew feared the same fate as the doomed souls
aboard the crewless ship—to be blown eternally by the Northern Wind's
chilly gusts into the afterlife.

Ialrist flew at a distance in front of them, while Corantha, atop Arax,
took up the rear. The two jägers had been instructed to keep an eye out for
danger. The captain stood at the bow and peered into his bronze spyglass,
searching the horizon for a specific rock formation. That place, he had
explained, would be the first sign that they were close to Gargantuan's lair.

"I don't like this," Kris said to Lian as the two carried harpoons from
below deck. "If the stories are true, then Gargantuan is far too large and
powerful to be killed by any jäger. Maybe it's not even possible for human hands to kill him at all. Some things out there are more powerful
than mere mortals. We should just accept that."

"You sound just like Smett," Lian teased, trying to sound lighthearted
despite the gravity of her words, as they returned up the steps from below deck. "I know what you mean, though." He thought of Hanon'ka's
incantation, and of the Water of Vision, and of Kesrondaia, the woman
of white. Before leaving Skargakar, magic had been a thing of stories—
bards sang about resplendent warriors and dark sorcery in their ballads—
and nothing more.

Now these legends had become reality, and if an extraordinary weapon
like Lian's spear or spirits like the woman with a dragon's aura truly did
exist, wouldn't it also mean that the horrifying evil from nightmares
loomed not far off? Adaron called Gargantuan the Firstborn and father

of all Great Drachen. If that were true—if Gargantuan were truly as old as the world itself—how could humankind be its downfall? How could the captain believe he could take down a demon?

And even if we could—should we? Lian wondered as he continued to load spears next to Kris. *We are only humans—and a few others. How could we ever extinguish a creature so old and so powerful?* It was one thing to kill a bronzeneck, a silverwing, or any other ordinary dragon. New hatchlings of those kinds were born every spring. But from everything Lian had heard, Gargantuan was unique. If they killed him, there would be no other Black Leviathan. Would extinguishing his life throw the Cloudmere off its equilibrium?

"What are you thinking?" Kris asked softly, unable to ignore Lian's worry.

"About what you said. There are greater things in this world than we can even imagine—ancient and precious things . . . and terrible things. I wonder if we should risk shifting the balance." He shrugged. "On the other hand, what else can we do? We're part of the *Carryola*'s crew. If we run into Gargantuan, we will fight him. He's already proven that he shows no mercy. If we don't fight back, we'll be as dead as the crew from the ghost ship. Our only choices are to kill or be killed. Would you sacrifice your own life to save a dragon?"

Lian assumed that Kris would argue his point. To his amazement, she just shook her head. "I don't know," she answered.

"There!" A call sounded from the bow.

Adaron pointed into the distance. He set down his spyglass and glanced over his shoulder toward the wheel. "Slightly portside, Jaular," he called to the Nondurier at the ropes. "There ahead. The ring of peaks I've been searching for. Four surrounding a fifth in the center. That's where we're headed."

Hanon'ka, who stood beside Jaular at the helm, gave the orders. "All men to the sails and the harpoons. Prepare for battle. Janosthir, load your thunder launcher. Lian, fetch your spear. Let's prepare to give Gargantuan everything we've got."

While Jaular steered toward the rocks, the men stirred from their nervous daze and set into motion.

"Come on," Lian said to Kris. "You'll be safest below deck with Smett and the two dragons."

They hurried down to the galley. Before separating, Kris grabbed Lian's hand. "Be careful," she said softly. In her eyes, Lian saw that she longed to say much more, but didn't dare.

He, too, had things he wanted to say. He wanted to tell her that the Four Winds had saved him from the Cloudmere's depths and that a woman of white named Kesrondaia watched over him. Higher powers guided him—though whether they were enough to save the *Carryola*, Lian couldn't say. It was all much too complicated to explain to Kris now. He forced a smile. "I will," he said. "And you keep your head down so it doesn't get snapped off. Understand?"

Kris nodded. "I'll do my best."

He squeezed her hand a final time and hurried toward his bunk to retrieve his spear. Sudden doubt washed over him. The Water of Vision had revealed a raging inferno with no survivors. Lian wished he could drink the water again, just one more time. If he could prepare, then maybe he could save at least a few lives. *I should never have given Ialrist the rest,* he thought. *There must be a reason why I found the source of magic on the island. I could have used it for good. Instead, I let them convince me that I would go mad.*

Maybe Ialrist had kept it. The Taijirin certainly liked to keep his options open. It would be a terrible loss to pour something so valuable into the clouds. *Should I search his chamber?* Lian considered as he reentered the canteen. Ialrist wasn't on board, and most others were occupied on deck. Nobody would even notice.

He shook his head. "What am I thinking?" he mumbled angrily.

He raced up the stairs and back on deck.

The *Carryola* descended until it floated a few dozen paces over the fleece. Before them, four giant stone spires shot into the air, surrounding a huge spire at their center. Lian could barely fathom how large the stone mass stretched beneath the clouds. The peaks were completely bare of vegetation, save a few scattered patches of moss. Along the mountainsides, strange plants covered the stone—thick and thorny shrubs, and bizarre, stunted, and gnarled trees with thick roots. Wine-colored leaves trembled on the branches, and small blue lizardwings, similar to Flicc in size, darted from branch to branch along the mountain edge. There was a strange and morbid beauty in the sight.

The central peak ended in a bare, blackened plateau, which tilted upward slightly and reminded Lian of a dark and powerful stone throne. Lian couldn't help but imagine a giant dragon ruling over the Cloudmere from atop the seat as it glared with evil satisfaction over its lofty realm.

"We'll stay outside of the ring," instructed Adaron, "and circle once. Keep a lookout for any cave or any entranceway into a valley. Gargantuan's lair must be here somewhere."

Jaular guided the schooner into a curve and led the *Carryola* once around the peaks. At their side, Ialrist rose to the mountaintop to get a better view. From behind the *Carryola*'s stern, Arax let out an agitated roar. The dragon seemed to sense its proximity to danger. Lian had always considered Arax to be fearless but now understood that the grayback had its limits.

Corantha answered with a wild howl, no doubt intended to inspire the dragon's courage. She wasn't intimidated by any foe, that much was clear, even if she were forced to fight the gods themselves. Filled with envy and awe, Lian marveled at the huntress, tattooed face and all. He wished that he could face whatever came with as much defiance and fearlessness as that brave warrior.

They soon returned to the front side of the stone formation, but no one had seen any opening or cave large enough to hold a monster of Gargantuan's size.

"Could you be mistaken, Captain?" Balen asked from his post at the ballista a few paces away.

"No. I saw this structure exactly. But something isn't right, yet." Adaron took a breath and closed his eyes. Lian, who stood at the bow clutching his spear, watched the captain's brow crease as he attempted to call forth the vision from his ritual.

"Clouds," the captain said, and he opened his eyes, nodding. "Contrary to most dragons, Gargantuan loves fog. He can see through haze as clearly as others can only see in the open air." He turned to Jaular. "We have to go under the fleece!"

The Nondurier laid his ears back. "You want us to attack from the clouds?"

"It's too dangerous," said Hanon'ka. "We need height and a good view to challenge a dragon this large."

"There's no need to worry," Adaron answered. "Gargantuan is not at home. If he were, he already would have made himself known."

"He could be resting in the depths," the commander argued. "What if our attack wakes him?"

"Or what if he's already lying in wait?" asked Balen. "Like a rock spider waiting for its pray to pass by."

Adaron's face darkened as the men admitted their fears, but instead of an outburst, he turned to the Sidhari. "Can you part the clouds? That way, we can see into the depths without risking too much."

Hanon'ka thought for a moment. "The fog in the Cloudmere is not a natural weather condition," he answered. "I don't know if the wind I call forth can influence anything, but I can try. I'd prefer anything over charging blindly into the unknown."

At the captain's nod, Hanon'ka directed his attention toward the mist at their feet. Standing just before the bow, he reached his hands out and began to murmur the foreign tongue of his folk to conjure the elements. He repeated the same words, over and over, calling forth the warm desert winds of his home.

Once more, Lian felt the beginnings of a breeze, until a fresh and astonishingly dry and warm wind surrounded them, carrying the scent of exotic spices.

Then the Sidhari directed the wind toward the clouds below. For an anxious moment, it seemed as though the thick white mass might swallow the wind away. Then the clouds began to shift, forming a tunnel that led a hundred paces down. At its opening, fog bubbled below, thick like syrup and unfazed by the gale.

"There!" Balen called, pointing into the depths.

They all saw it. A great opening yawned from the mountainside, large enough for a ship twice the *Carryola*'s size to pass through. Hanon'ka's desert wind revealed about half of its circular form.

"That must be it!" Adaron called excitedly. "The entrance to Gargantuan's lair. That's where we're headed."

"Captain," said Balen, "if I might make a suggestion. Send the kite first. We need the *Carryola* out here, where she has room to maneuver in battle."

The captain considered briefly. "Fine. So be it. Balen, you steer the *Carryola*. Dunrir, Lian, and Janosthir, come with me on the kite." Adaron whistled loudly and waved to Ialrist and pointed toward the cave.

Ialrist lifted a hand in confirmation and set out soaring toward the opening.

Lian and the others clambered on board the jäger kite. Lian regretted that Melvas wouldn't join them, but when he saw the heavy cylindrical weapon with a fire mechanism resembling a crossbow in the bearded Settlander's hands, and the haversack covered in dragon scales spanning his back, he understood why Adaron trusted his defense. If anyone could buy them time for a retreat, he could.

The Settlander grinned, revealing stained teeth, and shouldered his thunder launcher with a muscular arm. "Shall we, then?"

Lian, damned if he'd let the man sense his fear, forced a smile and gripped his spear with both hands. "I'll be right in front of you."

Janosthir laughed. "Better not stand *right* in front of me, or you'll only be standing until my first shot."

"Right, I see your point."

Dunrir gathered the sails and led the kite into Hanon'ka's wind current, which sent them gliding downward. They reached the cave entrance far too quickly for Lian's taste. Once close enough, he noticed wet stalactites reaching down, transforming the cave entrance into an unsettlingly sharp-toothed set of wide-open jaws. *Gargantuan's throat,* he thought, and a shiver ran down his spine.

The sight seemed to affect Adaron differently. Standing at the kite's bow, he peered with vicious anticipation into the rock tunnel. In the lantern light, the cave's vast walls were barely visible, which made it impossible to tell what awaited them.

Ialrist landed with a rush of wind to their side. "Are you sure you want to go down there, Adaron?" the Taijirin asked his old comrade softly.

The captain nodded. "I have to know if this is it—if we've finally found Gargantuan."

The Taijirin prince's eyes narrowed. "Then may the Illuminated Wings stand by us."

As the kite pushed through the entrance, Hanon'ka's gale forced them down the steep passageway. A cold and dry gust from the depths blew against them like death's breath from a tomb. More stalactites glittered overhead in the weak lantern light. Underneath the bow, fog cascaded sideways and disappeared into the nothingness. The inside of the mountain remained silent, apart from the soft groan of ropes from their kite's sails and the rush of blood inside Lian's own ears.

The tunnels abruptly fell away, and the ceiling disappeared into darkness. They arrived in a massive underground void. Although the room's size was impossible to measure in the darkness, a distant glittering in the light of their lanterns—*Probably crystal veins,* Lian thought—indicated the cave's limits. Their kite pressed onward, wisps of mist licking the keel.

They had only traveled a few hundred paces onward when a form came into view. Through the darkness, Lian could see a wrecked ship, around a dozen paces long, leaning against the rocks. "We are not the first here," Janosthir muttered, and he lifted the muzzle of his thunder launcher.

"The dragon isn't here," Dunrir added from behind them.

"Or he's toying with us," said Lian, immediately regretting the thought.

The captain, who stood leaning against the railing, straightened up. "We'll risk it. Janosthir, be so kind and give us some light, will you?"

"Aye, Captain." The Settlander set his haversack on the planks and knelt to open it. Inside, Lian spotted rows of fist-sized spheres stacked in wooden frames. The spheres were various colors—some silver, others deep black or bright white, or even faintly glowing blue as though carved from pure crystal.

With a practiced hand, Janosthir unlatched the end of the thrower, and a silver sphere rolled out into his hand. Carefully, he chose a white one, which glittered like a fist-sized sky filled with stars, and loaded it into the barrel. "Settlandish alchemy," he explained when he noticed Lian's perplexed glance. Then he stood up and released the weapon's safety cap with a crack. Pointing his thunder launcher into the air, he flipped a tiny switch and pulled the trigger.

With a dry snap, a line shot out, catapulting the sphere into the darkness. For a heartbeat, Lian lost sight of the sphere until an explosion of light in the middle of the cave blinded him. The sphere glowed like a sun, forcing Lian to look away. As they continued onward, the ball drifted down the tunnel in front of them and revealed what lay ahead.

Janosthir swore under his breath in Settlandish. Whatever the word meant, Lian agreed wholeheartedly.

The rock dome stretched around two hundred paces wide, and nearly as high. All along the ceiling and walls, crystal veins glittered. That much crystal ore would be worth a small fortune, but all four men's glances went to the mist-flecked ground.

A bizarre landscape stretched beneath them. At least two dozen ships of various types and sizes were scattered along the rocks—their hulls smashed and sails hanging in tatters from broken masts. One ship's hull was so rotted that it must have been at least a hundred years old, while others seemed much newer additions to this grotesque trophy collection. Amid the wreckage, Lian made out the sickening forms of piles of bones: skulls, arm and leg bones, pelvic bones, and rib cages. Scraps of clothing fluttered from some, and blades and jewelry shimmered among the remains. The entire room was a massive graveyard—a final stop for the victims who had ventured inside. It was a resting place, not just for the ships but for the countless humans, Nondurier, Drak, and Taijirin who had dared to enter.

For a long time, no one spoke. Eventually, the light of the alchemist's sphere went out, and darkness swallowed the resting place of all those drachenjägers from view.

"Janosthir," Adaron said, his voice dark and raw as though he, too, struggled against his feelings.

"Sir?"

"You have fire spheres in your haversack, don't you?"

"Yes, sir."

The captain turned to the stalky gunman. "Burn it all. Burn this whole damned place to the ground."

Janosthir needed four spheres to ignite enough of the wreckage before flames ate their way through the rest. Thick smoke lifted above and seared their eyes and throats.

"Take us back to the *Carryola*, Dunrir," sputtered Adaron.

"Aye," the Nondurier confirmed, coughing, and he steered the kite around.

"Was that wise?" asked Ialrist as they left the cave. "Gargantuan will be angry once he discovers his lair has been burned."

"Good," said Adaron as they left the mountain womb among the fog. "I hope he's angry. Fury will lure him here, and then we—"

A rumble rang from the distance, darker and more powerful than Lian had ever heard. It sounded as though a mountain fell into itself or as though the sky's pillars had caved in, as though the heart of the world had cracked open to spill out its darkest terrors.

"Lure him?" Ialrist frowned. "I think you're mistaken, Adaron. He's here already."

34

Gargantuan

Eleventh Day of the Seventh Moon, Year 841

"Prepare for battle! Secure main and side sails! Say your prayers and load the harpoons! It's fight or be damned!"

Once more in the air above the fleece, Captain Adaron sprang from the jäger kite to the *Carryola*'s deck and raced to the helm. Janosthir hurried toward the bow, and Lian and Dunrir secured the kite with ropes. If the *Carryola*'s crew were larger, Adaron might have sent the small vessel and her sister ship on ahead to assist Ialrist and Corantha from the sky, but now, all hands were needed on deck.

"Will you pray to your Winds for assistance and protection?" Dunrir asked as they pulled the lines tight.

"Why do you ask?" Lian answered.

"We Nondurier have no gods," he answered. "Pray for me, too, if you would."

Another thunderous rumble penetrated through bone and marrow from the fog below, and the planks underneath Lian's feet shook.

"I think I'll pray for us all," said Lian. He ran toward the bow, where

Melvas and Gaaki already manned the harpoon ballista. Hanon'ka stood with his arms raised, still controlling the wind.

The Sidhari lowered his arms, and the wind abated instantly. Then the Sidhari turned and hurried to the hatch that led into the belly of the ship.

. The menacing rumble sounded once more, closer this time. Lian heard the rushing wind of powerful wings whipping clouds. As he peered over the railing, an enormous black shadow passed underneath the *Carryola*.

Then the fog appeared.

From one moment to the next, out of nothing, mist gathered and thickened around the ship until the whiteness blinded them all.

"Ascend!" Lian heard the command yelled from starboard. "Jaular, steer us higher!"

"What is this?" Lian asked in confusion.

"Gargantuan's magic," Balen growled, and Lian made out his faint form as he and Dunrir took over the ballista from Melvas and Gaaki. Meanwhile, Srashi, Wil, and a few others returned from the masts, where they had secured the mainsails as they had during the battle against the great red. At Adaron's order, they hurried to the weapons at the stern, and Ialrist flew up to the crow's nest in order to attack from above when the time came.

Hanon'ka returned from the belly of the *Carryola*. He had removed his shirt to reveal a torso covered in the same tattooed symbols as his face. Amulets hung from his neck, chest, and back, made of polished wood, bone, and crystal beads. Only two weapons from his collection, jagged short swords, hung from his belt.

The Sidhari dropped in front of the foremast as the dragon surged up from the fog. The titan shot from the depths and rushed past, its wings conjuring a whirlwind far too close to the *Carryola*. Lian flinched and stumbled backward toward the railing as a blur of black and gray scales, the skin gnarled and pocked, reeled before his eyes. Heat seared his face. Leathery wings, as wide as the *Carryola*'s length from bow to stern alone, darkened the sky, and metallic black claws glinted in the light of the torches on board.

Once past the ship, the dragon barrel-rolled to the side and disappeared into the fog. Then a deafening roar sounded, causing Lian to buckle forward, gasping as he pressed his hands against his ears. Melvas and others, too, did the same. The Nondurier's ears flattened, and even Hanon'ka cringed. Only the Drak seemed unfazed by the sound.

"What is he doing?" Lian called as he stood up. "Why isn't he charging?" Apparently, despite his destroyed den, Gargantuan wasn't angry enough to strike.

"He's sizing up his opponent," Balen answered, reeling his harpoon ballista around as he struggled to take aim. "He's curious about us."

A drone sounded at their backs. As Lian turned, he spotted Adaron standing beside Jaular, blowing into the drachen horn that had riled the fireblood. The dragon answered the horn's call with another roar, this time farther off. Then it rushed once more past the clouds before the ship, a shadow of awe-instilling measure.

"He's toying with us!" Dunrir called from the ballista at portside.

"Not for long," Adaron promised. "Hanon'ka?"

"I'm ready." The Sidhari raised his arms and began to chant a new incantation. The words sounded wilder this time, more scornful, and the wind battered with an unusual fury. Then he sent the wind into the fog, tearing through the fleece.

The cleared air opened their view. From what Lian could tell, the *Carryola* had lifted up at least two thousand paces. The mountain formation that housed Gargantuan's den looked tiny from below as its peaks jutted through the white, and a black stream of smoke dissolved into the sky.

In the next heartbeat, Lian glimpsed the monster straight from his visions. The Black Leviathan glided in a wide loop past the stern, his massive body covered in thick coal-black scales. Enormous muscles rippled from his neck, wings, and legs, while red veins glowed like embers beneath the scales. The creature's massive wings stretched across bone frames ending in sharp spokes. The edges of the wings looked frayed, as though the dragon had endured battle wounds that had never properly healed. An irregular row of sharp bone plates ran from the massive skull down to the tail, which terminated in a flat, leaf-shaped blade.

Two curved horns protruded from the skull, each surrounded by four smaller ones. The beast's enormous eyes burned with an ancient fury. Behind rows of long fangs, a molten inferno boiled, and the beast's body excreted a stench that trailed in plumes of smoke as the great giant glided majestically across the sky.

"Gargantuan!" Adaron cried from the wheel. "So we meet again! I've hunted you all these years. Today, I will be your demise!"

The dragon turned his head as though studying the ship and its tiny captain, clad in black, with piqued interest. A deep, nearly amused growl escaped the depths of his throat. Then he flipped direction and shot toward the sky.

"Aim our bow toward him!" called the captain. "Hanon'ka, Janosthir, and all jägers: get ready!"

Lian crouched behind his harpoon with Balen and Melvas, while Dunrir and Gaaki waited behind the other. Janosthir set his thunder launcher onto the railing and took aim. Hanon'ka responded to Adaron's order with a mere twitch of recognition and spread his arms into the sky. Looking up, Lian spotted a cyclone in the clouds above his head, which gradually grew larger.

He also saw something else. At some distance from the cyclone, and barely visible, a small gray dragon hovered, awaiting a chance to strike: Arax and Corantha, two stubborn jägers, tiny compared to the enormous prey they taunted. The beast roared once more and charged straight toward them.

The hull groaned as Jaular forced the ship into a narrow curve with the sheer power of kyrillian.

"Now we'll show him what we're capable of!" Adaron called. "Fire! Let's give him everything we've got!"

Balen, Dunrir, and Janosthir pulled their triggers, and a blue ball of light and two black spears shot toward the monster. The first harpoon bounced off the dragon's breastplate, while the second sank into the tough flesh between two scales. Janosthir's fireball exploded against the beast's snout, at which the monster let out an enraged scream.

Meanwhile, Hanon'ka thrust his arms downward, sending a funnel of air toward the dragon from the center of swirling clouds. Losing his equilibrium, the monster fell sideways as his wings pulled upward. In his fury, his body glowed like an ember fanned by a gust of wind. His jaws opened wide, and a stream of flame spewed against the *Carryola*'s hull. Lian instinctively ducked behind the shields mounted at the bow, but the flames ran harmlessly over the armored hull. Gargantuan slipped beneath them, using the ship as a barrier from the approaching tornado.

"Raise the bow! Ballistae at the stern, fire as soon as you see him!" ordered Adaron.

Lian, who prepared to load the spear thrower, clung tightly to the railing as the ship pitched into a steep slant. The lines at the stern groaned as the men released their triggers.

"Both buoys sunk!" Wil called from the stern.

A sudden heavy blow shook the ship, and they dropped with a jolt. For a terrifying moment, the deck disappeared from under Lian's feet as the ship tilted to port, and he struggled to keep hold on the railing. His spear, along with others from the ballistae, slid along the deck past Hanon'ka, where their fall was stopped short at the helm.

"His tail smashed the hull!" Srashi called from the stern. "We're losing kyrillian."

"I'll try to level us," bellowed Jaular, who set to work to level the ship.

"Heave ho!" Adaron ordered. "Janosthir, try to do more damage."

"More damage. Ha," scoffed the Settlander. "The brute is as massive as a city wall." He opened the breech on his thunder launcher and loaded two more spheres. "We'll see if this gives him something to think about."

The dragon sped upward and flipped around to face them. Stretching out his neck, the beast stared at the ship through a single glaring eye. Then, he charged.

"Fend him off!" Adaron cried.

Dunrir reeled his ballista to face the beast, and Janosthir adjusted his position at the railing. Hanon'ka leaned port; his arms still stretched into the air as he swayed back and forth, eyes half-closed.

Fire, wind, and steel rained onto the beast hovering before them as it roared with rage. Chunks of hard scale flew as Janosthir's cannons broke through the beast's thick breastplate.

Gargantuan shook off the onslaught. In response, he beat his massive wings, conjuring a windstorm that tipped the ship farther sideways. He stoked the inferno in his throat once more, and flames shot across the deck. Screaming, men ducked for cover.

This time, though, Gargantuan had other plans. Lian watched as Ialrist swooped valiantly out of danger as flames shot past the crew's heads into the rigging and licked across masts and sails. Both materials were protected against fire, but the Black Leviathan persisted until the canvas burst into flames. Then the dragon whipped around and took off above them, slashing at the mast with outstretched claws that sent burning splinters raining onto the deck. At the stern, Lian heard shrill cries.

"Put out the fire!" Balen ordered. "Throw all burning parts overboard."

Lian, Melvas, and Gaaki jumped into action.

"He is too strong!" someone cried in panic. "We can't take him down."

"Silence!" ordered Adaron. "We just have to contain him. Then we can find his weak spot. Load the spears into the ballistae. The next time he passes us will be his last."

Ialrist appeared starboard. "I'll prepare to attack!" he called. "Maybe I can pierce through the muscles at the base of his wings." The Taijirin flew to catch the dragon before it could make another loop.

Corantha, astride Arax, chose the same moment to charge, a gray collection of claws, fangs, and blades that shot toward the beast. While Ialrist tried to avoid the monster's swinging tail, Corantha threw herself from her saddle and landed on the monster's back. Arax spiraled elegantly on his own axis and darted out of range of the larger dragon.

As Lian threw a last scrap of mast over the railing, Jaular steered the *Carryola* once more toward Gargantuan. Lian watched with amazement as Corantha worked her way toward the muscle fibers at the dragon's shoulders—just as she had done with the fireblood. In the meantime, Ialrist had landed farther down the dragon's back and made his way forward with his reaver in hand.

I should be up there, Lian thought in dismay. *I am a jäger. Why won't Adaron let me fight?* His gaze landed on his spear, which hung at the helm, all its magical powers momentarily useless.

As he considered convincing Balen or Dunrir to prepare a jäger kite, a harrowing howl tore him from his thoughts. Lian spun around to find Gargantuan faltering. Corantha, who knelt at the beast's left wing-base, had sunk a sword into the muscle, all the way down to the handle. Not far from her, Ialrist raised his reaver to do his part, and both jägers attempted to cripple the dragon's range of motion.

Horn plates appeared from nowhere across Gargantuan's back. Before anyone could register their meaning or purpose, the spaces between the black scales glowed red, and a cloud of scalding steam shot straight onto the slayers. The pressure sent Ialrist into the air, where he swirled helplessly in the heated air currents. A massive wing slammed against him, which knocked his weapon from his hand and batted him away like little more than a bothersome insect.

Corantha let out a terrible cry. Dropping her weapon, she tumbled backward, clutching her hands in front of her face. As a second burst of boiling-hot steam blasted her, she screamed again. Swaying, she stumbled on a horned plate. With a dismissive shake, Gargantuan threw her from his back. Still screaming and unable to remember her harness in time, she plummeted into the depths, where outstretched claws caught her and ripped her body to pieces.

As though struck by lightning, Lian recognized the scene from his premonition. The Water of Vision had revealed it all. *It's happening! It's really happening. We're all doomed.*

"We've lost Corantha and Ialrist!" someone yelled. "Our slayers are dead! Winds, stand by us!"

Howling, Arax pulled his wings in and shot into the clouds toward his mistress. His gesture showed heartbreaking loyalty, though Lian doubted there would be much to salvage of Corantha's body.

Adaron sprang from the helm with a wild cry. "Hanon'ka, Lian, it's on you now!" He grabbed the Sidhari's shoulder, then bent forward, picked up Lian's spear, and held it out to him. "We'll reel in the beast, and you'll end him with your spear."

Lian's heart beat frantically as he took the weapon. "I'll do my best," he promised.

The captain nodded and looked toward Hanon'ka.

"I'll protect the ship as well as I can," he said resolutely.

Both Lian and the first commander headed for the bow, still directed toward the dragon. Gargantuan, too, hadn't escaped the battle unscathed, Lian saw now. The beast's wings beat with less power, and the sword lodged in his shoulder seemed to cause great pain. The constant use of his inner fire, too, seemed to cause great stress.

Still, he turned toward his enemy. Just as surrender was out of the question for Adaron, the dragon seemed just as determined. His roar made the air shudder.

At Lian's back, he heard screaming and a scuffle. Turning, he watched in disbelief as Markaeth and Danark sped toward a jäger kite. The two prisoners must have managed to escape amid the chaos. Garon, the crystal carver, must have tried to stop them, but now the man fell to the deck with Markaeth's knife stuck in his throat.

"Rotten traitors and cowards!" Adaron cried. Distracted from his nemesis, he tore the sword from his belt and jumped down from the helm. His left arm hung limply at his side, his injury from the crew's uprising not fully healed.

"Danark!" Melvas ran toward them in an attempt to keep his brother from making any final mistakes.

"Stay here, Melvas," Dunrir ordered, but the young sailor wouldn't listen.

"Look out! He's coming!" Jaular cried from the steering ropes.

Lian pulled himself away from the battle at the stern just in time to see the powerful black mass plowing toward the *Carryola*, the beast's jaws opening wide. He threw himself onto the deck underneath the nearest shield.

A river of fire rushed over him; its heat robbed him of breath. It rolled over the deck, spread across the mast and helm, and made its way toward the stern. Men screamed, and Lian watched as a man covered in flames tumbled over the railing and into the depths.

Hanon'ka roared his powerful words to the sky as he stretched his right arm into the heavens and grasped the amulet at his neck with his left. Between his cramped fingers glowed a green fire that he released to the sky. The sea of flames was extinguished from one heartbeat to the next. Gargantuan, about to roll his enormous body into the deck, shot into the air as though propelled by a titan's fist. An anguished howl rang out, which grew when Janosthir quick-wittedly fired his thunder cannon into the dragon's weakly shielded belly. Boiling blood rained onto them as Gargantuan tipped sideways and fell into the *Carryola*. The beast's hind leg and tail ripped away a good part of the railing and destroyed the jäger kite in which Markaeth had tried to escape.

We're all going to die, thought Lian as he surveyed the devastation scattered across the burning deck. Melvas and Danark lay motionless. The sound of unrestrained sobbing came from the stern, and Adaron, who fought himself free from the rubble next to the destroyed kite, was smeared with soot, his hair half-scorched away, and blood streamed from his temple. Within his eyes, a seething scorn still raged unbroken.

"He's fleeing!" called Balen in disbelief. "Gargantuan is retreating."

"No!" Adaron cried, and he ran to the bow. He supported himself against Hanon'ka, who himself could barely stand. He had paid a price for the magic he had conjured again and again. "We can't let the monster escape," bellowed the captain. "This will be the final fight, as true as I stand here!"

35

The Way of Heroes

Eleventh Day of the Seventh Moon, Year 841

"Fire the harpoons!" ordered Adaron. "We have to keep him above the clouds. If the beast escapes now, this will all be for nothing. So many will have died for nothing."

Balen and Dunrir scowled fiercely as they followed the command. Lian could tell they would have preferred to give up, but the Black Leviathan was badly injured and more vulnerable than ever before. They had to end it now.

Lines shot out, and harpoons whistled through the air, sinking with a crack into the fleeing monster's back. Jaular, caked in blood and soot along with the rest of them, sent the *Carryola* barreling toward Gargantuan using the sheer power of kyrillian alone.

"Now two more harpoons," Adaron called to the men. "Or the ropes will break from the strain."

Lian and Gaaki helped Balen and Dunrir load the ballistae. Despite his weakness, Hanon'ka uttered a new incantation that called forth a wind against the monster. Though Lian felt the gust, the windstorm barely stirred the ship with all its sails scorched away.

When the dragon realized that Adaron wouldn't give up, he let out a scornful roar. Instead of falling into the clouds for cover or making an escape expected of any other dragon, Gargantuan spread his wings and allowed Hanon'ka's magic wind to propel him straight toward the *Carryola*. Using the wind's momentum, he whirled around and brandished his claws.

"Move!" cried Balen, running for cover.

Lian followed without taking his eyes off the approaching monster.

"Wait!" Janosthir called, aiming his thunder launcher. "I can get him."

Gargantuan opened his jaws wide, readying the flame in the depths of his throat.

The Settlander fired. The monster turned his head sideways at the last moment, and a destructive blue light exploded against his scaled cheek. Roaring, the beast's enormous body crashed into the ship, just right of the bowsprit against the railing. Pain from the uncontrolled collision seemed to rob the dragon of his senses. His front talons bored into the foredeck, and his tail slashed back and forth as he clung to the ship. Wood splintered, and the hull's scale armor shattered beneath the injured dragon's weight.

Lian searched for Janosthir amid the chaos but saw only his thunder launcher, now wet with blood, rolling across the planks. Then he spotted Gaaki, who whimpered as he dragged himself across the deck. The Drak's leg had been ripped open, and a shard of dragon plate protruded from his back. Lian wished he could help his comrade, but he couldn't risk leaving his cover behind the helm, where he now crouched beside Balen and Adaron.

Hanon'ka! he remembered. Where was the Sidhari, anyway? He scanned the deck but found no trace of him. He saw only Gargantuan, clinging to the rail, attempting to make his way onto the deck. The beast raised his head and roared.

"Get down!" cried Balen, pulling Lian toward him.

Flames shot over the helm and ignited the stern, where Lian made out the forms of Kettler, Wil, Srashi, and Sheshac. The men shrieked as fire poured over their shields. When one shattered from the heat, the Drak underneath—whether Srashi or Sheshac, Lian couldn't say—transformed into a living torch.

Adaron seized Lian by the collar. "You have to kill him," he growled, his eyes sparked with madness. "It's up to you. Kill him—or he'll murder us all." He closed a hand around Lian's own, which clutched his spear. "He'll murder Kris," Adaron urged. "The woman you love."

Lian started. "How do you . . . ?"

Adaron's mouth curled into a sly smile. "This is my ship. Nothing takes place on board without my knowledge. Did she really think she could keep such a secret from me?"

"But why—" Lian asked.

"I didn't interfere," Adaron interrupted, "because your love stirred old emotions within me. It reminded me of a time, many years ago, when I also knew love. But that love of mine is long dead, murdered by this monster. Don't let him extinguish yours, too."

As though to emphasize the captain's words, Gargantuan let out a roar, and more blows shook the *Carryola*. Lian felt the ship list. "He's smashing the kyrillian cases under the bow," Jaular called from above. "Do something, or we'll fall!"

"Go!" Adaron pushed Lian, who tumbled forward. "Show if you're truly the man you said you are!"

Lian's heart thumped wildly. His throat was parched and stung from inhaling hot smoke into his lungs. His insides felt as though they were balled into a hard knot, and only an act of will prevented him from cowering with fear as he forced himself into motion.

He inched past the wall of the helm, where Jaular clasped a laughably useless ax as he cowered next to Cabbyr. The pilot looked determined, while the younger sailor, pale from a long slash wound on his arm, looked desperately at Lian, who swallowed and directed his attention forward.

Oddly, Gargantuan seemed calm. Though Lian still felt the impact each time the beast's tail mauled the hull, his talons no longer tore up the deck, and he no longer roared. Instead, a deep guttural growl rumbled from his throat. When Lian peered around the corner, the beast turned his head toward the side to stare directly at Lian with his uninjured eye.

He's waiting for me! The realization was dizzying. Facing a raging dragon was one thing. How could he battle a titan that merely waited, calm and almost curious, for him to arrive? Was it because of his spear? Did Gargantuan know his weapon?

"Lian."

He turned his head toward the barely audible whisper and gasped with horror. "Hanon'ka!"

The Sidhari slumped against the helm rail. To Lian's amazement, his body wasn't burned, though the dragon's breath had blackened everything else around him. The amulet at his neck had ceased its glowing, and the crystal beads were dark and dull, drained of all their magic.

Just as the power had left his talismans, the Sidhari's own life, too, seemed to wane. Lian saw no obvious reason at first glance, but it was impossible to overlook that Hanon'ka was badly, even mortally, wounded. His dark skin had turned gray, his breathing was strained, and the fire in his emerald eyes merely smoldered as though he only remained conscious through sheer will.

"Lian," the Sidhari repeated faintly, and he ushered him forward with a barely perceptible gesture.

Lian glanced at Gargantuan, but the dragon calmly watched the two men before him.

Winds, protect me, Lian prayed silently. Then he rounded the corner and hurried to Hanon'ka's side. Crouching down, he set his spear onto the deck. "What is it? How can I help you?"

A mild smile crept across the Sidhari's dark cheeks. "You can't help me," he answered faintly. He lifted his hands off his stomach to reveal a thick splinter of plank that had pierced his gut. Wincing, Lian realized that the Sidhari's dark pants were soaked with blood.

"By all the Winds!" Lian whispered. "I'm so sorry."

"Don't be silly," Hanon'ka replied. "It's not your fault. And it . . . it's all right. He was a worthy opponent." Hanon'ka nodded toward the dragon, who still watched them silently. Lian wondered how severe Gargantuan's own wounds were. Was he close to death, too? Was that why he was so quiet?

"But as your mentor, I must . . ." The Sidhari stopped, breathing shallowly. His expression darkened, and he groaned. "I must tell you one final thing."

"Don't worry," Lian insisted. "I won't disappoint you. I know what needs to be done."

"What's going on over there?" Adaron bellowed in confusion from behind the helm.

"I don't know," Jaular called. "Gargantuan seems to be waiting for something. And . . . I don't see Lian anymore."

Lian heard the captain curse, but before he could answer, Hanon'ka grabbed him with bloody hands and pulled him closer. "You never had it in you," he strained to whisper. "I . . . recognized that. You're not a . . . dragon slayer."

"But—" Lian began.

"Silence," the Sidhari interrupted. "You have another talent. Find it . . . and use it. I can't . . ." His hand fell limply at his side. "Teach you . . ." His head sank back against the railing. "Any more . . ." The emerald light extinguished from his eyes.

Lian bowed his head and shut his eyes, but no tears came. Fire turned everything to steam.

"Lian!" the captain roared from behind him. "Where are you?"

Corantha. Lian's hand curled around his spear, and he stood up. *Ialrist. Melvas. Janosthir. Hanon'ka. And so many others. It's enough!*

"Over here!" he called, and he turned to face Gargantuan. "I'm here!" His fingers cramped as he clutched his spear's handle, and the runes awoke to life as he pointed the weapon toward the dragon, but it wasn't hate that ignited the weapon—for he felt no hate at the moment—it was the presence of the ancient and mysterious magic within the creature itself.

Gargantuan raised his head at the bow—as well as was possible as he desperately clung to the *Carryola.* A menacing rumble like the grinding of stones within a gaping abyss sounded from his throat and reverberated through every fiber of Lian's body. The beast's large glowing eye remained glued to Lian as he waited attentively.

He's killed so many. The image of the graveyard of wrecked ships and limbs rose in Lian's mind. *He deserves death more than any other dragon.*

Still, the great monster before him seemed to sense Lian's hesitation. Adaron, too, couldn't ignore it.

"Why are you just standing there?" the captain yelled from behind him. "Use your weapon to take the beast down! Gargantuan is wounded. Take your chance before it's too late!"

Lian looked at the blackened beast before him, a thing of legend that had terrorized the Cloudmere. The conflict plagued him: Was Gargantuan truly the monster? Yes, he had destroyed hundreds of ships and their crews. But had he really hunted them? Or, rather, had they hunted *him*? Hadn't Adaron hunted him for nearly twenty years? *Would Gargantuan have taken so many lives if we hadn't ventured so far into the Cloudmere and invaded his realm?* Lian wondered. He'd never heard of a single sighting of the Black Leviathan near land. The vast ether was his home, and the clouds far from every coast his hunting grounds. Had he ever done more than defend his territory against intruders and fight for his own life when necessary? People killed one another for far lesser reasons.

"By all the gods and demons!" the captain cried. "Pierce his damned heart with your spear!"

Lian glanced at the spear adorned in runes. What had Ialrist called it? One of the six drachen spears of the Theurgs of Fundur. *Six extraordinary warriors handled them, and their scorn for dragons flowed into the weapons, transforming them into the most powerful murder weapons ever made to kill Great Drachen.*

That was what Ialrist had told, but Kesrondaia's story about the weapon had been very different. Many generagions ago, a man brandished the spear to protect the innocent against evil itself. He fought to save lives, not to end them. He followed kindness and mercy, not lust and hate.

The spear's end, now directed at Gargantuan, began to shudder, and the runes flickered.

"Are you a coward or just a fool?" Adaron roared. "Do I have to do it myself, because you're not man enough?"

The enchanted weapon obeys the one who wields it, but the wielder must decide his motive.

There it was: Kesrondaia's voice, the woman of white with a dragon's aura. She spoke into his ear, quietly, but with more urgency than the captain's cries at Lian's back. She had said that he would have to decide how to direct his life. He had already decided once, when he'd saved Nock Nock from Karnosk and Srashi. Had that been a preview, a first taste, before the true test?

You're treading the way of heroes, Lian, but you have to decide for yourself if you want to become one.

He thought of Kris, and their talks together, and of Ialrist and

Hanon'ka. He thought of Adaron's mania, borne of a torturous pain that had grown into a vicious hate over two decades. It couldn't be right to follow a man so consumed by madness. That couldn't be a hero's way. Adaron's way led nowhere, if not into darkness.

Kindness and mercy . . .

Not lust and hate . . .

Lian looked upon the great creature before him and stared straight into Gargantuan's glowing eye. Some may have claimed to see evil or malice within the beast's glance, but Lian didn't see those things. The dragon's black, scaled face, and the glowing fire within his pupil-less eye, was far too exotic; it defied definition by a human's sense of feeling or thought. Fear of the beast came from not knowing. As soon as Lian realized that truth, he was no longer afraid. Gargantuan could have killed him a hundred times by now as they faced each other, and Lian didn't have the slightest urge to escape. In fact, the dragon had done nothing except wait for the man holding his spear to take action.

"That's enough," Lian said loudly, lowering the spear. "Enough have died. Let's end this here and now. Go now, and we'll retreat—and never return." Resolved, he threw his weapon to the floor.

"Has fog gotten into your brain?" Adaron shrieked. "Coward and traitor! I'll kill you, dragon companion!" Seething with rage, the captain stormed toward him, his broad sword raised to attack.

Suddenly, a figure swooped from behind him over the railing. With a gust from his tan wings, Ialrist landed on the deck. Standing in his half-torn armor, the Taijirin grabbed Adaron's shoulder. "Don't do it!" he cried.

"No one can stop me!" the captain spat. He whipped around and thrust his sword without sense or understanding.

Both men were stunned. Adaron and Ialrist had been the truest comrades to ever traverse the Cloudmere. Now, a blade protruded from the gut of one, stabbed by the hand of the other.

"You . . ." The Taijirin prince stared at Adaron. "Look how far it has come." Disappointment covered his face, and he collapsed to the deck. The captain let go of the sword to catch his friend, and they both sank onto the planks.

"Ialrist!" Adaron cried in horror. "Ialrist, true friend. I never wanted this. I swear to you, it wasn't deliberate. By the Three Gods, I beg you. Don't die!"

Ialrist winced and coughed weakly. He looked upon the man with his large, dark eyes. "Let's see if the Illuminated Wings take me this time." His eyelids dropped, and his body went lifeless.

"No!" Adaron cried. He tore his sword from the gash and threw it aside, then pressed both hands over the wound. "No, no, no, no! You can't die. Narso!" he bellowed, looking up. "Narso, damn it, where are you?" But the ship medic didn't arrive, and Ialrist, too, didn't stir again.

As though numb, Adaron studied his blood-drenched hands. Then he slowly turned, his face twisted with scorn. As he glared at Gargantuan, Lian saw sheer loathing in his eyes. "You!" he bellowed. "This is your dark doing. Your perverse magic. You brought me to this. You've robbed me of everything: the woman I love, twenty years of my life, my ship, and now my truest comrade. Are you satisfied now, you demon?" His voice grew louder until he was screaming. "Does your dark heart beat with joy? Do choruses of the damned sing within your blackened soul?"

Adaron bent forward and raised Lian's spear off the deck. "You've left me with nothing!" he shouted. "Naked and destroyed, I stand before you now, held up by hate alone." When he raised the weapon, the runes awoke with a gleam more powerful than Lian had ever seen before so that he had to look away. "And my wrath," spat the captain. "My wrath will be your downfall!"

He threw the spear with all the power his limitless scorn contained. The weapon whistled through the cold air and, with a crack of a thunderbolt, broke through the dragon's thick scales at his chest, burrowing into the black beast until only the very tip of its handle remained visible.

Gargantuan reared and raised his head into the air. His horrible roar expelled all the pain from an entire ancient life. The whole ship quaked, and Lian pressed his hands against his ears and moaned as he staggered backward. He leaned against the fallen mast and fell to his knees.

Adaron stumbled but remained standing, raising his arms victoriously. Slowly, he turned to Lian, his face distorted by maddened triumph.

In that moment, the dragon tilted his head down. With wide-open jaws, he charged for Adaron, devouring not only him but the entire bow of the *Carryola* as well, all the way to the keel. With cracks and bursts, the entire front end of the ship—bowsprit, harpoons, Adaron's and the slayers' chambers—was gone. Gargantuan and Adaron fell, swallowed up by churning gray clouds, united in death. The drachen spear from Theurgs of Fundur, Lian's inheritance and his last memento of Lonjar Draksmasher, fell with them. *Maybe,* Lian thought, *it is better this way.*

Epilogue

Eleventh Day of the Seventh Moon, Year 841

The *Carryola* set out from Skargakar on her final journey with a crew of thirty-six all those many weeks ago. After they collected the survivors, they were only ten. Besides Jaular, Kettler, and Narso—who had been knocked unconscious by a felled mast beam, but would recover— were Balen, Wil, Cabbyr, Srashi, and Lian. And Kris had survived. She, along with Smett, Flicc, and Nock Nock, had spent the entire battle in the safety of the galley and, apart from a few bruises and scrapes, had managed quite well.

As Kris appeared from the belly of the ship with Smett, Lian ran to her and wrapped his arms around her. At that moment, he couldn't care less what anyone thought or if his actions revealed that Kris was a woman. She had survived certain death. What did it matter if their feelings for each other remained secret?

Even though the *Carryola* had sunk drastically after losing her bow, Jaular managed to catch their fall using spare cases below deck. When Lian had first joined the crew, he had considered the extra cases an expensive and eccentric frivolity and had wondered how a dragon could ever pass through a steel hull covered in spikes to destroy all the kyrillian cases. He'd never thought that a dragon would destroy half their ship and was thankful for at least that part of Adaron's insanity.

Once they shook off the shock and horror, they collected the corpses under Balen's calm leadership and threw the bodies overboard before any scavengers got to them. No one on board had the energy for another battle.

So it came that Lian, Smett, and Kris stood over Ialrist's body, a few steps from the steep drop at the destroyed foremast. They had already laid Hanon'ka and Melvas to rest with the others over the railing at the stern. The Taijirin prince was the last—and for some reason the hardest—for Lian to part with. He and Ialrist had never been friends, or at least, Lian doubted that the Taijirin had ever considered him a friend. Still, Ialrist had always been there for Lian, from Lian's very first day aboard the *Carryola* until the moment he had prevented Adaron from attacking Lian. *You saved my life more than once.* Lian included Hanon'ka, too, in the thought. *But I couldn't protect you from death.* This realization was profoundly painful.

He bent forward along with Smett to lift the body. As he gripped Ialrist's arm, he froze. "He's still warm!" he cried. "Why is his body still warm?"

"By the Winds!" cried Smett. "The flutter-man is still alive." He raised his voice and cried out across the deck. "Narso! Cabbyr! Come here! Ialrist is alive! We need your help!"

Confused, Lian ran a hand over the Taijirin's body, searching for the stab wound that Adaron had inflicted. The wound had surely been deadly; there was no doubt. Aside from blood, he only found a red scar now, from a wound that had been closed for days. "What is the meaning of this?" he whispered.

Narso and Cabbyr hurried over. The medic groaned as he knelt, a bandage wrapped around his head, and despite his own suffering, he began to examine Ialrist. "What happened?" he asked.

"He was stabbed," explained Lian. "A sword pierced his gut. Right there." He pointed to the blood-drenched spot on Ialrist's body. "But the wound is already healed."

Narso surveyed the Taijirin's body with careful eyes. Then he loosened the fastening on the ripped harness. As he removed the torn leather armor and opened the Taijirin's vest, Lian's gaze fell on a faint golden sheen beneath Ialrist's shirt. A small amulet on a leather cord encircled his neck. A winged figure inside a ring of stars embossed the coin-sized bronze disk. When Lian touched it, a warmth emanated from the metal, and a deep feeling of peace came over him.

"A healing amulet." Smett chuckled and shook his head. "I've known this fellow for twenty years, but he never told me a thing about carrying a healing amulet. He sure could have told us about it. It could have saved a few others' arms and legs."

"Maybe its magic only works once," Narso suggested. "Maybe he saved it for a day like this one."

Hope stirred in Lian, paired with relief. "That means he'll be okay?"

Narso examined the Taijirin's body once more. "He's still sleeping—a healing sleep, most likely," he said. "I don't see any reason why he shouldn't recover, but I can't predict for sure when he'll wake up."

"As long as he wakes up, that doesn't make a difference," Lian said, and he grinned. "Should we carry him to his bed?"

"He'll be better off with us," suggested Kris. "The front chambers won't be inhabitable, if they're still there at all."

As they attempted to lift his body, Ialrist's eyes opened.

"Ialrist!" Lian cried. "You're back!"

The Taijirin seemed dazed at first, but he gradually began to focus on the figures before him with greater clarity.

"Back among the living," Smett said, grinning from ear to ear. "A remarkable feat, my friend, considering the sword that pierced your gut."

The Taijirin gave no reply and turned his head instead toward Lian, who knelt beside him. "Is he gone?" he asked hoarsely.

Lian grew grave. "Yes. They're both gone. Each brought death upon the other. I couldn't stop it."

The Taijirin sighed and closed his eyes. "So it shall be," he murmured bleakly. Then he opened his eyes and reached a hand toward Lian. "Help me up, please."

"Of course."

They lifted Ialrist to his feet. Lian would have liked to clap a hand on his shoulder to welcome him back to the living, but as the Taijirin prince gravely looked upon the wreckage on board the *Carryola*, it seemed the wrong thing to do. "The end of a bad voyage," Ialrist said softly as he looked upon the ruins with remorse.

"True, but it could have been worse," Lian said. "There are still a few survivors. And I'm indebted to you, once again." He looked at Ialrist.

"Thank you for interfering when the captain lost himself—and even more, for taking the blow for it."

Ialrist looked upon Lian with dark eyes, and a tiny hint of a smile crept across his face. It was a bitter smile. "During our last encounter with Gargantuan, twenty years ago, I saved the wrong man. I hope I chose the right one this time."

Lian opened his mouth to answer, unsure how to respond.

"I'm sure you did," Kris chimed in firmly. "Positive."

Acknowledgments

It's pretty strange how life can mimic art. Just as Captain Adaron wrestled with the Firstborn Gargantuan, I have also—for many reasons, including building a house—wrestled with this novel. All the more reason why I owe my deepest thanks to the people who supported "the crazed man through his final battle with the monster."

I thank Bastian Schlück and Kathrin Nehm from the Schlück Agency, for making this adventure into the Cloudmere at all possible. Andy Hahnemann, Hannes Riffel, and the whole team at FISCHER Tor were beyond generous when this mission began to develop in a direction that I (and they) hadn't anticipated. A huge "Thank you!" in your direction!

My reader Hanka Jobke gave tooth and nail to separate the good parts of the text from the bad with a slaughterman's thoroughness. It's an eternal challenge, by the way, because as soon as you resolve to start a new book project, and vow to avoid favorite words and phrases from the old ones, they creep back in, only to be cut out and thrown overboard once again.

Finally, I'd like to thank my family, who, with endless understanding and patience, accepted when I put myself into writing exile in the final weeks before submission. I can only promise that it'll go better next time!

(It's funny. That last part is often mentioned in an author's acknowledgments. You'd think that we professionals would have a better handle on our work. But apparently writing novels and hunting dragons have one thing in common: sometimes the beast just doesn't do what we expect him to.)

Glossary of Terms

Endar: the world encompassing the Cloudmere, its lands, and its many folk

Skargakar: coastal city that thrives from the fruits of jägers' toils

Kyrillian: violet crystals with buoyant properties

Lithos: floating rock masses, can be deadly to ships caught unaware

The fleece: the cloud blanket between the Cloudmere floor and the open sky

The Cloudmere: the fog-filled ether sea of Endar

Jäger: hunters of Great Drachen

Great Drachen: dragons great and small, and their majestic and terrible lore

The *Carryola*: a drachenjäger schooner

Jäger kite: smaller vessel used in battle against Great Drachen

Lonjar Draksmasher: Lian's father, former slayer of Great Drachen

Elven fire: mystical flames used to light ships and villages of men through the ages.

Firstborn: Gargantuan, the horn-crowned Black Leviathan, descendent of the Starborn, Ariocrestis the Wise

DRAGON SORTS:

Bronzeneck: known for its shimmering bronze scales

Silverwing: prized for its glimmering silver wings

Grayback: Corantha's dragon Arax; a type of raptor

Obsidianscale: heavily armored with black scales

Swingblade: possesses a deadly sharp blade on the end of its tail

Fireblood: known as reds, fire-spitters

Greenscale, shimmercomb, bluetail: types of lizardwings

Deities:

Illuminated Wings: revered by the Taijirin

The Three Gods: Indra, Jerup, and Vazar, revered by folk of former generations

Four Winds: revered by many along the coastline

Theurgs of Fundur: sorcerers who called themselves Theurgs, from the city of Fundur in the realm Quanish

Kesrondaia: the woman of white

Folk:

Taijirin: winged folk, known as *vogelfolk*, devotees to the Illuminated Wings

Sidhari: desert dwellers, devotees to the sands of Shaom

Nondurier: folk with heads of hounds, known for their nautical capacities, often called *houndlings;* devotees to the abilities of men and women

Drak: lizard-like scaled folk thought to have a propensity for dishonest dealings

human: folk hailing from the coastline, most devotees to the Three Gods or the Four Winds

Jägers of the *Carryola:*

Adaron / human / captain

Hanon'ka / Sidhari / first commander

Elrin / human / subcommander

Ialrist / Taijirin / slayer

Corantha / human / slayer

Lian / human / slayer

Jaular / Nondurier / head navigator

Urdin / human / carpenter

Bellem / Nondurier / sailmaker

Garon / human / crystal carver

Kettler / human / head slaughterman
Narso / human / medic
Smett / human / cook

Markaeth / human / second navigator and jäger kite pilot
Balen / human / navigator and jäger kite pilot
Kurrn / Nondurier / navigator and jäger kite pilot
Karnosk / Drak / jäger kite pilot
Dunrir / Nondurier / jäger kite pilot
Jakk / human / jäger kite pilot

Jarssas / Drak / slaughterman
Srashi / Drak / slaughterman
Hechler / Nondurier / slaughterman
Canzo / human / slaughterman

Cabbyr / human / medic's aid
Gaaki / Drak / medic's aid

Gandar / human / carpenter
Janosthir / Settlander / defense
Markol / human / cook's aid
Kris / human / cook's aid
Danark / human / crew
Melvas / human / crew
Aelfert / human / crew
Leachim / human / crew
Sheshac / Drak / crew
Lannik / human / crew
Wil / human / crew
Kylion / human / crew